HIGHEST PRAISE FOR
JOVE HOMESPUN ROMANCES

"In all of the Homespuns I've read and reviewed I've been very taken with the loving renderings of colorful small-town people doing small-town things and bringing 5 STAR and GOLD 5 STAR rankings to the readers. This series should be selling off the bookshelves within hours! Never have I given a series an overall review, but I feel this one, thus far, deserves it! Continue the excellent choices in authors and editors! It's working for this reviewer!"
—*Heartland Critiques*

We at Jove Books are thrilled by the enthusiastic critical acclaim that the Homespun Romances are receiving. We would like to thank you, the readers and fans of this wonderful series, for making it the success that it is. It is our pleasure to bring you the highest quality of romance writing in these breathtaking tales of love and family in the heartland of America.

And now, sit back and enjoy this delightful new Homespun Romance . . .

HEARTBOUND
by Rachelle Nelson

Praise for Rachelle Nelson's *A Cherished Reward*:

"ENCHANTING . . . a beautiful and poignant love story."
—*Affaire de Coeur*

"HEARTWARMING . . . enthra~~~
characters and endearing escapad~~~

"An entertaining and compelling~~~
reader long after the last page is t~~~

D0645696

Heartbound

Rachelle Nelson

JOVE BOOKS, NEW YORK

HEARTBOUND

A Jove Book / published by arrangement with
the author

PRINTING HISTORY
Jove edition / March 1997

The Putnam Berkley World Wide Web site address is
http://www.berkley.com/berkley

ISBN: 0-515-12034-0

A JOVE BOOK®
Jove Books are published by The Berkley Publishing Group,
200 Madison Avenue, New York, New York 10016.
JOVE and the "J" design are trademarks
belonging to Jove Publications, Inc.

PRINTED IN THE UNITED STATES OF AMERICA

10 9 8 7 6 5 4 3 2 1

This book has been written
in loving memory of
Virginia Pearl Bertha Krahn Greuel.
I hope you can hear me, Grandma.

Also . . .
To my favorite German,

Some might say I got my stubbornness from you.
But we prefer to call it persistence, don't we, Dad?
Thank you, for teaching me that I can accomplish
anything. Ich liebe dich.

To my best friend,

Remember all those purple hearts you painted on
your bedroom wall, so long ago? Who would have
ever known you would earn every one? Thank you,
Mom, for teaching me courage. I love you, always.

And for my husband and kids,

A special thank you for bearing with me through this
one. Y'all are the best.

Special thanks goes to Anna Maria Rodgers, who came to my rescue at the last minute. *Danke Shon*, Anna Maria, for letting me hear the music.

1

*T*HE WAR WAS over.

Tom Heart wondered how many times he'd have to repeat that fact to himself before it finally sank in. No more dodging cannon fire and belligerent Rebs. No more stepping over mangled corpses, eyes opened in sightless shock. No more stench-filled camps of disease and endless nights of nostalgia. Even six months after Lee's surrender it didn't seem real that the war had finally come to an end.

"What's the first thing you're gonna do when you get home, Lieutenant?"

Glancing at the eager-faced soldier marching beside him, Tom gave a short, rusty laugh. "Take a bath," he answered without hesitation. Hell, the dirt on his body felt thick enough to plant a crop in. He'd had enough of taking sporadic baths in whatever available puddle they could find. His old tin tub sounded heavenly in comparison.

"Not me." Gene Mason turned to walk backward in front of Tom, his knapsack and powder horn clapping against his bony hip, his musket strapped vertically against his back. "I'm gonna kiss the first girl I see, and marry the first one who'll have me." He raised the stump of what was left of his arm.

"A glutton for punishment, aren't you, doughboy?" Tom responded drolly, calling Gene by the nickname given to all Union infantrymen because of the globular buttons they wore on their uniforms.

Taking the ribbing in good stride, Gene flashed his customary grin. "Aw, don't tell me you don't plan on hanging up your bachelor's hat someday and sharing that big old farm of yours with a wife and a dozen kids."

"Not in this lifetime. I fought too hard and too long for my freedom. Why would I want to shackle myself to some woman?"

"I can think of worse things to get shackled to."

"Hah!" Tom threw back his head. "You haven't been around many women, have you, Gene?"

"'Nough to know they got fresh-cooked vittles waitin' at the end of a hard day's work, soft skin to smell when the stench of past battles overtake me, and a warm body on a cold winter's night." Gene inhaled a shivering breath. "Right now that sounds like heaven on earth."

Tom grimaced. War had turned a sensible young man into a sappy lunkhead. "More like hell in a handbasket. You just don't realize yet what you'll have to put up with to get all those so-called comforts. When they aren't nagging, they're crying. When they aren't crying, they're clinging. When they aren't clinging, they're withholding."

"Withholding what?"

Shaking his head in wry amusement over the twenty-two-year-old soldier's naïveté, Tom replied, "Their fresh-cooked vittles, soft skin and warm bodies."

"Well, after the years of misery I've suffered, I'd give my right arm for even a naggin', cryin', clingin' woman—if the Rebs hadn't took it first, that is."

His young friend deserved a lot of credit, Tom thought. He'd come to accept the loss of his limb much better than most soldiers. And it sure hadn't stopped him from lasting out the war.

As for the years of misery, Tom had known before enlisting that he might not make it out in one piece—if at all. But some principles were just worth taking that risk for.

Reaching the top of the ridge, Tom slowed his steps, then stopped. Below in a valley where the Rock River flowed lay the sleepy farming village of Ridgeford. Rooftops lined the edge of the woods like soft feather pillows against the headboard of a massive white-blanketed bed. Acres of birch, hemlock and oak trees behind slant-roofed buildings were still shedding their brittle leaves. And in between and beyond, Jersey and Guernsey cows dotted rolling hills in shades of white and ivory and vanilla, stretching as far as the eye could see.

God, he'd missed this place. The peace, the quiet.

"This is where we part ways, Corporal Mason," Tom said, breaking the stillness.

"'Pears so." Gene went quiet for a moment and squinted at the horizon from under the bill of his uniform cap.

Silence stretched between them, heavy with unspeakable memories, some nauseating, some tolerable, all best forgotten. If Tom could put every moment he'd endured up until now in a box and bury it, he would. More than anything he wanted to put the last four years behind him and pick up the pieces of his life before the war. So why couldn't he just walk off?

Gene breathed in appreciatively the crisp, reviving scents of autumn, then said, "It's hard to believe I'm standing here, a half a day from home. Alive. Sane." He pinned Tom with a steady look. "I owe that to you."

Tom frowned, shifted his weight from one leg to the other, shoved his thumbs into the scabbard belt around his waist. "You don't owe me anything."

"But I do, sir. I never would have had the guts you did, charging across enemy lines to rescue a bunch of strawfoots."

"Stop being so hard on yourself," he said gruffly, wishing Gene would quit making him into some kind of hero. Jumping into the fray had been an instinctive reaction, and a reckless one at that—nothing more. Had he known then that there were Johnnies hiding in the brush with heavy artillery, who could say if he'd have acted in the same way? "It was an ambush. Even seasoned soldiers found themselves in thick situations plenty of times." The memory of that particular skirmish at Brawner's Farm still made him queasy.

"Maybe so," Gene conceded. "But I bet you wouldn't of just sat there in a pool of blood, dumb as a rock, staring at your own arm laying five feet away while your buddies got plugged with minié balls."

"You were hurt and you were scared. Your mind shut down, that's all." Even the bravest of men had done worse in the name of survival, but Gene didn't need to hear the details. He should go home with at least a shred of his former innocence. Like all the other victims, he'd have to come to terms with the war and its effects in his own way, in his own time.

"That don't make me feel any less of a coward," he whispered. Then, with a swift upward glance into Tom's eyes, Gene regained his natural impassioned voice. "I would've either bled to death there on the field or gone mad in some Reb prison if it hadn't been for you. If there's anything I can ever do to repay you, just send word."

Tom couldn't see himself needing a preacher's son fresh out of combat anytime soon, but he nodded anyway, then gripped the young corporal's left hand and gave it a firm shake. "Find yourself a sweet-smelling warden who'll help you forget the last few years. We'll call it even, then."

Gene stepped back and saluted him. Tom's throat ached as he returned the gesture one last time before his companion headed through the village toward Minnow Falls. Only when his lanky form disappeared into the mouth of the covered bridge spanning the wide, current-bobbing river did Tom sling his haversack over his shoulder.

A brittle film of snow crunched beneath his worn soles as he fought the pull of gravity drawing his weary body down the hill. A bracing wind tugged at his woolen coat, copperheads jingled in his pockets.

He didn't understand the nearly suffocating tightness in his throat and chest. Thunderation, the war was over, he was almost home . . . he should be glad to be rid of his last reminder of the most exacting years of his life. It wasn't like he'd miss the kid or anything. To admit that he'd grown fond of the whelp would be the same as saying that he'd developed sentimental feelings.

That was impossible, of course. He'd learned long ago that feeling anything could destroy a man.

The land leveled at the base of the hill. Woodsmoke and meaty aromas from a dozen homes called invitations to him. Wrapping his collar tighter around his neck to ward off the late-October chill, Tom, as was his custom, headed in the opposite direction. The villagers would expect a recounting of the last four years, and the last thing he felt up to was being interrogated by well-meaning neighbors. All he wanted—all he'd ever wanted—was to be left alone.

What normally would have been a short ten-minute walk north of the village today seemed to take hours. Each step sent shards of agony through his thin boot soles. His cheeks and fingers stung from cold. The canvas haversack holding his mustering-out papers and a ratty shirt weighed like bricks across his back.

Tom ignored the discomforts as he trudged alongside the riverbank, heeding the lure of his farmstead.

Finally the shape of a familiar red-stained barn came into sight. Beyond that, Tom caught a glimpse of the house, a sturdy white frame structure that looked like an L lying on its back.

He didn't even try to stem the surge of pride rising inside him. Not many could claim of owning 140 acres of the most fertile land found in the Great Lakes region. Like most of the villagers, he was both businessman and landowner, but the farm was his greater source of pride. By thunder, every inch of soil on the place belonged to him. He'd earned it. Had bought and paid for it with his own sweat and blood after six years of backbreaking labor for the Central Railroad. If the Civil War hadn't interfered, he would have had time to figure out the secret to making the land produce and would now be counting profits from this fall's harvest.

Instead . . . he'd been made to start all over again. It was both rejuvenating and depressing.

He approached the side of the lofted barn, his mind filling quickly with a thousand tasks required to put the farm back into operation. Pungent scents of manure and fresh hay drifted through the cracks of the wall. He breathed deeply of the odors, then came to an abrupt standstill.

After nearly five years of sitting empty, the barn should have smelled musty and neglected.

Tom dropped to a precautionary crouch, straining to hear past the whistling wind.

A cough came from somewhere near the front of the barn.

He fit his rifle under his arm, his forefinger curved around the trigger. Keeping low, Tom moved stealthily against the stone foundation toward the noise, then rose and peered around the corner.

A boy stood just outside the doors, cupping water from the rain barrel into his hand. When he finished washing his hands, he scrubbed his face then blotted it with his coat sleeve.

"You there!" Tom shouted, stepping out into the open.

The boy spun around so fast he almost fell into the feed trough behind him. A shock of thick black hair falling over his forehead dripped with water. Dark eyes grew big when he spotted Tom, and he instantly flung his arms high in the air.

Tom's curious gaze traveled down the length of him. He wore a heavy brown wool coat over a flannel shirt and pants that left an inch of red socks showing between the hems and the top of his work boots. Taking note of the angular body lacking a man's developed muscles, and the absence of whiskers on the lean, oval face, Tom judged him to be around fourteen or fifteen.

"What are you doing on this property, boy?"

"J-j-just finished feedin' the oxen, sir."

"What oxen?"

"The o-o-ones insi-ide the barn."

There had been no livestock on the farm when Tom enlisted. He'd given the only animal he owned, his mule, to his neighbor Auggie Kirkmiller before leaving.

Tom scanned the empty yard, his blood heating at the sight of the changes. Someone had taken it upon themselves to build a henhouse and a smokehouse. That he'd intended to make the additions himself someday when he could afford it was beside the point. The idea of intruders tampering with his property while he'd been gone lit a fuse of outrage.

They obviously hadn't stopped there, either. Storm shutters painted a deep green had been hung alongside all three front windows of the house; now closed for the evening, the shutters blocked his view of the interior, but smoke curled from the stovepipe jutting out of the shaked roof.

"Who else is here?" Tom demanded, feeling violated.

The boy glanced nervously at the house, then back at Tom. "N-no one—" He gulped. "Sir."

He was lying. Tom saw it in his eyes, in the sudden locking of his joints. Distress fairly hummed in the air. The boy hardly looked strong enough to have done all this work alone. And Tom couldn't imagine the villagers being so obliging. He'd never given them cause to think he'd welcome any assistance where the farm was concerned.

So who was he trying to protect?

"No one, huh? Well, we'll just see about that, won't we?" And before the boy caught on to the warning, Tom leveled his rifle. "Into the barn. Now."

2

HE VIEW OUTSIDE Evie Mae's window hadn't changed a bit in the five minutes since Ginny Herz last looked over the placid village square. Ridgeford, the hub in a wagon wheel of farms spoking in all directions, had settled in with the falling of dusk. Center Lane remained deserted, the windows in Warren's General Store and Eischbach's Tannery were black squares in weather-grooved facades, and lights blinked like fireflies from Silver's Pub.

And yet, Ginny found herself repeatedly drawn to the spot, her nerves stretching tighter with each passing moment.

Evie Mae Johnson's curious gaze rested on her for several seconds before she returned her attention to the jagged-toothed plow blade clamped between her knees. "You're about as restless as a hen in a fox den," her friend remarked. "What's the mater with you today?"

Letting the gingham curtain settle back over the divided panes, Ginny resumed her place on the worn sofa and picked up the whetstone and iron wedge she had dropped moments before. The rhythmic grating of stone bar along dull blade didn't relax her as she'd hoped it would. "I am feeling . . . *ungelduldig* today." Since arriving in America nearly five years ago, she had made it a practice not to speak in her native Deutsch. But sometimes she found it difficult to express herself in English. This was one of those times. She had been feeling strange all day. Fidgety, impatient. For no apparent reason.

"Oh, no." Evie's hands stilled, her auburn brows lifted. "You aren't getting one of those feelings again, are you? The last time you did, we wound up keeping Margaret and her new groom up their entire wedding night with a shivaree."

Ginny shrugged. She gave another swipe to the splitting wedge. "It is the weather, I think. The coming of winter always affects me like this. Being caged inside instead of out in the fields, finding things to keep busy . . ." She shrugged again, not knowing how to explain her odd restlessness.

"As if you can't find anything to do with two growing children."

"The spinning wheel has been in constant motion," Ginny admitted with a grin. "David has gained another two inches in the last month and Doreen is needing more room in her bodices."

"I wouldn't know, but I've heard that it isn't easy for a mother to accept that her children are maturing."

Though Evie Mae was eight years younger than Ginny, she and the girl had become fast friends since the day Ginny arrived in Ridgeford over four years ago, and not a secret existed between them. In fact, the friendships she had formed with the women of the village were the one good thing that had come out of the war. "The years do seem to slip away." Somehow, though, Ginny didn't think the children's passage into their teen years was the cause of her unrest. "Speaking of the children, they must be wondering what is taking me so long. I had best get home." She set the iron wedge on the table with the other ice-cutting tools. "Oma will have supper ready soon."

"And we all know how upset your grandmother gets when someone arrives late to her table." Evie set aside the heavy blade then rose and brushed metallic flakes from the apron tied around her trim waist. "Thanks for helping me sharpen the tools, though. An extra pair of hands is always appreciated before the first good freeze."

"No thanks are necessary. We women must stick together."
The last four years had proven that. "Send word to the farm
when it is time to harvest the pond," Ginny said, collecting her
gloves and cape.

"If I don't, someone else will. You're the only one who can
talk Dolores into bringing her special recipe!"

Twirling her cape around her shoulders, Ginny giggled. The
taste of warmed beer did not appeal to her, but drinking
Dolores Silver's brew after cutting the ice had become tradition
to the rest of her female neighbors.

Just as she and Evie reached the doorway, an abrupt
cla—clang shattered the air. Ginny's startled gaze cut to her
friend. Both women at once recognized the rapid, repeating toll
of the school bell—a signal that the village women had
developed to report the arrival of one of their men, home from
the war.

Ginny couldn't move, she couldn't breathe.

Evie Mae flung the door open. Frigid air clashed with the
cookstove warmth inside the log cabin. "Someone's coming
across the bridge!"

A tingling spark flared inside Ginny. Her spirits began a
slow climb. "Can you see who it is?" The words came out in
a breathless whisper.

"It's too dark to see his face, but he's wearing a uniform . . ." Evie craned her neck for a closer study. Seconds
ticked by with agonizing slowness while she squinted at the
approaching figure.

Then her hand dropped, the corners of her plump lips
sagged. "Drat. It isn't one of Ridgeford's. Probably just one
drifting through on his way home."

The spark was doused, leaving a cold ache in Ginny's heart.
She looked away. She should have known it was too much to
hope for. Too much to expect. She'd been waiting so long. . . .

A consoling hand curved over her shoulder. "Be patient, my
friend. Maybe the next time the bell rings, it will be good
news."

"As long as it does not stop at three tolls."

The shadow that passed over her young friend's eyes filled

Ginny with instant contrition. "Oh, I am sorry, Evie. That was thoughtless of me."

"No need to apologize. It's been two years, after all." She smiled to hide her pain. "Someday a man'll come along who'll help me get over Alec's death. Meanwhile, stop fretting. They don't all come back the way he did."

Knowing that she had no words to right her blunder, Ginny let the matter drop.

Evie was already stepping outside when Ginny remembered the basket of Oma's new butter molds and she went back to retrieve them. A muffled squeal pulled her up short. She whirled around and gasped just as the soldier bent Evie Mae backward with one arm and kissed her.

"Evie?" Ginny hastened forward.

The soldier released her friend and gave a gallant bow. To Ginny, he tipped his hat, then swaggered down Center Lane, one sleeve of his dingy blue coat flapping against his side. It all happened in a matter of seconds.

"Are you all right? Did he hurt you?"

Dazed, Evie lifted one hand and nodded absently. Her lips were puffier than usual, her complexion flushed, her golden eyes sparkled. She had obviously not been hurt.

"Who was that man? Do you know him?"

Evie Mae shook her head, then grinned a silly grin. "No, but I'd pay him a dollar if he came back and did that again."

Choking back a chuckle, Ginny waited just long enough for the drifter to disappear from sight before she headed back to the farm. Her boots barely made a dent on the frozen road. She spied Dolores's ample figure through the pub window and waved, then further down poked her head inside the door of the combined smithy and stables. Sooty odors of burning coal, horseflesh, and hot biscuits assailed her. "Noble?" she called out.

His dark head appeared over the edge of the loft. "You headin' home, Miss Ginny?"

"Yes, Noble. Can you stop by the farm in the morning? Oma would like for you to take several crates of cheese with you to Minnow Falls."

"Will do. You be careful crossin' that bridge, ya hear? Them boards is mighty slick."

Ginny waved to let him know she'd heard, then let the door squeal shut. Once again she was grateful for the day the former slave had stumbled into their village. Not only was Noble a wonder with horses, but during the absence of the menfolk, he had appointed himself protector, errand-runner and handyman. Though the village women had become for the most part self-sufficient, it was comforting to know that in times of need, they had the giant of a man to rely on.

What really saddened Ginny was that they should have to call upon him at all. If the war hadn't taken all their men away . . .

She scanned the ridges on the way home with longing and found her thoughts straying to the soldier. Was he a son? A father? A husband?

Did it matter? He belonged to somebody, she was sure, a lost member of someone's family. And he had survived the war, was going home. Someone would not have to watch the horizon for his return much longer.

Would the day ever come when she stopped waiting and searching the horizon?

Would the day ever come when her family was complete again?

Ginny covered the distance to the farm in silent contemplation. Yes, she had Oma. She had the children. She had a productive farm and a bright future in this land of opportunity.

And yet . . . despite the many blessings in her life, there was still a missing piece, an aching void in her heart.

A void only one man could fill.

She tried summoning her most treasured image of him, the one that had sustained her during the bleakest hours. He had blond hair, she recalled, and eyes that most somber shade of brown—

Ginny halted in midstep, her mind stumbling. No, not brown. Green. His eyes were . . .

Ohhhh. Shutting her lids tightly, Ginny softly grieved. What color were they? *Gott* forgive her, but she could not remember. With each passing year, the memory had grown more hazy. The thought that it might disappear altogether filled her with such profound agony that she wondered if she could survive another year without seeing him. Touching him.

Or what if, like Evie Mae and Dolores and Mrs. Warren . . . and so many others . . . she had to live the rest of her life without him?

Swift tears scalded Ginny's eyes. She forced them back down, felt them clog in her throat. She must not let herself stop believing. The day he'd boarded the ship for America, he had promised that they would be together again. She would hold him to his word. No matter how long it took, or how difficult it became, or how desperately afraid she sometimes felt, she would keep the faith. It was all she had to hold on to.

By the time she reached the farmyard, Ginny regained a measure of the strength that had seen her through thus far. Entering the house, the spicy aroma of Bratwurst lured Ginny into the kitchen. After removing her cape, she snuck up behind her grandmother's plump form and kissed the wrinkled cheek.

Bertha Krahn jumped away from the cast-iron stove. "*Ach, Enkelin*, you give an old voman a fright!"

Ginny smiled. "You are not old, Oma, just well preserved." In fact, for a woman of seventy, her grandmother had more vigor packed in her stout body than most women half her age. "I have brought your butter molds," Ginny said, setting the basket on the counter. "And Noble said he will come by in the morning to take the cheese to market."

Eyes brown as crisp bacon assessed Ginny for a moment. Bertha set aside the fork she'd been using to turn the sausage and pressed her cool, broad hand against Ginny's forehead. Ginny smiled tolerantly at the maternal gesture. "I am not ill, Oma."

"You are flushed."

"I have just come in from outside," Ginny reminded her.

Bertha's hand fell away but her narrow lips, with the shadow of fine dark hair above them, still turned down in a sagging frown. Ginny patted the rawboned cheeks, wanting to ease her grandmother's concern. *Dear Oma, always needing someone to fuss over.* In truth, Ginny didn't mind. It was one of the traits she loved most about her Oma. And since Da passed on, Bertha was left with no one to mother but her granddaughter and great-granddaughter.

"Where are the children?" Ginny asked, pulling stoneware plates out of the glass-fronted cabinet beside the sheet-iron stove.

"David is probably in de barn milking de Jersey and Doreen is upstairs, trying on de *Kliedung* you make her."

"If you will tell them that supper is ready, I will finish setting the table."

Nodding, Bertha wiped her hands on her apron. The stairs, built against a wall of the sitting room beyond the kitchen, creaked with her ascent to the second floor as she went to fetch Doreen.

Ginny returned to the stove and picked up a slotted wooden spoon to ladle boiled turnips from a kettle into a bowl. Again, the old clumsiness that had been seizing her all day took hold. Her hand went limp. *Rubes* tumbled from the spoon, across the long countertop, and onto the puncheon floor.

"Sweet mercy," Ginny muttered her favorite American saying as she scrambled to catch the turnips rolling across the counter. She tossed them into a bowl for rinsing, then stooped low and threw those that had fallen onto the floor into the slop pail.

"Don't make any sudden moves."

3

$\mathcal{G}$INNY'S HAND STILLED at the sound of the deep-timbred voice behind her. Though the intruder made no further noises, she felt the threat of his presence fill the kitchen. Her senses became sharp and alert.

"Stand up, and do it slowly."

She obeyed even as her gaze swept the area for a means to defend herself and her family. A pot of hot water and a skillet remained on the stove, too far away. Neither were any knives within reach. Her only available weapons were her wits and the slop bucket clutched in her hand.

They would have to do.

In one swift move, Ginny threw herself around and flung the pail. Her target ducked as the object sailed harmlessly past him and crashed against the wall.

Before her failed attempt registered, Ginny found herself held motionless by a wicked bayonet rifle aimed directly at her middle.

"You missed," he taunted.

A stillness settled over the room. Ginny stared at him in shock. The grime on his face and a growth of dirty-blond whiskers framing his mouth obscured his features. His drab blue clothing was rumpled and worn. Brass buttons decorated the front of his thigh-length coat; twin patches curved over squared shoulders. A wide flannel bellyband wound around his middle, and the same yellow fabric had been sewn into the outside seams of his trousers.

He wore the uniform of a soldier.

A Union soldier.

The numbness holding Ginny motionless wore off and every nerve in her body came alive. "Thomas?" she whispered in disbelief.

His face lifted a fraction away from the rifle barrel he'd been sighting down. His lips parted in surprise. And from beneath the down-curved brim of a black hat, vaguely familiar eyes stared back at her, stunned.

He was one of Ridgeford's.

More importantly, he belonged to her.

His face blurred as Ginny's eyes filled with tears of recognition. A sob caught in her throat. She flattened her fingers over her lips. "Thomas!"

Tom's chest burned as though struck with grapeshot when the woman shrieked, then came flying at him. Heedless of the deadly weapon in his hands, she crashed into him with enough force to knock him off balance. The Springfield rifle clattered to the floor.

Stumbling backward, digging his fingers into the flesh around her narrow rib cage, Tom tried dodging the wild kisses she plastered over his face.

"Oh, Thomas, Thomas—"

Her arms flew around his neck, squeezing him so tight he swore there'd be bruises there for a week.

"I had almost given up hope of ever seeing you again," she half sobbed, half laughed against his skin. Each time he evaded one kiss, she smacked him with another. His eyelids, his nose, his cheeks, his ear . . . he couldn't tell where his skin ended and her lips began.

"Thunderation . . . lady . . ." Tom gasped, "are you crazy?"

He tried pushing her away.

She gripped him harder.

He twisted in the opposite direction.

She followed.

Finally Tom dove beneath her arms and made a desperate scramble across the floor. His heart slammed against his ribs, his breath came in great, heaving gulps as he slid up against the burlap-covered wall. "Lady," he panted, "you've got some quick explaining—"

A gasp from the direction of the stairwell cut him off. An old woman wearing a solid maroon gown and white triangular-bibbed apron poised at the base of the steps. Her eyes bulged. Her hands covered her mouth. A frilled cap curved on top of coal-and-iron-streaked braids coiled on either side of her head.

Beside her stood a young girl, a near replica of the woman standing close by with tears streaming down her face.

"It is Thomas come home!" the woman cried, gesturing wildly.

No sooner were the words out of her mouth than the girl squealed then launched herself at Tom. He caught her by reflex. Her slender legs locked around his waist, her fingernails bit into the skin at his nape. Gutteral sounds, like broken moans, spilled from her mouth into his ear.

Once more Tom found his face peppered with sloppy kisses. "Someone get this . . . this pint-sized mountain cat off me! Her claws are drawing blood!"

After what seemed an eternity the girl was removed. Free again, he wasted no time grappling for the rifle while still keeping the three intruders in sight. They weren't exactly the image of danger; none of them came any higher than his underarms, making him feel like the fabled Paul Bunyan among dwarves. But neither could he forget they'd practically mauled him to death!

Reassured by the fit of a weapon in his hand, he used the barrel of his rifle to motion this old woman toward the center of the room. "You, over with the other two."

"Thomas, do not be silly," the younger one said, chuckling as if he'd made a joke. "Put that gun away. . . ."

"Quiet! I'm the one giving the order around here."

Her jaw went slack. Then she snapped her mouth shut, but her pinch-lipped expression left no doubt that she wasn't happy. Who the hell cared? This was his house, by thunder, and no one told him what to do in it!

With one black brow winging upward, the old one marched regally across the room to join the others in front of the table.

Tom peeked into the sitting room, then up the stairs, then to his left into the kitchen area. "Anybody else going to jump out at me?"

"There is only myself and Oma and Doreen here. Thomas, please, you will frighten—"

"I said *quiet!*" He leaned against the wall, his nerves tense, his gaze darting from one female to the other to the other. Frighten them? he scoffed. Hah! Not a one of them appeared intimidated in the least. The woman was too busy raking him with disapproval, while the girl gave him a jolly grin over the pair of protective arms shielding her.

He couldn't help but feel as if that grin were meant just for him. But for the life of him, he couldn't figure out why.

Other than their different expressions, they were nearly identical images of one another. Same pale yellow hair plaited and strung up around their crowns, same softly rounded features.

The matronly one looked pleased. She was darker and stouter than the other two, and he could swear he saw just a hint of a mustache, but Tom detected a faint resemblance.

Since the middle woman seemed to have appointed herself the spokesperson, he focused on her. "Start talking, lady." His eyes narrowed dangerously. "And let me warn you, you better have a damn good reason for being in my house."

Her face pinkened. "Thomas, your language."

"To hell with my language! Tell me what in thunderation you're doing here!"

The woman didn't even have the sense to fear his steadily rising tone, a tone that not too long ago had made grown men quake in their boots.

Instead, she and the old woman exchanged puzzled looks. "Why, we have been waiting for you. I did not think you would mind that I brought Oma to live with us. She has been such a blessing to Doreen and me since—" Her tone dropped slightly to a grieving level. "My Da died, Thomas. I could not bear to leave her behind."

The more she spoke, the more confused Tom grew. The way she talked . . . Her low soprano voice held the mark of a native German. There was nothing special about that, for immigrants had been flooding into the States for the last decade—

Good God, she hadn't sailed over from Europe on one of those stinking ships, had she? "Who the hell *are* you?"

From beneath thick amber lashes, denim-blue eyes regarded him curiously. "What do you mean, 'who am I'?" She cocked her head to the side. "Thomas, do you not recognize me?"

Studying her, Tom racked his brain, trying to recall where he might have met her. He'd known a number of short, blond-haired, blue-eyed women. He couldn't match her face to any place or time, though. Yet she acted as if they'd been on very friendly terms. "I'm in no mood to play guessing games, so why don't you just tell me."

"It is me—Ginny."

She said her name as if it was supposed to matter.

"Your wife."

4

*H*IS WHAT?

No. Tom shook his head. He must have heard wrong. She couldn't have said . . . A chuckle of both shock and denial broke the imposing silence. "For a minute there I thought you said you were my wife."

The mere thought of the word made him shudder. There were incidents in his past he purposely blocked from his mind, sure, but marrying a German buttercup was not something he'd likely forget!

She and the old one exchanged puzzled looks. "I did," she said with a slow, singular nod. Then she pulled the young girl close and smoothed back her wavy blond hair. "And this is our Doreen. Doreen?" She gestured toward Tom. "Would you finally like to say hello to your *Vati?*"

A broad smile nearly split the girl's dainty face in two.

Tom's jaw nearly dropped to the floor. Blood rushed to his head. His nerves went numb by degrees. He recognized the German word. Daddy.

"Sweet mercy, Oma, I think he is going to faint!"

The comment registered a split second after she started forward. Tom jerked the slipping rifle back into place. "Get back!"

"But Thomas—"

She took another step, and Tom couldn't decide if she was extraordinarily brave or incredibly foolish. "I said get back. I'm not going to faint. I've never fainted in my life."

Lack of sleep was catching up to him—that's why he felt so blasted dizzy. Or maybe some of that lousy stew he'd eaten yesterday morning had poisoned his brain.

The woman made a drinking motion with her hand and told the girl, "*Liebchen*, bring your *Vati* a glass of water." Then she gently prodded her in the direction of the sink pump.

Tom recovered his scrambled wits enough to ask, "Is this a prank? Did somebody put you up to this?" If one of the villagers had made him the butt of one of their jokes, he'd kill them. Choke them with his bare hands. There wasn't a damn thing funny about planting a family in his house.

"A prank?" Deep lines grooved her brow as she stared at him. "It is not a prank. You sent a message saying you'd bought a farm in Wisconsin and would send for us as soon as your crops paid off. But then Da died, and I could wait no longer, so we came to America to be with you. Except, when we found your farm, you had already gone off to war." She lifted her hands away from her sides. "We only wanted to surprise you when you returned."

"Surprise me," he said flatly. She'd done that. Nothing—not Rebs darting out from behind stone hedges, not the sharp crack of a whip against flesh, not the feel of a grown man's tears soaking his shirtfront—*nothing* had ever taken him so completely by surprise as finding three females on his farm, one of whom claimed to be his wife. "Lady, just who do you think I am?"

She tilted her head curiously to the side. "You are Thomas Herz."

The lingering light-headedness fled and a swift flood of relief took its place. "Wrong. My name is Heart. Tom Heart."

"Heart in America, Herz in Deutschland," She countered with a careless wave. "It is the same meaning."

"But *not* the same man."

"Do not be silly." She gave him a disarming grin. "Do you think I would not know my own husband?"

Shaking his head back and forth, Tom whispered in awe, "You people aren't just crazy, you're out of your blasted minds!" Then he scooped his hat up off the floor where it had been knocked during her attack. "Now, I'll give you one hour to pack your things and get off my property."

Without giving them a chance to respond he spun on his heel and walked out the door.

Ginny stood dumbstruck, unable to do anything but watch Thomas disappear. However, she did flinch when the door slammed shut behind his fleeing form.

Of all the reunions she had dreamed of having with her husband, this certainly was not one of them—with Thomas nearly tripping over his own feet to get away from her.

A tug on her sleeve snapped Ginny from her stupor.

Where is Vati going? Doreen signed.

Bewildered blue eyes sought answers, answers Ginny simply didn't have to give. How could she explain Thomas's baffling behavior to an eleven-year-old, when she didn't understand it herself?

Did we scare him off?

"I think we shocked him," Ginny finally gestured.

Oma's plump arms wound around Ginny, surrounding her with the scent of baked bread and sausages. On any other day she would have found comfort in the familiar fragrance. But this was not any other day. In the last few, short minutes, her entire world had come crashing down around her.

Working down the lump in her throat, Ginny whispered, "He did not even recognize me, Oma." She twisted around and faced her grandmother. "Have I changed so much?"

"You did not expect to remain a sixteen-year-old bride forever, did you?" her grandmother replied in the thick accent of their native country.

Ginny brought her hands to her face, felt how pronounced her cheeks had become since the last time Thomas had seen her. She had been gently rounded with the child she carried then. Over time and after Doreen's birth, her figure had lost much of its plumpness, giving way to the curves of a woman. No, she was no longer the young girl he had left in Deutschland. "I suppose it is possible that he would not recognize me. It simply did not occur to me."

"*Enkelin*, are you certain dat is your Thomas?"

She pulled back far enough to meet Bertha's concerned gaze. "Oh, yes, Oma. Of course, I will admit that he looks a bit different than our wedding day when you saw him last. His hair is darker, and he is much thinner than I remember—" Ginny suddenly bit her lip, battling a swift attack of uncertainty. She had only lived with her husband for five months before he left for America. And of those months he had been gone often, fighting in the revolution . . .

Leaving her grandmother's embrace, she hastened to the window, lifted it open and threw back the shutters. He was marching across the yard toward the fields beyond the barn, his long-legged strides stiff and jarring. Of course, that was her Thomas.

Wasn't it?

Only a vague resemblance remained of the young stripling she had married, she conceded. Under the weariness and grime, she had tasted the salt of life and labor when she kissed his face. And beneath the coarse wool of his uniform she had felt the tightly controlled power of maturity. If she had met Thomas on the street, she might have passed right by him without knowing who he was. . . .

No, Ginny told herself. She would have known.

Like the first time she had seen him marching through her father's orchard so many years ago, she had felt a sense of connection the instant their gazes met. As if their hearts had linked, their souls united.

"There are differences," she granted, "but he is my *Mann*."

"Vhat vill you do? I have no vish to leave, and he cannot stay out dere. . . ."

Ginny turned her attention back to the window and watched her husband stomp a trench through the thin layer of snow that had fallen yesterday. Yes, what would she do? They had missed out on so much together . . . she had stored away every important event to share with him . . . had dreamed of the day he would take her in his arms and she would hear once more, "*Ich liebe dich.*"

I love you.

Were her years of faithfulness and loyalty and undying devotion to Thomas to end here and now, without him ever understanding the depth of her love?

Ginny let her hand fall. Her lips pressed together in fierce determination. No, by *Gott,* they wouldn't. "Well, I am certainly not going to stand by and let him walk away."

Armed with purpose, Ginny snatched her bulky cape from the coatrack by the door and wrapped it snugly around her. "The last time I allowed my husband to leave me I lost him for twelve years."

5

A STINGING WIND cut into his chapped cheeks as Tom advanced further into the field, no direction in mind. As long as it was away from that batty family of foreign nesters he didn't much care where he went.

The woman was an escapee from a lunatic ward. It was the only explanation he could come up with for her ridiculous claim.

A husband? A father? *Him?*

Like hell!

He cherished his freedom too much. In fact, there was no limit to the things he would do—had done already—to get it. He had sacrificed his sweat and blood. His dignity and his self-respect . . . There wasn't a price he hadn't paid to keep it.

And by thunder, no bit-of-fluff nester was going to pop into his life and announce it had all been for nothing!

"Thomas?"

Glancing over his shoulder, Tom growled. She couldn't give him two seconds' peace without chasing after him. What did she want now? Her cheeks were flushed, her pace eager, almost frantic, as she fairly flew across the field in pursuit.

"Thomas, wait!"

He gripped his rifle tighter and, numbing himself to the pain in his feet, forced his protesting legs to move faster. The feeling inside him had no name, but it meant danger. That much he recognized.

"Will you stop running and talk to me?"

From the corner of his vision he glimpsed a bundle in brown wool match his strides. "First, I'm not running, I'm walking fast. Second, I don't want to talk to you. You're crazier than a bedbug!"

The crunching of her boots against the snow ceased. "Has coming to America turned you into a coward?"

"A coward!" Tom jerked to a stop and swung around. She was a whole lot closer than he'd expected. So close that if she hadn't jumped back, the tip of his bayonet would have sliced off the tip of her upturned nose.

The near mutilation surprised him as much as her.

He recovered much faster, though. "Look, I don't know which one of you spun that cockamamie yarn, but it won't wash. I meant what I said—if your things aren't packed in one hour, I'm tossing them in the snow."

"You would turn away your own family?" she cried. "Where do you expect us to go?"

"Since you aren't my family, that isn't my problem."

She grabbed his sleeve when he attempted to spin away. "Now you listen here—I have traveled halfway around the world to bring our family together again, a family you left to the mercy of Prussian revolutionaries." Her furious breaths fogged the air with each exhale. Her eyes flashed like twin blades of a calvaryman's sword. "And while you have been off playing soldier the last four-and-a-half years, Oma, Doreen and I have worked these lands, brought them back to life, and made a home for you to come back to. The very least you could do, husband, is give us a proper welcome!"

He raised his brows mockingly. "Are you finished now?"

In answer, she released the grip on his coat and stiffened her spine.

"Good." He pinned her with a steady look. "Then let me put this in words you can't misunderstand. I'm *not* your husband—or anybody else's, for that matter. I don't have a wife, I don't have a daughter, and I for sure don't have an *Oma.*"

"*Liebling*," she said sternly, "I realize I have grown up since you last saw me . . ."

Grown up? He almost laughed. She had to be, what? Late twenties? Yet she was hardly bigger than her daughter!

"But I am your Ginny. And Doreen is our child. Sweet mercy, Thomas, she is eleven years old and has just now met her own father. Would you refuse her the chance to know you?"

Tom bent low, refusing to let her make him feel guilty for something he had no part of. "I don't have the foggiest notion what you are talking about, because I have never laid eyes on any of you in my life."

"But you sent me letters. . . ."

Letters? Tom crossed his arms over his chest. "Show them to me."

Grief slashed through the liquid blue of her eyes. "I do not have them anymore. They vanished, and I cannot find them."

"Ahhh." He nodded slyly. "How convenient—make the proof disappear."

"I do not need letters to prove you are my husband," she insisted. "I know. The moment you looked at me I knew."

"And how did you reach *that* absurd conclusion?"

She squared her shoulders. "My heart told me."

Now he knew she was mad. "Then your heart lied."

"But you are Thomas Herz."

"Heart! My *name* is Tom Heart! And I'm telling you, I'm not the fellow you are looking for!"

"You are Deutsche," she charged. "I can hear it in your voice."

Tom silently cursed the faint trace of his accent. Though he spoke three languages fluently, had often been requested to act as a translator between troops and officers, he hadn't quite been able to rid from his voice his German origins. Obviously she hadn't missed that telling fact. "I'm part French, too. That doesn't make me married to Josephine Bonaparte."

"You own a farm in Wisconsin."

"Along with hundreds of other men!" he cried with exasperation.

She tilted her chin in the air. "You went to fight in the war. You always fought in wars."

Tom sucked in, the volley hitting a little too close to home. A lucky shot, he told himself, turning to stare vacantly at the barn. She had no way of knowing that his life had been one battle after another—she couldn't know. Only his brother Matthew had known, for he'd fought the same battles. First for survival after the deaths of their parents, then for a country to call their own.

And Matthew had been the one to fight beside him for passage on a ship bound for America. The land of liberty, so everyone said, the answer to their dreams. His brother had been fortunate, though. It wasn't until after Matthew died that Tom learned they'd sold their souls to the devil, indentured to pay for the passage.

Joining the Union army five years later had been bittersweet revenge. He'd climbed the ranks quickly, took command of the Second Wisconsin Infantry. Earned himself commendations, awed his superiors. None of them had ever guessed that it hadn't been Yankee patriotism driving him to whip the Confederates, but a personal vendetta against bondage.

When was enough, enough? He was over thirty years old and fed up with living under another's control. Sick of having to fight for the God-given right to independence. He'd promised himself that if he made it through the war alive, he'd never fight again.

But unless he convinced this delusional woman that they were not, had never been, and never would be married, he feared he'd wind up battling for what he held most dear—his freedom.

"Lady," he sighed and rubbed his forehead, "over ninety-one thousand Wisconsin men fought in the war." The odds of making her see reason were pretty damn pitiful, Tom knew. Not one thing he'd said to her so far had made any difference. Yet he couldn't just give up. "Just accept that you've got me mixed up with someone else."

A glimmer of doubt entered her eyes. Tom's hopes climbed. Had he finally gotten through to her? Had he finally convinced her she'd accused the wrong man? She studied him for a long while, as if weighing the possibility.

Then, without warning, she flung her arms around his neck and dragged his head down to her level. Her lips crashed onto his.

Stunned, Tom reared back, pulling her feet off the ground. His palms fell flat against her back, just above the outward swell of stiff crinoline under her cape and skirt.

He tried pushing her away. She tightened her grip, her mouth ground against his. Fearing he might hurt her, Tom distanced his mind from the act. He could do that, had done it for years.

Her mouth opened and closed over his rigid lips, urgently coaxing a reaction he refused to give.

Notch by notch his will weakened.

With a moan of surrender, his fingers curled around her slim waist, pulling her closer. She smelled so good, like a fresh breeze after the bitter stench of battle. And she felt so warm, like a ray of sunshine in the dawn of winter. In the back of his mind, Tom knew kissing her back was a mistake, yet the strength to deny himself the luxury of holding something this soft and sweet, just for a minute, deserted him.

No, his strength had been stolen. By her.

Breaking the kiss, she whimpered against his mouth, "Oh, Thomas . . . I knew it was you." She slid down the length of him until her feet touched ground. Her head was tilted back, her eyes shut. Then amber lashes raised slowly, giving him a glimpse of a kindred hunger. "Only your kiss can make me feel this way."

He found himself mesmerized by eyes the dark blue of indigo dye. "What way?" The instant the words left his mouth, Tom damned himself for asking.

"Alive. Like a sonata that only you can play." She brought his limp hand to her lips and kissed his knuckles.

Oh, God. What was she doing to him? Why? "What do you want from me?" he whispered, his will dying.

"The only thing I've ever wanted, Thomas—" There was a catch in her voice. "To be with you."

And he got the sudden, sinking suspicion that this argument had been lost before it even started.

Tearing himself away from her, Tom dragged his hat from his head and clutched it in his hand. He stared at the bare, snow-laden branches of the maple tree in the center of the yard.

By thunder, it had been a long trek from Tennessee. He hadn't slept or eaten in nearly two days, he hadn't bathed in a

week. . . . The last thing he felt up to doing was pitting his
sluggish wits against her German tenacity.

He was just too tired.

With a resigned sigh, he said, "Fine. Stay the night if you
want, I don't give a damn anymore." He'd be in better shape to
straighten out this whole confounded mess in the morning.

A smile sunny enough to melt snow spread across her face.

Then she picked up his abandoned rifle, slid her arm around
his back, and steered him toward the house. "What you need is
a warm meal, a hot bath, and a good night's sleep."

Drained, he moved obediently, so accustomed to following
orders that a long time passed before he realized that he was no
longer in the army, and that the woman issuing them was now
his commanding officer.

Tom stood in the kitchen, feeling unaccountably out of place.
Ginny had disappeared somewhere. He told himself he didn't
care where she'd gone—after that little fiasco in the yard it
was best he kept his distance from her anyway.

Except she'd left him at the mercy of her relatives.

Still brooding over how he'd relented on letting them stay,
Tom washed off the worst of the travel grime at the sink, then
eased into the spindle-backed chair at the head of the table. The
girl, Doreen, quickly added another setting and Bertha heaped
his plate high with enough food to feed half a battalion.

Soon the delicious aroma of browned Bratwurst and tender
Rubes lured him out of his mood. There was even a fresh-baked
loaf of black bread. He didn't realize how much he'd missed
authentic German food until the feast was laid out before him.
Of course anything home-cooked would seem appetizing after
years of sheet-iron crackers and tinned beef. His men had
dubbed it "embalmed beef" because it had been soaked so long
in salt that it tasted like it had been packed by an undertaker.

Just as Tom picked up his fork, Ginny breezed in through the
front door, her brows knit together. "Has anyone seen David?"

He slapped the fork so hard against the table that it
ricocheted across the room. "Who in tarnation is David?" How
many people had she moved onto his farm?

"He is a young man I hired to help on the *Hof*. I cannot find
him anywhere, and I need his help."

Chagrin warmed Tom's cheeks. He'd forgotten all about the boy. "If he's tall and skinny and has black hair, you'll find him in the barn."

"I have looked in the barn."

"He's tied to a post next to the tack room."

Ginny marched over to his side. She plunked her hands on her hips, drawing Tom's attention to the womanly curves beneath her plaid dress and apron. "You tied him to a post?"

Quickly averting his eyes from her shapely figure, he mumbled in defense, "I thought he was a vagrant."

"Oh, sweet mercy!"

Her skirts twirled like a parasol as she disappeared out the front door, no doubt to rescue the hireling.

Tom rubbed his clammy palms against his pant legs, then felt his face redden when Doreen handed him a clean fork. He stabbed the tines into a turnip while Doreen and Bertha took seats on either side of him.

Half his plate had been cleared before he noticed that neither of his companions had touched their meals. Flicking glances at each of them, Tom found both staring at him as if he were performing a miracle.

He squirmed uncomfortably. He forked a chunk of sausage into his mouth, trying to ignore his rapt audience. The food became harder to swallow. They continued to stare at him for so long that he would have bet if they left the table, their eyeballs would stay behind. Hadn't they ever seen a hungry man before? What did they think they'd miss?

Movements captured his attention. He slanted a look toward Doreen. Her hands moved rapidly in a series of swishes and swirls. Bertha seemed to understand what they meant, for she nodded and responded with a big, white, slightly buck-toothed smile.

Tom's brows rose as he studied the girl. At his open regard, her lips curved in a shy smile. The boys better prepare themselves, he thought. In a couple of years she was going to be a hard one to resist—just like her mother. All sweet enchantment and raw temptation.

An image of himself tangled with Ginny in a lovers' embrace blinked in his mind.

Startled by the abrupt vision, Tom nearly choked on the bite he'd taken. He fumbled for the cup of coffee and took a deep drink of lukewarm brew, as if to wash down both the food and his wayward thoughts.

Keeping his chin tucked, hiding his face, Tom moped over the fact that his every expression—his very presence—was up for scrutiny.

The minutes dragged on like dead weights hauled across gravel, each strained second adding another painful nick to his normally thick-hided composure.

More motions from Doreen caught his notice. Tom realized she communicated with others through the use of her hands. "What's wrong with her?" he asked Bertha, waving the fork toward Doreen.

"She is happy to see her *Vati*."

Tom gritted his teeth. "I'm not—" He caught his slipping control. "Oh, never mind." Arguing up to this point had proven useless, anyway. But curiosity nagged at him. "Is she mute?"

"*Nach*, she can make sounds, but she cannot hear."

"She's deaf?"

"Since two. From de dot sickness."

That probably meant she'd caught measles, or a form of pox.

He felt a tug on his sleeve. Doreen pointed first to his plate, then to her mouth. A dainty, flaxen brow lifted in question.

"She asks if you would like more Wurst," Bertha interpreted.

Tom frowned at his half-eaten meal. Did they really expect him to eat while they watched his every move? He set his fork on his plate, his appetite disappearing.

Suddenly, it was all too much. The expectant faces; the awkward active silence; the foreign elements in what should have been a refuge.

He needed to escape.

Just as he scraped the chair back to rise, Ginny appeared with the gangly, black-haired boy at her side. The minute he saw Tom, he slunk back.

"Your bath is ready, Thomas."

There was a God after all.

6

*H*IS HEART SINKING, Tom absorbed the changes to the main room, feeling yet another link to his former life disintegrate.

The manly haven he'd left behind now looked like something that had jumped from the pages of a ladies' magazine. A prissy flowered sofa draped with a crocheted blue and green overthrow took over the spot his ratty leather chair once owned by the fireplace. The scarred rolltop desk below the front window had been moved across the room to make way for a spinning wheel, and a whatnot in the corner held a combination of European figurines and tiny teacups and saucers.

If not for the compelling presence of one familiar object, Tom would've run in the opposite direction. But in a niche by the chinked-stone fireplace his curved-back tub beckoned like a sultry mistress, steam rising from her surface in an invitation any man would find hard to resist.

Even him.

"Do I get an audience?" Tom grumbled, limping toward the sofa. He picked up a copy of *Godey's Lady's Book* then let it drop back onto the oval table with an old edition of *American Farmer*.

"David and I will hang curtains for privacy." Ginny set down the chair she had carried in from the kitchen. "Normally the tub is set up in the springhouse, but when the weather turns cold, we bathe in here by the fire. There is no doctor in the village so we must prevent illness any way we can."

David lifted a kettle from the hearth crane, where flames licked clear up into the chimney. After adding more hot water to the tub, he cut Tom a wide berth to help Ginny.

While they spread out a sheet, Tom strode around them to the shuttered window, saying not a word to the boy. Which was just as well. As skittish as David behaved around him, he'd probably jump out of his too-short trousers if Tom so much as peeped at him. "What happened to Doc Haines?" he asked Ginny, releasing the buckle of his scabbard belt then the fastener of his belly band.

"He joined the Union just as you. He did not return."

After setting both items on the deacon's bench below the window, his over-the-shoulder gaze strayed toward Ginny. David was tall enough to reach the ceiling but she needed the added height of the chair to tack up her corner of the sheet.

It should have been easy to ignore her, this slip of a woman who'd invaded his life. It wasn't. Not when fragments of moonbeams through the window danced in the loose upsweep of her hair. Not when smoky gold light from the hearth filtered through the sheet and illuminated her face, softening her features. Not when the wet hem of her dress weighed down the heavy fabric, enhancing her curvy figure.

Just a short while ago that figure had been stuck to his body like peel on an apple.

Tom tore his gaze away. Undoing the buttons of his uniform didn't take enough concentration to keep his mind from straying to that one brief moment in the yard. He'd let himself get closer to Ginny than he'd been to anyone in a long, long time. The edges of his coat spread wide as he flattened his hands against the windowpane and bowed his head. Maybe he was the crazy one. Any man with a lick of sense wouldn't be so aware of a woman intent on ruining his life. Why hadn't he just shoved her away? Instead, he'd stood there. Let her push her fingers through his hair. Let her press her body against his. Let her kiss him. . . .

Sensing more than seeing Ginny step down from the chair, Tom shook himself loose of the dangerous vision. Why had he ever touched her?

Straightening, he noticed David slinking away; strung sheets now isolated him and Ginny from the rest of the world.

With a grim frown Tom shrugged free of the tight coat. "What's the matter with that boy? He acts as if I'm going to pounce on him."

"It is a natural reaction from a child who suffered horrible beatings by his father."

In the presence of sliding his suspenders off each shoulder, Tom stilled. The loops fell heedlessly around his hips and rear. His blood turned to ice. "Beaten?"

"We found him two winters past hiding in the woods. Half-frozen, half-starved. Frightened out of his wits. In the years since he has lived with us we have done what we can to make him feel safe, but I am afraid we have not been able to ease his fear of men."

Knowing he hadn't helped matters by tying the boy up in the barn, guilt kept Tom quiet.

Ginny then made her way across the intimate enclosure. Reaching the part in the sheets, she paused. "Perhaps you will keep that in mind in his company and be patient with him?"

Tom let the query slide. He didn't plan on having them around long enough to have to exercise patience.

When she didn't leave, simply stood motionless, he wondered if she was waiting for him to answer. Tom couldn't say for sure. He refused to look at her. Every time he did his gut twisted in knots. His breath damned up in his lungs. His throat went dry.

Finally she said, "I will be back shortly with towels."

Alone at last he sat on the edge of the deacon's bench and removed his boots. One, then the other, thumped upon the bare floor. The effort sapped the last of his strength. Tom's elbows dug into his knees as he rested with the heels of his hands against his forehead.

This wasn't how he'd imagined spending his first night back

in Ridgeford. All he'd craved since his mustering out was silence and solitude.

Instead he'd found chaos and confusion.

On the other side of the sheet, dishes clicked together and murmurings drifted through the air, mocking his desires. He felt like a stranger in his own house. Nothing was as it should be. Not the rooms. Not the furnishings. Not the atmosphere.

Not even himself.

Because of Ginny.

With an annoyed growl he finished stripping off his woolen socks, trousers and cotton shirt. Well, he wouldn't have to put up with her much longer. Come morning he'd be rid of her. One way or another he'd get Ginny and her relatives out of his house.

He prized his freedom. And no German milkmaid with soft skin and an even softer smile was going to make him trade it for anything.

Ginny slid into the chair at the end of the table across from her grandmother. Doreen and David sat on either side of her finishing their supper. A plate waited in front of Ginny, but the thought of eating held no appeal. She rested her elbow on the table and absently rubbed her eyebrow.

"Does he still vant us to leave?" Bertha asked, pushing her plate away and lacing her fingers together.

"He said we could stay the night."

We have to leave the farm?

Ginny caught the motions of her attentive daughter and found herself gazing into a face riddled with shock. For a brief moment she almost regretted teaching Doreen to read lips. But the child had an insatiable curiosity, was eager to learn anything and everything, especially if it improved her communication skills. The lessons had helped pass the long winter days past. Even had she not learned to understand lip movements, a person's expressions oft times gave away their thoughts. Doreen read those expressions with amazing accuracy.

It is because of me, isn't it? Doreen pantomimed.

"No, Doreen," Ginny immediately responded. Whatever was

wrong with Thomas had nothing to do with their child. He had been just as thrilled as she when they discovered she would bear them a babe. "This is the first time he has seen you. Once he gets to know you he will love you as much as we do."

David set his fork carefully on top of his plate. "Miss Ginny? Is it me, then? If he's mad because I'm here, I'll leave."

"You will not! This is your home as much as it is ours. No one is going anywhere." Taming the frustrated rise of her voice, Ginny said, "Thomas is just confused. He is not acting like himself."

"Mayhap he is weary," Bertha suggested. "He has only just come home."

"Mayhap . . ." Ginny frowned. "It seems more than that, though."

"Vhat did he say vhen you spoke vit him?"

After a long pause, Ginny admitted, "He said I have mistaken him for another."

"But you said he vas your Thomas."

"He is." She was certain of it. Any doubts that she might have harbored disappeared the moment she had kissed him. No man had ever made her feel like Thomas did with just a kiss. "Yet he insists that he does not know me." She fell silent and pondered his odd reaction to finding them on the farm. *I don't have a wife, I don't have a daughter, and I don't have an Oma.* Ginny could understand him not knowing the others. Doreen had not yet been born and he had only met her grandmother that one time at their wedding. Bertha had not come to live with her and Da until years after Thomas left.

But she was his wife.

She twisted the ring on her finger. Two hearts, entwined upon a circle of gold. Heartbound, he had whispered twelve years ago beneath a September harvest moon. The word was even engraved inside the wedding band so she would never forget who she belonged to, he told her.

And she had never forgotten.

Had Thomas?

"Has it been too long, Oma?" She could barely bring herself to ask the question. She dreaded the answer. When he left Germany to find them a better life away from the revolution, she had not dreamed that the short time they expected to be apart would stretch into twelve long years. "After all we meant to each other, would he just forget me?"

Doreen's eyes grew big. *Like Herr Kirkmiller forgot his family when he came home from the war?* Her fingers moved rapidly as she finger spelled what she could not convey with motions.

Had the roof caved in, the three around the table could not have been taken more by surprise.

The villagers said Auggie Kirkmiller was not the same man who had left. They said the war had changed him. Their neighbor could not remember his mother or his farm—even his own name ofttimes when he first returned to Ridgeford a year ago. His service in the war and the loss of his sons had caused invisible scars that no one knew how to heal. Months had passed before he showed any signs of recovering, and even now he could not hold on to a thought for long.

"But . . . Thomas remembered where he lived, he remembered the village doctor. Why would he not remember his own wife?"

For a long moment Bertha did not reply. Ginny knew her grandmother was trying to form an answer in her mind, for she rarely wasted breath on meaningless words. She claimed that at her age, each breath was precious.

"War does strange tings to a man," she finally said. "Mayhap his heart led him home, but his mind has been left behind."

The more Ginny thought about the possibility the more it began to make sense. Fresh off the battlefields, could Thomas's mind have been scattered as Auggie Kirkmiller's had been? It would explain so much. His genuine shock at seeing them, his insistence that they were not a family, his tensing at her touch—

Oh, she'd known, *known* Thomas would not just forget her!

But if Vati is hurt where we cannot see, how will we help him get well?

Following her natural instinct when faced with a problem, Ginny offered a solution. "We simply love him."

What if he still does not remember? Doreen asked. *Will he make us leave?*

That thought was too upsetting for Ginny to consider. From the first moment she had seen Thomas marching through her father's orchard, he had been her greatest love. And when they agreed that a better life could be found across the ocean, she had survived on the belief that paradise would be waiting for her on the other side. That belief sustained her through the endless years of longing and loneliness.

The few letters she received early on in their separation confirmed her faith. That while she was bearing their daughter, Thomas had arrived in the strange new country. And while she and Oma pulled tiny Doreen from the clutches of death, Thomas had already begun preparing a home for them. And that he would send for her.

Two years she waited. Then the feeling set in—that if she was to be reunited with Thomas, she must arrange for passage herself.

Then Da . . . her vibrant, robust Da—stricken down in his prime. Left paralyzed and simpleminded. How could she have left him? The man who had raised and loved and nurtured her all her life? The strange sickness had taken away his ability to even feed himself. He would never have survived the journey, even had he wished to leave the fatherland.

Her father's death six years ago had freed her to make the journey, and after over a year of searching for Thomas, it had been a vicious blow to find not the husband she adored but an empty and neglected farm. Another four years she'd been forced to wait while the North and South waged a bitter battle, but she'd determined to make good use of the time. She put her heart and soul into all she had of her husband, into what he had begun for them. Their farm. They had labored over the land, built it into a success so that when Thomas did finally come home, they could rest the rest of their days making up for lost time.

Her reward? Ginny fought tears of discouragement. Thomas had come home without a memory. And if he made them leave now, all that she had done, all the years she had sacrificed to secure a future for her family, would be in vain.

She simply could not bear the thought.

Nor would she.

Ginny's lips set in a stubborn line. "You must not worry. I do not know what has happened to Thomas but we will not desert him in his time of need. We will be patient and understanding, show him how much we want and need him. Someday he will remember. And we will be a family, just as I promised."

It was the most risky promise Ginny had ever made, for she could not guarantee Thomas would regain his memory. But three people trusted her. She could not fail them. Nor could she fail Thomas.

She excused herself from the table, focusing her thoughts on the challenge ahead of her. She had listened to Mary Kirkmiller bemoan her middle-aged son's slow recovery often enough to understand that illnesses of the mind were not easily remedied.

However, come what may, Ginny would not let her husband carry his burden alone. As his wife, it was her duty to stand by him. Share all his blessings and help him bear all crosses. Believe in him when he'd lost belief in himself. She could do no less for the man who had come to America to build a better life for his family.

7

HE OPENED HIS eyes slowly, his senses relaxed by mist and hot liquid. A vision of shadow-splashed hair and candlelit eyes appeared before him like a dream. He blinked, bringing the vision into focus.

Ginny.

Tom lunged upright, jerking his knees to his chest. Rolling waves spilled over the rim and splashed onto the floor. "By thunder, lady, can't I have any privacy?" The murky water did little to conceal his body, and though he was by no means ashamed of it, neither did he appreciate a woman walking uninvited into his bath. Not this woman anyway.

She held out a short tumbler of amber liquid. "I thought a bit of brandy would help you relax."

Tom eyed her warily for several seconds before reaching for the offering. He sniffed at the heady fumes while she set the stack of towels down on the deacon's bench then took a bar of coarse soap and knelt beside the tub.

There was something different about her. He couldn't put his finger on it but she seemed more . . . confident. Almost as if she knew something he didn't. And secrets bothered him. Ranked right up there with surprises. A man had no way of preparing himself when he didn't know what he should be prepared for. That was how half his men had gotten killed.

Course, how dangerous could she be? Tom wondered, bringing the glass to his mouth. He choked on the first sip as her hand fished below the rippling surface. "What are you doing now?" he sputtered.

"Seeing to your comforts."

"That wasn't my comfort you touched," he barked, pulling himself into a tighter ball. "Just leave me in peace, will you?"

"It is my duty to attend you, Thomas." Nonplussed, she grabbed his ankle.

He resisted. "I can attend myself."

"I have missed doing so." She brought his foot forcefully out of the water until the tendon of his ankle rested against the rim. "Now stop fighting me. Lie back, drink your brandy, and enjoy being pampered." She gave him a crooked grin. "It will not happen around here often."

Tom sighed his exasperation and sank back. Why couldn't she leave him alone? Thunderation, he didn't have the strength for another battle. But other than physically removing her he didn't see any way of swaying her from her purpose.

The touch of her hand upon the soles of his feet drew a hiss from him. Tom took a generous swallow of the brandy to dim the pain. The liquor rolled smoothly down his throat.

"There are blisters all over your feet."

"And blisters under those," he said as she continued lathering his feet, then his ankles in turn.

Actually, Tom conceded, it was kind of nice having someone wait on him for a change. All right, he'd relax. Let her wash him. He figured she owed him anyway after living on his farm for who knew how long.

And as long as she didn't get the idea that he planned on letting her stay permanently, he might even let himself enjoy being pampered.

"How long have you been walking?"

He let his head droop back. The curved rim of the tub supported his neck. "Since I was one or so."

The soapy cloth stopped its circular motion. Her giggle trickled over him. "*Nach*, I meant how far have you walked since the war ended to reach the farm?"

It took Tom a moment to recover from hearing her laugh. He wanted to tell her not to do that around him. Somehow he couldn't find the words. Instead he said, "I know what you meant." Lazily, he brushed a shock of damp brown hair away from his temple. "It seems like forever but actually just since August. My regiment was one of the last to be discharged."

With each caress of the rag, the tension that gripped every muscle in his body started to loosen. Funny how something as simple as having his limbs washed could feel so soothing. "I already said you didn't have to leave tonight. You don't have to butter me up."

"I am not using butter, Thomas, I am using soap."

In spite of himself, a grin tugged at Tom's mouth.

"Was . . . was it as horrible as I have heard? The war, I mean."

Tom let his head roll limply to the side and he closed his eyes. Slick tin met his cheek. "It was worse than anything you heard." He didn't want to talk about the war, or think about it. In this tiny, sanctified corner of the world, he wanted to pretend it hadn't even existed.

"Many people in this area were against it," she said. "A recruiter was even killed in Dodge County after the draft began in '62."

He should have known Ginny wouldn't let the matter drop. The woman rattled on more than any he'd ever known.

"I must confess I was frightened," she went on. "It was much like the revolution in the fatherland. When we came to America, I did not expect to trade one war for another."

Neither had he. Opening his eyes, he peered at Ginny from beneath his lashes. She wasn't a classic beauty, but there was a wholesome sweetness about her, a gentle strength. What would drive a woman like her to travel across Europe, an ocean, and half a bullet-riddled country to find a man she hadn't seen in ages? He licked his lips, wanting to ask why she'd done such a dangerous, foolhardy thing. Except she might get the impression he cared. And he didn't. But he did want to know what made her think she'd find him here. "Look, if you're going to chew my ear all night, I'd rather you tell me how you wound up on my farm than listen to talk about the war."

"Oh, that is a long story," she said with a small smile and a negligent wave.

"So amuse me."

"Well, after we were granted admittance in Castle Garden, we journeyed here to Wisconsin, asking everyone we met if they knew where we could find Thomas Herz. For many months we searched for you. Nobody had heard your name, nobody had seen a man of your description."

A chill sped up Tom's spine at the thought that he bore even a vague similarity to the fellow she'd been looking for. Did she really believe they were one and the same? Or was she just afraid of being tossed out on her hoops?

Unaware of his thoughts, she went on.

"Finally we crossed paths with a worker from a railroad company who remembered you, but said your name was Thomas Heart, not Herz, and the last he heard, you were planning to buy a farm near Ridgeford. 'Heart' has always held a special meaning for you and me, so I knew we were talking about the same man. But when we arrived at the farm, we discovered that you had already joined the Union." She nudged his shoulder. "Lean forward so I can reach your back."

He scooted up and folded himself at the waist.

"Your shoulders are wider than I remember. You have not been eating well, though. I can feel your bones sticking out."

That didn't come as any surprise to Tom. He figured he'd lost close to thirty pounds by the close of the war since supplies had such a difficult time reaching the troops.

Her exploring fingers found the healed gash from his rib cage to his hip bone. "How did you come to have this scar?"

"Skirmish," he answered simply, trying to ignore the plea-surable sensation brought on by her featherlike touch.

"And these?"

The muscles in Tom's stomach clenched as she traced the gouged flesh across his spine, then the lighter scars branching from it, over his left shoulder blade. "I don't want to talk about it." He meant to sound harsh. Forbidding. But his voice came out in a husky whisper. His tongue felt thick and fuzzy. He had a disturbing idea that the brandy wasn't the cause.

"Lie back again," she ordered gently.

Strangely lethargic, Tom obeyed. To his relief she didn't pepper him with any more questions, though he could almost hear them whirring in her head.

As she reached past his neck to wash his chest, a renegade lock of her hair whispered across his bare shoulder. A scattering of goose bumps broke out along his flesh. His stomach muscles tightened. And against his will, a pressure began to build lower in his body.

Tom opened his eyes. He found Ginny watching him intently. Almost searching for . . . what? What was she looking for? His soul? If so, she'd be disappointed. He didn't have one anymore.

Again she surprised him.

"How could I have forgotten what beautiful eyes you have?" she whispered with awe, and a hint of . . . regret? "I see all the colors of autumn in them. Part green, part gold. Even a touch of russet."

He wished she'd stop looking at him. Wished more that he could stop looking at her. It was the liquor drugging him, Tom told himself. The liquor and the cleansing and the seductive quality of her voice. Her fragrance didn't help matters, wrapping around him like silken threads.

But in her darkening eyes, he glimpsed another power, more dangerous for its silent, stealthy assault.

Comfort. It radiated from her, surrounded him in a halo of warmth, soaked into his skin.

Of its own accord, his hand lifted. Water dribbled down his arm, dripped off his elbow, as Tom touched his fingertips to her lips. She didn't move. She didn't breathe. Neither did he. He couldn't. God, her lips were soft. He lightly traced the pale pink flesh. Softer than anything he'd ever touched in his life. And they tasted like . . . berries. Just like the elderberries that grew in the woods.

She brought her hand to his face. He turned into her palm. Closed his eyes. Felt the cottony softness of her palm curve around the sandpaper roughness of his jaw. *Hold me, Ginny. Just . . . hold me. I'm so tired of being along.*

Awareness struck him like a whiplash.

Tom wrenched his hand back, shot upright in the tub, and

bowed his back. What was wrong with him? He didn't need holding, hadn't for many, many years. He wasn't a helpless kid. He wasn't alone and scared. He was a grown man who'd fought damn hard for the peace and privacy she was stealing from him.

"Get out of here," he ordered hoarsely, ashamed of himself for letting her catch him at a weak moment. Again.

The faint smile she wore withered, hurt flickered across her face. "What?"

"I said *get out.*" A surge of blood rushed to his head. She recoiled as if he'd slapped her. But he had to get her away from him before he did something he'd really regret—like fall for her subtle charms. "Just leave me the hell alone!"

The derision in his voice cut through Ginny like a rusty blade. How could she have let herself believe, even for a moment, that her touch alone would somehow remind Thomas of the closeness they had once shared?

Pride kept her from letting him see the wound his words caused. She dropped her lashes, hiding her feelings. "There is no need to curse at me," she said quietly.

"I'll damn well curse whenever the hell I want to!"

Pursing her lips, she let the rag and soap plop onto his stomach. Rising with exaggerated care, Ginny picked up the bucket of fresh water and dumped it over his head.

He gasped as the freezing water hit his warm skin. A second later chills racked his body, yet at the moment Ginny did not much care. He deserved it. She had only tried to make him comfortable and he had cursed her for it. "I will not tolerate foul language, Thomas, even from you. Let that be a lesson."

Frustrated anger simmered within Ginny as she made a dignified exit, only to find Doreen and David sitting sprawled on their bottoms while Oma stood, her hand splayed across her bosom.

Ginny could not say who was more stunned, herself for catching them on the other side of the sheet, or they for being caught. "Have the three of you been eavesdropping?"

An answer wasn't necessary. Their guilty expressions told

Ginny exactly what they had been doing. How much had they overheard?

Narrowing her eyes, Ginny signed, "I believe it is your bedtime, Doreen. And David, if you want to go to Minnow Falls with Noble tomorrow morning, I suggest you, too, get some sleep."

"Yes, ma'am." Averting his eyes. David obediently headed for the stairs. Doreen hung back, her brows knit in puzzlement.

"Go on," Ginny motioned. "In the morning I will speak with you about respecting another's privacy."

Left alone with her grandmother, Ginny frowned. "Oma, I would expect such behavior from the children, but from you? You should be ashamed."

Bertha's hand fell to her side. She stiffened her spine and gave her graying braids a self-righteous toss. "How is a body to know vhat is going on in dis house if one does not keep her ears and eyes open?"

Ginny brushed past her. "*One* needs only to ask."

Bertha followed her to the staircase. "Den tell me vhat happened."

Pausing with one foot on the first step, Ginny sighed. "Nothing happened." Her gaze landed on the shadowy form visible through the sheer cotton. Delayed humiliation struck her full force. How could she have mistaken the glint in his amber eyes for that of longing? Thomas barely tolerated her presence. "He does not want me talking to him, he does not want me touching him, he does not want me near him. . . ."

Seams of worry appeared on her grandmother's brow and Ginny fell silent, aware that she had revealed more than she should have. Oma spent too much time fretting over who would take care of her granddaughter and great-granddaughter when she passed on as it was. Needlessly, too, Ginny thought, for Bertha Krahn was too stubborn to die.

Producing a feeble smile, Ginny said, "Forgive me, Oma, I do not mean to burden you with my troubles."

"*Unsinn*, Ginny. Your troubles are my troubles. Tell me vhat happened."

"He snapped at me and I took it to heart—that is all. Next time I will be prepared."

"Vhy vould Thomas snap at you?"

"One moment I was washing him, the next moment he cursed at me to leave him alone."

Oma's loud burst of laughter took Ginny by surprise. "Oh, *Kind*, do you not understand? Cursing is a sign of veakness!" Bertha tamed her chuckles and explained, "When a man feels tings beyond his control, he draws power where he can find it—your Thomas resorts to *Fluchen*." Brown eyes shining with amusement, she added, "Do not be offended by his profanity, use his veakness to your advantage."

Ginny's mouth went slack as Oma's meaning sank in. Thomas had not lost his temper because she had bathed his back or asked about his scars. He lost his temper because her touch had affected him.

The knowledge that she still had that sort of power over her husband both astounded and delighted Ginny. Grinning shamelessly, she confided, "Oma, I think you just gave me the answer I needed to help Thomas remember me."

Any hope of finding at least one area of his house that she hadn't invaded was quickly dashed the instant Tom entered his bedroom. Clutching his discarded belongings to his stomach with one hand, holding a flaming candle high with the other, he surveyed the room with a critical eye. She'd taken over even this space. Feminine articles were scattered everywhere—a brush, a hair collector, a tray of pins on the chest of drawers.

And against the far wall, piles of pillows concealed all but the top indention of the archer's bow headboard of his double bed. A thick peaches-and-cream crocheted quilt had been spread over the mattress, and smack in the middle was a distinctive lump.

Tom cautiously veered around a rack of sturdy shoes and umbrellas by the door. Reaching the side of the bed, he watched the even rise and fall of the quilt which was tucked around her neck. A fat white mobcap hid the back of her head.

"Wake up."

She didn't move.

Then again, why should she? She'd mucked up his homecoming in every other possible way. Never had he met a more mule-headed, unpredictable woman.

"Look, lady, this wasn't what I meant when I said you could stay the night."

She still gave no sign of hearing him. It figured. He'd get more reaction from a brick wall than he'd get from her. Hadn't he learned that already?

He debated on whether or not to sleep on the couch. The thin-cushioned chunk of wood and stuffing didn't look half as appealing as the bed.

No. By thunder, he'd let himself get maneuvered from one area of the farm to the other far too much. She'd not chase him from his own bedroom, too. He might not have been able to control his reaction to her nearness an hour ago, but as the water cooled his temper, so had it chilled his ardor. It wouldn't happen again. He wouldn't let it. The men of his battalion didn't call him the stone man for nothing.

Tom set the taper on the bedside table. "All right, lady, if you plan on sleeping in here, the least you could do is make room for me. You're hogging the whole bed."

Something must have penetrated her consciousness, for she stiffened. But she still didn't move over.

He rolled his eyes and sighed. A casual toss sent his bundle of dirty clothes over his shoulder. Gripping the towel around his waist, he swung the blankets back and slid between the sheets, trying to nudge her over with his body.

Muttering an impatient curse when she wouldn't budge, Tom flipped onto his side and pushed on her back. "Scoot over, will you?"

Finally the mobcapped head lifted and a pair of crinkled eyes peered over the blanket.

Tom's eyes widened in horror. Two rows of big white teeth surrounded by a gaping smile and what seemed an acre of thready wrinkles became visible over the edge of the quilt.

"Dear Thomas, I am flattered, but I do not tink Ginny would approve of her *Mann* sleeping mit her Oma."

Filling his shrinking lungs with air, he bellowed, "Ginnyyy!"

8

THE WILD CRY of her name sent Ginny tearing out of her room and down the stairs. Swinging around the newel post, she came to a skidding halt at the base of the steps and gaped in disbelief. Thomas stood at the entrance to her grandmother's bedroom—he wore nothing but a towel.

She blinked. A very *small* towel.

The corners barely met around his waist; the cloth parted high on his thigh, revealing a tantalizing wedge of hairy skin and a scandalous amount of pale hip. What details of his anatomy the socket lamps and scanty covering did not provide, her memory did. A short while ago she had caressed the same leg. Felt the firm muscle beneath. A sizzle skipped down her spine.

Boldly, irresistibly, her gaze followed the narrow line of fine hair that dissected his flat abdomen then spread across his heaving chest. The sight of his body now evoked an image of tangled limbs and breathless splendor. Her heartbeat picked up speed as desire flared anew within her.

"What the he—" He stopped the explosion in midsentence and jammed his arm through the doorway. "What in tarnation is she doing in my bed?"

Ginny reluctantly shifted her interest from Thomas to the figure doubled over in the bed. "Oma? It is where she sleeps."

"No, it's where *I* sleep!" He thumped his fist against his chest. "There are two bedrooms in this house—give her one that isn't mine."

Impervious to his bellowing, Ginny clasped her hands together at her waist. With a calm that belied the turbulent sensations within her, she said, "There are four bedrooms now, Thomas, and this one is Oma's. At her age she does not need to be climbing the steps. The rest of us sleep upstairs."

His face turned a mottled red. His mouth opened then clamped shut. Ginny imagined a string of profanity lay trapped behind his sealed lips. She bit back a grin.

Then he stormed past her, creating a twisting wind that fairly spun Ginny full circle. As he pounded his way to the second floor, she dearly hoped the steps didn't collapse.

"If I'd wanted a bed partner, I wouldn't have come home," he grumbled. Reaching the top landing he shouted over the balcony, "And she darn well wouldn't have a mustache!"

From above, a door slammed so hard the whole house shuddered. Ginny winced. Red-faced, she glanced at her grandmother. Rather than being insulted, Bertha was hunched over in the big bed, holding in her laughter.

"If you . . . vould have seen de look on his face vhen he climbed into my bed—I t'ought he vould jump out of his skin!" Another fit of laughter overtook her.

In spite of herself, a giggle slid past Ginny's lips. She knew she should not find humor at her poor confused husband's expense, and yet a picture of Thomas's reaction when he discovered himself in the wrong bed tickled her.

Bertha's chuckles died down and she wiped her damp eyes. "Mayhap you should check on *der Mann*, Ginny. Make sure he did not hurt somet'ing."

Ginny tried desperately not to laugh as she went upstairs. Once a single loft-style room, Noble had helped them erect dividing walls so she, Doreen and David each had privacy. She planned on taking full advantage of that tonight.

The door to the first bedroom cracked open and David cautiously poked his head out. "I heard yelling, Miss Ginny."

An ever present fear lurked behind his eyes, causing her heart to constrict. Much of what David had been through in his young life remained locked inside of him. The only reason she knew of his father's abuse was because the day she had found him, there had been deep welts across his narrow face. Months later Doreen had told her the welts had come from a razor strop wielded by his father.

"That is just Thomas being ornery," Ginny sought to assure him. "You have nothing to fear around him."

David dropped his gaze. "He ain't . . . uh, he ain't gonna cuff you, is he?"

"Sweet mercy, David, no! He may grouse and bellow, but he would never use violence to get his way."

"H-how can you be sure? He don't even know who he is."

"A violent man would have shot every one of us earlier. Thomas didn't."

The answer did little to pacify him, for he said, "Maybe not, but I'm just gonna lay here a while if that's all right, Miss Ginny. Just to be sure."

"If it will make you feel better. Just remember that dawn comes early, and Noble will be sorely disappointed if you don't join him." In the last year the giant black man had made remarkable progress with David, showing him that not all men were like his father. As Ginny proceeded down the corridor, she hoped he would someday feel as comfortable with her husband as he did with Noble.

She passed Doreen's room then opened the last door. It was easy to discern which room Thomas had entered, for his muted rantings had reached her all the way down the hall.

". . . damn pathetic when the master of the house can't even sleep in the master bedroom."

While he grumbled to himself, she folded her arms across her breasts and watched him send her frilly pillow sailing to the other side of the wide bed. Apparently he'd found the night-clothes she'd laid out for him, for a pair of faded red flannel underwear now covered him from waist to ankle. Ginny much preferred the towel.

His lips curled into a disgusted sneer when he flung the blankets back. "And pink sheets! If any of my men caught me sleeping on pink sheets I'd be laughed right out of the Black Hat Brigade."

He twisted around and caught sight of her standing in the doorway. His scowl deepened. "You're enjoying this, aren't you? You think it's funny that I almost wound up sleeping with your grandmother."

Ginny ducked her head to hide the telling twitch of her lips.

"I'm glad you find the most humiliating experience of my life so amusing." He crawled into bed, tossed one way, then the other, before finally settling down under the quilt. His damp, golden brown hair stuck to the pillow.

She hadn't taken two steps toward him before he lifted his head. "What do you think you're doing now?"

"The same as you—I am going to bed."

"If you climb into this one, I'm sleeping in the barn."

Undaunted, Ginny sashayed toward the open trunk pressed against the footboard. "Then I will come with you. However, I must warn you it is much colder in the barn. We should bring several quilts—"

"We are *not* sleeping together."

That is what he thought. "Thomas, you may snipe and growl all you wish, but I have spent twelve years sleeping alone. Tonight I am sleeping with you—be it in the barn, on the couch, or in this bed."

Leaving him no choice, Ginny extracted her sleeping gown from within the cedar-lined box and tossed the lacy garment on the bed. He watched her every move, brooding yet attentive.

Good, she thought, pulling the crisscross ties of her outer corset loose, drawing the ribbons slowly and, she hoped, provocatively from their bows. The longer he watched her the better her chances of success.

Never before had she deliberately set out to tempt her husband. It had not been necessary. Between the revolution stealing him away and the beckoning of America, she could count on one hand the number of times they had been intimate. And those times, Thomas always initiated their joining.

Yet her lips still felt swollen from his earlier kisses. Her fingertips still tingled from discovering the subtle changes of his body. And her blood, oh, sweet mercy, it had never run as thick through her veins as when Thomas looked at her then. If her husband felt half the desire she felt . . .

Holding his darkening gaze captive, she shrugged free of the vestlike corset then began unbuttoning her blouse. Did he notice that she had spent the last hour taking special care of her appearance? Brushed her hair until it crackled, then braided it in one long plait so that he could wind it around his hand like he used to?

The prospect gave her a giddy brazenness. She revealed one bare shoulder, then the other. The straps of her shift swooped low across the swells of her breasts. Her heartbeat quickened.

Ginny ran her tongue over her lips.

Thomas gulped.

The gown dropped to the floor, leaving her clad in her chemise and petticoats.

Then Thomas flipped the blankets over his face.

Ginny couldn't decide whether to laugh or clout him over his thick head. The plan had been so carefully laid out. And he was fighting her every step of the way.

But if he thought that she would relent just because he hid his face, then he best think again. There was too much at stake. She'd dreamed of being with him for too long to let even something as daunting as memory loss stand in the way of reclaiming his love.

She quickly shed her undergarments then tugged her nightgown over her head, allowing the soft cotton to shimmy down her body. Her legs felt like noodles as she approached him, her heartbeat raced. Reaching his side she peeled back the blanket, in spite of his firm grip. His eyes were clenched tightly shut. "Thomas?"

No answer. She did not expect one, though. And as she studied the man, this perfect stranger who was her husband, she marveled over the changes. His features had a hard, hungry look about them that had not been there when he left Germany. Smooth, olive-hued skin pulled tight around his lean cheeks. His firm lips were set in a perpetual frown. The dark blond whiskers around his mouth and on his chin gave him a rough, almost dangerous appeal he had not possessed before.

Her confidence plummeted. Twelve years was a long time.

What if she could no longer please him? What if he found her disappointing?

What if he no longer wanted her at all?

Battling a sudden attack of nervousness, Ginny took a deep breath of bravado then blew out the bedside lamp and plunged them into darkness. If she could make him curse at her, then she would know he was not as unaware of her as he pretended.

She crawled onto the bed, purposely dragging her body over Thomas's. He tensed beneath her. She suppressed a devilish grin. It seemed that some things between a man and wife could not be forgotten, no matter how dull the memory.

She stretched out beside him then turned to cuddle close against his side. She did not think he even breathed. "It feels so wonderful to hold you again." She drew a lazy pattern on his upper arm. "Late at night, I used to hold your pillow close . . . try to remember how you smelled. Try to recapture how you felt in my arms." She tasted the skin of his shoulder. Closed her eyes and inhaled the masculine essence of soap and musk, committing them to memory.

He rose suddenly and grabbed the pillow from beneath his head. Folding it, he shoved it between their bodies. Then he plopped onto his side. "The only thing that will be done in this bed is sleeping."

"Are you not going to curse at me again, Thomas?" she asked with feigned innocence.

"He—" His teeth clacked together and he ground out, "No."

Ginny beamed, pleased with her progress. Tonight she would content herself with sleeping beside her husband again. But tomorrow night . . .

"Good night, Thomas," she whispered to his back. "Welcome home."

9

*T*HE GIRL LED *him to the stone shed, tugging hard on the chains manacled to his wrists. The grandmother stood guard over the entrance, a cagemaster, her face distorted. The air smelled of freshly harvested wheat and crisp bank notes. From behind the stone shed came the woman, a sorceress in virginal white, her grip tight on the chains in one hand, a leather weapon in the other. Knots had been tied to the end of the whip.*

"No," Tom moaned, thrashing his head from side to side.

The girl pushed him forward and smiled a smile of silent evils. The grandmother cackled. The woman gave him a sensuous once-over, then licked her lips provocatively. "We have been waiting for you, Thomas."

Waiting for you Thomas . . .

Waiting for you, Thomas . . .

His eyes snapped open, the crack of a whip startling him awake. He waited for the sting of a leather tongue to nick his flesh. It never came. Nor had irons been clamped around his wrists. Yet the dream had felt so real.

Gradually the haunting vision faded as the room came into focus. Raftered ceiling, plain walls, shuttered windows.

A woman pressed against his back.

He went stiff as a gun barrel. He couldn't catch his breath. His heart thundered. His mouth felt dry. Alarmed by the intense urge to seek her softness, Tom stared at the closed door. Gritted his teeth. Counted to fifty. Tried every method he could think of in an effort to ignore the length of feminine hills and valleys stubbornly attached to him from neck to toe.

He told himself he didn't feel anything. Ginny's arm curled around his chest, her breasts flush to his back did nothing to him. Ginny's slender thigh draped over his hip, her pelvis nestled against his rear did nothing to him. Ginny's calf along his shin, her bare toes resting against his ankle did nothing to him.

He was the stone man. He *didn't feel anything*—not for Ginny.

She sighed softly.

With a growl of raw torment, Tom grabbed the frilly pillow and sprang from the bed. Damn her. He should have taken his chances with her grandmother.

Downstairs, he flung the pillow onto the sofa then fell onto the thin cushions. Twisting, squirming, he finally found a tolerable position on his side. He'd forgotten a blanket, but a fire still burned in the hearth and warmed his bare skin. As if it needed warming. He couldn't remember feeling so feverish in his life.

His gaze landed on the unemptied tub. A memory of Ginny sponging him down flashed through his mind. The faint touch of her fingers along his flesh, the incredible silkiness of her mouth, the invitation in her eyes. His blood quickened, his breathing grew rapid.

Tom cursed at the empty room and smothered his face with the pillow, wishing he could block out the picture.

Gene and his stupid speeches on women's virtues.

Ginny and those dratted eyes of hers.

She had to go. He had to get her out of here.

It wasn't because he was attracted to her, though, Tom told himself. Or because she tempted him with her womanly assets and imported charms.

He wasn't attracted to her.

And she didn't tempt him.

She was just the first woman he'd been near in months; any

red-blooded man would be aware of her. So she caused a stirring inside him unlike anything he'd ever felt before. So he couldn't explain why. Not everything in life came with explanations. Tom knew that all too well.

But it sure as thunder wasn't because he was attracted to her.

The stern mental scolding helped some. At least he wasn't breathing heavily anymore.

Groggy from lack of sleep, Tom rolled off the couch, wincing at the stiffness that had settled into his muscles. Yawning, he wandered into the kitchen. After searching the well-stocked shelves for several minutes he found a sack of coffee beans. He shut his eyes and breathed in the aroma of real honest-to-God coffee. Just as he'd brought out the grinder, Ginny's grandmother entered the kitchen.

"*Gutt Morgen*, Thomas."

He slanted a sideways look at her. Her brown eyes twinkled, her age-pleated cheeks were rosy. And why not? She'd probably gotten a grand night's sleep in *his* bed. "Mornin'," he mumbled.

"Should I expect anutter visit dis evening?"

To Tom's utter humiliation, a blush crept up his neck. "You always rise this early?"

"Of course. Dis is a farm. Chores must begin at sunrise."

And she was probably always this cheery, too, he thought, scowling. Tom directed a wary glance up the steps. "I guess that means the rest of them will be down soon."

"By de time breakfast is on de table, dis kitchen vill hear de clatter of feet coming down de stairs."

So much for his peace and quiet. "I suppose you've been taking care of them for a long time."

"Mmm-hmm. Since I came to live mit Ginny and *der Vater* vhen de baby grew ill. Fritz vorked de orchards, you ver in America. She needed help—but she vill never admit dat." The old woman smiled tenderly as she tied an apron around her ample waist. "Ginny is special. She is strong, sensitive. And stubborn? Ohhh, *Gott,* she is more stubborn even than *der Vater.*" Bertha wagged her finger at Tom. "My son vas de most hardheaded Bavarian ever known but Ginny is vorse." Not a gray hair stirred when she shook her head.

While the old woman pushed past him to dig potatoes out of the bin under the counter, Tom opened the drawer of the grinder, muttering, "Tell me something I haven't already figured out." But to his surprise he found himself intrigued. Bertha was giving him a better idea of what Ginny was like and he mentally filed each tidbit—to better understand how to get rid of her, of course.

"She loves to de bone," Bertha said matter-of-factly as she primed the pump attached to the sink. Then the lever stilled. The luster in her dark eyes dimmed, her voice took on a faraway tone. "I have alvays told her dat she loves too deeply. Someday dat vill be her downfall. . . ." Pulling herself from whatever cloud she'd wandered to, Bertha shrugged. "But she does not listen to an old voman."

"She doesn't listen to anybody. She hears what she wants to hear and believes what she wants to believe." As teeth-gnashing as he found the habit, Tom nonetheless recognized a protective barrier when he saw one. Except he didn't see what Ginny needed to protect herself from. He was the one with the most to lose.

"Dat is because she vas born *der Ausbesserer*." Bertha explained.

In the process of pouring freshly ground beans into the enamel coffeepot, Tom paused to watch the steel blade of a knife Bertha wielded make rapid dices through the potatoes. "A fixer?"

"Mmm-hmm. From de time she could valk, my Ginny believed dat nutting broke dat could not be fixed mit a sharp mind, a strong back, and much tender care."

"And I suppose she thinks I'm broke."

Bertha tilted her head to the side. "*Ja*, I guess you could say she does!"

"Well, I'm not. I've got my own mind, a strong enough back and I don't need any tender care. If she's looking for something to fix this time, she needs to look elsewhere."

"Thomas, I tink you are most in need of Ginny's fixing."

Scowling deeply, Tom walked the boundaries of his land, hoping the fresh air would clear his head. He tried to lose himself in the brilliance of the sunrise throwing diamond flakes on the snow. The peacefulness that stretched as far as the crow flew. The crisp flavor of approaching winter.

Bertha's words persisted, though, pounded at his brain until his head ached. So Ginny was a fixer, huh? She thought he needed fixing?

They were both absurd.

There wasn't a damn thing wrong with him. Just because he refused to claim a family that didn't belong to him didn't mean there was something wrong with him. He didn't want a family. Didn't want that sort of lifetime commitment, that . . . *sentence*. Was that so hard to understand? Apparently.

Clearing snow away from a small spot at the edge of the field, Tom scraped a measure of soil into his hand, held the cold grains in his palm. Now here was something that needed fixing. The land. No matter how rich the soil, no matter how diligent his efforts, he'd sat and watched crops wither and die from drought two years in a row. The third year, he'd managed to bring in a bumper corn crop, only to receive a pittance per bushel from the flooded market.

That which should have proven his success as an independent man instead served to remind him of his failures.

Then the war came along.

The rattle of an approaching wagon mercifully distracted Tom from thoughts of the war. It came to a halt in front of the house. Rising, Tom brushed his hands against the gold canvas strip running down the outside seam of his trousers. From the high seat of the wagon, a pair of midnight eyes studied him from a serious black face. Even across the distance between them, Tom could tell that this was not a man to tangle with.

For long moments they stared at one another, wary, assessing, before the driver's gaze swept the yard. Doreen had just come out of the house, swinging a small basket at her side. Spying the driver, she waved.

He lifted his hand in greeting while watching her open the gate to the chicken pen and disappear into the mesh-fenced area.

Then he turned his attention back to Tom and stepped down cautiously from the wagon. He was built like a brick house, with a wide chest and oak-trunk thighs, strengthening Tom's suspicion that this man could lay him flat with one swift blow.

"Who you be?" he asked in a voice that seemed to come from his gut. It sounded like a demand.

Tom squared his shoulders, refusing to let the man's size intimidate him. "I own this place."

A wide, blinding-white smile slashed across his face. "You be Mister Tom?"

"That's right. Who are you?"

"Name's Noble," he said, holding out a hand the size of the rear quarter of a butcher-ready hog. Tom returned the gesture, and nearly had his own hand crushed by the man's grip.

No man of his acquaintance fit a name better than Noble fit his. He carried himself with an air of confidence that could easily be misinterpreted as arrogance. Yet when he spoke, his voice was deeply mellow, with a definite note of Carolinian rearing, and as respectful as though he were talking to a preacher. "I work for Miss Ginny—and you, it seems. I bet she's just tickled pink you come home."

Tom flattened his lips, unsettled by the ease with which Noble insinuated that he and Ginny were a team. "By working for me, you mean on the farm?"

"Sometimes. Mostly I tend the smithy and stables and watch over the womenfolk." He gestured toward the frost-laden field. "You'll be amazed at how good Miss Ginny kept this place up while you been gone. She done you proud. Stood fast when folks tried talkin' her into leavin'. Fact, I thought you mighta been that fella who's been bullyin' her around."

"Which fellow is that?" Tom asked, unnerved by the idea of someone harassing Ginny.

"She ain't told you 'bout Marks?"

"We haven't exactly done much talking."

Noble let out a loud, robust laugh. "Nope, I don't 'spect you did, don't 'spect you did. Much more impo'tant things ta do with a missus than talk."

Tom didn't bother correcting Noble's mistaken conclusion. "I'd like to hear about Marks."

"He's been payin' visits to folks offerin' money fo' their lands. But Miss Ginny tol' him he had ta wait for you to come back."

"I won't sell."

"She'll be happy ta hear that. She's put her blood and sou[l] into these fields. Made 'em prosper, too."

Paling, Tom said, "That's impossible. They wouldn't produce a thing in the three years I sowed them."

Noble shrugged. "Miss Ginny just got this feeling—sai[d] corn wasn't the answer. Talked ever'body in these parts int[o] plantin' wheat."

"Wheat?"

"Yep. Grew like magic, too. Come harvest time, the Missu[s] Kirkmiller let ever'body take turns usin' her McCormick reaper. We reaped one neighbor's crop then moved on to the next. Then I took it into Minnow Falls and the army bought u[p] what we didn't need like hotcakes."

Tom turned his face toward the pinkening horizon. Why hadn't he thought to plant wheat as a market crop? But he knew why—because everybody advised him that corn had a highe[r] yield per acre and wheat was harder to grind. "What did it sell for?"

"Don't rightly know, 'xactly. But folks weren't losin' their farms no more. And they paid off what they owed for the seed after the first cradlin', so I s'pect it was a lot."

He could hardly believe it. He hadn't been able to save hi[s] brother so he'd sought to save their dream. And along came Ginny, stripping him of that chance.

His jaw went taut. A vein in his neck throbbed. Anger, swif[t] and deep, scored Tom's soul. Anger at the land, for no[t] cooperating with him, fighting his toils every step of the way. Anger at himself, for not thinking of planting wheat. Most of all, anger at Ginny for succeeding where he had failed. For making a bundle off of land that didn't even belong to her . . .

Without a word to Noble, Tom spun away, suddenly more determined to rid himself of Ginny's presence than ever.

He stormed past the henhouse, past the barn, past the maple tree. Just as his furious strides carried him past the front porch, he caught sight of Ginny stepping outside.

Tom stopped to glare at her. The smile she wore wilted. "Thomas?"

"You had no right—*no right!*"

"No right to what?"

"This is my land, Ginny, mine." He thumped his fist against his chest. "You had no right working it." He advanced toward her, clenching his hands at his sides. "I want to know why!"

She reared back as if the resentment inside him had scorched her, but she did not retreat.

"Was it so I'd feel indebted? Maybe support you and your family?"

"We meant no harm! I thought you would be pleased—"

"You thought I would *pleased* to come home and find a bunch of immigrants nesting on my farm, reaping profits from my fields, frittering away my money?"

"I have not 'frittered' away your money."

"What about all that new furniture? The oxen in the barn?"

"It is a woman's duty to furnish her husband's home! My Da was the finest wood craftsman in Bavaria. We brought with us his most valued pieces. And except for supplies, a pair of oxen, two swine and a *milch* cow, all the money is in the bank in the city. Not one cent has been spent that was not necessary and is not accounted for."

Baring his teeth, he demanded, "And just what in thunder did you expect in return?"

She brought herself up indignantly. "I expected nothing more than to have my family together again. I expected my husband to be proud that we fended for ourselves in his absence. I expected—" Her voice broke, then dropped to an agonized whisper. "I expected you to take me in your arms and tell me you loved me."

It was the last thing Tom expected her to say. His mind spun from the impact. But he quickly masked his surprise and bit out, "You could plow a field from here to Oregon with *that* expectation because it'll never happen."

"Where are you going, Thomas?" she cried as he turned sharply on his heel.

"To the village to find someone to take you and your interfering relatives off my hands."

10

$\mathcal{A}$LL THE WAY to town, Ginny told herself over and over that he did not remember her. That she had to be patient. Understanding. Compassionate and sympathetic and sensitive.

It was very difficult when he acted like such an *Esel*.

Moist puffs of air appeared before her with each deep breath she exhaled in an effort to calm herself. Ever since his return she had watched rage simmer behind his eyes. Felt the sharp lash of his wounding words. Heard him deny over and over again any connection to his own loyal family . . .

She tried to put herself in his position. If she had been away for many years, survived all manner of horrors, then come home to find people she perceived as strangers on her land, living in her home, how would she feel?

Probably very much like Thomas.

Frustrated. Confused.

Frightened.

Fear she knew. She had lived with it for so long that it felt like a companion. Each day as the war dragged on, she and the village women had gathered together, sometimes at Evie Mae's small cabin, other times at the pub or even the farm. A quilt would be draped across their laps. Needles darted in and out of squares.

At the first sound of the bell, light conversation died. All hands would grow still, then reach for and grasp tightly the hand nearest. Hearts pounded, throats went dry, eyes misted over. All would wait, and when the bell stopped at three tolls, the weeping would begin, and they would cling to each other in sorrow for another soldier lost.

By the time of Lee's surrender, the women of Ridgeford had sewn enough bridal quilts to fill the icehouse, shed enough tears to fill the Rock River.

Oh, yes, she knew fear well.

If she did not know her husband better, she would think him afraid of her. Recalling Thomas's actions of late, that conclusion did not seem so ludicrous after all. He was not the same man she had watched board a ship for America. What had the years done to him? What experience had been so damaging that it would erase his memory of her, of the love they shared, the promises they had made to one another? She wanted to ask him. Wanted to understand. But she didn't dare. Not in his present condition.

No, first she must stop him from evicting them from the farm.

Crossing the bridge, Ginny paid little attention to the wagon lumbering by her. Her thoughts remained soley on Thomas. The laws of the state escaped her, but she had the alarming suspicion that if he succeeded in pushing them off their farm, he would push them out of his life, too. Their marriage would surely be doomed then.

Just as she reached the stables, Evie Mae stepped into her path. "Ginny, was that Tom I just saw? You didn't tell me he was back!"

She slowed her steps, but didn't stop. "There has not been time. Something has happened to him—I will explain later, I promise. Right now I must stop him before he does something very foolish."

Leaving her friend standing openmouthed and astounded, Ginny finally caught up to her husband outside the threshold of Warren's General Store. She grabbed hold of him by the coat sleeve. "I cannot let you do this, Thomas."

"*You* don't have a say in the matter!"

"But a husband and wife should not live apart. . . ."

"Then consider us divorced!" With that pronouncement, he opened the door then slammed it shut hard enough to rattle the windows.

Ginny glared at him through the pane a moment before taking a deep breath and entering Warren's behind him. A counter ran the length of the store on the left side. On a stool beside the cash register sat a wren of a woman, engrossed in a crisp copy of *Ladies' Home Journal.*

The instant Vernice Warren spied them approaching the counter, the magazine dropped from her hands.

"Tom Heart! As I live and breathe . . ." Her work-worn fingers shot to the black ribbon at her throat. "Ginny, has the bell rung? I didn't hear the bell ring!"

"Thomas only just returned last evening."

"Mrs. Warren." Thomas tipped the brim of his hat in greeting. "Is Jonah around? I need to talk to him."

Vernice gave him a pitying look. "I guess you haven't heard. I lost Mr. Warren at the Battle of Shiloh."

"How about Sam, then?" he asked impatiently, speaking of Vernice's son.

"I'm sorry, Tom. Gettysburg."

Thomas was silent for a moment. Then he leaned his hands on the counter and braced his weight on one leg. "Maybe you can help me, then. See, I came home last night and found this family living on my farm—"

"Ohhh, and wasn't it wonderful?" The angular face glowed with pure delight. "Ginny, I am so pleased for you, my dear. I presume you made your husband's homecoming a memory to cherish?"

Ginny blushed at the fresh reminder of the lengths Thomas had gone to to avoid her.

Thomas frowned. "Yeah, she gave me a memory, all right."

Conspiratorily, Vernice whispered, "Your coming home is all she's talked about since her arrival. I must admit, however, that she somewhat surprised us. You never told us you had a wife and daughter. Of course, the way you always kept to yourself—"

"I never told anybody because I don't have either," he interrupted. His hands tightened around the counter edge. "And that's the problem."

As he launched into an accounting of how she and Oma and the children had "trespassed on his land" and "taken over his farm," a keen edge of panic sliced through Ginny's middle. Frantically, she waved her hands in front of herself. The minute she caught Vernice's notice, she pointed to her husband and shook her head with vigor.

Thomas swung around. Ginny locked her arms around her waist, tucked her chin against her collarbone and scuffed the sole of her high-buttoned shoes against the floor.

"What are you doing?" he asked, his brows narrowed.

Ginny batted her lashes with diabolical innocence. "Why, nothing, *Liebling*."

"Don't call me that."

"Yes, Thomas."

"Don't call me that either."

She smiled sweetly.

"Anyway," he went on to tell Vernice, "I've been trying to tell her that she's got me mixed up with someone else, but she won't believe me."

"Oh. Oh, dear," the tiny storekeeper twittered. "Oh, my. I am afraid I don't understand—" Vernice sought help from Ginny.

She pointed to Thomas, made like she was shooting a gun, then twirled her fingers near her temple. *The war has made him scatter-witted—*

Once again her husband jerked around. Ginny quickly latched on to a lock of hair.

"What in thunderation are you up to, Ginny?"

She pretended deep concentration on the limp yellow strand. "My hair is becoming a bit ragged, do you not think? Mayhap I should trim it. . . ."

"Dye it green for all I care, but quit distracting me—I'm trying to talk to Mrs. Warren here!"

The minute he turned back around, Ginny silently pleaded, *Do not pay any notice to what he is saying. Thomas is not right in the head.*

"Look, all it will take is a few simple words from you to

clear up this misunderstanding. Just tell her that I don't have a wife."

Ginny bit her lip and held her breath, offering a close-mouthed prayer that Vernice had understood her hasty—if confounding—explanation for Thomas's request. Even a hint of endorsement on her friend's part would seriously cripple her efforts to keep her family intact. Her husband needed her. He simply did not know that yet.

"I am afraid I don't know what you are talking about, Tom." Vernice raised her brows hopefully at Ginny. Ginny gave her an eager nod of encouragement.

Through gritted teeth, Thomas said, "Tell Ginny she's not my wife."

"Why would I do that?"

"Because she isn't!"

"But she told me she was. I have no reason not to believe her."

Relieved, Ginny released her breath in a slow, steady stream.

"You'd take the word of a woman you hardly know before you'd take mine?"

With a haughty look Vernice stated, "On the contrary, Tom Heart. I have come to know your wife quite well in the four years she has lived in Ridgeford whereas you I barely got to know at all."

Sighing in frustration, Thomas said, "Fine. If nothing else then, could you let Ginny and her family stay with you until I get this mess straightened out?"

Once more Vernice looked askance at Ginny. She shook her head briskly.

"I'm afraid I cannot do that either, Tom. There is scarcely enough room in our apartment for my daughter and me much less another family of four."

Ginny almost felt sorry for Thomas when he whirled around and stormed from the store. She hastened forward and clasped *Frau* Warren's rough hand within her own. "Please pass the word quickly that no one is to listen to anything Thomas says, nor are they to offer me lodgings."

"But what—"

"I do not have time to explain now. Will you please do this for me?"

"Of course, my dear, anything."

"*Danke Shon*," Ginny threw over her shoulder as she followed her husband.

Halfway across the lane he stopped so quickly that she ran into his back, then bounced off. "Stop following me, Ginny. The last thing I need is you traipsing at my heels while I tend to business."

"Then slow down so that I may walk beside you."

He raked his hands through his hair. "Just . . . go back to the farm!"

"Not until you forget this foolishness and come home with me." Ginny folded her arms across her chest, emphasizing her resolve. Once Thomas learned she could not be avoided easily, he would begin to see reason.

She would not give up until he did.

11

TAKING NOTE OF the stubborn stance and obstinate gleam in her eyes, Tom realized he'd have a better chance of fitting Lake Michigan into a bucket than convincing Ginny to leave him alone.

With a strangled sound, he spun on his worn heel and headed for the next store. She might not believe him, but once the people around here verified that he didn't have a family, she'd have no choice but to admit her mistake.

But Tom found the scenario at Warren's repeated at the tannery, the freight office and the cobble shop. The women now running each business denied any knowledge of his single status, claiming that he could have had ten wives and a dozen children for all they knew.

By the time he entered Silver's Pub, Ginny directly behind him, Tom's frustration had reached a rapid boil. Stiff-shouldered and tight-jawed he gave the same story to Hirham Silver's widow as he'd given to the other women he'd been forced to speak with.

Dolores was more blunt in her criticism.

"You oughtta be ashamed of yourself for not claimin' that sweet girl. Ginny's been nothing but faithful to your sorry hide and this is how you treat her? That there's your family and you're responsible for them, Tom Heart."

"Mrs. Silver, she's isn't mine!"

Throwing her shoulders back, looking down her bulbous nose at him, Dolores shot back, "Hummph. And to think folks is touting you as a big hero come home from war. Hummph. Some big hero you turned out to be. I ain't seen a coward so yellow since . . ."

But Tom was beyond listening. Twisting away from the bar he headed for the door. It was the second time in two days he'd been called a coward and he didn't have to take that kind of talk from anyone—especially not from a horde of sour-minded, sassy-mouthed women who didn't know beans about him.

Except what some interfering, trespassing, gold-digging immigrant had told them.

Outside the pub, the lid on his frustration blew. "What the hell kind of hogwash have you been feeding these people?"

"I have only told them the truth."

"As *you* see it! By thunder, isn't there anybody left in this village who can be reasoned with? Where are all the men?"

A veil of sorrow fell over her eyes. She pointed past the steeple of the Lutheran church. Spotting a half-dozen rows of grave markers, Tom sucked in a deep, swelling breath. "None of them made it?"

"Very few," she said. "There have been many tears shed in Ridgeford."

The sense of loss rising from deep in Tom's gut caught him off guard. It wasn't as if he'd been any closer to the men than he'd been to the women. He'd lived among them for three years, though. Suffered failed crops, lousy markets, and fickle weather with them. . . . A tiny part of him now wished he had gotten to know them better.

Now it was too late.

Tom shivered, then blew out a harsh breath. Stupid thoughts. He liked his solitude. Liked not forming ties. It had gotten him through the war, hadn't it? When half his regiment was wiped out by a Confederate cannon, he hadn't felt a thing, had he?

Even before that, though, the self-imposed isolation had been his friend. Kept him sane when he thought he'd go crazy.

Kept him tame when a wild obsession to run would have meant his death.

So why now? Why, after all the years since he'd gotten his emotions beaten out of him, did he suddenly care that he'd never see half his neighbors again?

His gaze shifted away from the cemetery and landed on the woman standing silent beside him.

Tom shut his eyes, a groan built in his throat. It was her fault. Somehow, he knew she was to blame for putting this chink in his wall of stone, just as she was somehow responsible for everybody refusing to take her in.

With a dark scowl, he shoved his hands into his pockets and started toward home. He didn't need to look behind him to know that Ginny was right on his heels. He hadn't been able to shake her since leaving the farm. She was worse than a damn thistle under his skin and twice as irritating.

Maybe if he ignored her, she'd go away.

He should have known better. She kept her pace sedate, and several feet separated them, but he could still feel her presence. It disturbed the hell out of him.

Tom picked up his stride, an unaccountable need to shake her off his tail gaining strength. The curious eyes of the village women marked his progress down Center Lane.

What the hell was he supposed to do now? Instead of being rid of his uninvited guests, he found himself stuck with them. He just couldn't bring himself to throw an old woman, a deaf girl and her mother out in the cold. Not with winter nipping at their heels. Yet nobody seemed inclined to take Ginny and her family in. All insisted they were his responsibility. It seemed that Ginny's open charm had gained her the loyalty of the entire female population while his reserve had earned him nothing but their contempt.

Before he realized it he was back at the farm, no closer to an answer than when he'd started out. Ginny kept up with him all the way to the barn. There, she stopped inside the doorway while he marched further into the dimly lit structure. If he didn't find something to keep himself busy he feared he might wind up wringing her neck for mucking up his life.

"Are you not coming into the house?"

"Nope."

She rubbed her arms through her cape. "But it is cold out here."

He didn't reply as he grabbed the first axe within reach.

"If you plan to chop wood, I can help you. I help David all the time."

"I don't need your help, I'm perfectly capable of chopping my own wood."

"Then I will keep you company."

He whirled on her, his temper snapping. "Don't you ever give up? I don't want your help, I don't want your company, I don't want your mollycoddling. Just . . . stay away from me!"

On his way back out her soft statement broke his stride.

"You are no longer a soldier, Thomas. The sooner you stop treating me like your enemy, the sooner we can get on with our lives."

He came to a startled halt, the accuracy of her statement hitting him in the gut like a cannonball. He didn't look at her. She didn't look at him. She didn't even touch him. And yet her observation stayed him as surely as if she'd laid a hand on his arm.

For a long time Tom stared straight ahead, unblinking, at a pine-covered bluff far in the distance. If she wasn't his enemy, then what was she?

It took every ounce of strength Tom could summon to walk away and not run.

Through the course of the morning, Tom felled four trees in the woods, used one of the oxen to haul them back, then spent the early afternoon chopping wood; it wasn't necessary, for there was already a ten-foot-high stack of firewood along the back of the barn.

Yet as if possessed by a demon, Tom lifted the axe, buried it deep in the wood, which splintered beneath the force of the blow, then stood another log on the block.

Over and over he hacked until split chunks of oak littered the yard.

Over and over he wondered what was stopping him from tossing Ginny out. He'd never asked her to come and make his house into a home. He'd never asked her to save his fields from ruin. He'd never asked her to wash his damn feet.

But she'd done all that and more. She'd said "to please him." Nobody did something just to make somebody else happy. Nobody was that selfless. No, they all wanted something in return. Germany had wanted control. The ship had wanted money. The factory had wanted cheap labor. And the Union, they wanted hired guns.

Tom closed his mind to the degrading memories before they could form. He was no longer at the mercy of another's demands. There were no legal contracts binding him, no irons chaining him to a debt long since paid. . . . He'd fulfilled all his obligations, and by thunder, he'd not wind up somebody's possession again. But unless he could find *somebody* to vouch for—

Suddenly Tom sank the axe head into the stump. Auggie, Auggie Kirkmiller would remember him.

12

*T*WENTY MINUTES LATER, Tom pulled the buckboard wagon to a stop. Calling the log building in front of him a house was stretching the term. The walls leaned at a precarious slant, the porch roof sagged, and weeds had taken control of the yard. It had been a long time since he'd seen the Kirkmiller's place, and though it had always been a bit run-down, Tom couldn't recall it being in such a sad state of disrepair.

He wrapped the reins around the brake handle then jumped to the ground. "Auggie?"

The mule penned in the small corral off the tool shack pricked up his ears. A pair of lazy-eyed hound dogs stretched out on the front stoop lifted their heads, then let them drop back onto their paws. Otherwise, nothing else stirred.

Tom kept his eyes peeled as he strode toward the open door of the shack.

Ten paces away from the wagon, a familiar rusty voice called out in alarm, "Lieutenant, get down!"

A sunbeam bounced off the deadly barrel of a gun. Instinctively, Tom dove to the ground just as a shot bit into a tree behind him. "Thunderation, Auggie, what are you shooting at?" Tom asked, wildly scanning the area to pinpoint the threat.

"Rebs."

Tom stomach-crawled toward the voice until he reached the shack and recoiled at the sight of the spare-built man crouching behind the corner. His tattered Federal uniform smelled as though it had never seen the inside of a washtub, and Auggie looked like he hadn't bathed in a month of Sundays himself. Dirt was crusted in the lines around eyes dark and beady. A scraggly brown beard covered his sunken cheeks. Savage caution emanated from him like a fume.

What the hell had happened to the hearty man he used to know? "Did you say Rebs?"

"They're hidin' in a trench 'tween the fence and the woods."

Giving the area a visual sweep, Tom's brow crumpled in confusion. There was no trench. There was no fence. Only the stubble of cornstalks remained in fields patchy with snow that the sun would melt by the end of the day.

"How long have you been out here, Auggie?"

Practiced fingers jammed one bullet after another into the Colt's chamber. "Can't 'member. Slimy sumbitches wiped out my regiment, though. Snuffed out every last one of the Second Artillery."

Oh, no. God have mercy, no. Tom shut his eyes with instant comprehension. Not Auggie. Not another one. He recognized the signs of a man crippled by war. Against his will, a parade of faces marched across his mind. A vision of Gene Mason stood out among the rest, face blank of all awareness as he'd sat in the midst of a blood-soaked battlefield staring at his detached arm. But Gene had pulled himself out of that pit of mindlessness.

It seemed Auggie Kirkmiller had taken a plunge. And it didn't make sense. Auggie had been one of the staunchest resisters of the war. Said there were better ways to settle a matter than killing over it.

"Why?" Tom asked hoarsely. "Why'd you join the fighting after you swore you wouldn't get involved?"

"Bastards took my boys, Lieutenant. Cut Andrew down like he was a piece of meat in a butcher shop and left my Alec to rot somewhere in Virginia. I gotta get my boys, bring 'em home for a proper burial. While I'm at it I'm gonna make the sumbitchen graybacks pay for what they done."

He knew then why Auggie had fought. To avenge the senseless deaths of his sons, neither of whom had lived to see their twentieth birthdays. A wave of sympathy crashed over Tom. Auggie's actions might have been admirable if they weren't so damn pitiful. The man was out here killing cornstalks to bring back his boys, but his boys were forever out of his reach.

Another two shots exploded into the early afternoon.

So much for leaving the war. It had followed him home.

Tom rolled to his feet. "Come on, Auggie, let's get you into the house before you hurt someone." He wrapped his hand around his neighbor's scrawny arm and tugged him upright.

Eyes turbulent as a tornado sky focused on Tom. "Andrew?" A gnarled hand reached out and touched Tom's face. "Is that you, my boy?"

Having seen cases similar to Auggie's, Tom knew he should have been prepared for the abrupt shift of mood. He wasn't.

"Where's your brother? Where's Alec?"

He had to swallow the choking lump in his throat before he could speak. Experience told him just to play along with whatever delusion Auggie was under. "He's fine, Pa. Told me to tell you he'd be home soon."

"'Bout damn time," Auggie said, pulling away. "Your mother's been worried sick. Now get your hinder in the house. Supper's gettin' cold."

Tom realized his neighbor was even more disturbed than he'd thought—the man's wife had died in childbirth fifteen years earlier.

Moving out of the imaginary war zone, he followed Auggie to the run-down house, where a woman in her late fifties had just stepped out the door. Auggie's mother's once vibrant red hair was now a washed-out pumpkin color, and her face had been weathered by age and hard work. She was just as gaunt as Auggie, too, not a spare ounce of flesh on her bones. "Tom Heart, I wasn't aware you'd made it back! Welcome home, boy."

"Thank you, Mrs. Kirkmiller."

"What brings you out this way?"

"I came by to talk with Auggie . . . he, uh, he thinks I'm Andrew."

"Half the time he thinks I'm a Blue Cross nurse. It'll pass once he's nipped a bit of Dolores's brew. Then I'll have a blubbering sot on my hands."

"Does that happen often?"

"Often enough."

The grief upon Mary Kirkmiller's face drove home the fact that soldiers hadn't been the only ones to suffer in the war. He'd seen men fight for many different reasons: honor, loyalty, liberation. Some with guns, some with voices, all with conviction. But for the first time Tom was being made aware of a different kind of courage, that of those left behind to watch their loved ones leave, knowing they might never survive. Women like Mrs. Kirkmiller and Mrs. Warren . . .

Ginny.

An emotion dangerously close to admiration unfurled inside him. The harder Tom fought it, the deeper it dug in its roots.

"Tom?"

The sound of his name jerked him from his thoughts.

"I'll take care of Augustuvus," Mrs. Kirkmiller announced somberly. "Go on home, now. Enjoy being back with your family."

Before Tom could protest that he had no family, Mary shut the door in his face. He stood on the threshold and watched through the dingy window as the old woman guided Auggie to a chair and wrapped a blanket around his shoulders. Tom wondered if Auggie would even recall his visit. Given the man's condition, Tom doubted it.

And it hit him that his last hope of anyone testifying that he wasn't Ginny's husband had just blown up in his face like a keg of dynamite. His former neighbors called a cemetery home. The village women supported Ginny. Auggie thought he was his son. . . .

With a sinking heart Tom made his way back to the wagon and climbed onto the seat. His shoulders slumped in defeat. He stared vacantly at the reins twisted around his fingers.

Everything was so different. . . .

Nothing was as it had been when he'd left. His house, the

village, his neighbors. His life. He sucked in a shuddering breath, then released it slowly. "Oh, damn."

With no sign yet of Thomas, Ginny ceased her restless pacing and perched on the edge of the sofa. Doreen then took up wearing thin the rag-woven carpet between the windows. Thomas should have been back long before now. He had been gone all afternoon. With each passing hour, a sense of unease intensified within Ginny.

Had it not been for her grandmother, Ginny would have already begun searching for him, but Oma insisted that Thomas needed time to put his thoughts in order and that Ginny must respect his wishes. Watching him ride away so soon after he had returned was the hardest thing she had ever done. But she knew she could not spend the rest of her life fretting each time Thomas walked out a door.

The sound of harnesses jingling in the yard brought Ginny quickly to her feet. Tossing the darning egg aside, she raced to the window and brushed aside the curtain just as Doreen wedged herself in front.

Ginny's joyous smile gave way to a disappointed frown, then a scowl of annoyance when instead of the ox-led buckboard, a familiar gleaming black buggy pulled by a pair of matching bays came to a stop in front of the house.

Bertha appeared behind Ginny, wiping her hands on he apron. The moment she spied the carriage, she sneered. "Vhat is *he* doing here?"

"I presume for the same reason he always visits," Ginny said flatly, letting the curtain fall just as C. R. Marks stepped out of the shay. Ginny had never cared to learn what the C. R. stood for, but knew that using initials was a common practice among gentlemen who thought themselves professional.

Marks was a professional nuisance.

In the last two years since the town forty miles to the north had petitioned to bring the railroad through, the founder of Marksville had persisted in courting the residents of Ridgeford, trying to gain access to their lands so that the railroad would have undisputed access from Minnow Falls, twenty miles south. Caught between the two townships, the citizens of

Ridgeford objected to lines being laid through the village and surrounding countryside. None objected more vehemently than Ginny, for the locomotives would be running day and night through the very same fields that had brought them such prosperity.

Unfortunately Marks could not seem to accept that some communities preferred farming to progressive industry.

She marched past her grandmother to the kitchen. "Please keep the children inside while I send him on his way."

"Do not go out dere, Ginny. I do not trust dat man. Make him wait in de cold until Thomas returns."

"We do not know when Thomas will be back." The sight of his face as he stocked the woodpile had ingrained itself in her mind. Eyes forbidding as red-hot coals. Jaw flexing with restrained anger. She could not recall one instance in their short time together when she had seen her husband so irate. But then, the years of their separation were a mystery she vowed to solve . . .

As soon as she dealt with a more pressing concern.

"You know as well as I do that if I do not go out there and speak with Herr Marks, he will insist on coming inside." And Ginny was not about to give the pompous man the satisfaction of knowing how disturbing his visits were becoming.

Throwing her cape around her shoulders, she stepped out the front door, shutting it firmly behind her just as Marks reached the porch.

"Good day, Mrs. Heart." He gestured pointedly at the door. "Aren't you going to invite me in?"

Ginny suspected the smile he gave her was meant to win his way into her good graces. Where this particular man was concerned, she had no graces—good or otherwise. He was a striking man, broad of shoulder, slim of torso, his tailored suit and raven-black hair equally as dark as his intentions. In spite of his fine appearance and courtly manner, greed lurked behind his deep-set brown eyes. "That will not be necessary. You have come to speak with my husband. He is not here."

"The two of you were spotted together in the village earlier, so I know he made it back from the war."

Had Marks resorted to spying? Her hold tightened on the

collar of her cape. "I did not say he had not made it back, I said he is not here. Not at the moment."

Marks scanned the area as if seeking proof himself. Other than a flutter of squawking chickens in the coop, and the Jersey flicking her tail in the nearby pasture, nothing stirred.

"When do you expect him, then?"

"Shortly," Ginny claimed, hoping he would not see the doubts warring in her breast.

Marks planted one foot on the bottom step. Resting his elbow on his thigh, he leaned forward. "I don't think you understand—I have business to discuss with him, business that can't wait any longer."

"I understand perfectly, Herr Marks. But your business will have to wait for another time."

All traces of feigned cordiality left his face. His eyes narrowed into slits. "The people of Marksville aren't pleased with the way you keep putting me off, Mrs. Heart. We've offered you a tidy sum for the center section of this property, and I can't guarantee how much longer their patience will hold out. The railroad intends to annul our petition—"

"And as I have told you during your previous visits," Ginny interrupted, "my husband has no interest in selling any section of Heart land, no matter how generous your offer."

He swaggered toward her. Her heart thudded, she forgot how to breathe.

"Let me give you a bit of advice, Mrs. Heart." He plucked at a lock of hair lying across her shoulder.

In spite of her effort to disguise her alarm, Ginny's eye twitched.

"Wives have ways of influencing their husbands to make, shall we say, wise decisions? It shouldn't be that hard for you to convince him to part with a few measly acres."

"My husband is not easily influenced," she retorted.

His gaze drilled into her, ground away at her composure. "Then I suggest you *find* a way to influence him—unless you want T. W. paying a visit. And I'll give you fair warning: T. W. isn't as pleasant to deal with as I am."

T. W. Ginny had never seen the man, but his reputation alone made her shiver down to her toes. None of the villagers believed the Brummers' house and outbuildings had accidentally caught fire in '62, any more than they believed the widow Welch's crops had developed an isolated infestation of weevils last summer. Farmers in the area had been careful to plow in the winter to destroy the harmful larvae.

And although no one could prove Marks was behind the disasters, it seemed too coincidental that each one followed his warning that if they did not sell voluntarily, "T. W." could persuade them.

But if he thought she would crumple at his threat, then he could think again. With false bravado, Ginny tossed her braid back and matched his steady stare with one of her own. "So you have said before. But Hearts do not respond well to threats either."

"Just make sure you pass my message on to your husband." Marks's hand fell away. His mouth formed a placating smile. "I will expect to hear from him very soon, Mrs. Heart. Good afternoon."

13

ONCE THE BUGGY faded from view, Ginny slumped against the door. The breath she had been holding since Marks put his hands on her escaped in a wavering trickle. All the man had to do was look at her and she felt soiled.

She pressed the back of her head against the grainy wood and shut her eyes. How much longer could she fend him off? She feared the day was fast approaching when the warning words became action. She—or rather *Thomas*—and Auggie Kirkmiller were the only landowners left holding out.

Recalling the possessive gleam in her husband's eyes after learning she had worked the fields, Ginny felt confident that Thomas would not part with even an inch of soil. And yet, in his present state of mind . . .

She stiffened with a sudden distressing thought. What if her husband's disdain for her was stronger than his attachment to the farm? What if he chose to sell to Marks? Where would that put her already shaky marriage? The farm was the only thing tying them together, and if he decided to sell, that connection would be broken. . . .

The door cracked open behind her and Oma's face appeared in the split. "I saw him leave. Are you vell?"

Moving away from the door, Ginny nodded. Bertha moved aside to let her in. The sight of a butcher knife gripped tightly in her grandmother's hand raised Ginny's brows. "What were you planning to do with that, Oma?"

"Carve Marks's heart out if he vould have harmed you."

Her grandmother laid the knife down beside a board of whey cream. Scattered about the table's surface were a dozen rectangular containers with Oma's distinctive medallion and a small cask of churned butter brought up from the spring. Several creations the size of gold bars already sat wrapped in salted wax paper, awaiting Noble's next trip to the city.

"I admit he is growing bolder in his threats but he would not dare harm me," Ginny claimed with all the conviction she could muster. "Thomas would not allow it."

"But Thomas is not here."

The statement held more than one meaning to Ginny. Even when he was home, he was not here—not the way she had anticipated.

"He will be, Oma." She could not allow herself to stop believing that her husband would come home. As long as she held on to that faith, one day she would reach the man inside.

Tom couldn't say how long he remained parked in front of the Kirkmiller place before urging the oxen in the direction of the village. But he'd come to one conclusion—he needed to put some distance between himself and Ginny until he could sort things out in his mind. Figure out what to do with her. And the only place he could think of to go where she wouldn't bother him was the stables.

Noble was in the corral, leading one of two black horses around the perimeter, when Tom finally pulled up. He wrapped the reins around the brake handle and leaped down from the box.

"Mistah Tom, this is a su'prise," Noble said, meeting him at the fence. "There sump'n I can do for you?"

Tom hooked his foot on the bottom rung and glanced around. The building stood about thirty feet high. New shingles covered the catslide roof and a fairly recent coat of paint protected the outer walls. Even the fence felt sturdy beneath his sole. It was a far cry from the Kirkmiller place, that was for certain. "Looks like you've done a fine job keeping this place up while I've been gone. I appreciate that."

"You come by to tell me I ain't needed no more?"

"Why would I do that?"

"Some folks don't cotton much to havin' a darkie 'round their womenfolk."

"Actually, the thought hadn't even occurred to me. I came by to find out if you'd mind having a bunkmate for a while."

"Anybody special?"

"No, nobody special—just me."

Taken aback, Noble asked, "What would you be wantin' to stay here wit me when you got yourself a family waitin' at home?"

Tom dragged his hat wearily from his head. "I wish everybody would stop saying that." He'd heard it repeated so often that it was beginning to sound natural. "Can I bunk down here or not?"

The question came out more curtly than Tom intended and Noble's brows rose at the tone. "Well, I cain't rightly stop you since this is your buildin'."

Relief rolled through him in waves. Tempering his tone he said, "I just didn't want to be any trouble."

Noble regarded him with a puzzled shake of his head. "Does Miss Ginny know you plan on stayin' here?" he asked in a singsong voice.

"Not yet, but I expect she will soon enough. News travels fast."

"Ahh, lovers' spat, huh?"

"Ginny isn't my lover, Noble—she isn't my anything." After eyeing the huge man for a moment, he sighed. "Why don't we go inside and make some coffee. I have a feeling this is gonna take some explaining."

Inside the combination smithy shop and stables, Tom spent the next hour delivering the details of his unwilling association with Ginny.

". . . so, simply put," he finished, "I find I've got myself a family that doesn't belong to me. But since I don't have any proof against her claim, it's come down to my word against hers—and hers is winning."

Noble let out a long, whooshing breath. "This is some powerful news."

"What I can't figure out is how every soul in this village can just believe her ridiculous story without proof."

"Why would she make up a story 'bout bein' married to you?"

"Maybe she's after money."

"Don't make no sense. If she was after money, she wouldn't have picked you—you were so far in debt it took all the profits from the first harvest to pay off what you owed."

The reminder was like carbolic acid to an infected wound, stinging Tom's pride. "Then for her daughter's sake," he countered. "It isn't unheard of for a woman to get pregnant, then either rope a man into marriage or claim widowhood. I'll wager she found herself in the family way, then figured she'd dupe some poor fool into thinking he'd done the deed. Who better than some brain-scrambled soldier fresh home from the war?"

But even as he spouted the charges, Tom couldn't reconcile the innocence he'd seen in Ginny's eyes with the picture he tried to paint of her. He was grasping at straws and he knew it.

So, apparently, did Noble.

He leveled a menacing glare at Tom. "You best watch who yo're disrespecting lest I forget the manners my mammy taught me." The low, almost inaudible warning came across with unmistakable clarity. "'Sides, Miss Ginny don't have a dishonest bone in her body," he continued amiably. "And any man with a lick of sense would take a woman like her for his own without a second thought. She wouldn't have to dupe nobody."

Then why had she chosen him? "Fine. If she is telling the truth, then there's only one problem. She's been waiting all these years for the wrong man."

After a long, pondering silence, Noble asked, "What are you tellin' all this to me for? You gotta know that I'm as fond of Miss Ginny as ever'body else in Ridgeford."

That was a good question. After all, he hardly knew the man.

But there'd been no place else to go after . . . "I stopped by the Kirkmiller place before coming here."

"Ahhh." Noble nodded, as if that explained everything.

"Maybe I just need someone to believe me," Tom said quietly. Then he laughed self-consciously. "Maybe I just need to hear someone tell me I'm not crazy."

"Well, how do you reckon on proving that?"

"The only way I can—I'm going to find her real husband." He turned to Noble. "And I'm going to need your help."

14

"*U*HH, I DON'T know 'bout that," Noble said, shaking his head. "Miss Ginny's been real good to me. She gave me a home, a job, my self-respect. . . ."

All the things Tom had needed to gain for himself, by himself.

Well, Ginny might have restored one man's self-worth with her good deeds, but bit by bit, she was robbing him of his. The farm should have been his fresh start, a place where he could build his future. If Matthew hadn't died, it would've been his future, too. That's all they'd talked of, dreamed of, worked for since their father's execution. Leaving Europe. Owning a place of their own. Making it into something they could be proud of.

Of course, neither of them had known one end of a plow from the other; ambition drove them more than any real talents. Ambition and, in retrospect, naïveté.

It should have been easy. Work off the contract they'd signed in exchange for passage. Tom should have known even then that nothing in life was easy.

Wrestling the memory into submission, he propped his forearms on his knees and steepled his fingers. "Look, Noble, I know you feel loyal to Ginny . . . but you were once a slave—I figured you of all people would relate to my need for freedom."

Noble hooted with laughter. "What would you know 'bout bein' somebody's slave?"

"I wasn't always a Northerner." Hesitantly, Tom confessed, "I spent some time in the South even before the war." Four long years.

"Not as some white man's slave."

No, he'd been given the sophisticated title of contract laborer. "Look, just because I wasn't forced to work on a plantation doesn't mean I don't know what it's like to have someone own me body and soul. Passage to this country wasn't free. Just like you, I had to pay a price."

Noble stuck a piece of straw into his mouth and leaned back, his elbows digging into the scarred top of the tool bench. Bridles, clippers, curry combs and tins of horseshoe nails surrounded him, both on the wall and on the bench top. "Did you, now?" His black eyes danced with mocking humor.

Without a word, Tom rose and unbuttoned his faded green shirt, then slipped his suspenders off his shoulders.

The instant he revealed the scars on his back the mirth faded from Noble's eyes. As an unspoken understanding passed between them, Tom wondered what memories he'd unearthed. Undoubtedly they were much the same as the demoralizing ones he fought to keep buried.

Neither crossed the line into forbidden territory, though. There were some things men just didn't go around divulging to other men. Like fear. Or shame. Or indignity. Unless he was deep in his cups, that is. Then even the most proudful sort tended to bare his weaknesses to anyone within listening range.

Tom didn't drink for just that reason. He would bet Noble didn't either.

Finally Noble cleared his throat and shattered the awkward quiet. "So what's that got to do with Miss Ginny?"

Tugging his shirt back over his shoulders, Tom once again hunkered down against the stall and stared at the scuffed toes of his boots. How could he explain to this man that the woman everyone in the village called friend scared the daylights out of him? "You ever been married, Noble?"

"Nope. Ain't found me the right woman to bed down with every night and wake up with every mornin'."

"My point exactly. Some men are cut out to have someone at their side from sunset to sunrise—I'm not. To me, marriage is no different than slave papers or labor contracts. They don't call it the bonds of matrimony for nothing. You marry somebody, you belong to them till death do you part. They expect you to be at their side every night, every morning. You have to tell them where you're going, what you're doing, and if they don't like your decision, they make you miserable."

"Ain't all marriages like that."

Tom rocked to his feet and braced himself against the gate. The black gelding within sidestepped and stirred up a fine powder of dust. "Maybe not. But I've seen enough of them to know that I don't want to take the chance of it happening to me. This is the first time that I've been free to do as I please," Tom said. "I can't give that up. But as long as everybody thinks I'm her husband, I feel as if I'm under some sort of restriction. Why should my life be disrupted because of another man's deed?"

Noble was quiet for a long while, seeming to mull over Tom's words.

Sensing that this man was the closest to an ally he had in this town, Tom swung his hand in an arc and pressed his advantage. "Think of it this way—she's waited twelve years to be reunited with her husband. A man she loves, a man she misses. A man she traveled halfway around the world to be with again. If she isn't made to realize that I'm not that man, think of what she'll be missing out on. And what about her husband? How do you think he would feel if he discovered his wife's affections were fixated on an impostor? This isn't just for my sake, it's for Ginny's."

"You ain't foolin', are ya, Tom? You really ain't Miss Ginny's husband."

Tom looked him directly in the eyes. "I'm not fooling."

Finally Noble sat up and rested his elbows on his knees. "Let's say I agree to help you. What's gonna happen to Miss Ginny in the meantime? Where's she gonna go? How's she gonna live? That farm's the only home she's known since she crossed the ocean, and I'll warn ya, she'll fight for the place, 'cause she believes with all her heart that it's hers."

Tom sighed. "There isn't much I can do with the land until spring, so she might as well stay on the farm while we begin a search for this Thomas Herz or whatever name he has adopted. Once he's found, she'll be his responsibility, and I can wash my hands of her."

Strangely, that decision didn't give him as much satisfaction as he'd thought it would.

It was near dark by the time he returned. Shadows and firelight spread a patchwork design across the yard as Tom parked the wagon in the barn. After feeding and stabling the oxen, Tom tied the black gelding Noble had provided him with to the porch, then quietly entered the house.

The aroma of fried pork cutlets and hot potatoes saturated the air. Lamplight spilled over the floor at his right.

Drawn to it, Tom clasped his hands behind his back and leaned his shoulder against the wall. David's back was to him as he fed a log into the fire. Bertha was spinning wool in the corner, the soft whirring of the wheel and the crackle of fire the only sounds in the room. Doreen and Ginny sat side by side on the sofa, leafing through a magazine. Ginny's hands moved gracefully as she silently communicated with her daughter.

An odd sense of peace crept into his soul as he observed the four of them. It seemed cozy somehow. Comfortable. Tom suspected that he could walk in here any night of the week and the same scene would greet him.

Was this what he'd been missing all these years? What Ginny seemed determined to snare him into?

He abruptly shoved away from the wall. Why'd he even come back here? It would have been better if he'd just stayed away. He didn't owe these people any explanations.

He was ready to turn away and slip out the door unnoticed, but Ginny's cry destroyed that plan.

"Thomas!"

A smile of pure delight broke out across her face, holding him captive. His gut twisted. That smile of hers was dangerous.

He wanted to tell her to stop it, and to stop looking at him with those trusting eyes. It shoved a sliver of guilt into his chest.

"Ah, Thomas, just de man I vas tinkink of—vhat color do you like best?" Bertha held up several swatches of colored cloth.

"Red, I guess."

"Hmmm, a fiery color for a fiery man, eh?" She winked.

Tom averted his face, trying in vain to hide the hot color rising up from his collar. Thunderation the old woman had an awful habit of embarrassing the socks off him with her outrageous comments.

"Come sit with us," Ginny invited, sliding over on the sofa to make room for him between her and Doreen.

His feet began moving further into the room before his brain gave the command. Tom caught himself too late to retreat. He'd been called a coward one too many times to suit him. Even so, he chose the safety of the deacon's bench rather than let Ginny's nearness unsettle him again.

Doreen's hands began to make those meaningless motions. Tom watched the girl, fascinated in spite of himself with her method of communicating. And it struck him as ironic that the quiet he'd craved for the last four years was hers for a lifetime. It didn't seem fair, he thought. He'd asked for silence. She hadn't.

Judging by the look of expectation on her face when she finished, she was waiting for him to reply. He didn't know what to say to her, or even how to say it, since he didn't know what she'd said in the first place. He, who had grown up understanding German and French, then spent hour after hour mastering English right down to the dialect, couldn't understand a few simple strokes made in the air.

Ginny broke the awkward hush. "She asks where you have been. We expected you hours ago."

Glancing into her eyes, he noticed lurking shadows that hadn't been there before. Had she been that worried about him?

A moment's remorse seized him. He tamped it down. They didn't need to know his every move. "You read to her like that every night?" he asked to change the subject.

Closing the magazine, she hesitantly replied, "I cannot read English, Thomas."

He felt like he'd said something wrong but didn't for the life of him know what.

"Doreen and I like looking at the pictures, though," she added brightly. "We make up stories about them."

"I figured these youngsters would be attending the village school this time of year."

"Doreen will, as soon as Sissy Warren gets her teaching certificate. We are without a schoolmarm until then. And David has promised to act as her interpreter. Isn't that right, David?"

From the boy's tightly strung posture, Tom got the impression he would have been much happier had Ginny not called attention to him. But he gave her a respectful nod then turned back to poke at the fire with an iron rod.

"*Kinder*," Bertha addressed the children. "Hilda needs milking *und die Erwachsenen* need privacy." She boosted her generous figure off the stool and ushered the children toward the front door.

As they bundled themselves into coats, Ginny licked her lips. She rose from the sofa and wiped her hands down her skirt. She suddenly seemed nervous. "Let me take your hat and coat. Are you hungry? Oma left you a plate on the stove."

He glanced into the kitchen, tempted. But he'd prolonged announcing his plans long enough. It was harder to tell her than he'd imagined it would be. Rising, Tom brushed his hand down his pant leg then cleared his throat. "I won't be staying. I only came back to get a few things."

He hated the look Ginny gave him. As if he'd just run her through with a bayonet. Her face had gone from a cheery pink to a bleached white color in the space of a few seconds.

And it would only get worse, he knew.

Bracing himself for her reaction, he blurted, "I'm moving out."

15

*B*ERTHA STOOD POISED at the door with her hand stilled on the latch. David's eyes were wide, darting between Tom and Ginny's rigid back.

Even Doreen's stricken gaze was fixed on him, telling Tom she'd understood more of the conversation than he'd intended.

"Moving out?" Ginny repeated with disbelief. "But you cannot leave, Thomas! What of your home? Your family?"

"Don't, Ginny," he warned low under his breath. "Don't make this difficult. Nobody wants to take you in and I can't stay here." Especially not after last night. Finding her all snuggled up against him had been staggering enough but the urge to pull her into his arms and keep her there . . . to lower his guard for just a little while . . . Hell, he hadn't come that close to losing control in ten years. Just the thought of what she'd read into a quick tumble made him shudder!

"But what will I tell—"

"Your loyal following?" he jeered, folding his arms over his chest. "Tell them whatever you want to tell them—you're good at that."

Although it didn't seem possible, she went even paler. Tom silently cursed his own callousness.

Suddenly Doreen broke the brittle tension by yanking the door open and bolting outside.

"Doreen, wait!"

"She cannot hear you, Thomas," Bertha reminded him tightly.

Tom didn't stop to examine his actions, he simply went after her. Reaching her at the edge of the field, he pulled on her arm. "Doreen—"

Whirling around, she wrenched herself away from his grasp and started motioning.

Tom followed the wild movements, trying to make sense of them. "I don't understand—"

She slapped her chest.

"You?"

She tugged at her ear, she patted her chest.

"You think I'm leaving because of you?"

She wouldn't look at him.

Gently tipping her chin up, Tom forced her to look at him. She glared back, her eyes moist, her lips pinched together so tight there was no color left in them.

"It isn't you," he said succinctly so she could read his lips.

She twisted around and folded her arms across her front.

Tom moved in front of her.

She spun the opposite way.

Thunderation, it was frustrating trying to talk to a deaf girl—a very angry deaf girl who refused to look at him so he could explain! At least with Ginny he could holler, giving her little choice but to hear him. But when Doreen ignored him, he might as well be shouting into the wind!

He lifted his hands and let them flutter onto her shoulders. She tensed beneath his touch. It didn't deter him. Near the tiny shell of her ear he whispered, "It has nothing to do with you. It's me, Doreen. It's me. I'm not a family man. I like going where I want, doing what I want, with nothing and no one holding me back. A family would hem me in. I'd feel obligated to stick around."

Even though she couldn't hear, he hoped she could somehow understand his need to be free.

Without warning she twirled to face him.

Now he'd done it—her hands moved swiftly in slashes and sharp arcs that, though he couldn't make out the words, communicated her message quite clearly.

She ended the silent tirade with her fists together, then executed an abrupt breaking motion. And as she stomped off, Tom wondered if she'd just cussed at him.

He started after her, then checked his steps when Ginny tore past him and followed Doreen into the barn.

When he turned around, he spied David standing on the porch.

"What the hell did she say to me?" Tom bellowed, hating the fact that Doreen's pain bothered him. What did it matter if she was angry, anyway? He didn't need to report his actions to an eleven-year-old!

David averted his eyes to the railing beneath his white-knuckled hands.

"Don't pretend you didn't see anything."

The boy's shoulder curled as if he were trying to crawl within himself.

Rage toward the man who'd broken his spirit welled inside Tom with such force it was all he could do to keep from retching. Why were maggots like David's father ever born? Worse, why did so many condone their abuse, or turn a blind eye to it? Nobody, *nobody* deserved to be treated like a whipping post.

Moving toward David with the same care he'd give a wounded animal, Tom stopped on the bottom step, blanking his face of any signs of aggression. "I'm not going to strike you, boy," he assured the boy quietly. "I've never laid a hand to a youngster before, and I'm not about to start now. I just want to know what's got her so hot under the collar."

Briefly David glanced at Tom, then back to the railing. "Doreen . . ." He cleared his throat. "Doreen's real sensitive." When David chanced another look at Tom, the fury simmering behind the boy's fear shocked Tom. "These are the most gentle, giving people I've ever known. They don't deserve to be treated the way you're treating 'em!"

As if suddenly aware of the emotion he'd revealed, the boy

ducked his head and took a backward step. "I'm sorry, sir. I meant no disrespect."

Once again Ginny had done it. The boy was so blasted devoted to her that he was willing to risk getting clobbered senseless for voicing his view.

Tom sighed. "Look, David, your obvious caring for these people is admirable and I respect your courage in standing up for them. But this is a complicated situation."

"Seems pretty simple to me. Miss Ginny loves you and you're breaking her heart."

He didn't have a single argument against that. That was what was becoming so complicated.

Tom rolled his clothes slowly, feeling strangely forlorn. He brought the shirt to his nose, inhaling starch and lye soap scented with lemon. It reminded him of Ginny. Strong and tart, yet so fresh and homey.

As if his thoughts summoned her, she appeared in the doorway. Her hair was tousled and damp spots blotched the shoulder of her maroon-striped gown. He suspected that Doreen had broken down in her mother's arms.

"Doreen is very upset."

He averted his eyes and shoved a stack of clean shirts into the haversack. Pants followed. "There's nothing I can do about that."

"You could forget this silly notion about moving out."

Swinging around toward the dresser, he opened the top drawer and sifted through her lacy camisoles to scoop up a pile of his socks. "I can't do that, Ginny. It just wouldn't work, us living in this house together. You, me, them . . ."

"What if I say that Doreen thinks you are leaving because she is deaf?"

"That's ridiculous—where would she get an idea like that?"

"I have told her all her life what a wonderful, loving *Vati* she has. So when you came back, she expected that you would be happy that we were here. But you are not. You are leaving. Doreen thinks it is her fault because she cannot hear."

Tom scoffed, "If she was my daughter it wouldn't make any difference whether she could hear or not. She could be blind and crippled, too, and I wouldn't care about her any less. But she isn't my daughter."

Ginny pulled back indignantly. "Are you accusing me of being unfaithful to you? Because I have not so much as looked at another since the day we met."

Two lousy days? Of course, they'd been the longest of Tom's life, but that was another issue. "I'm not accusing you of anything," he sighed.

"What if I say that we need you?"

"I'd say you've gotten along fine all these years without someone like me—why mess up a good thing?"

"Is there nothing I can say that will change your mind from leaving?"

"No, Ginny, nothing you say will change my mind. This is the best thing for all of us. I know you don't believe this now, but someday you're gonna thank me."

She tipped her chin up. "Where will you go?"

He could see the effort it took for her to hold on to her composure. Tight lips. Dimmed eyes. Stiff spine.

His guilt intensified. "I've made arrangements to stay in the stables with Noble."

"For how long?"

As long as it takes to find Herz. But he avoided telling her that the wheels had already been set into motion to locate her real husband. "Until other arrangements can be made."

She brought her hand to her mouth and turned away. "Where is the honorable man I used to know, Thomas?"

Oh, damn, she wasn't going to start crying, was she?

Buckling the strap, Tom steeled himself against the predictable show of emotion. "He isn't on this farm, that I can guarantee you." As for where Herz was, only time would tell.

The moment she left, the room went cold.

Yeah, moving out was the best thing. Being here was like having a noose around his neck, and the longer he stayed, the tighter it got.

His fingers brushed a leather pouch. Tom went still. He withdrew the pouch, loosened the string, and let the heavy object fall into his palm. The blue ribbon was crisp and new, the medal shiny and scratchless in contrast to the worn pocket he'd kept it in.

He lowered himself onto the bed and stared at the star-shaped Civil War campaign medal hinging from a spread-winged eagle.

Congressional Medal of Honor. The highest award given for bravery above and beyond the call of duty.

Tom rubbed the engraved word below the eagle. Valor.

The day that resulted in the medal was ground in his memory. No retreat, no advance, just stand and fire at the endless onslaught of Confederate battery coming out of the woods while men around him staggered backward and collapsed in bloody heaps.

It wasn't in him to just stand there waiting to die—no, he'd crashed helplessly through his own troops, driven by one determination—to strip the enemy of their firepower. The last thing he'd ever expected was to find thirty maimed and exhausted infantrymen being taunted by grayback gunners. He couldn't recall how he'd gained control of the cannon. Nor did he remember the Rebels retreating or leading the infantrymen safely back to the line.

But clear in his mind was the sight of Brigadier General John Gibbons, with his thick, frowning mustache and battle-blackened face, pounding him on the back and praising him upon their return to ranks.

He hadn't been brave. He'd felt reckless.

He hadn't been patriotic. He'd felt trapped.

It had been a big joke. A bandbox regular charging to the rescue of strawfoot infantrymen. The derogatory nicknames from veteran soldiers had ceased after that August day in '62. He'd become one of Gibbons's Regulars in the Black Hat Brigade. A title to wear proudly. With honor.

Lowering his hand to his thigh, Tom closed his eyes and clutched the medal so tightly it cut into his fingers. A man of honor took care of those who depended on him.

What would it be like to come in from a long day in the fields and find a woman waiting in the kitchen with a hot cup of coffee and a hearty meal? Lively conversation to fill the lonely quiet? Loving arms to welcome him at night and chase away the winter cold?

Ahhh, Ginny . . .

She insisted they belonged together. They didn't, though. He belonged to no one. And she . . .

She belonged to a man named Thomas Herz.

16

As Thomas wheeled the black toward the village, Ginny hugged her aching middle. One moment she was rejoicing over her husband's return, the next she wondered why he'd bothered coming back at all. If his intention had been to hurt her then he had succeeded. All it had taken was three little words.

"Did you not tell him about Herr Marks's visit?"

Ginny gathered up the tattered pieces of her soul and cast a swift look at her grandmother before turning back around to stare out the window. "It was not the right time, Oma."

"And vhen is de right time?"

In Thomas's present mental state, it was hard to say. One moment he seemed to know exactly where and who he was, the next he was denying any knowledge of his prewar life. Ginny simply could not predict which Thomas she would encounter. "If I told him now, he would not believe me, he would think I was only trying to hold him here. And he has made it very clear that I am the last person he wishes to be with."

"He must be told, Ginny. Only he can stop de riffraff. It is his signature dey vant."

"And what if he gives it?" she cried. "What if he decides to sell Heart land to Marks?"

"Den we farm on utter land."

"Leave Ridgeford? After all we have done to hold on to this farm?"

"Which is more important," Bertha chastised, "*der Mann* or *dien Farm*?"

Her husband, of course. The farm was nothing without him. And yet Ginny wanted to believe that deep down inside he remembered the dreams they had dreamed together. Of owning their own land, of making it prosper together, of building a future for their children. She wanted to believe that he would not part with one inch of the precious soil.

She'd also believed he would never forget her, and look where that had gotten her.

"You must tell him, Ginny. It is a husband's duty to protect his family."

"Thomas does not yet acknowledge that we are his family. Why would he feel obligated to protect us?"

"*Enkelin*," her grandmother said compassionately, "trust him in dis matter."

Therein lay the root of the problem, Ginny thought. How could she trust her husband with their future if he could not even recall their past?

"He doesn't remember you at all?" Evie gasped early the next morning after Ginny recounted the events leading up to Thomas's moving into the stables.

After spending a sleepless night devising and discarding ways to restore his memory, nothing short of tying him to a chair until he listened to reason sounded plausible. Pampering hadn't worked. Wifely wiles certainly hadn't worked. Nor had he been impressed by her improvements on his farm. She was out of ideas and needed an impartial opinion.

Seated at the small square table in her friend's kitchen, Ginny stared into the cup of coffee she had been nursing for the last thirty minutes. She barely noticed that it had grown cold. "Sometimes I see a glimmer of recognition in his eyes but it disappears so quickly that I wonder if I have imagined it."

Evie refilled her own cup, then set the china pot back down on a hot pad. "Ginny—" She paused with indecision. Then she folded her arms on the table. "You've told me before that you were only married five months to the man. How can you be sure you aren't wrong?"

"Because of the way I feel when I am near him. . . ." Ginny's breath caught as she searched for the words to explain. Finally, she gushed ahead, "It is as if half of my heart has been missing. The instant I saw him it felt whole again."

With a nostalgic smile, Evie replied, "That's how I felt with Alec. As different as we were, I could always count on him to keep me grounded."

"I wish I could count on Thomas, especially with Marks threatening us." The man's unsettling visit made returning her husband to normal more urgent. "My husband never ran from anything, he ran toward it. There was always something he wanted to conquer. And yet all he has done since he came home is run from me."

"Maybe it isn't you he's running from, but himself."

Suddenly Ginny jumped from the chair and slapped the table. "I hate what this war has done to him!" Turning away, she jammed one hand on her hip, the other through her tied-back hair. "And to us. I have spent years fighting to be with my husband, only to have him torn from me again and again."

"Have you talked to Bertha about any of this?"

"Some," Ginny admitted. "But I do not want her knowing the seriousness of my troubles, for she will only worry." With a weary sigh, she faced her friend once more. "Do you know what is the saddest part? Doreen feels she is to blame for his leaving."

"For heaven's sake, how could she have had anything to do with his decision?"

"She thinks that because she cannot hear, she is not what he expected in a daughter. Thomas himself told me that her deafness did not matter, but she is only a little girl. . . . It is natural that she crave her father's approval."

"Oh, Ginny, I wish I knew what to say." She shook her head and shrugged. "But to be honest, I don't know how to treat Mr. Kirkmiller half the time—and I've known him all my life! Shoot, we would have been in-laws if Alec hadn't died. But Tom? Well, like I've told you before, he pretty much kept to himself when he moved here, so he's practically a stranger to me." Offhandedly, Evie Mae added, "Course back then crops were failing left and right. Everybody was more worried about making it through another year than socializing with the new neighbor."

"At least your fiancé's father remembers who you are some of the time—Thomas refuses to acknowledge the fact that we ever met."

"Maybe Dolores will have a suggestion."

Ginny held on to that hope as she and Evie Mae made their way across the slushy street to the pub. Everyone went to Dolores with their problems, for she usually gave sound advice.

They found the robust pub owner in the back room, taking inventory of her supplies. Corked liquor bottles in various shades of brown and green occupied every inch of the floor-to-ceiling shelves. Assorted sizes of wooden kegs were stacked on either side of the rear door.

"Ginny's got a problem and she needs our help," Evie Mae announced without preamble.

Sending a sharp glance Ginny's way, Dolores lowered her bulk down the ladder and said, "By golly, it's about time."

After they made themselves comfortable around a table in the main room, Ginny explained the circumstances once more. Some called Dolores the town mother, others called her the general. Actually, Ginny thought her a bit of both. Beneath her generous bosom beat a nurturing heart lined in steel.

A pondering look crossed Dolores's harsh features as she stared into a morning cup of vodka-laced coffee. "I think he's got to remember, deep down inside, else why wouldn't he have married long before now? It's not as if gals haven't tried. Why, Margaret had her cap set for Tom since the day he bought the farm."

Ginny recalled the girl with a pang of jealousy. To say that Margaret had not been happy to learn that the man she had been pursuing was a husband and father described her reaction mildly.

"Course Tom was so wrapped up in his own self that he never gave her a second glance," Dolores added. "Pret-near broke her heart. I 'spect she finally got tired of beating a dead horse and that's why she hitched up with the first man sent home from the war."

"It was the quickest courtship in Ridgeford history," Evie Mae added. "Joseph Brummer didn't even have time to hang up his coat before Margaret dragged him to the altar."

And nobody had been more anxious than Ginny to see the girl wed. Oh, her friends assured Ginny that Thomas had shown no interest in Margaret, but an old insecurity reared, one that Ginny had been wrestling with since Thomas's letters stopped coming eight years earlier. That her husband may have found her love insufficient. That he may have turned his affections elsewhere.

Shortly after their home had burned down, Margaret and Joseph sold their farm to Marks. Though Ginny didn't wish their misfortune on anybody, it had been with a sense of relief that she watched their loaded wagon roll out of Ridgeford. "Well, I can understand women being enamored of Thomas, for he is a sightly man. But he is *my* man. Somehow I must win his heart back."

Dolores nodded decisively. "It's time for a village meeting. Evie Mae, ring the bell." As Evie scurried out of the pub, Dolores turned to Ginny. "We'll talk to the other women, see if they have any ideas."

By midafternoon, Ginny was overwhelmed by the support of her neighbors as they flowed into Silver's Pub.

"We came as soon as we heard. . . ."

"Congratulations, Ginny . . ."

"I'm so thrilled that your Tom made it back. . . ."

"You are so lucky, Ginny!"

She responded to each warm greeting. She knew every face. Many were widows of the merchants and closest farmers; others were sisters and mothers of slain or crippled heroes; the minority few were eligible maidens who crooned in sympathy over Ginny's plight.

By evening, not a chair remained empty, not a wall void of calico- and gingham-clad figures. No matter the background, religion, or political stand, these women had gathered together for one cause or another over the last four years: the birth of a babe, an illness in the family, a crisis on their home or farm, a funeral. She thought of them as her second family, bound together by circumstances beyond their control.

The knowledge that they had come to support her in her time of need left her feeling both humbled and proud. Someone in this room could help her find a way to save her marriage. Of that, Ginny had no doubt.

Dolores presided over the meeting. "Ladies, I figure all of you have heard by now that Tom Heart came home yesterday. What you might not know is that he lost his memory. He don't remember ever takin' Ginny to wife." Since all had been witness to Auggie Kirkmiller's confusion, not a voice rose to challenge Dolores's announcement. "Now, not a one of us would be where we are today if it wasn't for Ginny. So let's put our heads together and figure out how we can get him to remember her."

A tawdry comment from the far side of the pub caused a chorus of twitters.

Her cheeks pinkening, Ginny did not wish to admit that her attempts in that field had very likely been the reason her husband had moved into the stables.

"Do you have any daguerreotypes?" Auggie's mother asked. "During his bad spells, I show Augustuvus the boys' daguerreotypes and he often recognizes them."

"The only image I have is one I carry in my heart," Ginny replied.

"Letters?" someone inquired from across the room.

"I used to have several, but they disappeared shortly before we left Deutschland. The last message I received from Thomas was the one telling me he had purchased the farm."

"How 'bout gifts?" Elsbeth Eischbach asked. "Did Tom ever give you any gifts?"

"He gave me a spoon to honor our betrothal, but he does not believe we ever married."

"Your marriage license!" Vernice cried. "That would've had Tom's signature on it, proof that the two of you are married."

Growing increasingly discouraged, Ginny sank into a slatted pine chair. "In my family, the husband kept the important documents. Thomas took it with him when he left." The open discussion made her aware of how weak her position really was. After all, she had nothing to prove Thomas was the man she had given her heart to—except a feeling inside.

What if, for the first time in her life, that feeling was wrong? What if he wasn't her husband?

That's what Thomas seemed to think. Even Oma and Evie Mae questioned her—

Abruptly Ginny stiffened her spine. No, she would not accept that her heart could make such a dreadful mistake. The sense of rightness she experienced each time she shared his company was not a lie. Nor was the *Wiedererkennung* she saw in his amber eyes. And what of the powerful sensations he awakened within her when she touched him, or he touched her? Just because she could not recall feeling this strongly before did not mean it had not existed. They were simply memories dulled by time.

And forgotten by Thomas.

"You know him better than any of us, Ginny," Vernice cut into her ponderings. "Tell us some of the things he liked to do. Maybe that will help give us some ideas."

Ginny moistened her lips. "Well, we were only together a short time before he left for America, but I remember he enjoyed being outside." She closed her eyes, summoning a dim memory. "We would go on long walks through the forest. He would hold my hand, swing it back and forth, back and forth. He told me my eyes were like the moon-drenched sky . . . my lips were sweet as elderberry wine . . . then he would kiss me soundly right there under the stars."

Vernice let out a long, mopey sigh.

"Ohhh, Ginny, how romantic," Mary crooned.

Dolores snorted. "If my Hirham had ever took me for a walk and kissed me under the stars, I woulda keeled over dead from shock."

"I am beginning to wonder if Thomas will ever kiss me beneath the stars again."

The women's gazes traveled around the room, seeking one another, then finally settled once more on Ginny.

Her voice filled with mischievous determination, Dolores pronounced, "Don't you worry, Ginny, he ain't tangled with a village of women before. Once we got our minds set on something, not even General Grant and his whole Union army have got a chance of winning against us!"

17

"*ONCE YOU GET* to Minnow Falls, find Gene Mason and give him this," Tom said, handing a letter to Noble explaining his request. "His father is a circuit minister, so if anybody can get us information on immigrants named Herz, he probably can."

Noble stuffed the sealed missive into the pocket of his twill coat and climbed aboard the wagon. "You sure you want to do this?" he asked once he had settled onto the box seat.

"If you've got a better plan, I'd sure like to hear it."

"You could stop lookin' a gift horse in the mouth. Take what Miss Ginny's offerin'."

"Are you suggesting that I go along with her story?"

Noble shrugged nonchalantly. "Nobody'd ever have to know if you was or wasn't her real husband."

"I'd know."

Noble's full lips twitched.

Narrowing his eyes, Tom said, "Don't you go mistaking my meaning now. It has nothing to do with a code of honor or anything like that. It's pure selfishness on my part."

"Whatever you say, Tom. Keep an eye on the womenfolk while I'm gone." With a slap of the reins, Noble set the buckboard into motion. The wheels whipped up a spray of mud and Noble's laughter vibrated in the air like the rumble of a cattle stampede.

Tom shoved his hands into his pockets and scowled after Noble. Hopefully he would return with some lead on Herz, and Tom could get his life back to normal.

"Tom, just the man I was looking for." Auggie's mother glanced in the direction of the departing wagon.

"Where is Noble off to this early?"

"He's running an errand for me. He'll be back in a couple days."

"Oooooh," she trilled, a gleam in her eyes. Then her voice dropped to a sober level. "What I mean is, ohhh. That's nice."

"Was there something you needed, Mrs. Kirkmiller?"

"Actually, there is. Would you mind coming out to the farm later today? There is someone—I mean, something I'd like you to take care of."

"And what would that be?"

She blinked. "What? Oh, what indeed! I . . . uh . . ." She licked her lips, glanced across the lane.

Tom looked up in time to catch sight of Evie Mae Johnson flipping her hands away from her skirts. The instant she realized Tom was watching her, she grabbed hold of the woolen panels and began shaking them, as if ridding the hems of dust.

His brows lowered in suspicion. What in thunderation was going on here?

"I . . . uh . . . needyoutoshoemycow," Mrs. Kirkmiller suddenly gushed.

Tom gaped at the graying woman. "Sh-hoe your what?"

"Millie is very tender-hoofed. Noble shoes her all the time since my Augustuvus is not quite, shall we say, balanced."

Tom began to wonder if Auggie's mother wasn't the one slightly off-kilter. Shoe a cow? Rocking back then forth on his heels, he finally said, "All right." He had to see this for himself! Besides, he had nothing better to do with his time. "How about two o'clock?"

"Oh, no, no, no. It must be three o'clock." At Tom's perplexed expression, she explained gravely, "We must stick to Millie's schedule."

With a "ta-ta," Mrs. Kirkmiller swished away, leaving Tom to stare after the woman in utter disbelief.

Shaking his head, he entered the stables, muttering to himself, "It's got to be something in the water around here."

"I am nervous, Mary," Ginny confessed, smoothing down the wide velvet panels of her wedding dress. She had not realized how much her figure had changed over the years until she'd tried the gown on. The teardrop bodice and outer corset stretched tight across her breasts, and the waist needed a bit of tucking, but there had not been time for alterations.

She adjusted the crumbling wreath of dried flowers she had dug out of her cedar chest. "Mayhap I should have braided my hair."

"How did you wear it on your wedding day?"

"I left it down."

"Then leave it loose now. You said you didn't have a daguerreotype, so you need to look as much like you did that day as possible." Mary let the hem drop suddenly. "On the other hand, men tend to recollect the wedding night much clearer than they recall the actual ceremony. . . ."

She stepped back, and with her forefinger to her cheek, studied Ginny. "Hmmm. Raise your arm and put your hand to the back of your head. Yes, now lean to the right and throw your hip out just a bit. Very good. Now smile."

Striking the pose, Ginny grinned shamelessly.

"No, no, child! A small smile. An inviting smile. You want him unable to resist your charms."

Bowing to the widow's greater experience, Ginny let one side of her mouth curve, then lowered her lashes in what she hoped was a suggestive look. "Is this inviting enough?" she asked, barely allowing her lips to move.

"My dear"—Mary winked—"once he sees you, he'll toss you over his shoulder and you will find yourself ravished like one of those dime-novel heroines Vernice keeps raving about."

"I certainly hope so," Ginny confessed brazenly, longing for the early days of their marriage when her husband only had to look at her and she found herself ravished. Twelve years later she was being forced to use guile to get him to notice her. What a twist of fate.

The blast of a gunshot sent her jumping into the air.

Mary clucked her tongue. "That must be Tom coming now. I best go out there, we don't want Augustuvus killing him before he sets eyes on you."

Left alone in the shack, Ginny turned to the mule and resumed the languid stance. "What do you think?" She wiggled her brows. "Will he throw me over his shoulder or throw me out the door?"

A fuzzy brown ear flicked at the touch of a fly. She wondered if that meant the shoulder or the door.

Sweet mercy, she hoped this worked. If not, they would move to the next item on the list. The meeting last night had been more productive than she could have imagined. Every woman gathered in Dolores's pub had offered suggestions. Thanks to her friends, Ginny had a score of ideas to try on Thomas. She had narrowed the list down, choosing those she thought were best suited to the unflappable man he had become.

At the sound of approaching voices, Ginny's heart began to skip. She took a calming breath and waited for the door to open.

The instant Tom spied Ginny he threw back his head and laughed harder than he'd ever laughed in his life.

She stood before him in a costume of white silk and velvet. Shots of gold and red thread raced through the sleeves. Intricate embroidery patterned the hem of the tightly pleated skirt, which reached just below her knees. With her gold-spun hair pulled away from her face, and a circle of dried flowers around her crown, she resembled a Dresden figurine.

But her bare feet and ridiculous posturing ruined the elegant effect.

Once he realized that Ginny and Mrs. Kirkmiller didn't share his amusement, his laughter dwindled down to chuckles. "Ginny . . . *what* are you doing?"

Her arm drifted down to her side, her spine straightened.

"Thomas, this gown does not look familiar to you?" she asked in a small voice.

"Should it?" Tom instantly raised his had. "No, don't tell me—I've supposedly seen it on you before."

"Precisely—this is my wedding gown."

He planted his fists on his hips. "Courting the livestock, are you?"

She spread the panels of the skirt wide. Sunlight from the window behind her filtered through the material, making it almost transparent. "I had hoped this gown would stir your memory."

All traces of amusement fled as Tom's rapt gaze toured the silhouette of her body. The dress stirred something, but it damn well wasn't his memory. She had a figure to feed a man's fantasies for the rest of his lifetime and still leave him hungry. Generous bosom. Narrow waist. Wide hips, but not too wide. Just perfectly spanned for cradling against his—

Tom gulped down a thick breath as pressure built within him. His nerves quivered. His bones melted. Damn, and he thought she'd tormented him the other night, crawling over his body wearing nothing except a modest nightdress. This was the Ginny he'd felt in the dark but hadn't seen beyond his imagination. The sight she provided him with now was even more provocative than if she'd stripped down to nothing.

Pulling his mind from that treacherous path, Tom whipped away from Ginny and faced the older woman. "Mrs. Kirk-miller, just show me where the cow is."

"I don't have a cow."

"You asked me to come by and shoe your cow."

She shot a surprised look in Ginny's direction, then shook her head and clucked her tongue. "Oh, dear, this is more serious than I thought." To Tom she said in a tone usually reserved for a five-year-old, "Cows do not get shod."

"But you said Millie—"

"Millie is a mule, not a cow. The shoes get nailed to the hooves—"

Hot humiliation flooded his face and he wondered if maybe he'd misunderstood earlier. No, he'd distinctly heard her say "cow," but he wouldn't waste his time bickering. The faster he got the job done, the faster he could leave. "I don't need instructions on how to be a farrier." Thunderation, he'd been taking care of animals since he was a boy. One of his many odd jobs as a boy trying to survive on the streets of Strasbourg in Alsace-Lorraine. To prove his skills, he dropped a leather sack onto an upended crate and led the animal out of her stall.

While Tom withdrew an assortment of U-shape shoes, clippers, and picks from the farrier kit and laid them out on the crate, Mrs. Kirkmiller made some excuse about seeing to Auggie, then left him and Ginny alone.

He had three choices: waste time trying to get her to leave willingly, remove her bodily, or get the damn mule shod so he could leave. Since he didn't want to give Ginny the satisfaction of knowing how her presence stirred up a storm in his bloodstream, he decided just to do his job and get the hell out of here.

Bracing his back against the mule's rump, Tom grasped the animal's leg, lifted it so the hoof faced backward, and straddled the limb to pry off the cracked shoe.

Ginny wandered toward him. He caught the alluring sway of her hips at the edge of his vision. The size of the shed seemed to shrink from cramped to suffocating. "Get back before you get kicked," Tom barked unsteadily.

"I can hold Millie while you clean her hooves."

"She's too strong for you." Her straddling the mule's leg would only fill his head with wicked ideas. And he had enough of those churning in his mind already to keep him miserable for hours. "Besides, you'll ruin that . . . that thing you're wearing."

"I could take it off—"

"No!" Tom cried. Hell, that's all he needed! "If you insist on staying, just . . . keep petting her head. That'll distract her." And keep Ginny away from him, Tom thought.

Ginny followed his order but he was still too aware of her. Couldn't seem to concentrate enough on finding the right size shoes. Fumbled with the nails. Dropped the tap hammer twice. Worse, Ginny wasn't doing anything spectacular, just caressing Millie's muzzle. Her slender fingers toyed with the coarse mane.

Tom bent over the hoof and tried not to notice. But powerless against Ginny's guileless charms, he peered around Millie's rump to watch what she'd do next. She wrinkled her nose and rubbed it playfully against the mule's, then giggled when Millie tossed her head. A powerful longing built inside Tom at the carefree sound. It pulled him forward. He felt himself swaying. . . .

A lashing hoof caught him high on the thigh. He yelped in pain, his legs knocked out from under him.

With a harsh exclamation, Tom picked himself up from the dirt floor. In record time, he completed the chore, gathered his tools, and half stormed, half limped off the Kirkmiller property, cursing the day God gave women wiles.

The next morning he got cornered in the corral by Elsbeth Eischbach to chop wood. "Tom, I can't tan no hides if I ain't got no wood to boil the water."

Tom started to argue that the wood wouldn't be dry enough to burn, but one look at Miz Eischbach's forbidding expression shut him up. Bracing his weight on one leg since the other had a bruise the size of a saucer, he wound around his hand the reins of the black gelding he'd been exercising. "Isn't there someone else around here that can do it?"

"Only ones strong enough out here to wield an ax are David and Noble. Noble ain't here, and the roof sprung a leak on your house so David's busy fixin' that. Course, if you went home and fixed your own roof, that'd leave young David free to come by and chop my wood."

He was tempted to refuse Mrs. Eischbach just as she had refused Ginny lodgings. But after one glimpse at hands stained from years of being submerged in dyes and gnarled from rheumatism, he knew he couldn't deny her. With a disgusted sigh, he agreed to chop wood.

"Just make certain you don't cut the special trees."

"What special trees?"

"You'll know 'em when you see 'em."

And sure enough, a half an hour later he saw them.

"Thunderation . . ." Tom stared in disbelief. He let the ax slide off his shoulder and released his grip on the handle. The ax fell soundlessly onto the moldy leafage strewn over the forest bed.

Stunned, Tom wandered from birch to oak to maple, tracing the letters deeply chiseled into the trunks. *Ginny loves Thomas. Thomas loves Ginny.* A dozen trees bore the testimonies, each enclosed by the carved shape of a heart.

A sensation unlike anything he'd ever felt before built in his chest. How long had it taken her to carve into all these trees? he wondered in awe. Hours, probably. Nobody had ever gone to such trouble to catch his attention before.

Of course, it wasn't for him that she'd gone to all this trouble. . . .

It took him all day to hack every damn tree down.

Ginny picked up a piece of birch. Her shoulders slumped at the sight of the broken heart and splintered letters.

"I'm sorry, Ginny," Elsbeth said. "I told him not to cut down the special trees."

She glanced around the woods. Every tree that she had spent the previous night engraving had been chopped down to the base and split into logs for the tannery's fire pit.

It seemed a reflection of her ruined marriage.

"Did he say anything to you?"

"Not a word," Elsbeth said apologetically.

"How did he look? Pleased? Angry? Distant?"

"He looked kinda . . . troubled."

Troubled? Ginny smiled as she rose and brushed bits of bark from her hands. Troubled was a good sign. He might not yet realize it, but his wall was crumbling.

Two days later Tom was repairing a split board on the corral fence when Vernice Warren approached him with an invitation to dinner.

"Noble generally takes supper with us and with him off to the city, there's more than Sissy and I can possibly eat."

Tom hesitated, wondering if the invitation was as sincere as she made it sound. After the last couple of days he had a right to his wariness. "Did you invite Ginny?"

"Would you like me to?"

"No!" he burst out. Calming a surge of panic, he repeated, "No, I don't want Ginny anywhere around me." She was hell on his bloodstream.

"Why, Tom, you wouldn't be trying to avoid that sweet girl, now, would you?"

Like mortar fire, he thought.

"Well, you have nothing to fear. It will only be myself and Sissy."

He eyed her speculatively. What could it hurt? It was only supper. And he was getting pretty sick of biscuits and gravy, one of the only edible things him and Noble could cook. Just in case, though, he made Mrs. Warren swear on her husband's grave that Ginny would not be present—in any way, shape or form.

Mrs. Warren gave her oath that the only other female joining them would be her twenty-year-old daughter.

"Well, all right then," he accepted reluctantly.

At half past five that evening Mrs. Warren answered his knock and admitted him into the small quarters above the store.

"Oh, Tom, we are so pleased to have a gentleman over for company. Isn't that right, Sissy?"

Homely as a melon rind, Vernice's spinster daughter eyed him like a cat ready to pounce on a cornered mouse. Tom grimaced. Maybe this wasn't such a good idea. . . .

"Please pardon the apartment," Mrs. Warren said as she hung his coat. "Your Ginny is so much better at decorating than I. Why, that wife of yours has an eye for color and fabric that cannot be matched."

Tom's step faltered and he glanced around, expecting at any moment to encounter some physical form of Ginny. The living quarters were as small as Mrs. Warren had claimed, with only the barest of sturdily crafted furniture. But that didn't mean Ginny wasn't hiding behind either of the two calico-curtained doorways; one led to the kitchen, the other to possibly a bedroom.

When Mrs. Warren launched into polite conversation, Tom chalked his wariness up to paranoia. There was no sense in overreacting, he told himself. The invitation was just a neighborly gesture, nothing more. Perfectly harmless—as long as a certain German "fixer" didn't make an appearance.

Once they were seated around the maplewood table, Mrs. Warren said, "I hope you have a taste for shepherd's pie. It has been ages since we've cooked for someone other than ourselves." She flagged a napkin across her lap while Tom eyed the lumpy round loaf Sissy uncovered.

"Of course," Mrs. Warren continued. "your Ginny sets a much better table—why, that wife of yours can make pork fit for a prince!"

He couldn't decide if it was the second mention of Ginny that made him grimace or the toughness of the meat and crunch of half-raw vegetables in the pie. As a cook, Mrs. Warren couldn't hold a candle to Bertha.

Over the next half hour, the true reason for the invitation began to reveal itself. Tom heard so many "your Ginny's" and "that wife of yours" that his stomach began to roil. Then his head started spinning.

Tom shoved the chair back and wobbled to his feet. His face flushed and a wave of dizzying nausea gripped his middle. Oh, God, what had Vernice put in the custard dessert?

"Tom, you are looking quite green. Should I fetch your Ginny? That wife of yours is so much better at doctoring than anyone in the village."

He stared at the woman in disbelief. "You . . ." His stomach lunged. "You . . . did this on purpose . . ." He'd been hoodwinked! Worse, he'd let the prospect of a decent meal color his better judgment. But it seemed Ginny's friends were bound and determined to drive him back to her—dead or alive.

He barely made it out of the store before he lost his meal.

18

"*T*HOMAS?"

Oh, God, not Ginny . . .

He wasn't in any shape to battle her tonight—he just didn't have the strength. Rolling over on a blanket-covered pallet of straw, he flung one arm over his eyes and curled his other arm around his cramping belly. "Go away," Tom moaned in misery as Ginny set a basket down and knelt beside him. Her fresh scent made him all the more aware of the less than pleasant odor coming from the nearby slop bucket.

"The children and I have brought you something for your stomach."

"Haven't you done enough damage?"

"I had no idea they would make you ill."

"Well they did," Tom sulked. "And if I die you'll have everything you wanted."

"You are all I have ever wanted."

He clenched his eyes tightly shut, cursing the day he'd ever come home. He'd had more peace in battle than here.

His arm was drawn away from his face and a small palm flattened on his forehead. He opened his eyes to pixielike features wreathed in worry. Doreen. Beyond her shoulder he noticed David standing just close enough to guard Doreen, yet far enough away to keep out of Tom's reach. Tom's stomach knotted further at the mixture of wariness and pity in the boy's eyes. Maybe if he did meet his end, David would finally relax.

Doreen tilted her head to the side, then used her hands to talk to him.

"She asks if you are warm enough or do you need another blanket?" Ginny said.

"Why is she being so considerate? I figured she'd be gloating over my misery," Tom grumbled.

"Doreen cannot bear to see anyone in pain. She has a very soft heart, much like you."

"I don't have a soft heart," Tom denied gruffly. "I don't have a heart at all."

"Of course you do, Thomas, five of them."

His mind went completely blank at that comment.

"Your's, Mine, Doreen's, David's and Oma's." Ginny smiled tenderly. "Five hearts. Do they not call that a royal flush in cards?"

In his case, it was more like royal aggravation. "Why don't you show a dying man a little mercy and let me suffer in peace?"

"There is no reason to suffer. Here, sit up and drink this." She slid her arm beneath his neck to help him rise.

"I don't want anything from—" Another cramp seized his gut. Tom doubled over.

"Thomas, stop being stubborn." She held out a small brown bottle. "This will help ease the pain."

She was calling *him* stubborn? All right, so maybe he was being a little hardheaded, but only because Ginny was making him that way! Any sign of weakening on his part would only encourage her to continue this ridiculous game.

Fixing as menacing a glare on her as he could muster, he said, "You think you have the cure for everything, don't you? You think you can fix my aches the way you've fixed my house and my lands and my village and my life. Let me ask you something, Ginny—did it ever occur to you that while you've gone around 'fixing' everything the way you want it, you've completely taken away everything that I want?"

She blinked several times then glanced at the children who were ducking their heads. Her gaze returned to him.

There was no logic in the way she tenderly brushed his hair back after the caustic set down he'd given her.

Just as there was no logic in the way his pulse sped up at her touch.

"What do you want, Thomas?"

That question had never been asked of him before. His wants had always come last. And it stunned Tom to realize that he wanted everything just the way Ginny had made it.

Worse, he wanted her. Not as a warm body or a cook for his meals. He wanted her laughter. Her spirit. Her compassion.

Tom rolled back onto his side and shut his eyes. "I just want to be left alone."

He felt her watching him for countless disturbing minutes. Yet strangely when Ginny finally gathered the youngsters and left without another word, giving him what he wanted, he wrestled with the urge to call her back. To lay his head in her lap and let her soft touch ease all his aches, old and new.

His stomach gave another vicious heave. Oh, God, Tom moaned. He seized the small brown bottle she'd left behind. At this point he didn't much care if the elixir killed him—as long as his guts stopped hurting. He grimaced at the bittersweet taste then wiped his lips with the back of his hand.

Dropping back onto his pallet, he wasn't sure if the medicine really worked that well, or if his mind just tricked him into thinking so, but the queasiness and cramps seemed to disappear almost immediately.

Where had Ginny been after his first whipping? Or when that Johnny had pret-near sliced him in half? He sure could have used some of her magical remedies then.

Now it was too late. He was beyond healing.

Sunday, Tom waited for another attack. He was prepared this time. No matter who asked him to do what, he'd refuse. However, the day dragged on, as did the next, with no sign of Ginny or her fellow conspirators. But Tom didn't relax his guard.

By Tuesday he almost wished they'd hurry up, strike, and

get it over with. The anticipation was killing him. He knew it was too much to hope that they'd finally given up. Ginny didn't know the meaning of surrender.

So when he entered the stable late that afternoon and spotted a slatted crate just inside the doorway, his senses went instantly alert. Tom scanned the interior. Mounds of straw outside the stall gates, bundles of winter hay poking over the edge of the loft, toolboxes shut, and the forge cold. Nothing out of the ordinary.

Except a quizzical scratching from within the crate.

"Don't open it," he muttered to himself. "You don't want to know. . . ." But the not knowing would be worse, and he knew it.

Approaching the box cautiously, he flipped open the lid. Tom's eyes bulged at the sight of a furry black creature with a white stripe running down its back, staring at him with beady black eyes.

With a cry of disgust, he flung himself away from the box. The skunk flipped up its tail and let loose a fine, misty spray. Though it hadn't been a direct hit, the fumes were potent. Tom barreled out onto the lane, his eyes stinging, his nostrils burning from the horrendous stench. Blindly he stumbled to the horse trough. The thin layer of ice shattered as he plunged headfirst into the frigid water.

When he could finally see, he discovered Evie Mae Johnson standing a few feet away, her arms folded over her front, her brows raised. "Lose a tussle with a polecat, Tom?"

Amusement laced her voice. Instantly Tom knew she was the one responsible for the abominable stench clinging to every inch of his skin. "Evie Mae Johnson! What did you put a skunk in the stable for?" Tom cried.

"Somebody had to teach you a lesson."

"You call that a lesson? That damn thing sprayed the stables—where am I supposed to go now?"

"Try going back to your wife. It's where you belong."

"Don't you women have anything better to do than torment me?" She didn't need to answer, he saw it in her face. "I don't believe this," he spat in disgust, swiping his hand across his watery eyes, then slapping his thigh. "Look, Evie, I never asked Ginny to come here—hell, I didn't even know she existed until I came home. But even if I was a family man—which I'm not—I at least have the right to choose my own, not have one shoved down my throat."

"You still haven't learned, have you?" she asked.

It came as no surprise that she refused to listen to him. Nobody else had. Tom's neck went limp, his head drooped forward.

He gave a humorless laugh. "Learned what? That Ginny's on a one-way trip to bedlam and she's got all of you riding on her hems? Tell me something, how did she ever manage to earn such blind faith?"

"She saved this village from utter ruin, that's what she did. When the war snatched away all our men and everybody around here wondered how we'd get through the first year without them, Ginny came along and taught us that we were strong enough and smart enough to make it on our own. Everybody calls her the *Starkherz*, the strong heart. She doesn't quit, she doesn't give up, she keeps going. She's the spit that holds this village together and let me tell you something, any one of us would lay down our lives for Ginny. Yet all she wants is you."

"But I don't *want* her to want me!" Tom wailed.

Evie Mae raked him a disdainful look. "Then you're a fool, Tom Heart."

"Wait a minute!" he protested as she whirled away. "You don't expect me to sleep in there with a skunk, do you?"

Without bothering to turn around, she called out, "Sleep in the woods for all I care. It's where polecats belong, anyway."

Staring out the window of the general store, Ginny paid little attention to the chatter at the counter. Vernice, Dolores and Evie Mae had once again gathered to plot. Her gaze fixed to a spot in the distance, Ginny wondered why they bothered.

Her fingertips touched the moist pane. *Thomas.* Snow flurries hampered her view of the stables, but she knew he was in there. What was he doing this very moment? No doubt wishing her straight to purgatory, she decided.

Bits and pieces of conversation finally broke through her melancholy.

"I still can't believe the skunk idea didn't work," Evie Mae grumbled. "That was the best plan yet!"

"Well, we can't give up," Dolores said, her hand curved along her jaw, her fingers tapping against her cheek. "Tom can't get away with shirking his responsibilities. And long as he don't recall who Ginny is, he isn't going to go back to the farm."

Ginny moved to lean against the counter beside Doreen. Like the women, her daughter's elbows were propped on the long polished surface and her chin rested in her palms. And though Doreen couldn't understand everything that was being said, she wore the same thoughtful expression as the others.

Earlier in the week, she had approached Ginny with the knowledge that something was in the air. As soon as Ginny confessed that she and the women of Ridgeford had combined forces to bring Thomas back home, Doreen begged to be allowed to help. Knowing that her daughter had as much at stake as she, Ginny decided that including her might at least make her feel less powerless against the force tearing their family apart.

Doreen's input proved quite invaluable. Her creative mind invented the skunk idea; her irresistible smile convinced David to help build the box trap and catch the animal. It had been the perfect means to get Thomas out of the stables and back home where he belonged.

Unfortunately, Thomas had not seen it that way.

Ginny sighed forlornly. "I do not know what else to do. But I cannot continue imposing on all of you." Though she appreciated their devotion to the cause, for every forward step they made, Thomas bolted a mile back.

"Not that's enough of that kind of talk, Ginny Heart," Dolores scolded. "You've done so much for all of us, never asked anything in return. This is our chance to return the favor."

"Besides," Evie added, "so many of us have lost our own men. We can't just stand by and watch you lose yours, too, especially when he's come back hale and healthy."

"And more stubborn than I ever knew he could be," Ginny muttered.

Evie shook her head. "It just doesn't seem fair that after all the years you've waited for Tom, he won't even give you the time of day."

"Which brings us back to our original problem." Dolores began to pace the length of the counter, tapping her forefinger against her chin.

"I think we're going about this all wrong," Vernice said. "Maybe instead of trying to trick Tom into remembering Ginny, we should court him into falling back in love with her. That's what they do in the best classics."

Dolores snorted. "Shoot, it's been so long since I've been courted that I'd have to bring out an instruction manual. But I know enough that a man and woman have got to be together for the courtin' to work."

"Too bad there isn't enough snow or we could have a sleigh ride. That would put them together."

Several more suggestions came; a taffy pull, a husking party, a quilting bee. . . . Nothing seemed appropriate. But the thought of her husband seated in a room of women sewing on tiny squares of cloth made Ginny laugh.

Then Doreen stretched her hands in front of her and made a whacking motion toward the ground.

"A hoedown?" Ginny asked.

When Doreen nodded, her eyes bright, Vernice clapped in glee. "Oh, that is a splendid idea! We could celebrate your father's return!"

"The guest of honor couldn't very well refuse an invitation to his own party!" Evie Mae exclaimed.

"Especially if we have it in the stables," Dolores added with a sly grin.

Their enthusiasm was catching. Ginny straightened and said with a note of mischief, "Thomas always did love to polka. . . ."

Tom stiffened when the stable doors opened. He knew that nothing short of barring the entrance shut would keep the gaggle of meddlesome matchmakers from trying their utmost to drive him into Ginny's arms. It had gotten to the point where the mere hint of meeting anything in skirts had him running in the opposite direction.

"Wheeeew-weee, Lawdy, Lawdy!"

Hearing Noble's familiar voice, the tension drained from his shoulders. "You in here, Tom?"

"In the back." He turned back to the pile of straw, his nose curling at the acrid smell. Even though the doors and windows had been left open, the stables still reeked.

Noble approached, his expression understandably confused. "Wha'd you do to this buildin' while I been gone?"

"I didn't do anything." Tom sent a pitchforkful of fresh bedding soaring past Noble's head into the stall. "A skunk did."

"My pappy used to blame it on the dog." Noble grinned.

Tom glared at him. "I'm telling you it was a skunk. Someone let one loose in here the other night." If Noble made one wisecrack about Tom smelling of vinegar, he'd get a load of dirty straw dumped over his head.

"Now who'd do a fool thing like put a skunk in the stables?"

"Evie Mae Johnson. Where in thunderation have you been, anyway? I expected you back days ago."

"Wagon busted an axle four miles out of Minnow Falls."

"Did you find Gene Mason?"

"Yep. He said he'd see how many Herzs fittin' your age and description he could locate. He said lots of immigrants changed their names when they were admitted into the States, though."

"But they usually kept it pretty close to their real names. He didn't say how long this would take, did he?"

"A while, I 'spect. He'll contact you soon as he narrows the list down."

"Tom? You in here?"

Halting the pitchfork in midscoop, Tom glanced wildly around the stables for a place to hide. He jabbed the tines into the pile, then dropped to his knees and began digging. A man couldn't suffocate in a straw stack, could he?

His face a mask of bafflement, Noble stared at him. "What's the matter wit you, Tom?"

"Shhh. It's Dolores," Tom whispered, then dove into the cave he'd made. "Quick, throw some of that straw on me. Make sure I'm covered."

"What would she be wantin' wit you?"

"Just tell her you haven't seen me."

Shielded by the straw, Tom listened to the sharp click of boot heels crossing the floor. He couldn't make out the gruff murmurings, had no idea what excuse Noble came up with. As long as he got rid of the pub owner, he didn't much care, either. Tom wished he'd hurry up, though. His nose was beginning to itch, and stems were poking him in the ears.

Hearing only one set of footsteps return, Tom asked, "Is she gone?"

"It's safe; you can come out now."

Tom poked his head out and made sure Dolores was nowhere in sight before he crawled out of the straw stack. Standing, he brushed the fine yellow dust off his trousers.

Noble jabbed his hands on his hips and cocked his head to the side. "You gonna tell me what's goin' on 'round here?"

"They've been after me all week." He ruffled his hair and spit a stem out of his mouth. "I've been kicked by a mule, poisoned, sprayed by a skunk, and nearly froze my hind end off sleeping in the woods."

"Wha'd you go and do a fool thing like that for?"

"It was either sleep in the stables with the stink, sleep in the woods, or sleep in that house with Ginny. I took my chances in the woods." Tom grabbed the pitchfork. "I'm telling you, those women have waged a campaign against me to drive me back to the farm with Ginny. And she's masterminding the whole operation."

"Uh, then I reckon I shouldn't have told Miss Dolores that she could have a hoedown here."

Tom fell back against a stall post and gasped, "You didn't."

19

$\mathcal{T}$HE STABLES WERE ablaze with light from kerosene lanterns hooked to every available post. Fresh straw had been laid in the wide corridor between stall rows. Orange-hot coals in the forge lent a sultry odor to the crisp November evening.

Paying little mind to the plunk of fiddles being tuned and the gaping notes of an accordion, Ginny set a plate of Oma's apple dumplings on a saw board table with the rest of the cakes, pies, sweetmeats and crocks of punch.

I do not see Vati, Doreen sighed.

Craning her neck, Ginny searched the small gathering for a familiar lean form. "I am certain he is here somewhere. . . ."

Several women, dressed in their best starched calico gowns, were assembled together at the back of the building. More had taken seats alongside the dance arena. Young hunch-shouldered boys snickered in one corner while adolescent girls cast calf-eyed glances their way.

Thomas was nowhere in sight.

Ginny tamped down the sudden rise of doubt. Although he had managed to avoid every other situation that might throw them into each other's company, he would not miss his own homecoming celebration . . . would he?

Noble approached at that moment, looking very dapper in his black suit and sharply creased cravat.

"Have you seen Thomas?" Ginny asked hopefully as David helped relieve her of her cape. Then he reached for Doreen's and Oma's coats and hooked them on wall pegs with a dozen other winter garments.

"He's in the loft, Miss Ginny." Noble averted his face. "He won't come down."

"But dis *Zelebrieren* vas arranged in his honor!"

Noble shrugged his massive shoulders. "I'm sorry, Miss Bertha, but I already done tried tellin' him that. He says he didn't ask for no party and he don't have to go to no shindig he didn't ask for."

"Vell, he can be stubborn if he vants but no reasonable *Deutsch Frau* lets good polka music go to vaste. Come, David," Bertha commanded, seizing David's arm just as the fiddles began to screech, "give dis old voman a turn around de dance floor."

Ginny's emotions wavered between vexation at Thomas's childish behavior and profound disappointment that this effort, too, would be wasted. Parties were always an event to look forward to, but this evening she had come for the sole purpose of trying to spend an enjoyable couple of hours with her husband. To try and persuade him again that they belonged together.

Except her husband was not cooperating.

"Miss Ginny, try not to take this too much to heart," Noble said kindly. "Tom's just doin' what he thinks is right."

Studying Noble closely, Ginny once more wondered why lately he would not meet her eyes. Their relationship had always been one of open affection and respect. Did he think she felt it a betrayal of their friendship because Thomas chose to stay with him instead of her? Did he not know that she did not blame him for her husband's decision?

She curled her fingers over his thick forearm. "Noble? I do not hold any ill will toward you for being Thomas's friend. He needs someone near that he can trust. Unfortunately, that person is not me. Not yet, anyway."

He seemed to grow even more discomfited, shifting from

one leg to the other, fidgeting with his tie, before finally mumbling something about stoking coals in the forge.

The hour dragged on as Ginny sought to make sense of her chaotic emotions. Why was Thomas so determined to shoulder his troubles alone? Why would he not let her help him?

She mingled among the crowd, trying to keep up a pretense of gaiety. Neighbors from as far as twenty miles away had gathered to welcome her husband home and now all of them whispered about her being jilted. Most acted quite sympathetic but many of the younger set seemed pleased that her husband's attentions were not fastened.

After a mere hour her tolerance reached its breaking point. She spotted David at the refreshment table, taking a break from dancing.

"David, mayhap it is time we started for home. Would you please tell Doreen while I find my grandmother?"

He pushed away from the wall, alarm crossing his tanned features. "I thought Doreen was with you."

Ginny gave a puzzled shake of her head. "I have not seen her since the last waltz started."

"She wandered away when I was talkin' to Henry and a few of the boys. If she ain't with you, where is she?"

At the flash of panic in his brown eyes, she said, "Do not worry, David, she is here somewhere. Why don't you check the stalls? I will ask a few of the women if they have seen her."

But each query about Doreen's whereabouts led to an innocent question about Thomas, laying another bruise to her already battered heart. Ginny made excuses for Thomas's absence. Pride would not let her admit that he refused to come to his own party in order to avoid her, but inside she seethed with angry humiliation.

Ginny forced down the irritation and continued her search.

Up above, Tom gnawed on a hay stem and watched the goings-on. Ignoring the carefree laughter and rowdy clapping accompanying the accordions and fiddles proved futile. The women had turned his private sanctum into a three-ring circus.

His gaze found Ginny. He'd known the instant she walked in the door. His heartbeat picked up, his throat went tight, his palms went moist. He tugged the blanket around his shoulders closer to his neck and brought one knee to his chest. She was wearing blue tonight. Hoopskirts, too. The shiny cloth, silk he guessed, shimmered as she walked over to Dolores Silver. Whatever Ginny said into the woman's ear made her glance up in his direction.

Tom ducked back before they could see him, but he hadn't missed the look on Ginny's face. She'd seemed almost . . . depressed. Sighing, he let his head fall against the wall. He wasn't worth going through all this trouble, didn't she realize that? He could never feel for her what she felt for him—no, what she felt for who she thought he was.

It was Thomas Herz's fault Ginny fancied herself in love with him, not his. Tom had tried telling her in every way he could think of that she'd gotten the wrong man, yet she wouldn't listen.

Where was her husband, anyway? How could he have just left his family to wait and wonder?

Staring at the dusty rafters, Tom worked the piece of hay from one side of his mouth to the other. Maybe he should just confess that he was trying to locate her real husband.

Then again, what purpose would it serve? It would be just one more instance where she wouldn't believe him.

He could almost hear her now—"But, Thomas, why would you wish to search for a man I have already found?" And it would start another argument that he wouldn't win because he'd try denying their marriage, and that damned pained look would cross over her eyes . . . he couldn't stand the way her eyes went all cloudy.

The faintest of noises distracted him from examining the reason why. Next a pair of coiled flaxen braids appeared over the loft ledge. Doreen hesitated the moment she spied him. Then she surprised Tom by hauling herself over the ledge. He removed the stem from his mouth and silently watched her cross the straw-layered floor. She sat a few feet away, her legs tucked close to her chest.

After a while of their gazes meeting, then darting away, Tom finally jerked the stem toward the ladder. "Why aren't you down there dancing?"

She cocked her head curiously.

"Dancing." Tom wiggled his dangling fingers. "You know."
Wrinkling her nose, she ducked her head.

"Why not?"

She tugged at her ear, then shook her head again.

"Ahh," Tom nodded. "That's right, you can't hear the music."

He turned his attention back to the dancing. The lack of men didn't stop the women below from enjoying themselves, that was certain. Each held on tight to another and stomped around the makeshift dance floor with all the gusto of a bunch of lumberjacks.

And, Tom decided, lack of hearing shouldn't stop a young girl from dancing, either.

"Well, I can hear it." He unfolded himself and got to his feet. The blanket slipped to the floor. He motioned toward Doreen. "Come on, I'll show you."

She stared at him a moment, eyes as blue as Ginny's filled with unspoken questions. Finally, she reached up, placing her hand trustingly into Tom's. Stifling a warm surge of protectiveness, he pulled her to her feet. She was so small compared to him. The top of her head barely reached the middle of his chest. Her bones were tiny, too. Like Ginny's.

"Put your feet on mine—no, your feet." He tugged at the worn kidskin of her ankle boot and guided it on top of his Hessian. "Yeah, so you're standing on my toes."

She raised her brows skeptically at him.

"Don't worry, you're not hurting me." She couldn't weigh more than seventy pounds. "Now put this hand around my waist, and put the other one in my hand," he instructed, placing her hands at the proper places just as a new song began. "Hold on tight now, this is a lively one."

Sliding his upper body to the side as if entering the music, Tom felt her fingers clutch his for dear life. Doreen made a sound like a squeal.

"I won't let you fall."

Her tight grip gradually loosened as Tom kept a smooth pace with the boomp-ba-ba rhythm. She kept her eyes trained on his toes. His heels kicked up dust and chaff.

Eyes widening, she grinned up at him, blinding him with her smile. He saw Ginny in those eyes, saw Ginny in that smile.

"Fun, huh?" Could she hear it? Could she feel it? To Tom's astonishment, he could, and he found himself enjoying the music in a way he hadn't since . . . since he couldn't remember when.

Then Doreen's feet slipped off his, and a rare gurgle of laughter echoed through the slant-roofed beams. She stood before him for a moment, wearing a shy smile.

"Well, get back on," Thomas said gruffly. "The song isn't finished yet." She was having such a good time that he just couldn't bring himself to tell her the last note had faded away some time ago.

Ginny stood at the bottom of the ladder, trying to decide if she could endure Thomas's frosty attitude. The loft was the only place she had not yet looked for Doreen, and since she could not be found anywhere else, she knew she had little choice.

Gathering her courage, Ginny forced herself up each rung. Reaching the top, she peeked over the ledge.

She said not a word, could not have even if she'd wanted to, for a lump of emotion rose in her throat.

With her hand covering her mouth, her vision shimmery from unshed tears, Ginny's irritation with Thomas vanished as she lost her heart to him all over again. She watched in silent wonder as he twirled Doreen from one end of the loft to the other. The thick blanket of straw muffled the sound of his stomping feet.

There was something innocent and incomparably sweet about the rough and austere man teaching his little girl to dance, of having her stand on his toes while he whisked her from corner to corner. And she knew without a doubt that if she had not already been in love with him, his tender consideration with Doreen would have sent her spinning head over heels.

A moment passed before she realized that the fiddles had stopped playing. Ginny ducked unseen down the ladder lest her weeping alert him to her presence. She wanted nothing to spoil the fragile bond developing between father and daughter.

It wasn't much but it was a beginning.

David was waiting at the bottom. "Did you find her?"

Ginny nodded briskly. "I have changed my mind. I think we will stay for a little while longer."

Breathless, Tom slowed their pace, then stopped. Doreen looked at him, a question in her big blue eyes. "The dance is over," he answered with soft regret. Her expressive eyes clouded, as if she too wished the moment had not come to an end.

Then she eagerly began motioning toward the edge of the loft.

"No, Doreen, I'm not going down there. Those women are just waiting for a chance to make a fool of me—"

She shook her head vigorously. Bringing her hands together at the thumbs, she then spread them away.

Puzzled, Tom watched her repeat the motion several times. He just didn't understand her language, though. This signing stuff was as foreign to him as English had once been, and it had taken him years to master that. Frowning, he shook his head.

Her shoulders slumped. Disappointment pulled the corners of her mouth down. She drew her thumb along her jaw.

"Yeah, I shaved," he said, rubbing his smooth face. "What do you think?"

She laughed feebly, then shook her head. Her closed lips slanted to the side, her brows dipped. With her finger to her cheek, she pondered him a moment, then jabbed the finger into the air, indicating she'd come up with an idea.

Her hand raised, palm out. She curled three fingers over her thumb.

It took Tom a moment to realize that she was trying to spell something. "M?"

She nodded in excitement.

"M. Mmm . . ."

She raised the first two fingers straight up.

"Two. No, u. Mm . . . u. Mu, mu—muster! When did I muster out of the army?"

She doubled over, making those funny gurgling sounds, and slapped her knees. When she raised back up, he noticed she was biting the inside of her mouth to keep from laughing. And though she made no sound, her eyes danced. He couldn't help but find her enchanting.

Her hand formed a fist.

"You want to hit me?"

She pointed to the tip of her thumb poking between the first two fingers.

"You want to suck my thumb?"

Her hip cocked to the side, her eyes rolled heavenward.

"Okay, okay." This was sorta fun. Kinda like playing charades. He sounded out all the letters while she watched his lips. "M . . . u . . . c? r? d? t?"

She went ecstatic, and raised her fist again.

"T? Two t's M-u-t-t . . . mutt . . . mutt . . ." His startled eyes shot to her face. "*Mutter*," Tom said.

She brought a forefinger in a squiggly line down each cheek while turning her lips down sadly.

All traces of play drained from him. "Mother cries."

She folded her hands at her temple and tipped her head.

Tom whispered, "In her sleep."

She nodded a somber confirmation. Tom turned away. With his hands on his hips, he walked toward the loft hatch. He barely noticed when Doreen left.

For a long time after the stables cleared out and the sounds of revelry faded into the woodwork, Tom stared out the window at the sprinkle of white stars on black velvet. *Mutter cries in her sleep.*

Nobody had ever cried for him before.

20

LONG AFTER THE children and Oma went to sleep, Ginny lay awake in her big bed, wishing she held Thomas instead of his pillow. Only the faintest trace of his soapy scent clung to the slip case; she had not been able to bring herself to wash it yesterday with the rest of the laundry.

Sweet mercy, she missed him. The loneliness had once been but a dim pang. But ever since he'd come back from the war, it had grown in intensity until she wondered how she bore the pain.

When she closed her eyes, an image of Thomas dancing with Doreen took shape in her mind, filling her with bittersweet tenderness. In light of all Thomas had done to avoid the family, how had Doreen managed to coax him into dancing with her?

Throughout the evening, Ginny had bitten her tongue to keep from bringing up what she'd witnessed in the loft. She had preached to her daughter about respecting another's privacy for so long that it seemed hypocritical to press her for details. A potentially harmful situation would be another matter entirely, but keeping the dance with her *Vati* secret hurt no one. And Ginny could not fault Doreen for wanting to keep the experience to herself for a while. She had so little of Thomas to cherish. At least Ginny had memories.

She clutched the pillow tighter, buried her nose in the downy fold. Memories were a sore substitute for the flesh-and-blood man that used to make her body come alive.

Selfishly she pictured herself being swept into his arms. The fantasy came to life in her mind so clearly that she could almost feel his breath whisper across her temple. Smell the musky heat of his lean body. Hear the music in her veins and see the love in his amber eyes.

Oh, Thomas.

How had Doreen accomplished such a seemingly impossible feat, getting so close to the distant man?

Mayhap she should try to tell Thomas of Marks's visit. Use his possessiveness of the land to coerce him back. Ginny sighed despondently. That seemed so manipulative. He would not believe her, anyway. Not until he trusted her.

No, it was best she wait. He would regain his memory soon. He had to.

He just had to.

Tom watched the last of the women file into the church. The instant the doors shut and muffled organ music signaled the start of the service, he mounted the black. Tom checked the horse's high-stepping gait at the bridge, scanned the area to make sure nobody was watching, then sent the animal into a full gallop to the farm.

A late flock of geese arrowed across the cloudless sky as if pointing the way. Clods of rich soil spit out from beneath the black's pounding hooves. Nearly naked branches of maple and elm along the road provided perches to valiant blood-red cardinals content with the cold weather.

The road forked one way to the old Brummer stead, and Tom took the right path leading to his farm. He'd purposely waited until this morning when he could slip into the house undetected. With luck, everyone would be tied up listening to the sermon for at least a couple hours. That would give him more than enough time to search for something—anything—tangible proving that he and Ginny's husband were not one and the same.

Hearing that Ginny fell asleep with tears on her pillow had

been a wicked blow. But looking into that little girl's eyes last night? That had been a rude awakening. Ginny wasn't the only one suffering from Herz's neglect. Doreen needed her father as bad . . . well, as bad as he'd needed his. The difference between him and Doreen was that her father was alive. Somewhere. He hoped. He'd hate to be the one to tell them they'd waited all these years for nothing.

Pulling the black to a stop at the porch, Tom dismounted and loosely tied the reins to the railing.

It felt odd stepping through the front door, as if he'd entered a portal to the past. Not a sound disturbed the peace, not a soul came running at him to welcome him home. The stillness made him realize how thoroughly four people filled his house.

Tom cursed the peculiar void widening inside him. It had been this way before he'd joined the Union, it was what he'd craved for four long years. Solitude. Silence. The freedom to be his own master at his own leisure.

He snatched a piece of sausage from beneath a covered plate on the counter then mounted the steps and walked into her bedroom. Ginny's scent lingered in the air. A bit spicy, overwhelmingly sweet. He tried to remember a time when the room hadn't smelled of her but couldn't.

His gaze landed on the bed where she'd riled his senses. He brushed his hand along the quilt that must have warmed her last night. Had she cried for him?

Tom drew his hand back, moved to the trunk and lifted the lid. A horde of Ginny's treasures were stored beneath stacks of crisp, clean clothing redolent of cedar. Tiny booties he bet Doreen had worn; a chipped china plate that probably belonged to some distant relative; a pipe still smelling of cherry tobacco.

He picked up the wreath she'd worn on her head that day in the Kirkmiller barn.

He drew the yellowed ribbon between his thumb and forefinger, his blood beginning to simmer. Thunderation, she'd looked so tempting wearing the wreath and that silly white gown. Her pretty pink toes curling into the dirt beneath her feet. A mixture of virginal innocence and wanton wisdom.

Tom sucked in a swift breath and finished rummaging through the trunk. He felt like the skunk Evie Mae accused him of being, digging through Ginny's things. But if he was ever going to locate Herz, he needed to know as much about the man as possible.

More urgently now than ever.

Given Ginny's penchant for saving mementos, there had to be a clue in her possessions somewhere. The woman couldn't have kept her marriage alive all these years on faith alone.

Of course, the more he learned about Ginny, the more he suspected faith drove her every action.

Nothing of any use was found in either the trunk or in the drawers of the vanity table or between the cornhusk mattress and bedsprings. Where else did Ginny keep things of value?

The desk.

Downstairs once again, Tom glanced at the beautifully crafted wall clock with its pinecone-decorated chains and carved leaf design. Damn, he'd spent more time in the bedroom than he should have. With less than an hour left, Tom made a quick search of the cubbyholes and drawers. And as he flipped through ledgers, one of the totals at the bottom caught his eye.

As though clobbered with a beam, Tom sank onto the desk chair and stared at the staggering five-digit number printed neatly at the bottom. He flattened the ledger on the desk and studied the entries for last fall's harvest.

Twenty acres of corn, five of cotton, ten of flax, and eighty of wheat, of which over half had been sold. Flipping the pages backward he noticed similar entries for the previous years, including the dates of each harvest, the section of sowed and planted acreage, the amount of rain each season. . . .

She'd recorded it all. In German, of course, but she'd written down every single detail of the last four crops taken in while he'd been off fighting.

One thing became crystal clear as he absorbed Ginny's work. He'd done it backward. He'd planted too much of one crop, not enough of the other, and none at all of some.

The home place and garden took up several acres, and timberland consumed the rest, but using over a hundred acres wisely, Ginny had made him richer in four years than he ever imagined being in his whole life.

Ginny. A little bitty milkmaid with hands soft as down, a

spine of steel, and a heart of pure gold, had made it so that he'd never have to depend on anyone again. And she'd kept books on how she'd done it, so he could follow her example and double his account if he so chose.

Ginny. She'd made him a rich man.

Once Tom got over his astonishment that someone so tiny could create such an enormous impact, a glimmer of admiration, respect even, unfurled within him.

He wanted to do something for her. What would she want? An evening out? No, there wasn't any place to take her. Ridgeford had nothing in the way of cultural interests. New clothes? A house of her own? A diamond? No, he quickly decided, the only jewelry she wore was that ugly old ri—"

Tom slammed the ledgers shut and plowed his fingers through his hair. That damn ring was the bane of his existence. The only thing she wanted was the man who had put it on her finger, and she thought he was that man.

He had to find Herz. Had to prove once and for all that they were two completely different people. Then once Herz was found, if Ginny wanted half the profits from the farm, he'd gladly split them with her just to get rid of her. She'd done the work, but she'd done it on his land.

Spurred on by that decision, Tom tore through the house, rifling through every cupboard, every cranny, every shelf, looking for irrefutable evidence. Nothing. Not a blasted thing was found. As he stood in front of the whatnot, moving aside collectibles to peer into the corners of the shelving unit, the clock chimed once, warning him that it was eleven-thirty.

He figured he'd best scat before Ginny came home from church and caught him in the house. There was always next Sunday to return, and yet he'd checked just about every possible hiding place he could think of and his hands were still empty.

Well, almost. He set the porcelain figurine of a little girl sitting on a middle-aged man's lap back down between the two saucers—

Then froze.

His head whipped back around. A little girl. A man's lap.

The back of his neck prickled, the same way it had that day

he'd charged into the woods and found the men held captive. In surreal slow motion he watched his own hand reach for the figurine and tip it over. Curled edges of white paper blocked a hole the size of a silvery dollar.

A mixture of jubilation and apprehension started Tom's heart to pounding rapidly as he plucked the bent papers from the hollow base and returned the figurine to its spot.

The lost letters.

There were only a few, rolled together like a scroll and tied with a ribbon the same deep blue as Ginny's eyes. Tom brought them to the sunlight beaming through the window, and after glancing around to be sure nobody had come up unnoticed behind him, he untied the bundle.

The seams where the papers had been folded were very worn, even torn in several spots. As Tom opened them up, one almost fell apart in his hands. Obviously they had been read often. He could picture Ginny poring over the German words, memorizing every sharp curve of the handwriting, every sloping letter.

He skimmed over them in a hurry, committing them to memory himself. The first one told of Herz's journey on the steam ship. Tom forced himself not to remember his own degrading passage as he read of the comfortable berth Herz shared with five other people. What a luxury compared to the dank and moldy bowels he'd been packed into with hundreds of indentured servants and contract laborers. Thunderation, the fellow didn't know how lucky he'd been.

Between professions of love and devotion that made his stomach knot up, the next letter described Herz's arrival in the States. The paradoxical blend of nationalities he encountered traveling across the country. The difficulty in learning the strange new language being spoken around him. Herz's struggle to learn to speak and read English. He'd written that when he finally grasped it, he would teach Ginny.

Now Tom understood the sadness in her eyes when she told him she couldn't read English. She had been waiting for Herz to keep his promise. One of many, Tom thought scathingly.

Another missive told her about the rolling green hills, the abundant forests, the golden fields, the plentiful water and wildlife . . . all sights Tom had been denied until many years after his own immigration. But he found himself lingering on the more personal elements of the letters. *How are you faring, my darling? Our daughter must be quite a lovely young lady. . . . My heart aches for you. . . . My fingers long for the touch of your hair—*

At that, Tom growled in disgust and flipped to the last letter, not wanting to examine why the intimate portions of the missives bothered him. Why his chest felt clamped and his gut turned and the urge to burn the words hit him with the force of a lightning bolt.

The last one was short and terse. *I have purchased land in the southern section of a state called Wisconsin. I plan to build a home and put in a crop. I will send for you as soon as the first year's profits come in. Dein Dichliebender Mann,*

He signed with the shape of a heart.

Tom's stomach rolled with nausea. In his hand he held proof that Ginny belonged to another.

No, in his hand he held proof that he was a free man. Once the real Thomas Herz was found, all they had to do was compare the signatures. After twelve years, the man had to have changed somewhat, and since Ginny was fully convinced that Tom was her husband, the letters would be his ticket to liberty.

He retied the ribbon, then carefully tucked the packet into his inside coat pocket, where it seemed to sear the flesh beneath his shirt. So what if anybody noticed they were missing? Something had to be done to find Herz before the situation got more out of hand than it already was.

And yet Tom was left questioning who had stuck the letters in the figurine. According to Ginny, they'd vanished a while back. Had she lied? Her grief over their loss had seemed so sincere. . . .

But if she wasn't the one who'd placed them in the figurine, who was?

The minute Tom turned around he had his answer.

21

$\mathcal{S}$TANDING IN THE doorway, Doreen looked pale as mill-ground flour, her stricken gaze fixed on the hand Tom had tucked between his coat and shirt. Slowly, he removed his hand. Watching. Waiting. Wondering what she would do now that she'd caught him stealing the "vanished" letters.

Silence had never been so thick. Or so loud.

"*Heda*, Doreen," Tom cautiously greeted, lifting his hand.

The movement seemed to snap her from her trance. She flung herself across the room and shoved her hand under his coat, pinching the corners of the papers between her fingers.

Curling his body away, Tom refused to let her take them back. "No, Doreen, you can't have them."

She dodged around behind him, trying to snatch the letters from under his arm. "Stop it!" Tom swerved, evading her grasping hands. "Do you have any idea what these letters mean? They're my freedom, Doreen. The handwriting doesn't even resemble mine—"

She grabbed for his coat again. Little whimpering sounds came from her mouth.

"I won't keep them forever," he tried assuring her. "You can have them back as soon as I'm finished."

Earnestly she pointed to the figurine, then to him, then to herself, and closed her fist over her heart.

A little girl. A middle-aged man.

A daughter. A father.

Tom shut his eyes briefly, suddenly overwhelmed by remorse. But he had no choice. "I'm sorry. I really am. But I need them." Each one contained details that might help Gene track Herz's route and lead them directly to the man. And once his friend did find Herz, Tom planned on showing Ginny the letters. She'd have no choice but to accept he'd been telling the truth all along once she compared their penmanship.

It sounded so uncomplicated. So foolproof.

Until Tom glanced down and found himself confronted by a pixie's pale face, her innocent blue eyes silently imploring him not to take the letters . . .

Oh, thunderation! Didn't she understand how important they were to him? Did she realize that they could be the key to bringing back her true father?

Apparently not. The girl didn't seem to care about anything besides getting her hands on the letters. For whatever reason they were that important to her.

Tom bowed his head in defeat and reached into his pocket. "Here. Take the damn things." He just couldn't bring himself to steal from a child.

As he presented the bent packet, her mouth opened in shock. She took them reverently and with a great deal of caution, as if expecting him to snatch them back. She stared at them a long moment, kissed the folds, then threw her arms around his waist.

Tom felt as if the wall of his chest were made of glass and she'd just hurled a rock through it. It shattered in tiny pieces, taking nicks out of his skin.

Just as his arms were about to close around her, laughter coming from the direction of the front door sent Tom snapping self-consciously to attention. The action alerted Doreen, and she whirled around at the same moment Ginny appeared.

"Thomas!" she gasped, her face alive with surprise and joy. His pulse leaped uncontrollably at the way she said his name. She was the only one who ever called him Thomas, as if it meant something extraordinary.

They stared at one another, Tom dimly aware of Bertha and David filing in and the twelve resounding chimes tolling the noon hour.

The tension increased with each echoing *bong*.

He shouldn't have noticed how fetching she looked in her Sunday go-to-meeting clothes, but he did. She wore an outfit common to the women of her origins, yet on her it didn't look common at all. The brightly embroidered outer corset over a white scoop-collared blouse enhanced her bosom and slender waist. Her skirt barely reached below her knees, revealing a good two inches of finely turned calves encased in thick white stockings.

When the last chime ebbed, Ginny hastily looked away, a faint blush suffusing her cheeks. Her brows narrowed at her daughter. "Doreen?" She drew the name out both with her fingers and voice, in a tone mothers around the world probably used when they were fully aware that their children were hiding something.

Doreen shot a panicked gaze at Tom. He raised his brows and glanced at the ceiling, feigning ignorance. He didn't want Ginny knowing what he and Doreen had been up to any more than Doreen did. Then he'd have to confess that he'd been about to steal the letters for himself.

Doreen seemed to have understood his silent promise to keep the last few minutes a secret from her mother, for she smiled broadly at Tom, motioned to Ginny, then skipped off.

"Doreen said you were waiting for us to come home."

"I . . . uh, came by to pick up some extra clothes," he lied.

Ginny looked at his empty hands, then back into his face.

Tom mentally wiped his face clear of the guilt roiling inside him. Lying to her was getting harder by the day. "If you don't mind getting them for me, I'll be on my way."

Her lashes fell and she turned toward the stairs, but Tom hadn't missed the dimming of her eyes, the disappointment in her features.

The instant she went upstairs, he cast one last regretful glance at the figurine, trying to banish the knowledge that he'd just given away the only tangible evidence that he and Ginny weren't married because he couldn't resist a pair of innocent blue eyes.

He was really beginning to hate the color blue.

Feeling a desperate need to escape the house, to separate his confusion from the people who caused it, he stormed toward the door.

"You are leaving so soon?" Bertha asked in surprise. Her hands and apron were coated with flour and the white powder smudged her cheek.

"Umm, yeah, I just remembered I have something to do."

"But you forgot your clothes!"

"I'll come back another time." His hand closed around the latch.

Then Ginny's voice delayed him. He forced himself to release the latch. If he bolted out the door now, it would make Ginny suspicious. She was too astute, could read his face too well. And the last thing he needed was for her to learn of his weakness.

"Thomas, I hope you did not wish to preserve your uniform," she said, gliding down the stairs. "There was a bit of a mishap." Her fingers caressed the top garment of the stack of muted brown, green, and blue material in her arms.

Tom throat closed as he recalled those same fingers tracing the scars on his back. Rubbing circles on his arm. Threading through his hair . . .

He swallowed roughly. "Whatever it was, don't worry about it. It's just a shoddy."

"And I learned just how shoddy when I washed it. The fabric fell apart in my hands."

"No, I mean it's called a shoddy—made of reused wool."

"Sweet mercy, the army should have provided its soldiers with more durable clothing."

"Near the end of the war that's all we had." Tom paused to chuckle at a memory. "One time, my regiment was holed up in this bog down in Kentucky, and the skies opened up. General Dickson wound up standing there in nothing but skin because the rain just shredded his uniform."

She giggled at the image he'd painted. It made Tom aware

that he'd dawdled too long. He wasn't safe here. "Well, I suppose I'll be seeing you around the village." The way Ginny tracked his every step he could guarantee it.

"Would you care to join us for the midday meal?"

In spite of the urgency to get Herz's route down on paper for Gene while it was still fresh in his mind, Tom hesitated. "I better not. . . ." The entreaty in two identical sets of eyes made him falter.

He glanced at Bertha helplessly. She lifted one thick brow as if daring him to refuse the temptation of frying chicken and roasting corn he smelled cooking on the stove.

"Oh, all right—a few more minutes won't hurt."

He was wrong. The torture began the instant Ginny rewarded him with a winsome smile.

While Bertha, Ginny and Doreen combined their efforts to make the meal, Tom stood inauspiciously to the side, trying to keep out of their bustling way. After a while he found their lively chatter and welcoming smiles drawing him into the fold of their little family. He wasn't part of them, of course. He was an outsider. A landlord of sorts. Just letting them use his house and furnishings until Herz took over the responsibility.

The day would come when it was the other man they made feel welcome instead of him. When they cooked for him and smiled for him and provided for him everything the man could possibly desire.

Desire. Ginny would fulfill that part. She'd sleep in Herz's bed. Draw patterns on his arm. Whisper to him in that enticing German accent as she pressed her bare body against his.

The mental picture planted an unreasonable seed of loathing for Herz. What did he care if Ginny slept with the man? Tom swore under his breath and made a move for the door just as Ginny called his name.

"You have not changed your mind, have you?"

He halted for just a second, wanting nothing more than to leave and never look back. But one single unspoken word resounded in his brain—coward.

So instead he turned toward the table and hid his clenched fists behind his back. Out of the corner of his eye he caught a subtle movement by the sink. David, stiff as piano wire, was sidling several feet closer to Bertha, darting fearful looks toward Tom.

"I wish he'd stop acting like that around me," he told Ginny as he followed her to the table. "He makes me feel like a monster."

"It will help if you bring your hands out from behind your back. He fears you are hiding something."

The image that appeared in Tom's mind sickened him. But he masked his revulsion and eased his hands around to his front, revealing that they were empty.

"And do not scowl so, Thomas. You look as if you are on the verge of biting off someone's head."

That effort took a little more willpower but once Tom managed to force his features into a mask of cordiality, the boy visibly relaxed.

As Bertha served up the meal, Tom studied David. He reminded Tom too much of himself long ago. So much so that he felt compelled to draw him out of his reserve before it became a way of life.

"I saw you eyeing the black in the stables the other day," Tom said. "Do you ride, boy?"

David kept his gaze on his plate as he shrugged. "Sorta." He glanced at Ginny. After receiving her encouraging nod, he cleared his throat and quietly said, "Noble sometimes lets me ride with him but I'm not very good."

"Takes practice to get good at something. Why don't you take the black for a turn around the field."

"Y-y-you'd let me ride your horse?"

"Is there any reason why I shouldn't?"

His forehead crimped with uncertainty. Doreen tugged on his arm. When David began motioning, Tom figured he must be translating the conversation. Suddenly Doreen sprang from her chair and exuberantly dragged David away from the table.

Tom, too, deserted his meal to venture outside after the youngsters. Standing on the porch, he watched while the boy carefully mounted the black then pulled Doreen up behind him. A twinge of envy snuck into Tom's veins at their open, easy camaraderie.

After a few minutes, Ginny joined him at the railing.

Together they unabashedly spied on the young people loping through the field on the gelding.

"Those two are close," Tom voiced his observation.

"Inseparable," Ginny replied. "They trust each other. Sometimes I think more than they trust themselves."

As the comment sank in, Tom wondered what it would be like to have that much faith in someone. He'd never been able to trust anyone other than himself.

"David trusts you also, else he would not have dared accept your invitation." A note of smug satisfaction entered her voice. "I knew you had not lost your gift of making people feel safe."

Tom gawked at her. Him? Make people feel safe?

"Of course, you seem a bit out of practice, but I felt the same way. When Prussia and Austria brought the revolution to our peaceful *Dorf*, I lived in fear that my family would perish in the battles—until I met you."

The trusting smile she gave him made his chest swell with pride at the same time that his stomach knotted with anxiety.

"Then it did not matter where you went or how long you stayed away, I felt that no harm would come to me or them."

Closing his mouth, Tom turned his gaze back toward the youngsters, saying not a word. She had a tendency to give him admirable qualities he couldn't possibly possess. Virtues he didn't want. Honor and loyalty. Protectiveness and reliability. Why did everyone try and make him into some kind of hero? Matthew. Gene Mason. General Gibbons. Why couldn't they just look at him and see him for the selfish bastard he really was?

He squinted into the horizon, strangely disappointed that he wasn't worthy of the praise she lavished on him. Maybe her husband had been perfect, but Tom knew that he could try for the rest of his days and never match Herz's perfection. At least in her eyes.

With a tight frown he said, "I best head on back to the village." Then he stuck his fingers on his tongue and gave one loud, sharp whistle, calling for David to bring the horse back on around.

Ginny's hand burned an imprint on his arm. "Thomas, there is no reason for you to leave."

Studying her, Tom felt his heart shift in his chest. Felt his will weaken as her imported charms worked their power. Felt an attraction that had begun to take hold dig its roots in deeper and threaten everything he held dear. He set his jaw. "Wrong, Ginny, there's every reason."

As he mounted the black David brought around, he caught sight of Ginny's crestfallen expression. Tom forcibly swept aside a prick of guilt as he directed the horse away from her, away from the home she'd made of his farm.

He didn't have a choice.

He had his freedom to protect.

Every instinct within Ginny urged her to go after Thomas. She had watched him often enough to see the vulnerability behind his anger. The longing behind his fear. How could a man look at her the way Thomas did and not remember?

And yet whenever she got too close, he retreated. Not physically, but emotionally. He erected an impenetrable barrier between them, as if he needed to protect himself from her.

Why? What fear was so powerful that he could not trust the love they once shared to overcome it?

The sermon earlier that morning replayed in Ginny's mind as she watched her husband's form disappear around the bluff. *The heart of her husband safely trusts her so he will have no lack of gain. She does him good and not evil all the days of her life.*

Long ago she'd been entrusted with Thomas's heart. It belonged to her just as hers belonged to him. And all that she did was for his good as much as hers and their family's.

But her deeds were getting them nowhere.

Mayhap Dolores was right, Ginny conceded. Mayhap it was time to "bring out the big guns." Only then would they have a chance to come to terms with their lives—past, present, and future. And heaven help her when that happened, for she suspected that when all his barriers finally came tumbling down, there would be the devil to pay.

22

*T*HEY KIDNAPPED HIM.

Awareness hit Tom after a shove from behind jolted him from a sound sleep and sent him rolling across the loft floor. A blanket wound itself tighter and tighter around him. With one arm pinned across his chest, the other at his side, Tom ignored the stars swirling in his head and reacted instinctively, kicking free of the coarse wool trap. His heel connected with something fleshy.

"Augh! For pity's sake, hold him still—even barefoot he packs quite a whollop."

Startled by the sound of a woman's voice, Tom ceased his struggles. The moist heat of his own rapid breaths ricocheted off the blanket back into his face. *Dolores?*

"Here, wrap this around his ankles."

"You came prepared."

Evie Mae?

"I didn't expect he'd come along peaceably."

Feeling a rope wind around his feet, Tom once more began writhing in protest.

"Quit thrashing, Tom—I brought a mallet, too."

Tom settled considerably, not wanting to provoke Dolores

into using that. His heart slammed painfully against his ribs, his arm was bent at an awkward angle. "Whaa de 'el iz g'ing aan!"

"Can't understand a word you're bellowing so you might as well shush up and cooperate."

Cooperate? They expected him to just *let* them truss him up like a sausage?

"Maybe you should use the mallet anyway, Dolores. If you brain him a good one, it might make him remember and save us all this trouble."

"Nope. I thought of that, but Ginny made me promise I wouldn't hurt him."

Arggghhh! He should have known Ginny was behind this! When he got his hands on her . . .

They wound another length of rope around his body, restraining his arms. Just when he thought they'd heaped enough degradation on him, one shoved him flat onto his back.

"Now hold still, Tom—this ain't gonna hurt a bit."

It was his only warning before he felt a slender object slide along his blanketed ankles and up along the length of his body clear past his nose.

"As easy as roastin' a pig on a spit," Dolores pronounced. "You grab his head, I'll grab his feet."

Tom's feet rose, then his head left the ground, yet no hands touched his body. They'd tied him to a stick? Thunderation what were they planning to do to him, burn him at the stake because he wouldn't claim Ginny?

"My stars, what has Bertha been feeding this man?" Evie Mae complained as she hoisted him upward. "How are we going to get him down the ladder?"

That was a good question, Tom thought, second only to *Why in the hell were they doing this?*

"We could pitch him over the side. . . ."

His heart stopped.

"But if he got hurt, Ginny would never forgive us."

If he got hurt, Ginny was going to die!

"I know!" Dolores cried triumphantly. "We'll lower him down through the hatch. That pulley brings feed up into the loft, don't see why it can't take Tom down, too."

Oh, God, Tom thought, his heartbeat increasing to a painful

tempo. They were gonna kill him. His struggles as they dragged him across the loft floor didn't seem to daunt them, for they continued hauling him toward the opening. A blast of cold air ripped through the blanket, telling him they'd reached the mouth of the loft. Each screech of the pulley sent jabs of panic through his veins, yet Tom feared any movement on his part might send all three of them crashing to the dirt road below.

A few minutes later, they pushed him over the edge. As he swung to and fro and twisted in midair, Tom's life passed before his eyes. Not quickly as he'd heard it happened, but in agonizingly slow motion. He saw the tiny stone cottage where he had spent his early childhood; Matthew crouching beside him in a gutter, devouring bread swiped from a Munich bakery; the Manhattan shoreline at twilight; a sea of cornfields at sunset.

Then he saw Ginny. All big blue eyes and a smile of pure torture. A strength of will bendable but not breakable, much like the cottonwood trees that grew along the riverbank.

If he killed her, would the law consider his motives justifiable?

"Evie, bring the wagon around so we don't have to carry him."

A wagon? Where did they plan on taking him that they'd need a wagon?

Suspended by the pulley rope and unable to judge the distance to the ground, he didn't dare move, though every instinct screamed for freedom. Tom called upon every method of endurance he'd learned all those years ago, chained to the factory wall. He blanked his mind of all thought, forced his tense muscles to relax, his heart to pump evenly.

The rope suddenly went slack. Unprepared, his breath whooshed from his lungs as his back connected with a hard, flat surface.

A rocking squeak nearby gave him the first clue that they were about to move out, a gentle snap of reins, the second.

"Hang on, it's gonna be bumpy."

The bed started rolling.

A fleeting relief that he'd been safely lowered gave way to outrage. Adrenaline surged through Tom. He bucked and twisted against the bindings, but no amount of exertion would loosen the ropes keeping him tied to the stick.

His head dropped back against the wagon bed as the futility of his efforts sank in. By thunder, where were they taking him? To the farm? No, they would have crossed the bridge by now, and he neither felt nor heard the hollow clatter of wheels on wood.

Blinded by woolen darkness, he tried to picture the buildings along the route. The tannery? The general store? He couldn't tell. He couldn't even guess which direction they were heading without the daytime sounds to give him clues. But the wagon hit one rut after another until he thought his teeth would fall out.

He had no idea how much time passed before the wagon finally stopped. They were near the woods, though. He could tell from the sharp smell of decaying leaves.

Once more, hands grabbed his feet and dragged him along the wagon bed. Unladylike grunts accompanied plenty of shuffling as he was once again hoisted in the air.

"I'm going to have a permanent dent in my shoulder after this," Evie said.

"Just a bit farther and our part is done," Dolores replied.

Wood scraped along wood and he felt himself carried several more steps, heard the squeak of hinges. Then a barrier blocked the wind as if they'd entered an enclosure of some sort.

Then they dropped him. Tom's spine slammed against his ribs.

"He's all yours."

A prickling sensation crawled up the back of his neck as a faint waft of lemon and lye permeated through the covering.

Oh, no. Thunderation, no—they'd brought him to Ginny!

The numbing calm it had taken him years to develop completely deserted him. With a growl of pure helpless rage, he began writhing even as he felt her tugging on the knots. The stick busted, the ropes stretched then snapped. Each movement loosened the blanket a little more, increasing Tom's mobility. Finally he tore the blanket off his face and sucked in a deep draft of unfiltered air. It smelled dank and earthy. A brief glance at his surroundings revealed that they'd brought him to the icehouse near the river west of the village.

Tom staggered to the door just as the outside bar dropped with a fatal *phump*. "Let me out of here! Dolores? Evie?" He slammed his fist and the heel of his hand against the heavy oak slab. "You can't lock me up in here!" He pounded on the door until his knuckles bled.

Silence. So loud his ears rang with it. Not a sound penetrated the solid wooden structure.

He gave the door one last frustrated blow. "You won't get away with this!"

Then he paced the slatted floor. The icehouse had been built into the north side of a bluff. Square vents cut high into the walls and tacked over with screen were too small for him to squeeze through. Neither had tools been stored inside yet, for the cutting season didn't begin for another month at least.

His desperation mounted. He couldn't stay locked in here with Ginny. She had the uncanny power to wriggle beneath his coat of armor, melt the steel of his resistance. He tore off a loose board from one of the pallets stacked in the center and tried digging his way out. But the slats laid vertically on the floor for drainage couldn't be pried up to reach the dirt beneath.

The only way out was through the door. And only Ginny had the power to have it opened.

Slowly, dangerously, he fixed his gaze on the shadowy figure waiting across the shed. He hated the way the sight of her made the ground move beneath his feet. Despised the way his heart jumped into his throat and cut off his air supply. "Damn you, tell those meddling harpies to let me out," he ordered in a raspy whisper.

She stepped into a wedge of moonlight shining through one of the many ventilation windows above her head. "Not until we settle our problems."

His brittle restraint snapped. Throwing down the jagged board, he stretched his hands out. His fingers curled like talons. The urge to throttle her rose inside him, propelled him forward until barely a foot separated them.

She didn't even flinch. Just watched him. Her eyes so big

and fearless, her posture proud. He'd never met anyone with Ginny's pluck.

Just shy of throttling her, Tom growled his frustration then let his hands fall to his sides. His short fingernails dug into his palms. No matter how furious she made him, no matter how tempted he was to put her out of his misery, he just couldn't bring himself to physically hurt her. "You . . . are really, *really* getting on my nerves."

"Am I? Well, the feeling is requited, Thomas, for I am becoming quite annoyed with you, too."

His jaw dropped. "What did you have me kidnapped for, then?"

"It was the last suggestion on the list."

"Ohhh, Gawd! You made a list of ways to torment me?" He dragged his hand down his face. "Just what do you hope to gain by locking us in here together?"

"Time and privacy to help you regain your memory."

"There is *nothing wrong* with my *memory*—yours, on the other hand, is as loose as a button."

The heat of her anger seared him from head to toe as she gave him a scathing once-over. "I am not the one who does not remember leaving behind a wife and child."

Tom threw his hands up in exasperation. "I can't remember something that never happened!"

"Look at me." Her hand grasped his jaw. "Look at me!"

The instant Tom met her gaze he knew he was in trouble. He couldn't explain the softening in his chest. Nor did he want to. But he knew that it was not a good thing.

"Look at me and say the laughter we shared, the tears we shed, the dreams we dreamed never happened. Look at me and say that taking me to wife, creating a child within me never happened."

At that moment, looking at her, into her furious and so damned compelling eyes, he couldn't say anything. The words, "It never happened," locked in his throat. Dumbly, he shook his head.

"Because deep inside, you know the truth. The heart never lies." She sounded so sure it was chilling.

Tom tore himself away from her hold and began to pace.

"All right, let's test this outrageous theory of yours. Ask me something—anything."

"Thomas, it would be pointless—"

"Just ask me."

"All right, how old are you?"

Suddenly trapped, Tom silently cursed the question. All he knew was that Matthew had been a baby when they'd been taken to the orphanage, so that would make him . . . "Thirty-two," he said, trying to put as much conviction in the answer as he could muster.

She shook her head. "You are thirty-one. Where were you born?"

"Alsace," he said without hesitation. He knew that for sure.

"Frankfurt. What is your eldest brother's name?"

"I don't have an older brother."

"Thomas, you have six of them. See, I told you that you did not remember."

Tom threw himself against the wall, dimly aware of the pain shooting up his spine. Oh, God, he was getting a headache. Anything he said she would twist to suit her own purposes. "What did I ever do to deserve this?" he implored to the rafters.

She took a step toward him then stopped and spread her hands away from her sides. "If you had not been so intent on avoiding me, I would not have been forced to take such drastic measures."

"So you get your cohorts to kidnap me from my bed?"

"This was my last chance of getting your undivided attention. Had my friends not, you would have only fled again."

"Doesn't that tell you something?"

"It tells me that you are afraid of being near me."

Had Tom stepped on a Ketchum grenade, he could not have been more fully blown away than he was by Ginny's accusation. He turned his head and pinned her with a ferocious glower. "*Afraid?* Do you know who you are talking to? I was a soldier in the Union army, a decorated lieutenant in the Black Hat Brigade. I have braved circumstances that would make an iron man tremble—I sure as hell am not afraid of you!"

Her voice rang with quiet challenge. "Then prove it, soldier boy."

23

*A*LARM SURGED THROUGH Ginny's veins as 170 pounds of pure male indignity advanced toward her. It might have been amusing, for Dolores and Evie Mae had not even given him time to dress, and he wore only his faded long underwear. However, there was nothing remotely funny about the expression of wild rage on his rugged features.

Oh, sweet mercy, what had she done?

She had hoped to provoke Thomas into some reaction, yes, but how could she have forgotten that this was no longer the gentle soldier she once knew?

Then there was no time for misgivings. Ginny gasped as his mouth swooped down upon hers. His lips were hard, unforgiving. As if he were trying to punish her for loving him. And his fingers tore through her unbound hair, trapping her in place. Did he not know that it was not necessary? She had no intention of going anywhere—ever. He was the one who kept running.

He was not running now.

In fact, Ginny suspected he was trying to drive her away—with his smoldering eyes and savage mouth—before he lost control. But she wanted him to lose control. Wanted him over the brink of rational thinking and steely reserve.

She wanted him cursing.

With nothing to lose and everything to gain, she returned his kisses with equal fervor, wanting to punish him back. For making her wait. Making her wonder. Making her doubt.

Wedging one hand between their bodies, she slid it roughly up his chest, felt his heart batter against her palm, matching the radical tempo of her own. She clutched the collar of his union suit, holding fast, not about to let him escape. The man kissing her was not one who needed understanding or patience or compassion. The man kissing her was one who needed a strength of will equal to his own. And she vowed to show him that no matter how hard he pushed, or how fast he ran, he could not hide from the feelings they once shared.

By the time she finished with him, he would know he belonged to her.

But as his mouth left hers, Ginny's plan began to disintegrate under an onslaught of raw sensation. Greedy, openmouthed kisses scorched the sensitive cords of her neck, her throat, her chin, leaving her skin steaming. She could almost see the mist rolling off her flesh. Ginny arched her neck, relishing the scrape of a day's growth of whiskers. And when Thomas brought his hand to her breast, she arched, aching, wanting. A liquid puddle of heat and need spread through her womb. Her knees buckled. His arm curled around her waist, catching her tight against his whipcord hardness. Had her body's cry for his always been this strong? Had she always felt this urgency to be claimed by Thomas?

Then there was a subtle shift in mood, as if Thomas had become aware of his own roughness. The bruising edge of fury gave way to almost timid need when his mouth closed once more over hers, no longer punishing but clinging, as though he'd never been loved before.

And Ginny gave what he sought, projecting all the love she had stored inside for the last twelve years into this elusive moment. Her grip loosened from his collar. Her fingers brushed his mustache, then touched the corners of their joined lips. He tasted her, soothed away burns caused by whiskers and desperation. And tears stung the back of her eyes at his infinite tenderness.

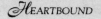

In a thick and husky baritone, he said, "You taste like wine."

Ginny's breath caught. She pulled back and asked, "Like elderberry wine?"

"Mmmm-hmmm."

Did she dare . . . ? Could it be . . . ? "And my eyes?"

"What about your eyes?" he asked without much interest.

"Are they blue as a moon-drenched sky?"

"Sure, Ginny." He lowered his mouth again. "Whatever you say."

The tears sprang forth, blurring her vision. He was remembering.

Thomas was remembering.

She might as well have shot a spear of lightning into his loins, for no kiss ever jolted Tom like the one Ginny gave him then. He swore the earth moved each time her tongue swept through his mouth and tangled with his. Anxious, wild. Coercing a response from him he couldn't find the will to fight.

A storm brewed deep inside him, twisting within his loins like a tornado picking up speed and whipping a fever through his veins.

Though his mind screamed a warning, desire took control when she pressed herself tighter against him. The pliant flesh of her breast hollowed beneath his knuckles. Her hips fit snugly between his. The scent of her filled his nostrils and the moist honey of her mouth stirred up needs long neglected.

He could count on one hand the number of women he'd bedded since the war. Sure, there had been the usual trollops following the camps, but unlike the men who served under him, Tom rarely found the idea of lying with a woman who serviced entire battalions appealing.

But Ginny appealed to him. She'd been teasing him with her sassy spirit and dogged determination for the last couple of weeks. Putting dents in his armor. Whittling away at his self-control . . .

Tom fought the swell of need building inside him. If he let go now, she'd own a piece of him no one had ever owned before. And he'd never be free of her again.

"Damn you, Ginny," he cursed, pulling back. He snagged

her slender hands within one large palm. "You are not going to seduce me."

Though her shallow breaths matched his own, a glint of humor lurked behind the desire in her eyes. "But, Thomas, you are the one who first kissed me," she pointed out.

He released her as if she were the lit fuse to a powder keg. He'd walked right into an ambush. Cursing under his breath, Tom marked falling into her trap as one of the stupidest things he'd ever done. If he knew Ginny—and he felt he was beginning to know her quite well—she'd never let him forget his moment of weakness. As if he could, anyway. She had a way of haunting him. "Only to prove I'm not afraid of you."

"Mayhap at first but you cannot deny that when you kissed me, something special happened."

"The same thing happens with most of the women I've kissed."

It went very quiet, then.

After a lengthy, inscrutable study, she sighed and crossed to a dark corner of the shed.

He stared after her, both puzzled and disappointed by the sudden lack of interest. Why wasn't she pressing her advantage? As thin as his restraint was, she had only to touch him again and she'd get just about anything she wanted. Instead, she seemed to have given up. So why wasn't he relieved?

Tom wheeled around, disgusted with himself. According to Noble, he should just take what she offered. He was so tempted. Never more so than this moment. But she wasn't the type of woman he could have, no strings, no questions. No, she believed in love and emotional commitment and happily-ever-after. Attachments he'd spent years avoiding. If he took her now as his body demanded, she'd expect a whole lot more in return than he was willing to give.

Flint struck rock and the odor of burning paper drifted toward Tom. Glancing over his shoulder, he watched Ginny sink to the ground in front of a pile of burning boards as if settling in. It was then that he realized she hadn't given up, she'd just shifted tactics. She could have taught his commander, John Gibbons, a few things with her attack and retreat strategies. "How long do you plan on keeping me locked in here?"

"As long as it takes for you to decide to come home," she said frankly, bringing out a basket from the shadows. "I have brought provisions if you are hungry."

She really was a piece of work. Here he was, trying to get his blood to return to normal flow, and there she sat, pulling paper-wrapped packages out of her basket as if nothing had ever happened.

As if she hadn't just rattled him to the very core.

"Oma packed your favorite potato salad and . . . hmmm, bread, cheese—she makes the best cheddar in the state."

"I may be stuck in here with you, but I don't have to listen to anything you say," he grumbled loud enough for her to hear.

Ginny, of course, ignored him. "Oh! And Doreen made you apple fritters. She must have remembered me telling her how much you liked them," Ginny went on, setting each item down on a checkered cloth spread out in front of the small fire. "You are aware that we would have lost her had it not been for Oma. You really must thank her sometime for saving our daughter's life, Thomas."

He refused to respond. In fact, he refused to give any sign he'd heard her at all.

Clad only in his flannel underwear, he rubbed his arms to ward off the chill he now felt. His conniving captors hadn't even given him a chance to get dressed.

"Did you know that 'Doreen' means 'gift from God'?" Ginny rattled on. "I believe He gave her to me so I would always have a piece of you near me until I could join you again."

Tom tightened the blanket around himself when his teeth began to chatter. He swore that nothing she said or did would coax him over by her. He'd rather freeze to death than seek warmth from Ginny's fire. He'd rather starve than eat Ginny's food.

No matter what, he wouldn't go near her.

"I would like to have more children. David and Doreen are growing up so quickly. Did you notice that he is growing a mustache like yours? No? Well, when you get home, mayhap you could mention how dashing it looks on him. He is quite proud of it. In fact, you may as well give him his first shaving lesson since you are the closest thing he has to a father."

Finally sighing, Tom accepted that short of gagging Ginny, she couldn't be shut up. He closed his eyes and shook his head. A chuckle escaped from his mouth before he could stop it. "You just don't give up, do you?"

With a light shrug, she stated, "I cannot. My Da used to say that love is a rare gift, that once you find it, you must never let it go." She went still, stared at her hands. Her voice dropped, heavy with sorry. "I miss him, Thomas. I miss the sound of his laughter. I miss the way he smelled of sawdust and apples. . . ."

He envied her that. If anybody asked Tom what his father had smelled like, he wouldn't be able to tell them. It was a good thing that question hadn't been on Ginny's test.

She snapped herself out of the reverie and giggled. It sounded forced, though. "The day we married he threatened to cut your heart out if you hurt me. You replied that you would provide the knife."

One of the burning boards popped and sent a spray of hot ash into the air.

"There were times when I hated you, Thomas. Even as I loved you, there were times I was so angry with you for not being there. For not writing more. For taking so long to send for us. And then I grew angry with myself because I knew you were trying to do what was best for us."

Against all wisdom, Tom looked at her. She sat with her back and shoulders pressed tight against the wall, her knees brought up to her chest. Dancing flames exposed her somber features and turned her yellow hair to gold.

"It is just that . . . sometimes the waiting grew unbearable. The nights were always cold. And lonely."

Tom swallowed and glanced away. Lonely, he knew.

"I am still cold, Thomas. So very cold."

He wanted to tell her it was her own fault for locking them in here. He wanted to tell her to suffer, just as he was suffering. But he couldn't. Because he knew the cold, too, and it didn't come from the outside. It was a cold of the soul.

And before he stopped to think about what he was doing, he

rose and crossed the shed and lowered himself onto the floor beside her. She laid her head trustingly against his chest. She fit naturally against him, as if they'd been made for each other.

As he held her, Tom stared at the moon and stars through the window, trying to ignore the flood of tenderness that filled him. The sensation felt at once safe and dangerous. Warm yet chilling. He wondered if she could hear the heavy thumping in his chest.

"*Ich liebe dich*, Thomas. Through everything, I have loved you. And I have missed you so desperately."

Her staunch loyalty earned her Tom's respect and disdain. His envy. Did Herz realize what a lucky man he was? Did he even care? In his opinion, the man had deserted her. Ginny would never believe that, though. Gruffly he told her, "You don't fight fair, lady."

"The war is over, Thomas." She lifted her head, pinned him with a look of complete bafflement. "Who says we have to fight at all?"

Now there she was wrong, Tom thought, closing his eyes. The war wasn't over, it had just begun.

Worse, it raged inside him.

24

$\mathcal{G}$INNY STARED AT Noble with her mouth agape and her heart dropping to her stomach where it settled like lead. "What do you mean he left?"

Noble's gaze dropped to the toes of his boots. "Just what I said, Miss Ginny. He tore into the smithy shop, said he had to tend to important business in Minnow Falls, took the wagon and left."

Dolores punched her fist into her palm. "I knew something was wrong the minute I opened the doors and he came flying outta the icehouse like a swarm of hornets was after him."

"What business would he have in the city?" Evie Mae asked.

Ginny could not say anything. She had been asleep until her friends arrived at the appointed hour to unlock the shed, so she could not vouch for whether an important matter had called Thomas away or not. But she wondered why, if business was all there was to it, did Noble look so guilty? What was he hiding from her?

She turned partly away and folded her arms across her stomach, cradling a heavy sense of apprehension. He had said nothing during their time in the icehouse about going to the city.

Upon further reflection, she realized he had said very little at all after breaking off their kiss. But her elation over a fragment of his memory returning dimmed her recollection of anything but the hope that soon it would be fully restored, and she and Thomas could begin making up for lost time.

Why had she not taken his uncustomary silence as a warning? Thomas was rarely silent, he never had been. And since returning from the war he had been even more vocal. Especially when the discussion veered anywhere near their marriage. "Did he say when he was coming back?"

"'Fraid not," Noble answered.

"Noble, please saddle me a horse."

"Where are you going?" Evie asked.

"After him. I am tired of Thomas running away from me. If I must drag him back to the farm and lock him in the house until he accepts I am his wife then I will do so."

"But Miss Ginny, you cain't ride. You don't know how!"

"Then I will learn," she stated, starting toward the corral. Something so minor as not having ridden a horse before would not keep her from forcing Thomas to acknowledge his feelings for him, not after the progress they had made last night. Even if he did not remember their past, he could not deny the attraction between them. The rest would come in time.

A hand closed around her upper arm, halting her steps.

"Ginny—" Dolores began. "You didn't see him—me and Evie did. Even we didn't dare say a word to him. Sometimes when a man's got a stinger in his back end, it's best to just let him be till he works it out."

"But he was remembering," she cried. "He kissed me and he said my lips . . . and my eyes . . ."

"Chasin' after him won't make him remember any faster," Dolores scolded. "There's a time to take action and a time to sit back and wait. Now's the time to wait."

Clenching her teeth, Ginny declared, "I have waited for twelve years!"

"And waitin' a couple more days ain't gonna make any difference. When he settles whatever is bothering him, he'll come back around."

"What if he does not return?"

"Then you're gonna have to learn to accept that, Ginny. You've done all you can do. We all have."

Ginny pressed her lips tightly together and stared first at Dolores, then Evie Mae, through blurry eyes. When she saw Evie's auburn brows raised in pity, she realized her friends were in complete agreement. They wanted her to give up. Give up hope, her husband, her dreams of the future. Did they not understand that those things were all she had to hold on to?

Her head acknowledged that if the time ever came when none of her efforts paid off, she would survive. The children and Oma depended on her. Her heart, though . . . her heart just would not accept life without Thomas. She had loved him for too long to imagine coping without him.

But she had imposed on her friends long enough. Now she must win her husband back alone.

"Mayhap you are right, Dolores. Mayhap I should give him time."

"Do you want company?" Evie asked as Ginny turned away.

Ginny swallowed. "*Danke*, but I think I would like to be alone for a while." Her head high, her shoulders thrown back, she started the long, lonely walk back to the farm to wait for Thomas.

Tom stood back and admired the dun mare he'd brought back from Minnow Falls. He wasn't an expert on horseflesh, but the mare had let him keep his seat during a trial ride, and she appeared healthy. It still rankled that Ginny's genius with the crops had given him the funds to afford not only the mare, but two additional horses for the stable and a new plow. However it didn't bother him enough to let the money rot in the bank.

Unfortunately, even the two-day trip to the city didn't help him put her out of his mind. She drenched his thoughts. Not a moment passed that he did not think of the courage it took to bring her family to a new country. Not a moment passed that he did not think of her dedication to a man she hadn't seen in over a decade.

Unbidden, an image filled his mind of how Dolores and Evie Mae had found them the next morning. Ginny all nestled in his arms where she'd eventually fallen asleep. In spite of himself, he recalled too clearly how right it had felt holding her until dawn. How soft her lips had been. How quickly he'd responded to the challenge she'd flung at him and the instantaneous pleasure it brought.

No woman had ever rattled him like Ginny.

He wished he would have learned sooner that the best reaction to her was no reaction. Keep calm and unruffled, because she fed off his frustration. Don't carry on a conversation with her, because she'd only insist she knew him better than he knew himself. Don't tell her where he was going, because she'd only follow. And most of all, don't get within ten feet of her.

Because now that he'd tasted her, he wasn't sure he'd have the willpower to resist her again.

"Now that's one fine-lookin' piece of horseflesh." The stable door banged shut behind Noble, grabbing Tom's attention. "Looks like the trip was worth you racing outta here like the devil was after you."

Tom frowned, pushing the disturbing thoughts of Ginny aside. "Let's just say it wasn't a complete disappointment."

"No word on Herz yet?"

"None." Tom grimaced. "We seem to be slamming into one stone wall after another. Gene only found ten Herzes—none named Thomas, none even coming close to our mutual age and description." He picked up the flat brush and began stroking the mare's coat clean of the dust she'd collected during the ride back. "I'm hoping the route information from those letters will help speed things up.

"Meanwhile, Gene has broadened the search to include immigrants with names beginning with H who have settled in the area during the last twelve years." It was a big stretch of time to cover, but Tom grimly realized he didn't have any choice. The longer Ginny stayed under the delusion that they were married, the faster he saw his life spinning out of control.

"Ever'body's been asking 'bout you."

"What did you tell them?"

"That an old army friend needed you." Noble shoved his hands into his twill pockets, straining the suspenders over his massive torso. "Ain't ya gonna ask 'bout Miss Ginny?"

The brush picked up speed across the mare's coat. "I thought we agreed that Ginny was a closed subject?"

"She came lookin' for you."

"I expected she would."

"Wish you'd just tell her that you're lookin' for her husband. I don't like lyin' to her."

It dismayed Tom to admit that not being honest with Ginny didn't sit well with him either. "I told you that I can't do that. The way my luck has been running lately, she'd find some means of stopping the search. Then I'd wind up living with *you* the rest of my life."

"Not if you come to your senses and claim her."

"Tom! Noble!"

Tom offered a mental word of thanks for the interruption until he glanced over his shoulder and spied Evie Mae racing across the road, her calico skirts and petticoats tangling around her legs.

"You have to get to the farm. Ginny needs you!"

He shut his eyes and groaned. "Miss Johnson, whatever scheme you women have cooked up this time, just forget it."

"It's David. He's been hurt real bad." Evie Mae bent over, breathing raggedly. "That land grabber . . . he came back . . . David's hurt, and Ginny's beside herself. You've got to go to her, Tom, she needs you."

The wild panic in Evie's eyes alerted Tom that this was no ruse. "Noble, meet me at the farm." Without another word, Tom swung his leg over the mare's bare back and sent her galloping recklessly across the bridge.

He didn't stop to think that he'd never ridden bareback before. Even when the horse nearly spilled him to the ground twice, he didn't consider stopping to saddle her. All he could think of was the fact that Ginny needed him.

When he reached the farmhouse, he didn't bother knocking, just barreled inside. David lay on the kitchen table. Doreen stood near his head, holding his hand, brushing his thick black hair away from his temple. Silent tears tracked down her cheeks; her tortured gaze never left David's ashen face.

Ginny stood on the other side, pressing a wad of blood-soaked cloth to the side of his head. Bertha had unfastened his suspenders and unbuttoned his shirt, baring his scrawny chest, also spattered with blood.

For a brief moment time took a backward spin. The boy on the table wasn't David, but Matthew. Limp, lifeless. Reeking of the disease eating away at his young body while Tom stood by, helpless. The memory of cradling his brother's head in his lap sent a forgotten shaft of guilt through him. He'd promised to take care of him. He'd let him die instead.

Noble crashed through the doorway. "Miss Ginny? How bad is it?"

She became aware of their presence with a start. Worry had been etched into her wholesome features, making her look older somehow.

Tom pulled himself together. He might not have been able to do anything for Matthew, but this wasn't the hold of an immigrant ship, either. Other than shifting over to make room for Tom at the table, Ginny barely acknowledged his presence.

"Has he come to at all?" Tom asked, drawing David's eyelid back.

"No. His head was bleeding badly but I think I have stopped it."

"His pupils are dilating, that's a good sign." He ran his hands along David's angular body, feeling an unnatural slant on David's left arm. "Hopefully he'll stay out for a few minutes longer. His arm is broken above the elbow, and we'll have to pop the bones back into place. Bertha, I need some long strips of linen. Miss Johnson, you take Doreen outside and find several sturdy sticks to use for a splint."

"But she won't leave David's side."

"Make her. I need to set his arm and it isn't going to be pretty. If David wakes up, the last thing I need is Doreen falling to pieces." Right now she looked fragile enough to shatter.

Once Evie Mae tugged the reluctant girl out of sight, Tom told Ginny and Noble, "You two are going to have to hold him. Ginny, lie across his chest and make sure you keep his other arm flat. Noble, you hold his legs down—even unconscious, this is gonna hurt him like hell."

For once Ginny didn't scold him for his language. She and Noble moved into position. As gently as he could, Tom straightened David's arm. David whimpered. Ginny cooed to him in German, told him it would be all right, that she loved him, that she was so very sorry they had to hurt him more.

Tom forced himself not to listen to her soothing voice. He focused his concentration on the boy's arm. If he popped it too hard, he feared he'd do further damage. He wasn't a damn doctor, and his only experience came from the rudimentary care he'd performed on the battlefields until field surgeons arrived on the scene. But if they tried taking David to a doctor in Minnow Falls, the jarring from the wagon might hurt him worse. Neither did Tom have any way of judging how serious his head wound was.

He grasped David's arm on either side of the break, took a deep breath, and pulled the bone apart then straightened it and let go. He heard the gruesome click as the bone fused together just as David screamed. His whole body bucked, nearly throwing Ginny off.

She righted herself and strove to keep him calm. Her tears fell onto David's neck. Tom's heart twisted.

His hands shaking, Tom awkwardly patted the boy's shoulder with one and brought Ginny close to his chest with the other. Their pain seeped into his numb shell and spread through his chest.

David finally went limp.

"I'm sorry, Ginny," Tom told her.

She wiped her eyes. "It had to be done. It is only that . . . he is like my own. His suffering is my suffering."

"The worst part is over, Miss Ginny," Noble said.

"As soon as Doreen and Miss Johnson come back with the sticks, we'll wrap his arm."

"His head is bleeding again."

Tom examined the gash just above David's left ear. The area around it was swollen and bruised. "Looks like he'll need a couple of stitches. Noble, you ever sewn anybody up before?"

Bertha bustled in with strips of cloth draped over her arm, and a basin of water. "I vill tend his vound. Make Ginny sit down before she falls."

Tom slid one of the chairs behind Ginny's thighs and guided her down onto the seat. He didn't think she noticed, for her hand never left David's brow, her eyes remained fixed on his face. For the first time, Tom realized the depth of her love for the boy. And David wasn't even hers. Yet she had taken him in, nurtured his broken soul, accepted him without reservation. And somehow she'd made him feel safe, as if he truly belonged to her.

She treats me the same way, Tom thought. In spite of his cutting temperament, she still tried to make him feel like he really belonged to her.

But he knew it was a lie, even if Ginny didn't.

"How in thunderation did this happen to him?" Tom asked.

Just then, Doreen and Evie Mae walked through the front door, postponing any explanation. Tom left Ginny to comfort David while he chose the best of the sticks and broke them into the proper lengths.

He waited until Bertha finished her stitching to apply the splint, then took David upstairs where he could rest. Ginny said not a word to him as she pulled a chair up beside the narrow bed. Doreen sat on the mattress next to David and held his hand.

Knowing there was nothing left to do but wait until David revived, he went back downstairs to find out how the "land grabber" and David's injury were tied together.

25

$\mathcal{E}$VIE MAE AND Noble were sitting at the kitchen table. He didn't know where Bertha had gone, but expected she would be joining Doreen and Ginny soon. The four of them were closer than skin on a coon. He was an outsider.

"I want to know what happened here," he told Evie Mae.

"I guess Marks ran out of patience."

"Marks?"

"C. R. Marks—the founder of Marksville, who's after your farm." Evie Mae waited expectantly. "Didn't Ginny tell you about him?"

Tom shook his head. "Noble mentioned something a while back about a fellow wanting to buy my land, but I didn't know he was still interested."

"Not just interested, determined. And he doesn't want all the land, just the strip that runs up the middle. He's petitioned for the railroad to lay tracks connecting Minnow Falls to his town, but he needs your acreage."

"Why doesn't he just bypass Ridgeford?"

"Because Marksville sits smack between the Rock River to the west and miles of marshlands to the east. The only solid path is from the south, and Ridgeford is in the way."

"So what you're saying is that unless I sell my land to Marks, his town won't get the railroad."

"Exactly, and his town will go under because it needs the money the railroad will bring in. But we don't want locomotives passing through Ridgeford at all hours of the day and night—we like our village just the way it is, especially since the land is worth more being farmed."

Tom's bank account verified that. But even if the last harvests hadn't been so prosperous, he didn't fancy having railroad tracks laid down the center of his property.

"Ginny and the Kirkmillers have held out for two years," Evie Mae added. "And I expect that Marksville is about to lose the opportunity."

"So he takes it out on the children?"

"From what I've been able to get out of Ginny, Doreen had gone to fetch firewood and caught a man skulking out behind the barn. When she tried to run, he grabbed her arm and started hauling her up into his buggy. Next thing she knows, David's racing around the corner and tries tackling him.

"But the fellow got himself a hold of a whip and started hitting David with it. That's when David fell and hit his head on the wheel. Then the horse bolted and the buggy ran him over. The fellow just kept on going."

Tom absorbed the news with a mixture of admiration and outrage. Knowing David's history, it must have taken a load of courage to attack a man—any man. Yet for Doreen's sake, he'd done it. The thought of what might have happened to Ginny's daughter if David hadn't been there left Tom feeling queasy.

Then guilt set in. David had gotten hurt protecting Doreen at the cost of his own safety. It shouldn't have happened. Tom should have been here. He never should have left the responsibility of his farm on a fourteen-year-old's narrow shoulders. His land wasn't worth a young man's life.

"Did the youngsters by chance get a look at the fellow?"

"I don't think so, but you can ask them later." Evie Mae rose and shook her shirts so the heavy pleats fell straight to her ankles. "I'm going to see if Ginny needs any help."

After Evie Mae excused herself, Noble bowed his back and clasped his hands between his knees. "What are you figurin' on doin', Tom?" he asked quietly. "Marks ain't never hurt nobody before so I s'pect that means he's gettin' desperate."

His mind churned with a dozen forms of retaliation, not the least of which was tracking Marks down and giving him a five-knuckle lesson on the wisdom of involving innocent children in adult affairs. But he couldn't leave Ginny and Bertha and the kids alone. Besides, from what he gathered, the man who'd caused David's injury was just a lackey. Taking out one man wouldn't solve the problem, for Marks would undoubtedly send another ruffian in his place. And John Gibbons always told him, "Battles should be fought in your own territory whenever possible, because you don't know what you'll find in the enemy's backyard."

"I'm figuring that a message needs to be sent to Marks. Let him know in no uncertain terms that my property isn't for sale. Meanwhile, I best stick around for a while in case this fellow comes back. And if he does, I'm gonna have a little talk with him on how to treat children."

Tom glanced up and caught the self-satisfied grin on his friend's face. "You can quit smirking, Noble. This isn't permanent. I can't very well throw them out while we're looking for her husband, but neither can I leave them here defenseless."

"What are you gonna do if we can't find Herz? It's been over three weeks and your friend hasn't come across anyone that even resembles you."

Tom stroked his chin and stared at the knotty pattern of the table. "I haven't thought that far ahead."

Ginny quietly shut David's door and pressed her forehead against it. He had awakened briefly, and though he would not admit to any pain, he spoke coherently. For that she felt a huge wave of relief. Thoughts of what could have happened filled her mind. David might have been killed, and it would have been her fault.

She didn't hear Thomas come up behind her, but when she turned around, he was there. She wanted more than anything to lean on him. Trust him to take control of this matter. But his arms were folded across his chest, his feet spread in a combative stance.

"Why didn't you tell me about the railroad mess?"

Another layer of guilt piled onto those Ginny already carried. "I did not want to add to your burdens," she said feebly, trying to brush past him. She did not have the strength to engage in a battle with him tonight.

He grabbed her arm in a gentle but firm grip. "This is my land, damn it! I have a right to know when somebody is threatening what belongs to me."

She stared at him agog. "The land? Is that all you care about? A young boy is lying in there injured!"

"Don't you think I know that? If you would have told me about Marks, maybe none of this would have happened."

Suddenly it was all too much to bear. The grief, the guilt, the pressure . . . "When should I have told you?" Ginny bit out. "When you were running off, trying to get rid of me? When you were hiding in the stables? When you fled to the city?"

He winced. It gave Ginny small satisfaction. Conflicting emotions, too jumbled to sort out, assaulted her. Part of her wanted him to feel as much pain as she'd felt when he'd left for Minnow Falls without a word, another wanted to run straight into his arms and cry her relief when David hadn't been fatally injured. She tempered the second urge and dropped her gaze. Thomas had once told her that her strength was one of the traits he had fallen in love with.

Again she was reminded of the difference between the man she had married and the man he had become. Her husband had always left the responsibility of running their home to her, a duty she had embraced with loving pride. And she had thought herself lucky that he was the type of man who could encourage her independence, yet make her feel useful. She had taken it as a compliment that he trusted her abilities.

And now . . . he barely tolerated her. Each time she got too close to him he ran.

Tightly, she said, "Thank you for tending to David. I will not impose on you any longer."

"I'm not leaving."

The announcement fell on her like a load of ore, knocking her stunned and breathless.

She sent a sharp glance to his face. His sloping jaw was set at a stubborn angle she recognized immediately, for she had used that same expression often herself. He had made up his mind and nothing would change it. Until lately, she had rarely seen such a stubborn streak in her husband. "But you said it would not work, all of us living together."

"I don't have a choice anymore. After what happened today, there's no telling what lengths Marks will go to to convince me to sell, and I can't risk leaving the four of you here alone."

Ginny tamped down the thrill his words caused. If she had learned anything, it was not to read more into the things Thomas said than what he intended, for she would only set herself up for disappointment. "We all have choices, Thomas. Some are harder to make than others because they mean sacrifice."

The color left his tightened face and he sucked in, as if she had pricked his heart. The thought gave her a measure of consolation. She had begun to wonder if he even had one anymore.

Swiftly his mask of indifference fell back into place. He loosened his grip on her arm, his hand dropped to his side. "I'll make my bed on the sofa until the matter with Marks is settled."

"And then?"

Silence met her question, lasting for several long, tense moments. Thomas finally sighed. "I don't know, Ginny. I just don't know."

Tom stepped into David's room. Not much more than the bed and chest fit inside the cramped quarters. He doubted a word of complaint ever fell from the boy's lips, though. David tended to treasure any generosity handed to him, which made Marks's attack doubly enraging.

Doreen sat on the edge of the narrow bed. Midafternoon sunlight spilled through the unshuttered window, turning her crown of yellow braids to a polished gold. She looked very young and vulnerable as she smoothed the pillow beneath David's head. And so much like her mother that Tom's throat tightened.

Catching sight of Tom, she jumped to her feet and rushed

toward him. Her arms wrapped around his waist. She pressed her cheek against his middle. Awkwardly Tom patted her back, making an effort to give her the comfort she seemed to seek. Again that possessive sensation claimed him. He set her gently away and cleared his throat. "How are you feeling, boy?" he asked David.

"Fine, sir." The tight lines around David's mouth were the only sign of discomfort.

"I see. You're pretty used to getting run over by a wagon, then, huh?"

David's face turned red. His gaze briefly shifted toward Doreen before his lashes fell over his eyes. "No, sir."

Tom bit his tongue as instant understanding hit him. The discussion would go no further in Doreen's company. Turning to her, he nudged her toward the door, conveying the only way he knew how that he wanted to speak with David alone. She seemed to understand, for she cast a worried look David's way. He nodded and gave her the briefest of smiles. Then she slipped out into the hall, shutting the door behind her.

"Now, why don't you tell me how you're really feeling?"

After a lengthy hesitation David licked his lips then said, "If I ever told my pa that I hurt somewhere, he'd make it hurt worse."

His voice changed pitch on several words the same way Tom's had at his age. As if he couldn't decide whether it belonged to a boy or a man.

Ginny's words echoed in his mind. And for the first time, Tom noticed the fine beginnings of a mustache above David's lip. It seemed too soon—he was just a boy. But a very old, worn boy. Sadly Tom realized that David had been robbed of his youth, and it sickened him to know that an adult had taken it from him. An adult he should have been able to trust . . .

His own father had been stern, but Tom couldn't imagine feeling compelled to hide from William Heart as David had hid from his father. In fact, before David had come to the farm, Tom doubted that he'd ever known the feeling of having supper with a family. Or received a nod of encouragement. Or had his hair tousled affectionately . . .

Tom controlled the fury building inside him and said, "I'm

not your pa, David. You can tell me anything and I would never hold it against you."

"No, sir. I don't expect you would." Another moment passed while David seemed to wrestle with his emotions. He finally lifted his head and looked Tom directly in the eyes. "My head hurts some. My arm, too."

Tom nodded gravely. "That's to be expected. Can you tell me what color shirt I'm wearing?"

"Blue."

"And how many fingers am I holding up?"

"Four."

"Good. I don't think there's any permanent damage, but you'll be sore for a while. And you'll have to wear that splint, at least until Christmas."

"But I can't chop wood with one arm. And I've got the animals to tend . . ."

"I'll make sure your chores get done." And gladly. He needed every excuse he could get to keep himself busy and away from Ginny until spring when the fields could be plowed.

Denying his weakness for her was pointless. But at least he'd come to his senses before she dug her way too deeply into his system. As long as he kept uppermost in his mind the price he'd have to pay for a small physical indulgence, he could manage to avoid her.

Eventually she'd give up this crazy notion that they were married.

Meanwhile he held on to the hope that some word on Herz would turn up soon. Then he wouldn't have to worry about keeping his distance from her. From what he'd seen, David hadn't left him much to do. That didn't bode well. A man with too much time on his hands usually found himself in trouble.

"What about Miss Ginny and Miss Bertha and Doreen? That man said he'd be back—"

"I'll take care of him, too," Tom stated.

David seemed to relax, as if he'd been carrying the weight of the world on his shoulders and Tom had just lifted the load.

"Tell me something—what made you think you could take on a man with a whip alone?"

"Didn't have time to think. He was hurting Doreen."

Simple words, yet they carried a wealth of meaning. Little details that held no significance before now slipped into place. The protective stand David took behind Doreen. The gentle consideration he revealed by including her in all his activities. The genuine interest he showed in everything she said and did.

"You care about her deeply, don't you?"

"More than anything."

"Well, that was a real honorable thing you did—reckless, but honorable."

Color rose in his lean cheeks at the praise. "I couldn't let her get hurt." He looked at the sling supporting his arm. "Same as you, 'spect."

"Any particular reason you think that?"

"She told me what you did, about the letters. Letting her keep them and all. She says they bring her good luck."

"Why didn't she ever tell her mother that she took them?"

"Miss Ginny never asked her."

"Didn't it occur to her that Ginny would be hurt by their disappearance?"

"She didn't mean any harm!" David hastened to say. "She just wanted something of you. Miss Ginny had memories; Doreen didn't have anything." He inhaled sharply, cast a wary look at Tom. "Are you gonna tell Miss Ginny?"

And what, spill Doreen's secret? Betray a little girl's trust? As David had said, the letters were all she had of the father she'd never known. Even he wasn't that cruel. "Tell her about what?"

"About Doreen taking the—" At once David caught on to Tom's pretense. He grinned timidly. It was the first smile Tom had seen from him since they'd met, and it inexplicably lifted his spirits.

Figuring they'd said all that needed saying, he reached for the doorknob. "You'd best get some rest now."

Tom walked out of the room and met Bertha in the hall. In spite of the shadows of concern she spared for him a cheerful grin.

"What do you have there?"

She lifted the cover off the tray, releasing a fog of heavenly aromas. Hot bread, wedges of yellow cheese and a bowl of beef broth.

"Mmm-mmm, you sure know how to reach a man's heart."

She popped the cover over his knuckles when he reached for a cheese slice. "I brought dis for David. You go downstairs and eat."

"If you keep feeding me so well I'm going to start busting buttons."

"I have never known a man who could resist good cooking— or a good cook." She winked. "You know vhat dey say . . ."

"No, Bertha, what do they say?"

"A voman who can satisfy a man's stomach, satisfies utter hungers, too!"

Tom gave a startled cry when she swatted his behind in passing. As he headed downstairs, a disturbing thought occurred to him. If Ginny had half the talent in the kitchen that she did in a bedroom, he was in for a bigger battle than he'd ever imagined.

26

$\mathcal{T}$OM LEARNED OVER the next couple of weeks that instead of worrying himself ragged over how he was going to keep avoiding Ginny, he should have worried more about the relatives.

Doreen followed him everywhere. He couldn't even make a trip to the outhouse without finding her waiting outside the door. It got worse after David's headaches stopped and he felt normal again, in spite of his broken arm. Because where Doreen went, David went, so Tom often felt like a train engine dragging two cabooses behind him.

He glanced over at the young pair standing near the newly constructed stall penning the dun mare. Doreen was petting the horse's nose. David smiled with shy tenderness at something Doreen signed to him, then scattered a handful of straw into the stall.

Tom studied the snow runners he'd been measuring to fit the wagon for winter travel. The snows would begin to fall in earnest soon. Another trip to Minnow Falls would be wise to stock up on supplies before the weather made travel too hazardous. And while he was there, he'd check with Gene for news of Herz.

Yet he found his thoughts dwelling not on preparations for the trip, or even on Ginny's real husband, but on what Doreen had said to put that smile on David's face. It was one of secret pleasure. Of humble favor. Of understanding.

Doreen constantly tried talking to him, too. It wasn't so bad when David could interpret, but when they were alone . . . he felt like a fool—a very inept fool. He spoke three damn languages and yet he couldn't understand half of what Doreen told him.

Thunderation, he understood Ginny's body language better than he did Doreen's. Since he'd moved back to the farm, she pretty much kept a safe distance from him, but he felt her watching him, her eyes wistful, her head tilted to the side, a dreamy expression on her face.

He often wondered if she thought of him the way he thought of her. Did the same things play on her mind as they did on his? Did she recall the feel of loose hair dragged between fingers? The haunting song their lips had sung when they met? And did she lie alone in that big bed upstairs, hungering for a warmth that started deep inside, then spread outward until not an inch of skin was cool to the touch?

Not once since his return had she brought up their marital status, or the icehouse folly. But any time she spoke his name, she did it in that soft voice that made him imagine hauling her off into some dark corner and finishing what she'd started that night.

Tom lunged off the stool and laid the bulky skids on the workbench for further sanding. The pegboard behind displayed an assortment of awls, hammers, and drivers. A pile of scuffed sandpaper lay neglected next to a scattering of smithy-forged nails.

Why did he stay? Why didn't he just move back in with Noble? After all, the threat was past now. All it had taken was a polite but firm letter of refusal to the upstanding citizens of Marksville. They hadn't contacted him since. So why was he sticking around?

A clanging of the metal triangle rang across the yard, announcing supper. Great, Tom thought, both grateful for the interruption and eager for another of Bertha's tasty spreads.

One advantage he'd discovered to having Bertha living on the farm was the array of stick-to-the-ribs meals she stuffed him with. Nobody left her table without an empty plate and a full stomach.

No wonder Ginny's figure had such definition, he mused. He never could stand a scrawny woman, and though Ginny wasn't pudgy, either, she had a nicely rounded figure that nipped in where it should and filled out where it was supposed to. Unfortunately, Tom noticed that more often than was wise.

After removing his heavy leather apron, Tom headed out of the barn. Doreen led the procession toward the house. David lagged behind, his brows knitted together with thoughtfulness.

"Something on your mind, boy?" Tom asked casually.

David slanted a glance at Tom, then stared ahead. "I couldn't protect her. She needed me and I couldn't keep her safe."

Tom didn't know what to say, given his own conflicting emotions where Doreen's mother was concerned. "If there's one thing I've learned, boy, it's that German women have independent streaks a mile wide. Those women in there are born survivors. Not much gets thrown in their way that they can't handle."

"But what if something like that happens again?"

"About all you can do is watch out for them, then trust your instincts. But if it's Marks you're worried about, you can rest your mind. The only way he'll get his hands on Heart land or anything on it is to fight me. He's probably decided it isn't worth the hassle. By now the railroad has probably rejected their petition anyway."

"Does that mean you'll be leavin' soon?"

"And have to eat Noble's cooking again? Nah, I'll take Bertha's over his for the time being."

They reached the house, and David hesitated before opening the door. "Mr. Heart?"

Tom's brows rose in question.

"It's nice havin' a man around to talk to. I mean, I talk to Doreen all the time, but some things . . . well, there's just some things girls don't understand."

He clapped David on his good shoulder. "You're gonna learn

that men don't understand women half the time, either. They're one of life's greatest mysteries."

Thunderation, Tom thought, half the time men didn't understand themselves.

Inside the house the scents of home greeted them—hot bread and meat and fried apples. Bertha bustled around the stove, steam from the bubbling kettle curling wisps of hair around her wide face.

"Der you are! I t'ought I vould have to send a search party for you. Wash up and sit down before supper gets cold."

It was the same thing she said before every meal and Tom found it strangely comforting. Then Ginny claimed his attention, her welcoming smile brightening a dark place inside him. She seemed to have a knack for doing that more and more lately.

"Where has Doreen gone off to?" she asked.

Scanning the room, Tom caught a flash of braids in the sitting room. "I'll fetch her."

He stepped into the living area where Doreen looked like she was searching for a place to hide. He tapped her on the shoulder, making her jump.

"Come on, Doreen, suppertime," Tom motioned.

Her head shook back and forth in quick, narrow jerks. She acted as if she were being led to the gallows.

"What's the matter with you?"

She gestured toward the table where a fat copper kettle acted as a centerpiece. The aroma alone made Tom's mouth water.

"If you don't sit at the table, you'll hurt your grandma's feelings. You don't want to do that, do you?"

After a moment's reluctance, her shoulders slumped and she took her seat beside Ginny. Tom rubbed his hands together as he slid into his own chair. He glanced down into the bowl in front of him. His eager smile wilted. Fat chunks of ham swam in a thick green pool of—something. "Hmmm, Bertha, this looks . . . colorful," Tom improvised.

"It is *Erbsen Suppe*. Put some meat on your skinny bones."

Or hair on his chest. And he already had plenty of that.

Tom picked up his spoon, trying very hard to keep his face

bland. He sniffed what could only be described as a bowl of wet mold. It smelled a whole lot better than it looked, though.

Encouraged, Tom shoved a spoonful into his mouth. *Ewwww!* He tried—and failed—to conceal a face-distorting grimace. Pea soup was more disgusting than bully soup, and he never thought anything could taste worse than that!

He glanced around to make sure nobody had seen his expression. Fortunately, slicing the bread kept Ginny too occupied to notice, and Bertha was filling David's bowl, but Doreen sat with her head ducked and her shoulders hunched. The little stinker was grinning into her bowl. She slanted a glimpse up at him that plainly said, "I tried to warn you."

Bertha winked at him. Tom gave her a strained grin, then forced himself to swallow the mouthful. He tried valiantly not to gag as it rolled down his throat. His stomach rolled, rebelling.

After that first bite, he ate only the chunks of ham, but once no more meat could be found, Tom found himself dragging his spoon through the rest of the soup, trying to figure out a way to get rid of the rest of it without having to ingest it.

A sharp jab to his shin grabbed Tom's attention. Doreen jerked her head toward Bertha, who was engrossed in a conversation with Ginny at the opposite end of the table. Beside Tom, David's attentive gaze darted back and forth between him and Doreen.

She kicked him again, then pointed to her lap where she'd clamped her empty milk glass between her thighs. Tom raised his brows and nodded in silent tribute at her ingenuity, then drained his own glass and followed her lead. At regular intervals he tipped his bowl so the soup plopped into the cup.

"My goodness, Thomas, have you finished already?" Ginny exclaimed.

He blanched when Bertha instantly dipped another generous ladleful of soup into his bowl. David ducked his head, but the boy's quaking shoulders told Tom he was enjoying his predicament. Doreen made that funny gurgling sound, and he gave her a mock scowl, which made her laugh harder.

Ginny glanced at her in surprise, but said nothing.

And Tom wondered how he was going to get rid of the soup

in his glass along with the heap in his bowl. He suffered through the rest of the meal in silence while Doreen and David fought to hide their amusement. The moment Bertha took the kettle away, Tom set the glass on the floor, up against the fat plank of the table leg. With an exaggerated sigh of satisfaction, he patted his belly. "That was delicious, Bertha. I must have fed my eyes before my stomach though, because I'm about to burst."

He could have killed the kids when they exploded into full-fledged laughter.

Thankfully neither Bertha nor Ginny caught on. Bertha was too busy preening under the praise, and Ginny . . . Ginny was giving him a tender look that made his chest swell and put goose bumps on his arms.

After supper, Tom found himself wishing the family didn't feel so obliged to give him his privacy. Sitting alone in the sitting room, which had become his bedroom, he tugged off his boots and listened to familial chatter as they put the kitchen to rights.

He knelt in front of the fireplace and stoked the burning logs until they gave off a red-hot heat. He hoped it stayed warm enough for Ginny and the youngsters upstairs. He hadn't built a fireplace up there since it had only been a storage loft until they'd moved in. He'd often seen Ginny take coals from the stove and put them in a bed warmer to run across the sheets.

Maybe he should start gathering stones. It wouldn't be that much trouble to put in a central hearth—

Thunderation, he had to stop thinking in such permanent terms. Next winter there wouldn't be anyone living upstairs to need warming.

As he returned the poker to its stand, he started at the sight of Doreen standing behind him. She withdrew a hefty hunk of bread from behind her back and held it out to him.

"Oh, Doreen—" he tore off a chunk of leftover roasted beef and day-old bread with his teeth—"you are a savior." He chewed and swallowed, then added before ripping off another bite, "I've eaten some pretty disgusting things in my time, but that soup beats all."

The vigorous nod of her head indicated that she agreed wholeheartedly.

"I give you my solemn promise that I will never, ever make you eat anything you don't like." She grinned, made several motions, then stunned Tom by kissing his cheek.

As Doreen skipped up the stairs, Ginny entered the sitting room, pulling her apron over her head. Tom shoved the sandwich between the folds of his blanket and assumed a mask of nonchalance. Ginny didn't seem to notice, though. She headed straight for the stairwell, and Tom found himself wishing she'd stay and visit—just for a little while.

"Ginny."

She paused with her hand on the railing. Tom wasn't sure he liked this new caution he sensed in her. She was the type of woman who charged into situations without reservation, whereas Tom found himself dissecting every situation: who, what, where, when, why. . . . It wasn't something he'd always done, only since Ginny had come into his life.

And he realized that he, at least in part, was responsible for this unsettling wariness in her eyes.

"Why does she do that all the time?" he asked, compelled to dispel her unease around him. He wanted her accepting that they weren't married, not afraid to hold a conversation with him. Maybe by the time this was all over, they could even be friends. Or as close to that as Tom ever allowed.

"Why does who do what?"

"Doreen. Why does she move her hands like that in front of me?"

Ginny strolled closer. "She wants only to talk with you, Thomas."

"But I don't understand her."

"That is because you do not know the language." Ginny leaned her hip against the sofa.

It took all of Tom's willpower to concentrate on her words rather than the inviting curve of her waist, and the blood-heating profile of her breasts beneath the yellow-and-green checked material.

"A teacher for the deaf in Deutschland stayed at the orchard for a while. He taught Oma and me a special language of the hands that we have taught Doreen. She can also read many lip movements, both in English and Deutsche." She licked her lips, then hesitantly offered, "We could teach you to sign, if you would like to learn."

"I'd like to learn," he found himself saying. After a few seconds another idea occurred to him. "Maybe we could work out an exchange."

"Did you have something special in mind?"

"Would you like me to teach you to read English?"

The brilliant smile breaking out across her face took Tom's breath away, then Ginny seemed to catch herself. She tamed the spontaneous response. It felt almost like a reward dangled in front of him, then quickly snatched back.

And it left him feeling oddly dark and empty inside.

"I would love that more than anything," she answered in a husky whisper that made his blood thicken.

"Tomorrow evening, then? After supper?"

"Fine," he said, surprised at how much the idea of having her teach him to sign appealed to him. Might as well, he figured. The weather was beginning to hamper his outdoor activities so the lessons would help pass the time. And who knew? It might come in handy, being able to communicate with the deaf. If next season's crops didn't pay off, he could hire himself out as an interpreter, as he'd done before he'd enlisted and during the war.

An uncomfortable silence stretched between them. Finally she moved away toward the stairs, allowing him to breathe easier.

"Oh, Ginny, one more thing . . ."

"Do not worry, Thomas," she said, a faint trace of laughter in her voice. "You will not have to eat *Erbsen Suppe* again."

As Ginny ascended to the second floor and Tom settled onto the cushions it dawned on him that she didn't miss a detail.

Safely inside her bedroom, Ginny pressed her back and shoulders against the door. A wicked smile of victory spread across her face. Thomas might be winning the battles, but she would win the war.

27

THANKSGIVING, TOM LEARNED, was not a quiet affair in Ridgeford. Never had he seen so many people making themselves at home in his home. Ginny seemed to have invited half of Dodge county over for the feast she and Bertha had spent days preparing. With the exception of Noble, Auggie, and a handful of boys, including David, all the guests inside were female. Tom didn't have anything against them personally. He just didn't trust them. Their underhanded tactics to push him and Ginny together were still too fresh in his mind.

As he suffered through a day filled with speculative stares and gossip, he decided that he would have much rather had a private supper with just Ginny, Bertha and the youngsters. The thought caught him off guard. Over the last few days they'd fallen into a comfortable routine. The days started off with a breakfast fit for a prince, followed by morning chores and afternoons spent between the barn and the stables making repairs or modifications to the structures. Then after supper he filled his evenings with the family and lessons.

He admitted that he looked forward to the lessons more than he probably should. Ginny often had to curve his hands the way the certain words required. It gave him a perfectly

legitimate reason for being close to her. At first he'd shot away
from her like she was a match and he the fuse to a stick of
dynamite. He stopped doing that when her eyes clouded over
with hurt. She tried to hide it, would smile over the sorrow, but
they were only ghosts of the smiles he was used to. And Tom
found himself wishing for those beaming grins that lightened
his spirits and kept him drawn to her in spite of himself.

They were dangerous thoughts for a man who wanted
nothing more than his freedom.

He pushed away from the wall, ready to escape into the barn
for a while. Auggie headed him off at the door. Hazel eyes
glittered with irrational zeal, his matted hair stuck out from his
scalp in all directions.

"Got me a Reb yesterday, Lieutenant," he said over the pipe
shoved between his teeth. A match flared and tobacco glowed
from within the corncob bowl as Auggie sucked and puffed
through the stem. "Caught the sumbitch sneakin' around by the
springhouse."

Oh, no, Tom thought, growing cold with dread. "What did
you do to him, Auggie?"

He grinned. "Shot his damn kneecap off."

Well, that was better than what Tom had imagined. And he'd
gleaned enough of the conversation throughout the day to
know that it hadn't been a resident of Ridgeford injured; the
women would have been gossiping about it. Even so, the poor
fool. "Did he say what he was doing on your land?"

"Do you ask what a cow's doing when she's taking a pee?
Hell, Lieutenant! The damn grayback was settin' to bushwhack
me! 'Cept *I*"—Auggie wiggled his prematurely graying brows
and jabbed his thumb into his chest—"got to him first. The
sumbitch won't be pokin' around my land no more."

Mary Kirkmiller saved Tom from replying when she took
Auggie's arm and led him into the sitting room. Tom used the
chance to slip out the door undetected.

Or so he'd thought.

He hadn't been in the barn more than five minutes when the
doors squeaked open and Ginny glided in on a ray of dingy
sunlight.

"Thomas, what are you doing out here? We are getting ready to serve pie."

"Figured I'd start for Minnow Falls in the morning, so I'm attaching the runners." He had removed the wheels yesterday and the box was propped on sawhorses. He glanced up. Her hand trembled a bit as she tucked a loose curl behind her ear. She wouldn't meet his eyes, though, and that wasn't a good sign. Gruffly he added, "Do you think you and Bertha and the kids can be ready by dawn?"

Her eyes widened, glistening with surprise and some other unnamed emotion. "You wish us to go with you?"

"The snows will be hitting soon. I thought you'd like to get some marketing done. And Christmas is just around the corner. The boy needs new trousers, Bertha said she's got holes in her kettles—"

Ginny shushed his nervous chatter with her fingers to his lips. "We will be up, ready and waiting for you."

Then she tilted her head low and kissed him very softly, very sweetly. . . .

With an over-the-shoulder grin, she glided out the doors. And the cold casing in Tom's chest, a sheath of ice that had been so much a part of him he had forgotten it existed, began to melt.

Caught in the twilight of sleep, Tom batted at the ticklish sensation beneath his nose. Smacking his lips, he rolled onto his other side and sought the pleasant oblivion of sleep. Again, something soft and fuzzy brushed his nose, then retreated.

He cracked open one eye and found Doreen laughing mutely at him. She tucked the goose feather under her arm and signed for him to get up, then indicated the quilt he'd burrowed under.

"Are you calling me a worm?" he asked, deciphering her signals the best he could.

You said we were going to the city today. Can we leave now?

He glanced out the window at the pitch blackness. The sun hadn't even risen yet.

"Oh, all right," he sighed in resignation. He wouldn't be able to get back to sleep anyway. It had taken him long enough to finally fall into a decent slumber as it was. "But you'd best let me get dressed first or I'll create a scandal." He didn't know gestures for all the words yet, but got his meaning across by plucking at the collar of his faded red underwear. Then with a mock scowl he tweaked her nose. "Fetch me some coffee, girl."

Just as Tom slid his brown homespun trousers over his hips, a hard pinch to his behind sent him jumping a good foot in the air.

Bertha stood wearing a completely unrepentant grin. "Dis old voman loves to know she can still make a grown man blush."

Flushing fiercely, Tom quipped, "You are incorrigible."

Black eyes twinkling, she said, "Ja, but let dat be our secret." She held out a fat tin mug steaming with fresh coffee, a bribe, Tom thought. He couldn't refuse. As he took the cup, something unspoken passed between him and Ginny's grandma—a mutual respect for her years and his youth.

And Tom looked at her wrinkled face and lively eyes, at her plump and motherly figure, and thought that her departed husband had been a very fortunate man. "Pretty lady," he said conspiratorially, "if you can make a stone man blush, I imagine you set mere mortals afire."

For the first time since he'd met her, Bertha was the one turning crimson.

Soon after one of the fastest meals he could remember, they bundled up in their winter wear and climbed into the wagon. Even the leaden layer of clouds blocking out the sun couldn't dim his good cheer.

In the bed of the wagon, David, Doreen and Bertha chatted with their hands and voices but Tom barely noticed. His gaze kept straying to the woman beside him. The big beaver hat and thick wool coat she wore covered all but her face. Wind nipped at her cheeks and upturned nose, turning both a becoming pink.

Funny how such wholesome looks disguised a heart of pure mischief. Thinking back to all that she'd done to "remind" him of a past romance, a warm, tingling sensation invaded his chest, alarmingly close to where his heart had once been.

He squirmed uncomfortably on the seat. By thunder, if Gene didn't find out anything about Herz soon, Tom wondered if he'd be able to survive the winter unscathed.

Reaching Minnow Falls late that morning, Tom parked the wagon in front of the two-story brick building. The eight-foot-wide sign was boldly painted JANSON'S EMPORIUM.

"You go on in and get what you need," Tom told Ginny as David helped Doreen and Bertha alight. "I need to speak with an old friend."

"You do not wish to come with us?"

"I'll be there shortly."

She kissed his cheek, letting her hand drag down the side of his face. Their gazes met and held. The unconcealed love in her eyes drove a spike of guilt into the steel wall of his chest because of what he was about to do—had, in fact, begun a month ago.

Tom averted his face. He had no choice. Finding Herz wasn't just for his sake anymore, it was for Ginny's and her family's, too.

Once the quartet disappeared into the store, Tom stepped down onto the road, shoved his hands into his coat pockets and turned the opposite way.

It felt strange walking into the church. The echo of his footsteps sounded abnormally loud on the bare wood floor as he strode toward the raised pulpit at the end of the aisle. Sunlight filtered through the stained-glass windows, sending a kaleidoscope of colors onto the polished cherrywood pews. The door to his right was ajar, and he spotted Gene inside, bent over his father's desk. The twig pencil made scratching noises on the paper in front of him.

"Am I interrupting?"

"Lieutenant!" Gene closed the frayed black Bible and rose to grasp Tom's hand in welcome. "No, you aren't interrupting, I was just working on my Sunday school lesson."

"I had to come in for supplies so thought I'd stop by and see if there was any news on Herz yet."

"Not yet. I'll be heading for Germantown on Monday to follow up on a lead. An immigrant farmer named Herzel. He fits your age and description—" Gene broke off and caught his lip between his teeth. "There's just one thing, Lieutenant."

"Why do I get the feeling I'm not going to like what you're about to tell me?"

Gene suddenly seemed interested in his arrangement of a cup of pencils. Finally, he looked directly at Tom and squared his shoulders. "Herzel's married. Been married ten years and has five kids."

Tom's stomach plunged as he stared at Gene. Married? Five kids? "That's impossible—that's illegal! He's already married to Ginny."

"Let's not jump to any conclusions. There's no guarantee that this is Herz."

"But if it is, how am I supposed to tell her that the man she's spent half her life waiting for went and started another family?" It would kill her. Completely destroy her. Tom twisted away, rubbing his jaw. He tried to gather his thoughts. This was one complication he'd never considered. "When will you know for sure?"

"A couple of weeks—by Christmas at the latest."

He had a little over three weeks to try and find the words to tell Ginny that not only had he been searching for her husband, but that he might have found him—married to another woman.

"Thanks, Gene. I'd appreciate hearing from you as soon as you know."

In boots that felt as if the soles were made of iron, Tom trudged along the walkway toward the emporium to collect his "family."

Wet snow began to fall on the way home. Ginny scooted closer to Tom as the wagon wheels jumped over another frozen rut. He stiffened. After tucking the lap robe around his legs, she brought a second blanket snugly around his shoulder and held it there while he handled the reins.

In the bed of the wagon, snug between sacks of feed and dry staples, flats of jars and bolts of cloth wrapped in a protective layer of oilskin, Bertha, David, and Doreen huddled together beneath a blanket.

"You have been strangely quiet, Thomas," Ginny said, laying her cheek against his shoulder. "Is your friend well?"

Tom turned and stared at her profile. She was so pretty. How could Herz be such an idiot? This woman had given everything up for him, had raised their daughter alone, had saved the farm she thought belonged to him—for what? So he could cast her out of his life like old news?

He directed a blank gaze back toward the distant bluffs. "Yeah, he's fine."

That damn Herz didn't deserve her. Didn't deserve Doreen either. Why had he ever thought launching a search for Herz would be a good idea?

Oh, he knew it was unconfirmed that Herzel and Herz were the same man. But if it was true . . .

He began to wonder, what would it matter if Ginny never knew what had become of the man she'd married?

Doreen fell back against the sofa, holding her stomach, her eyes crinkled in mirth. Monotone giggles reverberated in the cozy room. David also glanced up from the hemlock branches he was bunching together to give Thomas a crooked grin. Even Oma, weaving tiny loops around her knitting needle, chuckled.

"What?" Thomas cried with a perplexed lift of his thick brows. "What did I say?"

"You just asked her if she wanted a drink of dirt."

An endearing tinge of color crept up his cheeks. "I meant to say a drink of water."

"Water and dirt are nothing alike," David pointed out.

"You haven't been to the Mississippi yet, have you?" Thomas countered with a grin.

Ginny set aside her magazine and leaned closer to her husband. "Here. Let me show you." She took his hands in hers. As always when she touched him, a forbidden charge of awareness swept through her. She tamped it down, knowing that if she allowed the feeling to rise, the result would be another endless and miserable night.

She guided his hands in the correct pattern to symbolize water. A silhouette of their joined hands cut through the bright light shed from the blaze in the fireplace. Both, it seemed, caught the glitter of her wedding ring at the same time. He captured her hand in his, turned her fingers to the firelight, and studied the ring. Ginny's breath caught in her lungs. Even as Thomas frowned, his thumb stroked the golden band.

Then he pulled away, got up, and left the room.

Ginny picked up her magazine and sought a diversion. But she could not concentrate on the sketchings or occasional familiar word printed in English. She could not forget the image of Thomas's expression as he stared at her ring.

Had it stirred his memory? For that one brief moment, did he recall the brightness of the harvest moon, the scent of summer heavy in the wind, the exchange of their vows and the joining of their hearts?

As the days of full winter bloomed and Christmas drew near, she had been witnessing a gradual change in Thomas. Though he continued to hold much of himself back, she often found him watching her. There was a softening in his eyes, though it was tainted with something else. Something she didn't understand. Almost a sadness.

Would he ever open up and share the secret fear that kept the wall between them? What would it take to get him to trust her with his love again?

She wanted to shake him, force him to see that fighting her was only making matters worse, not better. And yet she knew if she did not tread lightly she could very well drive him back to that isolated tunnel he was emerging from.

From the direction of the spinning wheel came a single cough, then another, which led to a string of thick hacking. "Oma, would you care for a cup of hot tea?" Ginny asked with a worried frown.

"Mayhap mit honey," her grandmother answered, holding a handkerchief to her mouth. "Mein t'roat feels a bit sore."

In the kitchen, Thomas stood at the counter drinking a dipperful of springwater. As if nothing had happened, Ginny handed him the teakettle for filling while she brought out the tea tin and tiny cheesecloth strainer.

"How do you do it?" he asked, working the pump handle up and down until water gushed out the spigot.

Ginny gave him a puzzled look. "I boil the water and tea leaves then let it steep—"

"No, that's not what I mean." He set the kettle onto the stove, then crouched low to feed logs from the wood bin into the mouth of the iron stove. "You don't quit. You don't give up. You keep going in spite of all the odds against you."

"But have you not done the same thing, Thomas?"

"No, Ginny, I haven't done the same thing at all. I just learned not to care anymore."

Deep into the night, an agonized cry jolted Ginny awake. She leaped out of bed and slid down the hallway. Disoriented, she checked Doreen's and David's rooms first, but found both children sleeping. Wild panic rushed through her as another cry split the darkness below, a cry of such intense pain that her stomach muscles wrung together.

Her bare feet skimmed down the steps and Ginny fell to her knees at the landing. Her nightgown tangled around her legs as she half ran, half crawled across the floor. Her knee banged against an object in the way and sent it skittering until it hit the hearthstones. The label on the bottle caught Ginny's notice briefly before a keening moan once more stole her attention.

"I am here, Thomas." Her hand skimmed over his back, shoulder, chest. Seeking his face. Smooth cheek, bristly chin, chapped lips.

Her palm smoothed his thick hair back out of his eyes, over his brow, across his temple. "Thomas, *Liebling,* it is a dream."

Oh, sweet mercy. She did not know what to do! His face was a twisted mask of torment, his body taut. The smell of brandy was sharp on his breath.

Though her friends imbibed during the ice-cutting party and were quite amusing to watch, only once had she encountered one who had binged to Thomas's extent. The day her mother died her Da had consumed half a jug of vodka traded by one of the *Dorfbewohner* for apples. Ginny had only been nine, but she recalled nonsense pouring from his mouth as he whined and blubbered his sorrows before finally falling into an oblivious sleep. The next morning he could not remember any of what he had said, or felt.

What sorrows did Thomas feel compelled to drown? Why could he not let her be strong for him? He used to. She had always been the strong one. . . .

Suddenly his arm lashed out, knocked her to the floor. Then Ginny could not think at all, for the man staring down at her

with menace blazing in his amber eyes was a complete and
utter stranger.

A moment passed before he could focus, but when he did, he
recoiled. Ginny lay beneath him. At her throat lay the sharp
blade of the knife he kept beneath his pillow. What had he
done?

"Thomas?" Her voice was tinged with alarm.

Tom threw himself off her, flipping onto his side, onto the
fire-warmed floor. He breathed in great, heaving gulps of
soot-scented air. What the hell had he done? The last thing he
remembered was pacing the room restlessly, unable to sleep,
thoughts of Herz heavy on his mind.

As a last resort he'd scoured the cabinets in search of the
brandy Ginny had pampered him with his first night home.

After that he drew a blank.

He heard a scrambling behind him. Then Ginny was
gathering him into her arms. He tried to fight her, resist the
comfort she tried to provide. But his strength was gone, his will
weak.

He was so tired of being alone.

"Ahhh, Ginny . . ." He swung his arm around her neck,
drew her roughly against him, and held on for all he was worth.

And as she stroked his sweat-dampened hair back, the
terrors of the night came back to haunt him. All the anger and
the rage and the helpless despair he wouldn't let himself feel
came back and hit him with the force of a cannonball.

He'd known this would happen. Letting her into his life
pulled down all the barriers protecting his emotions. It felt like
every bone in his body was splintering.

His voice was thick with torment. "Oh, *God*, Ginny, it
hurts."

"I know, *Liebling*."

"They all wanted out, something better . . . so many hopes
crushed . . . and the others, all dead . . ." He knew he wasn't
making any sense. He wanted so desperately to tell her about
the ship, and Matthew, and the years in the factory . . . a war
that had taken the life out of the country. But the words were
as broken as the memories, coming only in flashes.

"Let me help you."

He turned anguished eyes on her. "There's nothing even you can do."

Her own eyes were moist, revealing her own despair. "I can be with you."

"You don't want to go where I've been. It's dark and lonesome. It's mean and ugly."

"Then let me take you away from there."

Indecision waged a merciless battle. Finally the need to feel safe won over the need to be free. He closed his eyes and laid his cheek against her breast. Felt the life pulse against his skin. A comforting warmth surrounded him, the scent of clean skin erased the stench of battle. The soft touch of her hand calmed the turmoil inside him.

Throughout the night all she did was hold him, rock him, brush his hair away from his face, murmur soothing words in her native tongue, much like he imagined his mother would have done had she survived his brother's birth. Ginny's lyrical voice touched something deep inside him. Drew him out of the pit of agony, washed away the cutting edge of panic.

After a while the clamp around his chest loosened, releasing all the bitter agony locked inside. And something new and fragile and frightening began to sprout in its place.

28

"GINNY, WAKE UP."

Fuzzy-headed, Ginny batted at the annoying voice bursting into her dream.

"Come on, Ginny, there's something I want you to see."

She reluctantly lifted her lashes, then blinked several times. Thomas had stepped straight out of her dream into reality— into her bedroom. She came wide-awake. "Is it Doreen?"

"No, it's a surprise."

"What kind of surprise?"

"Just come with me."

He held up her wrapper, helped her slide her arms into the loose sleeves, then waited for her to leave the room before following. The house was bathed in darkness, only a wan glow of moonlight washing the furniture. His fingertips pressed lightly at the small of her back, prodding her toward the kitchen. "Where are you taking me?"

"Not far. Hurry, or you'll miss it."

Puzzled, she watched him open the front door. He moved up behind her, then pointed outside. "Look."

Ginny gasped. "It is snowing!" Though she had watched it snow countless times before, never had it looked as enchanting as it did now in the predawn light. The flakes seemed to glow as they drifted in a slanting pattern.

She leaned back against his chest. He stood stiff and unresponsive for a moment before his arms slowly crept around her waist.

His chin rested atop her head. "When I was a boy," he said in a low, melodic tone, "I used to wake up early every Christmas morning, hoping it would be snowing. It just didn't seem like Christmas without snow."

Ginny angled her head. Morning whiskers shadowed his face. His eyes held that sleepy cast she had come to adore.

"I hadn't thought of that in a long, long time. But watching you and Bertha in the sitting room making gifts, smelling the evergreen boughs over the fireplace, it made me remember what Christmas used to be like—I guess I just wanted you to see it."

Ginny swallowed her tears. Whatever Thomas had tried to drown in drink the other night seemed to have passed. And as she watched the eddying downfall of snow, the love she felt for him took on a dimension she had not dreamed possible, so deep and soul-stirring her breast actually ached. At the same time, it seemed so much more fragile and new.

"Are there any candles in the house?" he asked suddenly.

"Of course. We always make several batches to spare using the lamp oil. Why?"

"I want to look for a tree today. You, me, the children, Bertha—"

"Not Oma. She has been coughing the past few days, she does not need to go out in the cold."

"Then maybe she'll make us up some cider for when we get back. We'll put the candles on the tree."

"And bows," Ginny exclaimed, catching his enthusiasm. "There is a box of decorations in the root cellar."

"I'll put some coffee on, you wake up the youngsters."

Releasing his hold on her, Thomas reached for the grinder while she started toward the stairs. Rather than feeling the usual emptiness when they parted, Ginny experienced a sense of closeness to her husband she had never, ever felt before. At the bottom of the stairs, she stopped and said, "Thomas? Thank you for sharing the snow with me."

He rewarded her with a tender smile that sent her senses spinning. "It was my pleasure."

"We'll have to keep an eye out for the buck that made these tracks," David said, pointing out a parallel set of prints to Tom.

"You can tell the difference?"

"Sure! See how deep they are? And see the shaving on the trees? That's how they sharpen their antlers. The buck's about a ten pointer from the looks and height of those marks. Good eatin' if we can find him."

Impressed, Tom asked, "How do you know so much?"

"Used to spend a lot of time in the woods."

"Ginny told me that that's where she'd found you."

"It was more peaceful there." David picked up a stick and sent it flying. "He wasn't always mean, ya know. My ma ran off when I was too little to remember her. My pa, well, I think she took everything that made him a kind man with her when she left."

"I'm surprised you aren't more bitter."

"I was for a while, but Miss Bertha says everything happens for a reason. Now I figure I never would have run off if my pa had been gentle. And I never would have met them." He waved toward Ginny and Doreen, who were lying flat in the snow, waving their arms and legs. "They've given me more love in the last couple of years than I ever knew in my whole life."

Their lazy paces matched as they studied a group of snow-laden hemlocks, though Tom's concentration wasn't on which one to cut for decorating. Had all that he'd endured up to this point in time been to teach him how to appreciate how good life could be? "Have you ever gone back?"

"Once, last fall. Found the cabin burned down with my pa inside. I think he set the fire himself."

A fitting end that the man should die as brutally as he'd lived, Tom thought callously. All he'd done was cause a young boy pain and degradation.

"Mister Heart?"

David spoke so quietly that Tom would have missed hearing him had he not trained himself to catch the slightest sound. But he did hear, and the query rocked him to the core.

Peeling bark off a twig with his thumbnail, David sidled a glance at Tom. "Think maybe my pa died so you could take his place?"

Long moments passed while Tom let the unexpected question digest. "I think I'd make a lousy father, David," he finally replied. "I holler a lot."

"Miss Ginny says you're just ornery."

A rusty chuckle came loose from Tom's gut. He stared at his snow-crusted boots. "That sounds like something Miss Ginny would say."

"'Sides," David added somberly, "I wouldn't pay no mind to the hollerin'. It's the hittin' that hurts."

Tom had no idea how to take the comment. He'd never thought about being a father before. He'd been alone for so long, relying only on wits and determination to see him through, that he wasn't sure he'd have the skills it would take to make a good parent.

Then as if to pin him into a corner, Doreen approached him from the other side and tugged vigorously on his sleeve.

Vati, help me make angels in the snow!

Balking, Tom shook his head and signed back, "We're supposed to be looking for a tree."

"Thomas, when your daughter asks you to make angels, you should oblige her!"

A snowball smacked him in the back of the head. Whipping around, he caught sight of Ginny ducking behind a juniper bush, scrambling for more ammunition. The next snowball that came flying splattered against the front of David's coat.

Tom chuckled at the look of stunned amazement on the boy's face. "David, she's just declared war."

Tossing the ax onto a mound of needles and leaning his rifle against a hemlock tree, Tom scooped a handful of snow and packed it tight. Ginny squealed and raced for cover.

David, too, had armed himself and was chasing Doreen across the field. Another snowball wholloped Tom in the thigh.

For the rest of the morning he allowed himself to re-create his childhood the way he would have wanted it. Out here in the fragrant evergreen woods of Heart land, there were no dirty gutters to scrounge through, no peddlers throwing rotten apples at hungry little boys, no brother wasting away to skin and bones in his arms. Just carefree laughter and merry frolicking that sired gladness in his heart and brought a lightness to his soul, both of which he had thought were forever lost to him.

Panting from pleasant exertion, Tom scouted the edge of the woods for moving targets. Somewhere in the forest, boyish laughter rang as David no doubt hit his mark. Ready to come to his defense, Tom stepped out of his cover just as a bundle of wool topped with cornsilk hair slammed into his shoulder and tumbled him to the ground.

"You cannot hide from me, soldier boy!"

The world instantly narrowed down to him and the woman on top of him. Two heavy coats lay between them, but the bulky material did nothing to guard him from the sweet heat of Ginny's skin, the branding fit of her curves.

"Who says I want to hide from you?" he confessed, startling himself as much as Ginny.

She cupped his jaw with freezing, wet mittens. He stroked the side of her cheek. Then Tom lifted his head from the icy snow and touched his cold lips to hers. The kiss, though achingly brief, warmed him faster than any fire.

Staring at his face, she said in a voice shaky with emotion, "*Ich liebe dich,* Thomas Herz."

The faint smile of contentment ebbed away at the sound of the name she called him. Love glistened in her eyes, glowed in her cheeks. But it was love for the man she thought he was—a man who'd deserted her twelve years ago and never looked back.

Why couldn't that love belong to him instead?

His chest painfully barren, he drew a lock of her hair away from her lips. "Heart," he whispered sadly. "My name is Tom Heart."

"Oh, my goodness!" Bertha exclaimed as they tromped in later that morning, toting a seven-foot hemlock on their shoulders.

"We'll have to move your spinning wheel, Bertha."

"But vhere vill I sit vhere I can have a good view of your handsome hinder?"

Tom pinched her fleshy cheek, mentally thanking the old

woman for giving him something to smile about since Ginny's unwitting reminder that she wasn't his for the taking.

Somehow, he had to tell her about Herz. And soon.

Unfortunately she didn't give him much of an opportunity. When he wasn't building a stand for the tree, he was hauling crates of ornaments from the root cellar, stringing popcorn, dodging Doreen's energetic help, or getting his hand rapped with the spoon Bertha used to keep him from picking at the golden brown turkey she'd pulled out of the oven.

At the end of the holiday feast they retired to the sitting room, stomachs full, spirits content. A Yule log was lit in the hearth. Candlewicks glowed yellow and blue from the sweeping branches of the fragrant hemlock tree loaded with woven wreaths, calico figures, and tiny wooden soldiers that Ginny's father had made.

Tom relaxed on the sofa with Ginny beside him, his arm draped across the back of the cushion. Doreen sat at his feet, staring in awe at the beautiful tree they'd decorated. No matter what the future held, these audacious nesters had given him a memory to cherish for the rest of his life.

"Mr. Heart—"

"Can't you call me Tom?"

"Uh, sure. Mr. Tom."

Tom shook his head and rolled his eyes. The boy was hopeless.

"Me and Doreen found something special for you. We hope you like it."

David rose from his cross-legged position in front of the hearth. He opened the door to the springhouse off the kitchen. A short-legged, fat-bellied black puppy came skidding into the sitting room, tail wagging so fast his whole body shook. As if it had been rehearsed, the puppy headed straight for Tom and attacked his hand with sloppy licks.

Tom glanced around, blinking in surprise.

"We found him wandering around lost in the village," David said. "Miss Ginny didn't think he belonged to anybody so she said we could keep him. But me and Doreen wanted you to have him. He'll keep you company in the spring when you're plowin' the fields."

He was so touched he couldn't say a word. Holding the puppy under its belly, he felt the warmth of its tongue lapping his nose. "I've never had a dog before," Tom finally choked out.

What will you name him?

Looking into the bright eyes, one brown, one a silvery blue, Tom said without a second thought, "Blue. His name is Blue." Laying the dog in his lap, he pulled Doreen close, then motioned to David and embraced him. "Thank you."

Bertha then pressed a paper-wrapped bundle into his hands. Tom knew before he opened the gift that he would find the red shirt she had been making. Stitched on the rounded collar were his initials.

"A fiery color for a fiery man," she reminded him, returning his hug.

"I have a little something for you also, Thomas."

The gift from Ginny wasn't wrapped in paper, but carefully protected in a leather case. Tom stared first at the compass, then at Ginny.

"So you will always know where home is."

He took her hand, pressed her knuckles to his lips. Then he cleared his throat. "My turn." Tom rose and pulled several items out of the deacon's bench. He'd found the gifts yesterday in Vernice's store. The minute he'd seen each one, he'd known whom they were meant for.

David opened his box. He saw the bridle, then read the note attached to it, which read: THE REST OF THIS GIFT IS PENNED IN THE BARN. His eyes bulged.

Doreen opened her box. She clutched the musical figurine of a father dancing with his little girl and she wept.

Bertha laughed upon opening hers. She flipped a gaudy orange feather boa around her shoulders and slid the matching garter up her thigh over her woolen stockings.

And Ginny . . . Ginny went speechless as she opened hers.

"Oh, Thomas . . ." Her voice broke; her eyes went all misty. Suddenly she sprang from the chair and bolted up the stairs.

His heart stopping, Tom jumped off the sofa and raced after her. He found her digging frantically through the top drawer of her dresser.

"It's just a spoon, Ginny."

"It is not—it is just like the one you gave me upon our betrothal!" She held both spoons in the air. "See, they are the same!"

The color drained from his face. "It's just a coincidence—"

"Dolores said that deep down inside you remembered. . . . I doubted her—but this is proof! You do remember!"

Tom swallowed roughly, suddenly feeling sick inside. This illusion had gone on long enough. He should have told her, had been wrong not telling her about the search. By keeping it secret, he'd unwittingly given her false hope that eventually he'd become everything she'd ever wanted—the man she'd married.

Sighing, he closed the space between them. Clasping her hand in his, he sank onto the bed, pulling Ginny down beside him. "Ginny, look . . ."

Beaming, she waited for him to speak. In her hands she clutched two silver spoons engraved with apples and leaves. She held them as if she'd never let go. Just as she held on to her hopes and her dreams and her beliefs.

Oh, God, how could he tell her that the man she'd pinned her whole life on might never want to see her again because he'd traded her for another woman? Worse, how could he not? She deserved to know the truth—even if she didn't believe him.

He cleared his throat and stared at the spoon he'd given her, willing the words to magically flow from his mouth. *I'm not your husband, Ginny, I'm just a worn-out soldier who's fought too long to give a damn anymore.* But he did give a damn. Had from the moment he'd laid eyes on Ginny, though he hadn't accepted it then. Else he would've kicked her out on her hoopskirts and never thought twice.

And somehow, over the days and weeks, she'd thrown herself at him again and again. Opened up a piece of him that had been closed for so long . . .

Tom's shoulder slumped. He couldn't, he just couldn't break her heart. Not tonight. It was Christmas, for God's sake.

He'd tell her later. When he wasn't such a damn coward.

29

THE END OF December brought more than a chill to the body, it brought a chill to the soul. Ginny could not shake the sense of unease that the nagging cough plaguing her grandmother would not go away. It had grown steadily worse since their return from the city, sapping the vigorous woman of strength and color.

Is Oma still in bed? Doreen asked when she reached the bottom of the stairs. The shadows under her sleepy eyes testified to her lack of sleep.

Ginny cast a worried glance toward the closed door of Bertha's room. She suspected that today would be one of her grandmother's bad days, which had grown increasingly more frequent as the month waned. "Oma needs rest today. Would you help me make apple pancakes?"

Working together in companionable silence, Doreen whipped the batter while Ginny fried pork sausages. As long as she kept busy, the worry did not consume her.

Breakfast was not the gabby affair she had come to treasure. Ginny strove to keep conversation light and off Bertha's poor health but it seemed uppermost on everyone's mind. She often caught Thomas and the children glancing at Bertha's door as if they, like she, expected the old woman to appear at any moment in her usual chipper form.

Forcing herself to eat, Ginny watched her daughter drag her fork through the puddle of maple syrup on her plate. She wiped her mouth with a napkin then gained Doreen's attention.

"Is something wrong with your pancakes?"

Doreen set the fork down and sighed. *They do not taste like Oma's.*

"I used her recipe . . . David, do they taste strange to you?"

He cleared his throat, shifted in his chair. "They're fine, Miss Ginny. They're just missin' Miss Bertha's special flavor, that's all."

Ginny knew what they meant. Bertha put a little bit of herself in everything she cooked, a dash of zest, a heaping spoonful of love. That flavor could not be duplicated regardless of another's talent. "If you wish to be excused, you may go about your chores," she permitted.

They rose from their places and bundled themselves in their coats and mittens, then solemnly left for the barn.

"How is she this morning?" Thomas asked once they were alone.

She gave him a tired smile. "Resting."

"Which is what you should be doing."

Ginny shrugged lethargically. The last thing she could endure right now was lying in her big bed alone. It allowed for too much thinking. Too much longing. She'd hoped that Christmas day had somehow broken down the invisible barrier between her and Thomas but he seemed even more distracted lately. Mayhap it was due to Oma's illness, yet Ginny sensed something deeper occupied his thoughts. "I will rest when Oma recovers. The alumroot plasters are not working."

Thomas crossed his forearms, then rested them against the table. "You can't keep going like this, Ginny. You've been up nearly three days straight—"

"How do you know?" she asked with wry amusement. "You sleep on the sofa."

"I hear your footsteps in the night."

Surprise fluttered through Ginny at the soft confession. "I was not aware of that."

"I notice a lot of things you aren't aware of."

The flutter became a tremor. What things? she wondered. Did he know that she dreamed of him? Did he know that she still hugged her pillow, wishing it were him? Did he know that her heart lodged in her throat whenever she looked at him?

If he did, he gave no sign.

Averting her eyes lest he see the longing in them, Ginny rose and gathered the sticky plates, all as untouched as hers. "After you left, I used to pace the cottage, wondering if you'd made it safely to American shores. It woke my Da every time." With fond remembrance, she scraped the dishes then carefully set them in the basin of water to soak. "Then one night, he never awoke."

Her forehead crinkled as old grief mingled with new. "If anything happens to Oma . . ."

The look in her husband's eyes held such sympathy that it tested Ginny's composure to the limits. She wanted promises, not pity.

She grabbed several large onions from the bin and set them on the counter. "Onion syrup. That is what she needs. And a poultice."

"She's seventy years old, Ginny. As sickly as she is, she needs a miracle."

Looking directly at her husband, Ginny stated, "Then I will pray for one."

His lashes fell over his eyes, hiding his lack of faith.

"Miracles happen all the time," Ginny declared, stripping the onions of their outer skin. "A miracle saved our daughter's life. A miracle brought us prosperity. A miracle ended the war and brought you back to me. All you have to do is believe."

With a heavy sigh, Thomas pushed back the chair and rose. "I'll fetch some snow. We'll make the syrup."

Her gaze followed him as he wrapped himself in his Union coat then braved the frigid cold outside. My doubting Thomas, she thought, shaking her head. Did he not know that faith accomplished wonders? She had never wavered in her faith that she and Thomas would be together again. And though the situation had not turned out exactly as she had expected, it was enough that her husband had come home from the war, in one piece, unlike the other few who had returned. At least she and

Thomas had a chance to repair their relationship. That was much more than many of her women friends had.

A bout of muffled coughing from the other room turned her thoughts back to her grandmother. Pulling a knife from the chopping block, Ginny keenly felt Oma's absence in the kitchen. She was used to bumping into her grandmother as she bustled from stove to sink to counter. Used to watching her as she churned butter. Used to hearing her low laughter and heavy Deutsche accent as they chatted at the table. . . .

Her eyes began to water as she sliced the pungent onions. A sob caught in her throat. A tear fell. Then another, and another, until the knife's steel blade became nothing more than a blur of liquid silver.

Bowing her head over the counter, Ginny prayed for a miracle.

Two days later Tom set the hammer on the workbench as if it were made of glass, then ran his hands along the interior of the casket, searching for any rough patches that needed smoothing. An ache developed in his chest at the thought of how Ginny would fare when Bertha passed on. It was inevitable.

Although he'd made a point of going along with her fantasy that Bertha would recover, he'd seen enough death to know that the old woman's breaths were numbered. Ginny had to know deep down inside that this was one thing she couldn't fix. Yet like everything else, she denied it, protecting herself from the unpleasant facts of life.

With a soul-wrenching sigh, Tom draped a piece of canvas over the coffin, wishing he could spare Ginny this pain.

"Mr. Heart?"

He turned his head slowly. David stood two feet away, holding tight to Doreen's hand. She looked so frail standing next to the boy, her eyes huge and sorrowful. She regarded Tom as if he had the power to change destiny.

"What are you two doing out here? I've told you before not to chance wandering around in this weather." Even now mighty winds hit the side of the barn, bringing more snow to the two-foot drifts already dumped on the ground.

"Miss Bertha's asking for you," David said. His gaze fell on the canvas covered box. "She isn't gonna get better, is she?"

"I don't think so, son."

His Adam's apple worked its way down his throat. His eyes remained dry.

"But we're doing all we can. Let's go see if she needs anything, all right?"

David nodded, then drew Doreen behind him. Tom followed, ducking his head against the gusts to avoid the stinging flakes. As they plodded along the trench dug from the barn to the house, using the guide rope to lead them, he felt Doreen slip her free hand into his.

Three sets of boots tramped snow into the kitchen. After divesting themselves of their bulky outerwear, Doreen and David went to stand in front of the fireplace while Tom headed for the closed door beneath the stairwell.

The room smelled of sickness and onions. A single oil lamp burned on the bedside table. A piece of ribbon marked a page in the German Bible, and a glass of water shimmered in the wan light. Bertha lay on the right side of the bed, the quilt molding to her plump figure. Feverish patches were the only color on her otherwise pale and sunken cheeks.

Sitting beside her in a chair pulled up to the bed, Ginny prayed softly, "Our Father, who art in Heaven . . ." Their hands were linked together, as if Ginny could somehow keep the old woman alive by touch alone.

When she finished, Bertha looked up and smiled. "Your hair is vhite, Thomas."

Self-consciously, he ruffled the icy flakes from his hair. "We'll probably get another foot of snow before nightfall."

"Ginny, leave us a moment. I vould like to speak mit *dein Mann.*"

Ginny released her hands. As she passed Tom, he was struck by her drawn and haggard appearance. He stopped her, touched her cheek. She shut her eyes and leaned into his palm for just a moment before leaving the room.

Bertha patted the bed. "Come sit." When Tom did as she bade, she asked, "Do you vemember de first time you came to my bed?"

"You won't ever let me forget it," he said with a lopsided grin that belied his concern for Ginny.

"You are such fun to tease." Her brown eyes glittered, whether from amusement or the fever Tom couldn't determine. Maybe both. "Ve disrupted your life, did ve not?"

He licked his lips, unsure how to answer and wondering where the conversation was leading.

"I have always vanted only de best for my Ginny, do you understand dat, Thomas?"

"Yes, ma'am," he replied.

"You are de best tink dat has happened to her in many years." A stream of wheezing coughs interrupted her sentiments, and Tom supported her back, rubbing soothing circles. He felt so damn useless.

Once she regained control of herself she clasped his hand tightly. "Do not leave my Ginny, she needs you so."

"I won't, Bertha."

Shutting her eyes, she smiled her approval. "Gutt. Dis is vhere you belong anyvay."

The promise weighed heavily on his shoulders as he walked out. Ginny stood alone in the sitting room, slowly turning the hoop of the spinning wheel with her finger.

He hated seeing her this way. Like the weather and like Bertha, she had gone from bad to worse. Her melancholy put a vacant glow in her lively eyes, widening the hole in Tom's heart.

From the thump above, he figured the children had closeted themselves in one room or the other, trying to soothe each other's fears. He glanced upward, wondering if he should talk to them, even though he had no idea what to say. No, he told himself. They had each other, they'd be all right for now.

Ginny, though, who was everything to everybody, had no one.

A few swift strides carried him across the room. He wrapped his arms around Ginny in an awkward offer of comfort. She instantly turned into his arms.

With her face buried against his chest, she said, "The alumroot plasters are not working, nor are the onion syrup and poultices. . . ."

Tom smoothed his hand along her spine. Thunderation, he wasn't any good at this. But he didn't know what else to do to ease her grief. "Noble's already gone to fetch the doctor, but he's probably stranded like everyone else."

"I hope the snows let up and he arrives soon, or I fear . . ."

The consequence remained unspoken, as if by not voicing the fear she could prevent the worst from happening. "We're doing all we can, Ginny."

"She has always been there when I needed her most. When my mother died, when we married, then when my father died and Doreen was so ill. . . . She is slipping away and I cannot seem to stop it."

Shame coursed through Tom as his body grew aware of her lush figure and reacted to it. He held her as close as he dared, the top of her head tucked under his chin, and sought some distraction from the pressure building in his loins. "I heard somewhere that when one life ends, another begins."

"Do you believe that?"

In all honesty, Tom wasn't sure what he believed anymore. Meeting Ginny had pitched him into such a state of confusion. He'd tried so hard to push her away. But when she'd drawn back there was an ache in his soul. Against his will she'd awakened tender feelings inside him, making it harder and harder to remember why he so desperately wanted his freedom.

It wasn't important what he believed, though, only what Ginny did. And right now, she needed her faith in miracles restored. Brushing loose strands of cornsilk hair away from her face, he cupped her cheek and whispered, "I'm beginning to believe that anything is possible."

Ginny had never noticed before how frail Oma's hands were; they'd always seemed so strong. They were the hands that kneaded the bread they ate each day. Created perfect molds of cheese and butter that brought extra coins into the house. Spun wool into thread for the clothes they wore, slapped a knee with amusement, wiped a tear away, gave a squeeze for comfort, spoke wise words to a deaf girl . . .

They were the hands of a provider, a mentor, a mother. Ginny brought one to her mouth, pressed her lips against the knobby knuckles. How important these hands were. Now they were on fire.

The rattling in Oma's chest stopped for a moment, and Ginny prepared herself for the fit of thick coughing that would follow. Her own lungs shrank and filled painfully, as if she were the one straining for breath. Ginny wished she could take her grandmother's illness onto herself, if only to ease the old woman's suffering. Night fevers had quickly drained her of resistance, daytime coughing of strength. Ginny hoped for the best, but feared the worst.

"Ginny?"

She sprang forward, smoothed the iron-gray hair away from Oma's crinkled face. Such a dear face. She memorized every detail. Her dark brows and sparse lashes, the thready lines of her eyelids, her rounded nose and flat lips and the fine mustache between.

"I am here, Oma."

"*Enkelin*, I must . . . leave you now."

Ginny felt her chest cave in. "Noooo, Oma, noooo." Panicked tears sprang to her eyes as she stroked Bertha's hair, her cheeks, willing her own strength into the weakened body.

"Do not . . . cry for me," Bertha huffed. "Opa is vaiting, Fritz is vaiting. I must . . . follow my heart."

"But I cannot let you go," Ginny said in a desperate whisper. "I need you. Doreen and David need you."

"Doreen and David . . . have each utter. You . . . have your Thomas."

"*Ich liebe dich,* Oma. Do not leave me."

"I alvays said . . . you loved too deeply," she wheezed. "*Kind*, if you . . . love someting . . . you must learn . . . to set it free. Dat is de . . . greatest . . . love of all. *Ich liebe dich . . . meine geliebte Enkelin. Auf Wiedersehen . . .*"

It was dark. So dark he couldn't see her face. But he knew she was crying. It was the kind of silent crying that no one heard, but each tear that fell shaved off another piece of his heart.

Tom curled his hands over her shoulders, felt her sorrow become his own. "Ginny?"

In a voice devoid of emotion, Ginny told him, "She said my grandfather was waiting for her. And my father . . . She said I must let her go." Bowing her head, Ginny softly wailed, "I do not know how-ow."

His chest hurting for her, Tom wrapped his arms around her and whispered, "One finger at a time."

30

*B*ERTHA KRAHN WAS laid to rest on New Year's morning beneath an oak tree as solid and sturdy as she'd been all her life. And the tree grew on a bluff overlooking the farm so she could always watch over Ginny. Tom wished with all his heart he could've at least given the old woman a proper burial. But until the ground thawed, a coffin covered with rocks to keep animals from desecrating her body was the best he could do.

He settled his hat on his head then took Ginny's cold hand in his own. She didn't resist as he led her away from the grave. In fact, she hadn't shed a single tear since the night Bertha died. That worried him more than anything given Ginny's usual open expressiveness.

They worked their way down the hillside, the mourners walking behind them. He doubted Ginny noticed, but her closest friends had come to pay their respects: Evie Mae and Dolores, Mary and Vernice and Elsbeth. And Noble, of course, standing like a silent guardian in the background. He'd arrived late last night with the doctor in tow. Though the weather had calmed considerably in the last two days, snowdrifts five feet high still prevented him from arriving in time to possibly save Bertha.

Before they entered the house, Tom bent low and whispered into Ginny's ear, "Will you be all right for a moment? I need to talk to Noble."

She didn't look at him but she nodded. It was better than nothing. At least he knew she'd heard him.

He waited until Evie Mae guided her inside and shut the door then turned to his friend and grasped his hand. "I'm sorry you went all that way for nothing."

"Just wish I coulda got here sooner."

"I'm not sure it would have helped."

"How's Miss Ginny?"

"I don't think it's hit her yet. She's walking around in a daze. I can't keep her out of Bertha's room. . . ." Tom shrugged helplessly. Ginny was the one good at comforting, not him.

"This may not be the right time, but I thought I'd tell you—the man in Germantown wasn't Herz."

His knees nearly buckled with relief. Herz hadn't left his wife for another woman, hadn't started another family. Anger set in. Where the hell was he, then? His wife needed him!

"Noble, tell Gene that I want him found. Tell him to hire a goddamn detective if he has to, I don't care if it costs me every cent I've got. I want that bastard found."

And when he was, Tom would make Ginny a widow.

Day after day Tom watched helplessly as Ginny blocked out reality. She kept making onion syrup. The kitchen reeked of onions but if he tried to take them or the knife away from her, she yelled. Screamed. Lashed out at him with her fists.

Or she'd withdraw.

He often found her sitting beside Bertha's bed, staring at the empty spot. Sometimes David and Doreen sat with her, but not for long. She scared them. This wasn't the mother they knew and loved, just a shell of a woman wandering around in a state of shock.

Huge purple circles colored the skin under her eyes from lack of sleep. She was losing weight. She never smiled. Or laughed. She'd say one thing then do another, as if unable to hold on to a single thought for long.

Her friends came to visit regularly, but she remained as

unresponsive to their efforts as she did to his. Even now, while Dolores kept up a steady monologue with Ginny at the kitchen table, all she did was stare at her hands.

Doreen came to sit by him on the sofa. She picked up one of the magazines and set it in his lap. Knowing that she needed this small pretense of normalcy, Tom forced himself to finger spell the English word of the picture she pointed to. She in turn taught him the gesture, but his heart just wasn't in it. David joined them a little while later and they sat until long after nightfall, talking about nothing and everything.

The instant Dolores rose to leave, Tom jumped from the sofa and cornered her in the kitchen.

"Can't you do something for her?" he whispered desperately.

"There's nothing that can be done," Dolores told him. "We've all been where she is at one time or another, Tom."

"So have I. A long time ago, I lost my brother. It hurt."

"Ginny's gonna hurt, too, it'll just take time for her to feel the pain."

"But she's usually so strong—"

"Everybody's got their breaking point—she reached hers. She's just lost someone very close to her and she's handling it the only way her mind will let her."

"I can't stand seeing her this way, there's got to be something I can do!"

"Just be with her. This'll run its course, and then she'll need you to lean on. In the meantime, Vernice sent over a pot of stew for supper. Do you need anything else?"

I need my Ginny back. Tom shook his head. "No, but I appreciate your asking."

He shut the door behind Dolores and immediately sought out Ginny. She was in Bertha's room, as he'd figured she would be.

He watched her from the doorway, his chest hurting so bad for her it felt bruised. His "fixer" was broken, and he didn't know how to put her back together again. "Ginny?"

"Our lives will never be the same, Thomas."

"Nothing stays the same, Ginny. Everything changes."

"I am coming to understand that."

Tom's brows rose. Was it good or bad? He held his breath, divided between hope and dread.

"Knowing I would soon be with you gave me the strength to endure my Da's death, Thomas. But you are not you. And Oma is gone. . . . Nothing is as it should be."

He rounded the bed and wrapped her in a tight embrace. For countless moments she clung to him. "Tell me what I can do, Ginny."

"Love me, Thomas."

"Ginny . . . you don't know what you're asking." The request was so simple. And yet so complicated.

"Please. I need to believe in something—even if it is a lie. I need to feel alive."

His hands trembled as he tilted her head back. Her eyes were filled with pain. Despair. Loneliness. He only meant to offer her comfort. But the moment his lips touched hers, the kiss became something more. Urgent. Wild.

And he knew he'd give her the moon if she asked for it.

Sweeping her into his arms, he carried her up the stairs.

Even when the mattress dipped beneath Ginny's back, she clung to her husband's neck, fearing that if she let go he would leave her again. And she needed him. She had always needed him, but now she needed him more than ever. With her grandmother's death such a crushing blow she felt as if the foundation of her life had given away beneath her. And Thomas, for all his differences, was the force that kept her from crumbling. More so now than ever before.

He claimed her mouth with an urgency that astounded her. His passionate kiss seemed to contain a lifetime of neglected longing. Then his mouth softened, became almost reverent.

Submerged in a sea of feeling, Ginny was only dimly aware of him peeling away her clothing until a chilly draft of air skipped over her body. Thomas quickly covered her with his own lean length. He touched her as if she were made of glass. His fingertips brushed across her flesh, each leisurely caress blazing a path of liquid heat.

Ginny followed his example. Unbuttoning his shirt and spreading the edges wide, she trailed first her fingertips, then her lips along every inch of skin between his neck and midriff, cherishing the masculine essence of him.

Following the spread of fine golden hair over his chest, she measured the breadth of his shoulders, marveled at the power flexing beneath her hands. Her fingernails lightly traced the path of branching scars on his back. She kissed one thin white line on the crest of his shoulder. Her lips lingered on the marred velvet flesh. "How could anyone have been so cruel to you?"

With his thumb poised on the frantic pulse at her throat, he whispered against her damp neck, "It doesn't hurt, Ginny. It hasn't for a long, long time."

"Then why have I felt your pain?"

He would have drawn back had she not caught him around the neck in an unyielding hold. "Do not deny us this."

A moment's indecision flickered across his face. She teased the corner of his mouth with her tongue, drew his upper lip into her mouth, felt the rumble of his surrendering groan quiver against her chin. His roaming hands caressed the backs of her thighs, her buttocks, her hips. Ripples of pleasure stronger than she remembered ever feeling followed his touch. She refused to ponder the remarkable skill of his hands. Did not wish to consider how he had gained knowledge of sensitive areas even she had not known existed.

She only wanted him to continue exploring each secret pulse point and bring to life her deadened nerves. And he did until not an inch of her body escaped the attentions of his hands and mouth.

Trembling with need, Ginny anxiously tugged at the waistband of his trousers. He granted her wish to feel nothing between them but skin, then levered himself over her, bracing the weight on his arms. Unbridled desire left his green-gold eyes glazed as he stared at her.

Why did he hesitate? Did he fear he was taking advantage of her? Did he wonder if she understood that this would change everything between them?

She knew. It would make their relationship either better or worse. But as she had pledged long ago, better or worse was part of the commitment. He was worth the risk.

Seeking to convince him that she had all her wits about her,

Ginny said, "We may have changed, Thomas, but one thing always has and always will remain the same." She pressed her fingers to her swollen breast, then to his rigid chest. "We are joined at the heart, you and I. Connected by a string that nothing can break. Not time. Not distance. Not wars . . . *Ich liebe dich*, Thomas. I know you do not remember, but I have loved you always."

And if he rejected her now, she did not think she could survive the loneliness.

She watched the struggle on his face, saw the effort it took him to hold himself in check. Then a strange peacefulness passed over his features, relaxed his taut planes. He kissed her with an aching gentleness and entered her. Instantly Ginny felt the sheer perfection. The rightness. A love so powerful that tears blinded her to all but the man sliding within her. Splendor built with each excruciatingly tender stroke until every nerve in Ginny's body hummed.

And she discovered a newness to loving Thomas, as if she'd never loved him before, never made love with him before. She could not place the difference, nor did she want to examine it. She only wanted to revel in the sonata her body sang as he brought her to the peak of pleasure.

Their muffled cries soon combined as sheer sensation drove them over the brink of control and sent them spinning into bliss. Then, as the heady euphoria of fulfillment subsided and their racing hearts became one, matching each other beat for beat, Thomas opened his eyes and Ginny opened hers.

He gazed at her in shock; misty-eyed, she gazed back at him in breathless wonder. Love filled her heart so full she could hardly breathe. Had it always been this powerful between them?

Clenching her eyes shut against the tears threatening to spill, she rubbed her cheek against his slick chest, listening to the thundering beat of his heart. Her breath came out slowly tremulously. "Tell me you feel it. Please . . . tell me you remember."

Then he said the words she had begun to think she would never hear.

"I remember."

31

SHE WENT SO still that if not for the slight stiffening of her body he would have thought she'd fainted.

Tom eased his weight off of her and stared at the ceiling. What had he done? Staggered from the emotional impact of their joining, the words had slipped out before he'd completely thought through the consequences.

Then suddenly her face appeared before his eyes, her expression reflecting such hope and disbelief that his heart twisted.

And in that instant he knew not a moment's regret. He couldn't give Ginny back her grandmother, but he could give her something she wanted with equal intensity—a man who loved her.

Himself. For what that was worth.

He swallowed roughly, then repeated, "I remember."

Her shoulders quaked from the force of her sobs. Acceptance, grief, joy. He simply held her while her healing tears trickled onto his bare skin, caught in his chest hairs, burned holes into his soul. He didn't know how else to comfort her. Ginny was the comforting one, not him. He wasn't any good at that kind of thing. But he rubbed her back, said not a word, just let all her tears pour out. And hoped it was enough.

"I cannot tell you how often I have dreamed of you holding me like this."

Tom clutched her as tightly as she clutched him. "I can't tell you how many times I've wanted to hold you like this."

"What stopped you, silly?" The chuckle in her voice sounded like music.

"I couldn't let myself get close to you. It's safer existing in numbness, and you began to make me feel alive. It's not an easy transition."

Soberly she asked, "Because of the war?"

Never before had he been as tempted to purge himself of the story of his indentureship than at this moment. But Ginny . . . his arms tightened around her. She needed to forget. She needed warm, loving arms, not cold, hard facts. "Partly."

To his relief, she didn't press him for explanations he wasn't prepared to give. It was just too soon, his emotions too fresh. Powerful.

He'd tell her later—when his body stopped humming from the magic of their union. When his brain had time to sort out the magnitude of his lie without the fog of passion clouding his thinking.

"How much do you remember?" she asked tentatively.

"Only bits and pieces."

"Like what?"

Calling upon chips of information gleaned over the last two months, Tom bluffed, "You look like your mother."

"Except for my Da's chin," she claimed with a watery grin.

"Yes, you have your father's stubborn chin. And your grandmother's mustache."

"I do not have a mustache!" she cried with mock indignation. "Unlike you." She scrubbed the bristles under his nose and around his chin playfully with her short nails. "Your whiskers feel like a curry brush."

"Do they hurt you?" He tipped her chin up, saw the red patches around her mouth, down the slender column of her neck.

Allowing her lashes to fall, she admitted, "Mayhap a little."

Remorseful, Tom attempted to soothe the burns he'd caused. Nothing tasted as sweet as Ginny's skin. Reining in the desire beginning to stir again, he caught her neck in the crook of his arm and tugged her close to him once more.

While he stared at the raw-wood rafters, she sighed content-edly and laid her cheek against his chest. "Thomas?"

His lips curved. He loved the way she said his name. Made it sound like an endearment. He wondered if he should call her something special. Except he really didn't know any sweet terms that fit a stubborn, independent, persistent German milkmaid. "What, Ginny?"

"I miss Oma."

"I know. It'll get easier, though."

"As long as I have you to lean on it will."

The weight of her dependence on him filled him with both pride that she thought he was worthy enough and fear that he'd let her down. "I know I'm not everything you always wanted but I hope you'll give us a chance."

"Not what I wanted?" She lifted her head. "Oh, *Liebling*, you are so much more than I ever dreamed!" Her hand fit along the slope of his jaw, her fingertips stroked his earlobe. "The love I felt long ago was gentle and comforting. It gave me something to reach for. The love I feel now is powerful and fills my veins with lightning. It gives me something to hold on to."

Tom shut his eyes and swallowed, then roughly said, "I can't promise it won't be hard—just don't ever give up on me, Ginny."

"Never." She settled back into his arms. Plucked at the hair on his chest. "Just do not *ever* leave me again, Thomas."

Pulling her close, he whispered, "I won't." It had nothing to do with the promise he'd made Bertha, either.

Tom awoke with a feeling of satiety and peace of mind he hadn't felt in years. Had he ever felt so whole? So alive? His head rolled to the side and Ginny filled his vision. Her lashes rested upon her cheeks, a tiny smile curved her lips. She still looked exhausted but it was a peaceful exhaustion.

He drew his finger down her cheek, savoring the softness of her skin. Seeing her like this was worth any sacrifice he had to make.

Tom slid a niggle of guilt to the back of his mind and locked it away. Herz was never going to be found. What harm could there be in being her husband? It wasn't like he was taking over Herz's identity—he'd never claimed to be anyone but Tom Heart. Someday she'd love him for who he was. He'd see that she did.

Sliding out of the bed, Tom dressed and carried his boots downstairs so that the thumping wouldn't wake her. The kitchen was more empty than he'd imagined it would be. He was used to greeting Bertha first thing in the morning. Used to her outrageous flirting. Used to her companionship as he made coffee.

No time for coffee now, though. No time for mourning either. If he was going to seize this new beginning with Ginny, there was an ending he had to deal with first.

Out in the barn, Tom led the dun out of her stall and saddled her with haste. She pranced backward at the first blast of cold air when he opened the barn doors. "I know, girl, the last thing I wanted was to leave my warm bed, too. But this is important."

Important, hell. It was life and death.

The dun responded to his urgency and galloped into town, her hooves thudding solidly on the packed road. The sun hadn't even risen yet, but fingers of dawn splayed wide across the horizon, casting purple shadows over drifts of snow.

The village was just beginning to stir. Wisps of smoke from the chimneys evaporated above the treetops, whose branches bowed under the ivory weight they held.

Tom pulled on the string dangling from a hole in the smithy door. The bar inside lifted. He led the dun inside, then strode purposefully toward the back of stables warm from the body heat of animals snug inside their stalls.

At the clomping sound his boots made on the wood floor, Noble started awake.

Tom planted his feet in front of his friend's face. "I want the search called off," he said without preamble.

Noble's ebony lashes rose and fell several times before his bleary-eyed gaze trailed up from Tom's mushy boots to his heavy coat and wind-tossed hair. After a long, speculative look, a grin stole across his face. "So ya fin'ly come to your senses."

"Can you get a message to Gene?"

"I'm wearin' a mighty solid path 'tween here and the city—"

"I'd do it myself but I don't want to leave Ginny alone this soon after Bertha's passing."

Instantly sober, Noble rose to a sitting position, his hand resting limply on his upraised knee. "She takin' it hard?"

Tom hunkered down. "She's coping, but it's going to take a while for her to get back to her usual self. I need to be there for her." Ginny had stuck by him through his healing process. He needed to give that back to her.

"She really got to you, didn't she?"

"Is it that obvious?" Tom chuckled. On a serious note, he admitted, "I love her. I didn't want to, didn't plan on ever loving anybody, but Ginny . . ."

"Don't leave ya much of a choice, does she?"

Tom laughed. "No, she doesn't." And it felt good. Better than good. It felt . . . right. Tom could no longer imagine not going to bed with her every night and waking up beside her every dawn. She was all the things he'd shut out from his life. She was everything he had needed a long time ago, but wasn't there. She brought out the good in him. Made him smile. Made him feel like a success even when he failed. With her, he didn't feel tied down or trapped. She showed him a freedom in accepting her love, a freedom of the soul he had never before experienced.

Fate had brought Ginny into his life, and by thunder, he'd do all in his power to keep her there.

Snapping himself out of his mental wanderings, he asked, "So when can you leave?"

"Well, let me up so's I can get dressed first. I ain't about to freeze my hind end off, even for you."

The last chain snapped, freeing Tom from the wall he'd been shackled to for as long as he could remember. And all he wanted to do was run—straight back to Ginny.

"Thank you, Noble. You've been really tolerant of me."

Flipping the blanket off his massive body, Noble grumbled, "Somebody's got to keep fools safe from themselves."

Back at the farm, Tom was greeted by a miserable bawling. One glance at the darkened house told him Ginny hadn't yet wakened. After the turmoil of the last couple of weeks, she needed sleep as desperately as the Jersey needed milking.

Tom curried and fed the dun, then tied the cow's lead rope to a post. As he milked the cow he couldn't get rid of the stupid grin he wore. Why had he spent so much time fighting her?

David came barreling through the doors, his face wild with disbelief. "I've been lookin' all over for you—something happened to Miss Ginny!"

Tom shot up so fast the milking stool flew halfway across the floor. The cow kicked the bucket, spraying milk all over the walls. "Is she all right?" What the hell could have happened? Less than an hour ago she'd been sleeping contentedly in their bed—

"She's . . . hummin'! And smilin'!"

Once his heart started beating again, his chest swelled with humble pride and a crooked grin tugged at his lips. "She is, huh?"

"Ya gotta see her. I ain't seen her this happy since the day you came home."

Yeah, he had to see her. He'd never had anybody humming and smiling after a night spent with him before.

She was standing at the stove, singing a lively polka tune in German. The instant she heard the door she turned around and saw him.

Tom's blood rushed through his veins, there was a roaring in his ears. She glowed. He'd heard men crudely boast of women they'd been with blooming with color in the aftermath of lovemaking, but Tom hadn't witnessed it himself until now.

Until Ginny.

And her eyes sparkled. He knew it would be a long time before she fully recovered from her grandmother's death, but this was the first sign of life he'd seen in weeks. He couldn't stem the tiny surge of masculine arrogance that maybe he'd been partly responsible.

Setting the bucket down, Tom swaggered across the kitchen

to stand in front of her. She didn't touch him. He didn't touch her. He just looked into her shining eyes and she looked into his. That invisible string she claimed connected them reeled him in and wound around him.

Her cheeks turned even rosier, her lashes dropped. If Tom didn't know her better he'd have sworn she was embarrassed.

He gave her a lopsided grin and took the fork from her hand. Then he swept her into his arms and twirled her around in a circle. She squealed in delight.

Lowering her until her feet touched the floor, he kissed her tenderly, felt her mouth cling to his for several long, heart-thundering seconds before he released her. "Welcome home, Ginny."

32

$\mathcal{H}$E'D ALREADY FIGURED out that the women of Ridgeford were a conniving bunch, but as Tom drove another wedge into a frozen block of ice, he couldn't help but reflect on how he'd gotten himself maneuvered into this latest scheme.

Dawn had barely broken over the horizon when Ginny had jostled his shoulder. "Wake up, Thomas! It is harvest time!"

"Harvest?" he'd wailed petulantly, trying to burrow further between quilts still warm from their combined body heat. "It's the middle of winter."

She flipped the blanket off his face. "The pond, silly! We must break the ice and store it in the shed or we will have no ice in the summer!"

Brows wiggling, he countered, "Why would we want to spend the whole day cutting ice when we can spend it lighting fires?"

"It will be fun, you shall see."

Only Ginny could find enjoyment in backbreaking labor. With a resigned sigh, he pulled her into his arms. "I always knew you were crazy."

The devilish gleam in her eyes turned tender. "Crazy for you." She brushed his lips with her fingertips, then lowered her mouth over his. . . .

And that was all the persuasion he'd needed. Except now, instead of lighting fires with Ginny back at the farm, he was suffering frostbite on his rear end in the middle of a frozen pond.

It was the second harvest of the season, the first having taken place before the blizzard hit and Bertha grew so ill. Around him, Ginny and her friends worked together like a well-oiled machine. She'd told him it was tradition, and watching their competent teamwork, he could understand how they'd managed to bring in four successful crops during his absence.

Young and old and in between, each of the ten villagers present performed a task according to their ability. Evie Mae and Dolores handled the horses. They began at one end of the pond, guiding their teams across the ice. An apparatus much like a plow, only with flat, crescent-shaped blades, scraped the snow toward the banks. Once the surface had been cleared, another two pairs of horses, one starting at the north end, the other heading from the east, dragged a hacksawlike blade across the ice, scoring it into blocks.

He learned quickly that his opinion didn't count, either. Only his brawn. With a loud crack, the block he'd been splitting separated from the mass. Behind him, Vernice and Mary used long iron poles to propel the ice down the watery channel, where Doreen and David sank grappling hooks into the blocks and hauled them up a plank ramp.

At the end of the day, when the last foot-by-foot square had been towed out for transporting to the icehouse tomorrow morning, a victorious whoop rent the air.

Even Blue caught the excitement, bounding between the horses' legs, yapping up a storm until the mighty swish of a long-stranded tail sent him reeling end over end into a snowdrift.

Muscles Tom didn't even know he had felt as if they'd been put through a meat grinder as he picked his way around the bank. A goodly distance away from the pond, a huge bonfire shot a fountain of golden sparks skyward. The "petticoat crew," as he'd begun to think of the women, were gathered around a smaller fire where a bubbling cauldron gave off a fine, yeasty mist.

He laid his wedge and hammer in the wooden box housing the rest of the tools and made the mistake of heading toward them. "Looks like you got a head start on me," he observed, taking a sip of the warm beer Mary Kirkmiller handed him.

"It's part of the tradition."

"Look, ladies, we got us a man in our midst," Dolores slurred.

The sound of her voice was Tom's only warning before the horde of women descended on him. In a matter of moments he was surrounded. Hands pawed at his coat, tousled his hair. Horrified when Dolores crammed her wet, beer-flavored mouth onto his, Tom glanced wildly around for Ginny.

She wedged herself between the tight gathering of bodies and came to stand at his side. Amusement danced in her eyes. "My friends, I am afraid you must find your own man. This one belongs to me."

Her arm circled his shoulders in a possessive embrace that gave his spirit wings. How did she do it? How did she manage to capture him and set him free at the same time?

"Ain't no fair, Ginny," Dolores whined. "Friends are suppo—*hic*—supposed to share!"

As she led him toward the wagon, Tom shuddered. "I thought they were gonna rip my clothes clean off me."

Ginny planted the heels of her hands on the tailgate and boosted herself into the bed, then ran her palms up his chest. "Hmmm, I cannot say I blame them," she said in a sultry whisper that sent Tom's blood pressure soaring. "A man as fine as you creates quite a stir among women long without male companionship."

Her words inflamed banked needs. He wrapped his fingers around her wrists. "Don't, Ginny. There's only so much a man can take."

"Tell me when you have reached your limit," she purred.

His desire mirrored itself in her eyes. Tom felt himself sink into the dark abyss of denim blue. He combed his fingers through the hair at her temples, knocking the hood loose so it fell around her shoulders. He couldn't seem to stop touching her.

Slurred voices and inebriated giggles faded as the world

narrowed, becoming only him and this beautiful, strong-hearted woman.

Their lashes lowered, their faces drifted toward one another—

"Okay, let's go home." He grabbed her hand, whistled at David to collect Doreen and Blue.

Giggling, Ginny protested, "Thomas, we cannot leave them here." She made a sweeping gesture toward the passel of stumbling women. "In their condition, one may fall into the pond."

Damn. But Ginny was right. He'd never be able to live with himself if something happened to one of the women because of his own selfishness. "Let's load them up in the wagon, then. The sooner we get them back to their places, the sooner we can return to our own place."

"You said 'our.'"

"Did I?" He grinned like an idiot. Yet that's how he felt right now. Like a mindless idiot. All she had to do was look at him and he was tempted beyond reason. But when she touched him . . . thunderation, he was as lost a cause as Southern succession.

His thoughts were so fixed on the night ahead that he practically tossed each of the women into the wagon bed. Then, with David's help, he unhitched the other horses from their traces. They could leave the wagons behind until morning. He had more important things planned for tonight.

Once all the gear had been gathered, he sent David and Doreen on ahead with the animals, to the village.

Tom then climbed into the wagon and followed. Ginny curled up beside him, leaning her head on his shoulder. He reached over and tugged the blanket closer around her neck. The temperature had dropped with the fall of darkness. The last thing he needed was for Ginny to catch a chill.

"I did not realize how much I missed being outside until today."

The fresh air had done wonders for her, too, Tom noticed. Beneath her hood, tousled flaxen hair bunched around her face. Healthy color stained her cheeks. Her eyes were bright and temporarily clear of grief.

She looked young and refreshed and tempting as hell.

Needing a distraction from her irresistible charms lest he tumble her in the closest snowbank, he searched the darkness for the youngsters. "I don't see the kids. Are you sure Doreen is ready to ride by herself?"

"She is fine, Thomas. David is with her, he will not let anything happen to her."

The wheels rolled with a steady rumble over the frozen ruts. Behind them, the women let loose a chorus of drunken laughter but Tom and Ginny paid no notice.

"He's in love with her—did you know that?"

Her mouth dropped opened in shock. "But they are only children!"

"He's a young man. Bright, ambitious. And she's a beautiful girl. So much like her mother that I'm sure she knows exactly what she wants, too."

"I know what I want right now." Her mouth latched onto his earlobe.

"Behave yourself or we'll never get home."

With a cheeky grin, she settled back against his side. "Now that you mention it, I was not much older than David when I fell in love with you."

A sharp twinge of jealousy joined the pained jab to his chest at the reminder that she'd loved another man.

But maybe Bertha was right. Maybe everything did happen for a reason. If Ginny had never loved Herz so completely, so blindly, she might not ever have moved heaven and earth to be reunited with him. Would not have mistaken Tom for him. And Tom would never have known what he had been missing all these years.

To his way of thinking, Herz had his chance and he'd missed it. Now his loss was Tom's gain.

Shaking his head, Tom decided that their optimism must be rubbing off on him. He tightened his hold on Ginny's hand, brushed his lips across her temple. "You've done a fine job raising her."

"It means much hearing you say that. I had hoped you would be proud of her."

"I wish I could've been there to watch her grow up." And he meant it. He wished he could've seen Doreen's first tiny steps—though knowing her exuberance, she'd gone straight from a crawl to a run.

"You are here now, that is what matters." Cocking her head to the side, Ginny ventured, "Would you like to have another baby, Thomas?"

A picture of Ginny swollen with his child made Tom's spirits soar. Just as quickly, a curl of panic wended its way through his blood. It was one thing adopting a ready-made family, another starting one from scratch. Especially under the circumstances. What if, by some cruel stroke of fate, Herz came back to claim Ginny? Or what if he lost her in childbirth like he'd lost his mother? He didn't voice either of those fears, but did admit another. "I don't know if I'd make a very good father."

"Of course you would, silly! You are the most gentle man I have ever known."

Tom's brows rose in amazement. "Me? Gentle?"

"Oh, you try to hide it, but I know how often you look in on the children during the night to make sure they are warm. I also notice how you are very careful not to raise your voice around David, and how you pretend to love Doreen's burned bacon. And what of the way you stand in the cold when the puppy needs to go outside?" She brushed a strand of his wind-blown hair back over his forehead. "And I have not begun to describe the gentleness you show me—in public and in private."

"Has anyone ever told you that flattery will get you anything you want?" he accused with an amused grin.

"I have learned a few tricks from my friends," she quipped.

Tom lost his grin at the sight of two carriages in the distance, one a gleaming black buggy, the other a more ragged-looking shay. Both blocked the mouth of the bridge, barring their path home.

Ginny must have seen them, too, for she laid a mittened hand on his sleeve. "Thomas? That looks like Herr Marks's buggy."

"Who does the other carriage belong to?"

Just then, two men alighted from the vehicles, one from one, one from the other. Like their own wagon, the wheels had been removed and replaced with skids.

"That first man is definitely Marks. I have never seen the other one before. What if he is T. W.?"

"Who's T. W.?"

"He is the man they send to persuade the landowners to sell when they balk."

"Why didn't you tell me before?" he demanded.

"Because I thought the situation had been taken care of! After all, we have heard naught from Marks for weeks!"

He shook his head in exasperation. "We really need to work on your timing."

"Tom Heart!" a voice rang out.

"Stay here—" A burst of inebriated laughter from the bed of the wagon interrupted his speech. "And by thunder, keep them contained or I'll bind and gag them!" The last thing Tom needed was for the village women to interfere in this situation the way they'd interfered in his and Ginny's relationship— although they deserved a round of thanks for that now.

Walking toward the duo was like being caught in a snow- storm naked. The only weapon on his person was the knife strapped to his side. As Tom approached, he figured he could take on the first one easily. But the brute at his side would give even Noble a helluva contest.

Tom directed his attention to the first man but kept alert to every move the other made. Right now his attention was fixed on the bevy of boisterous beauties draped over each side of the wagon.

"Can I help you gentlemen?"

"I had hoped we could form an alliance, Mr. Heart, but it seems you are reluctant to do business with the good people of Marksville. That wasn't very neighborly of you to return one of our men with a bullet in his leg."

Got me a Reb, Lieutenant. Caught him sneakin' round by the springhouse. Any sympathy for the victim Tom had felt upon hearing Auggie's boast scattered in the wind. He didn't bother correcting the man by telling him Auggie had been the sharp- shooter—it was a moot point. "Didn't seem very neighborly of your hireling to sneak around on private property."

"You appear a reasonable man, Mr. Heart. . . ."

Tom coiled in readiness when the man reached into his pocket. But instead of the firearm Tom expected, the man held a wad of rolled bills in his palm.

"Tell me how much you want for your property—I am sure we can come to an agreement."

"You're wasting your time, Mr.—"

"Marks. I am the founder of Marksville, to the north. This is Mr. Henry, my associate."

Tom slanted a glance at the big bear of a man beside Marks. Henry grinned at Evie Mae, who was waving her hand alongside the outer frame of the wagon, inviting him over. The gleam of hunger in his eyes was unmistakable.

"I am offering a peaceable solution," Marks said. "Just name your price."

Rather than repeat that he wouldn't give up his property for all the gold found in Sutter's Mill, Tom assessed the dyed black beaver-fur coat Marks wore and the glitter of gold cuff links visible between his sleeve and glove. Because of this man's greed, Doreen had been scared witless and David injured.

One glance at the hulking Henry, though, made Tom reconsider starting what would surely become a brawl. He couldn't risk the safety of his family or any of the women temporarily under his care.

After studying the women, then sizing up Marks through narrowed eyes, he hedged, "Are you a gambling man, Mr. Marks?"

The digressive question took him by surprise. "I am known to engage in games of chance now and then—if the stakes are high enough."

"On my wife's finger is a very unique ring—Ginny, come here, please?"

She said something to her friends, then slipped down from the box and strolled gracefully toward Tom. The gaze she turned to him held questions he couldn't take the time to answer.

"Give me your ring."

Immediately Ginny covered the band.

"Just for a moment," Tom assured her, even though his heart wrenched at the thought of returning another man's ring to her finger. "You'll get it back, you have my word."

Magic words. Without hesitation she twisted the band off her finger, leaving a pale reminder on her flesh.

A lantern hung from a wrought-iron holder on Marks's buggy. Tom held the golden circle up to the light. "If you can guess which of these obliging ladies is holding this, I will *give* you the deed to my farm—all one hundred and forty acres."

Ginny gasped.

"Toss my land in the pot, too, Tom!" Mary Kirkmiller cried.

After sparing a grateful look at Mary for her supportive consent, Tom continued, "If you guess wrong, neither you nor any hirelings in your employ will ever so much as breathe on a wind blowing through Ridgeford."

A glitter of contemplation appeared in Marks's black eyes. Henry, unable to resist the scent of the women, lumbered toward the wagon.

"Oh, my, you're a whole lotta man, aren't you?" Dolores leaned over the side and purred to the giant. Her voice was slurred, her eyes glassy as she ran her hands up his barrel-shaped chest. "In case you ain't noticed, I'm a whole lotta woman."

When Dolores winked lazily, Tom grinned at the man's expression. He looked ready to erupt, probably very much like Tom suspected he looked when Ginny turned her charms on him.

"What about the woman holding it?" Henry asked, licking his fleshy lips. "She part of the deal, too?"

"That's entirely up to the lady. But my wife—" His voice broke on that one word. He tugged Ginny closer to his side in a possessive gesture. "My wife will not be among the participants." Addressing Marks, Tom said, "Your odds are one in four, Marks."

"And if I don't agree to the bet?"

"Then you'll be dodging bullets every time you so much as pass within twenty miles of this village."

Marks motioned for Henry to join him a few feet away. Snippets of their conference drifted toward Tom.

"Last chance . . . petition . . . thrown out tomorrow . . ."

". . . kill him?"

At that, Ginny stiffened. Tom squeezed her hand, silently communicating for her to trust him. He knew what he was doing—he hoped.

The minutes crawled by while they waited for Marks to either accept or decline the proposal. Tom wished Noble was back from the city. He'd feel a helluva lot more confident with a bit of Noble's strength in his corner if the need arose. But he didn't expect his friend back until late the next evening.

Finally Marks faced him once more. With a simple nod, he gave his agreement. With Marks's permission, Tom asked Doreen to gather Vernice, Evie Mae, Dolores, and Mary together and give one of them the ring.

Tom wasn't sure who enjoyed the ploy more—the women-smitten men or the men-starved women. He witnessed more wanton winks and seductive smiles than he could shake a stick at. As if in competition, the bolder one woman got the bolder the others got, until Tom wondered how Marks and his cohort walked straight, much less thought straight.

Beside him Ginny covered her mouth with her hand, stifling her giggles. But her dancing eyes revealed that she was enjoying the game as much as if not more than her flirtatious friends.

Finally Marks pointed toward Vernice Warren, who had remained the tamest of the four—which didn't say much. She immediately went tight with guilt.

Ginny gasped.

Tom's heart stopped pumping. His farm—all that he had built both for himself and in memory of his brother, all that he hoped would make him worthy in Ginny's eyes—was gone. Ashes.

And all because he'd tempted fate.

33

*N*OT A *SOUND* broke the tension as Tom watched Vernice slowly unfold her palm. Ginny clutched his hand, her nails biting into the skin on his knuckles.

It was empty. Tom closed his eyes momentarily. Vernice didn't have the ring. He still owned 140 of the most fertile acres in the Great Lakes region. He still had something to offer Ginny.

But . . . if Vernice didn't have the ring . . . One glance at Evie Mae Johnson's mischievous grin and Tom wondered how he hadn't figured it out before.

Then she smiled. Through closed teeth, Evie said, "Gentlemen?" She opened her mouth. Ginny's ring fell into her palm.

A sudden gust of relieved laughter burst from Ginny's mouth.

"You cheated!" Marks blustered.

"Nobody said we had to hold it in our hands," Evie pointed out, wiping off the ring and turning it over to Ginny.

Tom forced himself not to watch her jam it back on her finger. Instead he kept his attention trained on Marks and his bear-like accomplice. They argued the entire time it took them to jostle into their respective buggies. Only when they'd disappeared into the black mouth of the bridge, and the clattering of wheels faded into the night, did Tom release a shaky sigh of relief.

"I am so proud of you."

He lifted his head and looked at Ginny. Her eyes were filled with adoration.

"It would have been so easy to bring harm to them, but instead you used Marks's own greed against him. You beat him at his own game."

"I've seen enough blood shed in my lifetime. I had no wish to spill more."

"But you were willing to risk your farm! What would you have done if he had chosen Evie Mae?"

"Then we would have started another farm," he said with forced optimism. "It doesn't matter where we go, Ginny, as long as we're together."

Her smile took his breath away. She was a compelling combination of soldier of fortune and angel of mercy. Someone who hunted down their quarry with fierce determination, only to disarm them with sensitivity and kindness. She would not only withstand the worst life had to offer, but make the best of it.

How could he ever have thought sharing his life would be degrading? She never tried to enslave him, as others had done. She only wanted to be his helpmate. "What did I ever do to deserve you?"

"You were born under a lucky star," she said flippantly.

"You have no clue what you've done for me, do you?"

With a puzzled expression, she shook her head back and forth in quick, tiny movements.

"No one has ever loved me the way you have, Ginny." He took her palm, laid it flat against his chest. "I didn't have a heart—you gave me one."

With a sad smile, she said, "Four of them."

"I didn't have a soul—you found me one."

"It was at home where you left it."

Leaning low, he drew her face close. Their warm breaths mingled, creating an intimate steam in the wintry air. She did this to him—lit a fire in a place that had needed fire.

And he knew in that moment that he never wanted to feel the cold again. "Marry me, Ginny."

"Silly Thomas, we are already married."

No, Tom thought, she had married a man who walked out of her life a dozen years ago, never to be seen again. Either Herz decided that marriage to Ginny wasn't for him, or he was dead and they hadn't located the source to confirm it. If that was the case then any children Ginny might bear with him would carry the disgrace of illegitimacy. If Herz had started a new life with no intention of sending for his German bride, then Ginny would never learn of it. He'd make sure of it. Why give her cause for more anguish? "Wouldn't you like to be married on American soil?" he tempted her, knowing her affinity for their adopted country.

"But there is no ordained minister in town," Ginny pointed out. "The women take turns preaching on Sunday."

He cocked his head and raised one amused brow.

Ginny giggled. "When they are sober, of course. We like to maintain some sense of tradition on Sundays. However, they do not have the authority to conduct a wedding."

"Then I know of a minister in Minnow Falls. I'm sure he won't mind making the trip out to perform the ceremony, and if he isn't willing, then we'll find someone else who does have the authority."

She studied him curiously. Tom's heart picked up speed as he waited for her answer. After several moments of her remaining silent, he dropped his gaze. What the hell ever made him think she'd want to tie herself to him after all he'd done to drive her away?

Holding his chin, she forced him to look at her. "This is truly important to you?" she asked. "Exchanging our vows again on American soil?"

"I just want to make sure you'll always be mine."

She tilted her head to the side. "Of course I will. We are heartbound, remember?"

Her smile was so enchanting that he swore his heart leaped from his chest and fell into her palm. He'd never felt like this before. Completely wanted, in every sense of the word. As if he belonged to her. "Well? Will you marry me or not?"

Ginny didn't need to think twice about her answer. And as spring struggled to make its entrance through the thawing ground, Ginny wondered if anybody had a right to be as happy as she was. She had two wonderful children, a prosperous farm, and a loving husband who proved to her daily that the best things in life were worth waiting for.

Humming an old German ballad, she finished packing a basket with enough edibles to tide over two ravenous men until they reached Minnow Falls.

She still found it hard to believe that Thomas was determined to see them married again. But she had to admit, since she had consented to exchanging vows for the second time, the last of his reserve had slipped away.

Over the last two months, he had grown increasingly considerate of her, much as the old Thomas had been, and yet there was a difference. She found herself willing to lean on him so much more now than when he was younger. Back then it seemed she had needed to be the strong one, for he had been consumed with his dreams. Striving for perfection and unable to handle failure.

They had complemented each other, though. If he neglected something in the pursuit of his goals, she gave it attention. If he failed to accomplish a task to his satisfaction, she fixed it.

Now, he was the one being attentive. He was the one making things better. He was the strong one. He seemed more courageous in his wants, made her feel that whatever life doled out, they could brave it together.

This was the man she'd always thought he would become. And now that he had, well, sweet mercy, who could ask for more?

A whistling from the direction of the front door attracted her attention. Thomas walked in. As always, her heartbeat quickened at the sight of him. The winter months had added weight to his undernourished form and given his muscles more substance. His light brown hair, though collar length in the back, was kept trimmed around the clean-shaven face she woke up to every morning.

Smiling brightly at her good fortune, Ginny lifted the basket in one hand and picked up the marketing list with the other. She felt a burst of pride in herself as she scanned the English words, and gratitude toward Thomas for teaching her the language of their adopted country.

He'd been right, all those years ago. America was the land where dreams were made.

"The horses are hitched and itching to go."

Handing him her list, she said, "Do not forget the taffeta. I need it to finish my wedding costume."

"Are you sure you just don't want to go with me? We could ignore all this hoopla your friends have got cooking and have Reverend Mason perform the ceremony in his church."

"Now, Thomas," Ginny chided, "everybody is anxious to see the ceremony."

"If Evie Mae is planning a shivaree, I swear I'm gonna lock *her* in the icehouse! The last thing I want on my wedding night is to wind up listening to someone beating on kettles when I'm trying to make lo—"

"Thomas!" Ginny whispered loudly as Doreen walked in.

He ran his hands up her hips and cradled her against him. "She can't hear us, Ginny."

"No, but she can read your lips, silly!"

"So can you. Tell me what I'm saying right now."

She pressed her hands against this chest, stopping him from kissing her lest he begin something they could not finish. "*Liebling*, I have a hundred things to do before the planting season, and you are keeping me from getting them done!"

"Maybe when we start sowing one field, we could start sowing another." He winked.

Ginny's eyes widened as his meaning sank in. Then she threw her arms around him and buried her face against his shoulder. Each time she had brought up having another baby, Thomas found a way to avoid the subject. He never explained his reservations, except to say that it simply was not the right time, they would discuss it after repeating their vows. Sometimes Ginny wondered if he worried about misfortune falling on another of their children as it had on Doreen. If so, he seemed to have put to rest his concerns. Or mayhap he simply accepted that everything in life happened for a reason.

Angling her face so she could look into his, she could not resist teasing him. "Mayhap the crops will be especially plentiful this season. Twins do run in your family, if you recall."

The expression of startled horror on his face made her laughter peal across Heart lands.

It took Tom several minutes to recover from the powerful sensation Ginny's laughter created. He cupped her cheek with his hand. The feeling inside seemed too good and pure to last.

"What is it, Thomas?"

"What?"

"You are looking at me strangely."

"I . . ." No—he couldn't let himself think that way. This would last. If he ever slacked in that belief, Ginny would take up the reins. She had enough faith for the both of them. His voice dropped to a shaky whisper. "*Ich liebe dich*, Ginny. More than anything that has come into my life, I love you."

"And I love you, *Liebling*. Now hurry and go so you can hurry and come back."

Chuckling, Tom kissed her tenderly, wanting to always give her the peace she gave him. "I miss you already."

David raced through the door just then. "Mr. Tom, there's a man outside who says he's a friend of yours."

Tom didn't bother asking who; his eyes were on Ginny. "Tell him I'll be out in a minute." He couldn't resist one last taste of her. She welcomed him as she always did. Matched his greed. Dragged her fingers through the hair at his nape while his own hands cupped her bottom and drew her tight against him. The fever she created in his heart and loins warmed him from the inside out.

And he knew if he didn't leave now, David would get an eyeful of something boys his age only dreamed of.

Just as he began to pull back, he felt Ginny stiffen in his arms. "Thomas?" she gasped.

Alarm slammed into Tom when he saw the ashen color on Ginny's face. He slowly twisted and looked over his shoulder.

He always thought when a man took a shot, it would hurt. It didn't. It turned him numb.

In the doorway, standing beside Gene Mason, a stranger leaned heavily on a gnarled switch cane, his face a frozen mask of fury.

"Get your hands off my wife."

34

$\mathcal{G}$INNY LET HER hands fall slowly from Thomas's shoulders. Her gaze never left the irate man a few feet away. Looking at him, she felt nothing except a vague sense of detachment, as if the blood in her veins had turned to a misty fog and she no longer had control of her own functionings.

"Step away from him, Ginny."

The German accent, tamed but still evident, sent a bolt of unease down her spine. How did he know her name?

Brows knitting together, she sought Thomas's gaze. He would not meet her eyes. His face had gone white as one of Oma's mobcaps, too, though his expression was unreadable.

Out of habit, Ginny took charge of the situation and turned to the visitors in the doorway. The one missing his arm seemed as perplexed as she. The one wearing a thick flannel shirt and twill trousers acted alarmingly possessive. It was he she sensed posed the greater threat. "What do you want?"

Sparse brows lifted a fraction. "To collect you, of course. Did you think once Herr Mason told me you were in America searching for me that I would not come for you?"

"I do not understand. I have never met Herr Mason. Why would I ask him to look for you?"

"You didn't, Ginny," Thomas said softly beside her. "I did. I . . ." He swallowed roughly. "I launched a search for Thomas Herz last November."

In gradual waves, a roaring began in her ears. She felt the color leave her lips and a lightness fill her head. "But . . . *you* are Thomas Herz."

"No, Ginny." When he lifted his gaze to hers, she saw such profound despair that her soul began to weep. "My name has always been, and always will be, Tom Heart."

Tom caught her limp body just before she crumpled to the ground. Wild-eyed, he sought help from Gene.

Herz came forward instead.

"Get away from her!" Tom snarled, cradling Ginny possessively against his chest. "You lost the right to touch her when you deserted her twelve years ago."

Pain slashed through the man's small hazel eyes, then quickly vanished. "Did Ginny tell you that?"

"No," Tom spat. "You had her convinced you'd bought land and were farming it. That you planned to send for her. We know the truth, though, don't we, Herz?"

"Lieutenant?" Gene interceded. "What's going on?"

"Damn it, Gene! Why wasn't the search called off?"

He shook his head in confusion. "What are you talking about, sir?"

"Noble left a message with your father two months ago, telling you to call the whole thing off."

Gene blanched. "My father is a traveling minister. He'd already left for his circuit by the time I got back from checking out another futile lead. I never received any message."

And it was too damn late to do anything about that now. The damage was done. Jerking his thumb toward Herz, Tom asked, "How did you find him?"

"I kept going over the names. He goes by T. W. Hurts, H-U-R-T-S. He was under our noses the whole time—right in Minnow Falls. I just didn't realize it. I mean, I was looking for a farmer. . . ."

Oh, God, T. W. Hurts. Thomas Herz. Marks's hireling and Ginny's husband were one and the same.

"You son of a bitch." He sneered at the man through a haze of pure loathing. "Get off my land."

Herz reached for Ginny. "Not without my wife."

Tom clutched her tiny frame tighter against his chest, leaving no question in Herz's mind to whom she belonged to now. "If you think I'm just gonna hand her over to you after all the misery you've caused—as if abandoning your pregnant wife isn't bad enough, you nearly killed two innocent children!"

"I had no idea those children were nearby!"

He probably had no idea one was his own flesh and blood, either, Tom thought with disgust. He'd been too busy kicking puppies in his lifetime to give any consideration to the daughter he'd left Ginny to raise by herself.

Aghast, Gene asked, "Good God, Lieutenant, what has he done?"

"He's a ruffie-for-hire. He's been the one responsible for convincing the local farmers to sell their lands to C. R. Marks—unwillingly, I might ad."

"I had no choice. The job paid good money. All I needed was a little more time and I would have had enough to send for Ginny."

"Twelve years wasn't long enough? What the hell kind of man are you?"

Herz seemed impervious to Tom's scorn. "I had already been saving to send for her when Herr Mason notified me that Ginny was here. I have come to take her home."

"She doesn't love you anymore, Herz. She won't go with you willingly."

"Then you do not know my Ginny as well as you think. She loves to the bone. And once I explain why I did not send for her sooner, she will forgive me."

That's what scared Tom the most.

Panic and desperation wove their way through every fiber of his body. "What do you want—the farm? You can have it. Every last fertile acre. Just walk away and pretend you never met Ginny."

"I cannot do that. The land means nothing without the woman I love."

The words lit a fuse. The keg of pent-up loathing inside Tom exploded as he sent his fist crashing into Herz's jaw. Herz reeled backward and landed on the floor in a heap of flannel and twill, while his cane skittered across the bare floor.

Raking Herz with a look of pure loathing, he stated, "She doesn't need your kind of love."

Herz rose wobblingly onto one arm and touched his torn lip. A trickle of blood ran down his chin, but Tom didn't feel any satisfaction, only a powerful contempt and a spread of foreboding he couldn't corral. And as he shook out his fingers, he wished that Auggie had saved them a whole lot of grief by aiming higher.

He sat at one end of the sofa, his thin shoulders hunched around his face, a ragged straw hat dangling limply from his fingers. Her trembling hands clenched tightly in her lap, Ginny sat at the other end, waiting for him to speak.

Funny, she thought with a peculiar sense of surrealism, the two men had very little in common physically. Thomas had a full scalp of thick light brown hair; Herz was bald, except for a ring of limp strands around the back of his head. Thomas had a sloping jaw and clean-shaven cheeks so his whiskers wouldn't chafe her face; Herz had a double chin and sideburns. But the eyes were the biggest difference. Thomas's were the color of copper pennies, shiny and new; Herz's were a dull green-brown of failure.

Thomas resembled the man she'd married more than the man himself did.

"Did you lay with him?"

The moment she had been dreading would not be put off any longer. Memories assaulted her. Her nostrils flared, her eyes stung, her lips trembled. "Yes," she whispered, her throat burning with unshed tears.

His eyes closed. His throat worked as if it hurt him to swallow. "How could you, Ginny? Did our vows mean so little?"

Her mouth fell open with disbelief. Then shame filled her every pore for causing him pain. "It was not intentional. When I came to America, I mistook another man's farm for yours." Ginny ran her tongue over her dry lips. She twisted the ring on her finger, hoping to find courage in the entwined hearts engraved in the band. "I . . . I believed he was you." Even to her own ears, it sounded like such a weak excuse for committing the unforgivable. Yet it was her only defense.

Murky eyes mocked the faith she had held on to for so long. The faith she had clung to during the most trying times in her life. Faith that he would be building a future for them.

Suddenly, all her confusion and rage and heartache came gushing forth. "Why did you not send for me? I waited and I waited—you promised to send for me and you did not!"

He said nothing. No explanations, no assurances that he had not forgotten her, nothing. And she knew from his silence that he had not tried to contact her. "You never had any intention of sending for me, did you?"

"Not until I had something to offer you." Anguish tinged his accent as he went on. "But it seems you found another who could. Tell me, was it his handsome face or his padded pockets that attracted you?"

She did not waste her breath correcting his mistaken impression that her relationship with Thomas was based on greed. He had no idea of Thomas's sad state of affairs before he had gone off to war, nor did she think he wished to hear of it. Instead she asked a question of her own. "Would you rather that your daughter and I be living on the streets? That nearly happened. Would have had I not found this place." And had Thomas not taken them in.

"But you do not belong here, Ginny, and you do not belong to him." He rocked the hat upon his balding pate and rose to his feet, leaning heavily on the cane. "Now if you will please gather your things, I wish to leave this place."

Ginny sent him a startled glance. He still wanted her even after she had been unfaithful to him?

Misunderstanding her surprise, his mouth settled into a grim line. "Do not worry, Ginny. You will be free to return to your lover's arms soon enough."

"What do you mean?"

"By the time the season ends, you will be a widow. That should please you greatly."

* * *

Entering the bedroom he shared with Ginny, Tom took in the sight of the open trunk, the neat pile of clothes beside a small case on the bed.

Her back stiff, her head bowed, Ginny took special care folding one of her blood-stirring outer corsets and laying it precisely in the bag.

His hands went sweaty. His throat went dry. His heart started to thunder in his chest like the hooves of a runaway horse.

"What are you doing, Ginny?"

"Packing."

"Why?"

"You never lost your memory in the war," she stated flatly, without looking at him.

"I never said I did, Ginny. You came to that conclusion. Nothing I said made any difference."

"But you said you remembered!" she cried, twisting around at the waist and facing him. Her forehead was crinkled as she fought the truth, yet her eyes reflected anguish. "And I believed you . . . the spoons . . . the spoons were the same!"

Confession time. No excuses, no postponements. Tom knew there was no way of avoiding it—not anymore. "I never had time to fall in love with a little orchard girl and give her spoons, Ginny. I was too busy trying to survive."

She watched him with a look of the lost. Bewildered. Betrayed. Knowing she needed to hear the truth, Tom sought to get his thoughts in order. "My mother was Austrian, my father French, from Alsace. His name was William Heart. He was killed for treason shortly after my mother died in childbirth."

Tom forged ahead before he changed his mind. "I had a brother once, too—one brother, Ginny, not six. Matthew and I spent a lot of our childhood in orphanages but mostly we kept to the streets, getting by the best we could. We always dreamed of some place to call our own, where we couldn't be persecuted like our father had been for what we believed in.

"One day we met up with a man who convinced us that a whole new life waited for us in America. He would buy our passage, and we would work it off when we got to the States. We thought this was the perfect opportunity, so we agreed.

Except my brother didn't live long enough to carry out his dream. He died on the ship. Since his passage had already been paid, I became responsible for both his contract and mine."

Recollecting the longest four years of his life, Tom shuddered and wandered to the window where Gene's carriage stood out in the yard like an omen. And he knew that if he and Ginny had half a chance of staying together, he had to be completely honest with her—and himself. "The man I was sent to wasn't very nice," Tom went on. "He beat the people that worked for him, Ginny, he beat them really bad."

"The scars . . ."

"Anybody who tried to escape before they'd paid off their passage got chained to a wall inside the factory and beaten. They were made examples to the rest of the laborers who might try the same thing. There was a boy about Matthew's age who'd made a run for it. He got caught. He was so skinny . . . the whipping would have killed him—"

"So you took it instead?"

Tom flattened his hands against the sill but said nothing.

"How many times?" she demanded. "How many times did you pay for another's flight?"

"You learn to turn off the pain, Ginny. You learn not to feel anything. And I didn't—not until you came into my life."

"Why did you deceive me? Why did you tell me you remembered when you couldn't have possibly . . . ?"

"Because I'm a selfish bastard who didn't have a soul to care a whit about me until I met you. I didn't want to lose you."

"But you knew all along you were not my husband."

"Ginny, I tried from the start to tell you that you had me mixed up with somebody else—"

"And I would not listen. Oh, *Gott*, why did I not listen?"

Barging forward, Tom seized her cold hands with his own. "Ginny, this doesn't have to change anything. The man deserted you. Any court in the nation would understand and grant you a divorce. Then we can get married. Nobody would ever have to know."

"I cannot, Thomas," she whispered in agony.

He stared at her with incredulous shock. Didn't she realize what he had given up for her? Didn't she have any idea what it had cost him to bare his deepest wounds to her? Didn't she care that he'd opened himself up just to let her inside a place closed to any other human being? "Why not?" he cried as claws of fear scored his soul.

"I have to go with him. I have no choice."

"We all have choices, remember? Some are just harder to make than others because they mean—"

Tom let the sentence go unfinished as tiny seeds of dawning burst inside him.

Because they mean sacrifice.

And Ginny wasn't willing to sacrifice Thomas Herz. Not for anything. Not even for him. Especially not for him. "You are honestly going to leave me for that sorry deserter?"

"I must. No matter his reason for not sending for me, he is my husband, Thomas, in the eyes of God and the law."

"What the hell does that make me?"

She stared at him through eyes moist and filled with desolation. "My heart," she whispered.

He was waiting for her in the carriage below.

Kneeling beside the open trunk her father had made, Ginny let her hand linger on the tiny pearls of the wreath she'd planned to wear next week on her second wedding day. And it occurred to her that she had very nearly committed bigamy.

Why had she blinded herself to the truth all these months? Why had she not heeded the warnings of her mind each time she noticed a difference between the Thomas she once knew and the man she accepted as her husband?

No, she knew why. Because she needed to believe that her love for her husband had been everlasting. Because she could not bear the fact that he would forsake her. And later, when Thomas had "recovered his memory," she believed him because she wanted to believe him. Because she could not accept that she had fallen more deeply in love with him than the man she'd married.

She had betrayed her vows. She had committed unpardonable sins. And now, knowing she must somehow repair the damage she'd caused before Herz died, she must betray her heart.

Ginny closed the trunk, gave one last fond look around the room, and with traveling case in hand, descended the stairs. The sight of him standing by the window in the sitting room filled her with such pain she could hardly bear it.

Heartbound to one.

Duty bound to another.

Then he turned and looked at her. A thousand unspoken words hung in the air between them. His silence frightened her more than any amount of angry bellowing.

He is dying, Thomas. My husband is dying. Please understand. . . .

"Ginny, if you walk out that door, don't bother coming back."

He might as well have sliced open her chest and taken out that which pumped life into her body. For now she felt empty inside, so empty.

She blinked. She swallowed. She turned to Doreen. "It is time to go, *Liebchen.*"

I do not want to leave.

"Doreen, we must."

But I do not want to leave Vati!

As Doreen rushed toward him, Tom instantly knelt and caught her in a rough embrace, burying his face against her shoulder. His nose stung and his eyes went blurry.

"Go with your mother, girl." He couldn't bring himself to tell her to go with her father. In his mind, he had become her father, her daddy.

She backed away from him, blue eyes shimmering with tears and denial. Suddenly she dashed into the sitting room. She returned holding the figurine, and to Ginny's utter horror, she smashed it to the floor. Lying in the center of the shards was the packet.

"My letters!" Ginny gasped.

Doreen ignored her as she tried to force the letters into Tom's hand. *Show her! Show her the writing!*

Shaken, Tom pushed the letters back into her hand. "I can't, Doreen, because I never wrote them."

She backed away, her expression a mixture of disillusionment and pain. Then she threw the letters at his feet and dashed out the door.

With one last, lingering stare, Ginny also turned and walked out of his life.

Deadened legs carried Tom to the doorway. He leaned his shoulder against the frame. As he watched the buggy fade from view, he couldn't believe Ginny would do this to him. To them. Take Doreen, leave David, split their family into "his" and "hers" when it had become "theirs." Take all the happiness they'd found together and just crush it under her foot like an ugly bug.

Tom whirled around and slugged the door.

How could she do this? And why had he refused to listen to his instincts? It had always been Herz who Ginny truly loved, not him.

He punched the door again. The wood splintered. A bone in his hand cracked. He didn't feel any pain. Maybe later he would, but not now, not while he was this numb.

Fine. To hell with her, then. He'd never wanted a wife in the first place. Never asked her to invade his life. Had, in fact, done everything he could possibly think of to drive her away from him.

He was glad she'd gone back to that miserable fool, glad! Now he finally had what he'd always wanted—his freedom.

His forehead hit the busted door. So why'd he feel like crying?

35

*I*T MATTERED LITTLE where the carriage took them. Ginny only knew it was taking her away from Thomas.

Nach, she corrected herself. Not Thomas. Tom. Tom Heart. Fresh pain ripped through her at the memory of his face when she'd walked out of their home. She had made him promise to never leave her—and she had been the one to leave.

She turned her gaze to the sullen man sitting at her side; she could not bear to say his name. Every time she even thought it, it was not his face she saw in her mind, but another's.

How was it possible that he could be her true husband? How could her heart have betrayed her like this? Made her believe that as long as one kept hopes and wishes and dreams alive, all would come true?

As if sensing her despair, Doreen gripped her hand tightly for support, and together they stared out the window. After a while, certain landmarks began to register to Ginny's mind and she recognized the route to Minnow Falls. How different the scenery looked since the last time she had made the trip. Marshes of slender, brown-coned cattail stalks were half-hidden in a haze of fine drizzle. Bare, drab-barked trees seemed shrouded in a mysterious mist. Geese flying in V formation through a cloud-riddled sky called out the lonesome wail of the lost.

Herr Mason finally left them off in front of a windowless stone structure. The base of the building was water-stained and gave off a fetid odor.

Her husband led them through an alleyway. Reaching a rear addition built of logs, he unlocked a door and it swung open on leather hinges.

Ginny received her first glimpse of her new house. Scouting out the one-room dwelling, she tried not to compare it with the rambling home she'd left behind. *Open fields and sawdust and baked bread. Distant bluffs and cows lowing and hands learning to sign . . .*

Her husband's quarters held many conveniences lacking on the farm, the most notable being an indoor water closet, visible through an open door to her right—the only door in the house, for that matter. A single bed was pushed up against the same wall as a ceiling-high mahogany clothespress and a shiny sheet-iron stove Oma would have drooled over. Crates beside it were sparsely stocked with jars and cans. In the middle of the room a plain round table constituted the dining area.

He said nothing to her as he dropped her bag on a rag rug just inside the door and limped heavily into the room. In fact, he had said nothing at all since leaving the farm hours earlier. The presence of Gene Mason in the carriage left them no privacy, but now she wondered if he planned on giving her this silent treatment as some sort of punishment.

Ginny shut her eyes against the remorse twisting inside her. She did not blame him if he never spoke a single word to her, though. How he must have felt, finding her living with another man. . . .

"Doreen Herz, you will respect another's privacy in this house!"

Her eyes snapped open and she saw Doreen leap back from the blaze of anger in her father's eyes as he slammed shut the door to the tall clothespress. But Ginny did not know which part of the statement startled her more—hearing Doreen called

"Herz" when they had called themselves "Heart" for so long, or the disparaging tone Herz used in speaking to his daughter.

"Why are you shouting at her? She cannot—" A frantic tugging on Ginny's arm interrupted her.

I want to go home.

This is our home now, Liebchen, Ginny silently replied.

But I do not like him! And I have nowhere to sleep!

We will make a pallet on the floor in front of the stove for now. Tomorrow I will speak with him about the sleeping arrangements.

I want to go back to the farm, Doreen begged. *I want to see Vati.*

She did not bother correcting Doreen for continuing to call Thomas Heart *"Vati."* Herz had been the one to sire her, and yet Thomas Heart at least cared enough to speak with her. And teach her to dance. And ride a horse. *Mayhap he will visit you, or you can visit him. Would you like that?* Ginny asked.

David, too? And Noble and Dolores and Evie . . .

Out of the corner of her eye, Ginny noticed her husband's thinning brows rise in horror. "What is she doing with her hands?"

Ginny glanced at him in astonishment. Had he not gotten her letter telling him of Doreen's deafness? "She is speaking, husband."

"With her *hands?*"

"She suffered an illness that took her hearing and nearly took her life. We will be happy to teach you the language she understands so you can communicate with her."

"Mime like the heathens?" He shook his head in a staunch refusal. "I am too old for such nonsense."

From the unyielding distaste on her husband's face, Ginny knew that from this point forward, the only communication her husband planned with his own child was through her. The realization planted a seed of resentment.

Protectively, she turned to Doreen and signed, *Go on and try to get some sleep. It has been a long day, and I need to speak with your father.*

Doreen's baffled gaze turned to the man now slumped in a plank-wood rocking chair by the window. His fingers rested lightly over his mouth, his attention was trained on the noisy street below. Her thoughts were clearly reflected on her face. How could this dreary, brooding man truly be the father Ginny had so often boasted of?

Despondently, Doreen made herself as comfortable as the hard stone floor would allow. Ginny brushed the hair out of her big blue eyes and tucked the thin blanket around her neck as if she were two instead of almost twelve. *Everything will look better in the morning; you will see.*

Though Doreen nodded, she did not seem very confident.

Sighing, Ginny approached the window where her husband still stared out of the dingy pane at the rain-soaked alley below. On a scratched oak stand beside the table, a lock of her hair tied with a blue ribbon lay next to a half-melted candlestick. She had forgotten that he had requested the memento before sauntering out of the orchard. And it surprised her that he had kept it.

"Try to remember that Doreen is very confused right now. She does not mean to pry into your things, she is only curious. And she does not know where her place is in your house."

"There are not many places to choose from. But I do not want her in the clothespress. I keep a loaded gun in there."

Ginny could see why, living in this section of the city. As if on cue, a rowdy blare of revelers drifted down the littered alley. "What ever happened to the farm you wrote of?" Or was that just one of her husband's many dreams? she added to herself.

A muscle tightened in his jaw. "I lost it in a title dispute. After spending over a year clearing the land, building a house, putting in crops . . . I lost everything." With a self-deprecating snort he said, "I promised you paradise. I have nothing to give you but poverty."

"Do you not know that it would not have mattered where we lived or how much we had? I only wanted to be with you. We would have gotten by somehow."

His waxen face turned ruddy. "You would have wished that I bring you to this"—his wave encompassed the cramped quarters, where the smell of stale liquor seeped through the cracks in the walls from the pub in front. —"after seeing what he could give you?"

Fixing on him a steady look of reproach, Ginny said, "What I wish is that you would have had more faith in my love, husband. Our lives would have been much different."

Because now it was too late. Her love belonged to another.

The last of the snow had melted and the ground had thawed enough to begin breaking sod for spring planting. Tom threw himself into tilling the soil, clearing it of rocks, raking it smooth of clumps. He didn't keep track of the days anymore. They crawled by one after another, bleak and insignificant, each an endless ordeal. He couldn't find the old ability to shut off the pain. His chest hurt constantly with a dead ache. His throat always felt tight and raw.

But at least the hard work kept the nights at bay.

They were the worst. He moved back into the downstairs bedroom to escape the memories. It didn't help. The barrenness just followed him. And he'd stare at the ceiling for hours on end while the house rang with a quiet so loud it gave him headaches. Silence had become his enemy.

"Noble asked me to go to the city with him tomorrow," David said one morning at breakfast. "Is it all right if I go?"

Neither really knew why they'd fallen into the habit of talking in low, almost whispered tones—when they talked at all. Most times they just had nothing to say.

But Tom found a strange sort of comfort in the boy's company. The thought of losing that even for the day filled him with both envy and resentment. He knew David saw her when he went to Minnow Falls. "You plan on taking the wagon?" he asked.

"Yeah. Why, you needing anything special?"

Her name was on the tip of his tongue. He shoved a bite of tasteless eggs into his mouth and forbid himself to think it much less say it out loud. "Stop by the emporium and pick up a new plow blade if you've got time. The other one's so rusted I can strain rocks through it."

David cast him a timid glance from beneath his black lashes. "You want me to pass on any messages to any person in particular?"

Tom's chewing slowed to a stop. A thousand different words

flickered through his mind. They all narrowed down to one simple request. *Come home.*

He dropped his gaze to his plate, then shoved himself away from the table. He felt David measuring his progress as he calmly strode to the front door. Pausing with his hand on the latch, he said, "If you happen to see a little girl with flaxen braids, you might want to tell her . . . tell her to make sure she wears her coat. It's been unnaturally cold lately."

"Doreen, will you help me fix supper?"

Her responding motions were slow and listless.

"Oh, Doreen, I miss them too."

As the days became weeks, and the weeks became months, Ginny began to wonder exactly what it was about Thomas Herz she had fallen in love with in the first place. What she once considered his gentleness of spirit had in truth been a lack of ambition. His penchant for dreaming had been an aversion to honest work, his willingness to let her handle their affairs and mend his mistakes, an avoidance of responsibility.

The only reason he had come for her was because he was dying of a lung disease brought on by working in the lead mines after losing his farm—and because she had been in easy reach, a mere twenty miles away. Had she still been in Germany, Ginny doubted she ever would have known of his ill health. He would not have sent for her. Not only did he feel as though he had failed her, but he was simply too weak to earn the money needed for the passage. Odd jobs, he'd told her with strange vagueness, got him by. So she began to cook for the pub below, and Doreen helped her mop the floors early in the morning, which brought in much needed coins.

Once again she had been thrust into the role of the strong one.

But she performed her duties without complaint, as wife and mother and caretaker, hoping the work would somehow ease her guilt each time her soul wept for another.

Her only links to Thomas Heart now were Noble and David. Noble brought David to the city as often as the weather permitted. But they weren't the same, those infrequent and all-too-brief visits. And now Thomas Heart had begun preparing the fields for spring planting, the visits had decreased, for David was needed on the farm.

David says Sissy Warren keeps coming to call on Vati.

The thought of Sissy Warren and Thomas together made Ginny's spine prickle with jealousy. Only she had no right. She was married to another.

But David says Vati will not talk to her. Do you think Vati misses us as much as we miss him?

Ginny often wondered the same thing as once again she began searching the horizon by day, this time seeking Thomas Heart's lanky form. And she found herself longing for the lazy winter evenings when they had gathered in the sitting room in front of the fire, looking through magazines and making up stories, laughing at his blunders.

Unlike Thomas, Herz barely acknowledged their existence, and that alone seemed to drain the spirit out of Doreen.

Ginny knew how she felt. She was married to Herz. Had once cared for him as deeply as it was possible for a bride to care for the man whose name she bore. But he rarely spoke to her now. When he did, the conversations were terse and unforgiving. Filled with defeat and condemnation, aimed both at her and at himself.

And she wished she could somehow find the same energy to repair her marriage now as she had once used trying to make a stranger remember her.

That evening Herz pushed away the food tray, telling her in his own sullen way that he was not hungry. Just then a round of thick coughs echoed in the room. The disease had progressed at an alarming rate in the last month. His face was pasty. His cheeks sunken. His thinning hair limp and dry.

He looked a hundred years older than he was. And after the bout of lung fever with her grandmother, Ginny knew that his health would not hold out much longer. If ever they would make peace with each other, it must begin tonight.

Ginny set the tray on the floor and sat on the bed near his hip. "We cannot go on like this, Thomas Herz. You are my husband. I am your wife. After all the love we shared, why are we making each other miserable?"

He shut his eyes, as if to avoid the conversation.

She refused to let him block her out this time. She took his veined hand in her own, studied the chipped, jaundiced nails and bony knuckles. "I made a terrible, horrible, dreadful mistake. I admit that. But we have both made mistakes. Can we not put the bitterness between us aside and make the most of our last days together?"

Opening his bleary hazel eyes, her husband gazed upon her for many long moments. Finally he said, "You are beautiful, Ginny. No man can resist you for long. Eyes the color of a moon-drenched sky . . . lips sweet as elderberry wine . . ."

Ginny's eyes misted over.

And the threads of forgiveness began to weave into a fragile truce. She had devoted her life to him based on a young girl's adoration. He had allowed his promises to her to weaken his character instead of making it stronger.

They talked long into the night, of their hopes and dreams, of the past and for the future. And they talked of the child they had created together, and the children they should have had. And just as the dawn broke through and bathed their tiny house in gold, Ginny lay beside her husband and heard him whisper, "I loved you the moment I saw you."

"And I, you."

"I wanted only to be worthy of you."

"And I, you."

"I regret only one thing, my Ginny. That I could not be the man you believed I was." He pulled the tail of her yellow braid through his fingers. "Follow where your heart leads you, Ginny. You are no longer bound to me."

For the first time in twelve years, Ginny kissed her husband hello. She also kissed him good-bye.

36

*T*OM RESTED THE plow blades in the furrowed soil and mopped his brow with a soiled kerchief used a dozen times that afternoon already. The ox hung his head, pulling the yoke tethers tight against its sweat-slicked back.

"We'll finish turning up these last two rows then call it a day," Tom told David who met him coming down the next row. Lowering his kerchief, Tom wondered if David heard a word he said. His gaze was riveted to a point beyond Tom's shoulder.

"It's Miss Ginny. . . ."

Twisting at the waist, Tom felt his insides lurch. She stood at the edge of the field, her hands clasped loosely in front of her. She looked lonely. Apprehensive. He'd rarely seen her unsure about anything before, and the change irritated him. Tom frowned and glanced away, fighting the swell of longing trying to rise inside him. She wasn't supposed to matter to him anymore. Shoving the rag into his back pocket, he struggled to keep his voice bland. "What's she doing here?"

"Maybe she changed her mind and left Herz," David speculated.

And hell had frozen over. Tom's lip curled into a sneer. Not even knowing that Herz was "T. W." would have persuaded her to forget her vows to the worthless man. Not that Tom would have ever told her. Countless times he'd been tempted to approach her with the truth about her husband. Tell her that Herz was far from the saint she considered him. Except, after his actions when she left, she might think him a spurned lover trying to separate her from her one true love. Tom's pride had already been stomped on and ground into the dirt—only a fool went back for a second helping.

No, if she couldn't see Herz's true nature for herself, then she was more naive than he'd been for thinking she would have settled for him. He was better off without her, anyway. Someday, maybe he'd even stop missing her.

A flash of calico brought his attention off to the side, to the young girl racing across the field. The genuine joy on her face melted a bit of the frost clinging to his soul. Tom knelt and caught Doreen as she dove into his arms. He hugged her close. Inhaling the scent of her quiet innocence reaffirmed his decision to keep Herz's second identity secret. For Doreen's sake, if for no other reason.

"How are you doing, pretty girl?" he signed.

Sniffling, she gestured back, *I have missed you.*

"I've missed you, too." He wanted to ask her if her father was still ignoring her, as David had reported, but he held his tongue. As long as Herz wasn't hurting her, he'd keep out of their family business. After all, he was just an outsider. Again.

Come say hello to Mütter. She has missed you as much as me.

Tom doubted that but could no more resist Doreen tugging him across the field than he could fight the invisible pull drawing him closer to *her.* When they reached the edge of the field, Doreen finally released her hold on his hand.

With mixed emotions he watched her and David silently drift away. Part of him wanted to call them back, force them not to leave him alone with this woman. Another part was grateful that they'd spared themselves from witnessing the hostility he couldn't hide. "Well, well, if it isn't Mrs. Herz. To what do I owe this honor?"

She met his stare for several long, indecipherable moments before her tawny lashes fell over her eyes. She looked pale.

Worn. And still so damn beautiful she took his breath away. He hated that she still made his hands sweat and his heart race and mouth go dry. "That husband of yours is wearing you out," he said snidely, his own words creating a sickening image.

With a proud tilt of her chin, she stated, "My husband is gone."

"Left you again, did he? Don't expect me to feel sorry for you, you made your choice."

She drew in a sudden breath, then glanced across the freshly turned soil at Doreen and the boy who were lavishing his horse with affection.

"I have come to see David. I brought him a new pair of trousers."

"Now's a fine time to remember him—after you just dumped him."

A flash of anger appeared in her dark blue eyes, turning them the same stormy color that haunted his nights. "He wished to stay with you. David's choice broke my heart, but what should I have done, ignored his wishes and forced him to go where I know he would have been miserable?"

Had she been miserable? "That never stopped you before. You paid no attention to my wishes—" Tom cut himself off before he let slip that her leaving actually made any difference to him. He'd given her the power of knowing he cared once, he'd not make the same mistake again.

"Will you deny me a visit with him?"

"David makes up his own mind. But don't be surprised if he doesn't want to see you. I sure as hell don't." And as he strode away, he wished he could make himself believe that.

Over another bland meal that evening, David unwittingly skewered Tom with guilt when he told him that Ginny's husband didn't leave her, but that he'd died.

"I don't think they have any place to go. Herz didn't own any property and from what Doreen says, he didn't leave them much money."

"What did she do with the money I put in her account?"

"Miss Ginny won't touch it. Says it don't belong to her."

But she was the reason he had money to give her, Tom thought with a second's astonishment. Only a second's, though.

"Fine, let her stubborn pride keep her warm then. She isn't moving back in here. Doreen is welcome to visit anytime she wants, but I don't want her mother stepping one foot back on this property. She made her choice. She can live with it."

David ducked his head, making Tom regret his harsh tone. Taming the swift rise of temper at any mention of *her*, he asked, "What did he die of, anyway?"

"Doreen said when he lost his farm, he started working in the lead mines. Got the black lung, or whatever it's called."

Sadistically Tom hoped it was a long, painful death. After the years of torment he'd put Ginny—

Tom cursed, her name hitting him like a sledgehammer to the chest. He'd promised himself he would never say it, not even think it. Course, he'd always been lousy at keeping promises to himself. If he'd been good at it, he wouldn't be suffering now.

Striding purposefully down Center Lane, Tom ignored the women talking in huddled groups. Ever since word got out that he was actually the bachelor he had claimed to be, he'd been finding himself dodging one marriage-minded spinster after another. He didn't know what gave them the impression he'd welcome the attention, but by thunder, he'd lock himself in the icehouse before letting any one of them get their man-hungry claws into him.

He'd considered surrendering his freedom papers for shackles for a woman only once. And she'd betrayed him.

The bell in Warren's store made a tinkling sound above his head.

"Do you still love him, Ginny?"

Tom froze. The conversation coming from the next aisle gripped him in iron manacles, leaving him no choice but to wait for her response.

"With everything that I am. But it makes no difference. I hurt him. He cannot forgive that, nor am I certain he should."

"Do you want us to help you get him back again?"

"Not this time," she replied with a note of decisiveness. "My grandmother once told me that if you love something you must set it free. That that is the greatest love of all. If Thomas Heart ever takes me back, it must be of his own will. And if he does not, it is no less than I deserve for the pain I have caused him."

The news that Ginny was setting him free shook Tom to the core. With every ounce of strength he could muster, he tore free of his own immobility. He turned on his heel and walked out the door, forgetting what he'd needed to pick up in the first place.

As Ginny kneaded bread at Evie Mae's table she tried not to notice the laughter of young love blossoming in the living area. Evie Mae and Thomas's friend Gene Mason were trying to teach David and Doreen how to play monte, using Indian corn as markers to place their bets.

Watching Evie Mae and Gene become smitten with each other over the last several weeks had brought a bittersweet ache to Ginny's breast. Her friend deserved every happiness; her fiancé's death had been a terrible tragedy for her and she had longed to find a man who could help her get over him. The one-armed soldier who put a sparkle in her eyes that very first day he walked into their village seemed the perfect man for the job.

Ginny tried to give them privacy, but that wasn't always easy. And she wondered where she and Doreen might live should the courtship result in marriage. The tiny cabin was hardly big enough for three people, never mind four.

Though she had little appetite, she nibbled on a pickled beet. As much as it irked her pride, she would have to withdraw some of the money Thomas Heart had put in the bank months ago and either find a place to let or have a small cabin built. She could not expect her friends to keep boarding her and Doreen, and come September . . .

She touched her belly and felt swift tears sting her eyes. How she longed to tell Thomas that he would become a father. Though she and Herz had shared a bed, they had not shared their bodies. At first he had claimed bitterly that he could not bear to touch another man's leavings. Then he had simply been too sick. Ginny thought it a blessing of sorts. After the symphonies she and Thomas had created, she could not bear another man's hands on her—even if they had belonged to her real husband.

Yet the hostility Thomas harbored toward her forbade such a confession. His reservations about having children had only just been broken when their lives took such an unexpected twist. If she told him now, he might feel honor-bound to provide for his child. But what of the emotional toll of living a life split between parents? It was difficult enough for Doreen and David, dividing their time between the farm and the village. . . .

An eruption of laughter jolted Ginny from her troubling thoughts and she glanced up in time to see Gene press a playful kiss to Evie Mae's cheek.

Her emotions, already so unpredictable, took a swing for the worse. And Ginny knew if she did not get out of the cabin this very moment, she would disgrace herself by bursting into a fit of tears in front of friends and family.

Snatching her shawl off the back of the kitchen chair, she curtailed her urgent pace and slipped outside. She came to a sudden stop on the stones.

He was sitting on the ground, his back and shoulders tight against the logs of Evie's cabin, his knees drawn up to his chest, his gaze directed toward the heavens as if waiting for direction from above. An errant spring wind ruffled the lock of light brown hair falling across his brow, yet he seemed not to notice that it got in the way of his vision.

What was he doing here? After taking such great pains to avoid being within a field's length of her, why was he now sitting alone outside Evie Mae's cabin? It was no secret that she and Doreen were staying here. In a town as small as Ridgeford, surely he must have heard.

Softly the door clicked shut behind Ginny. The look he turned on her was so filled with pain that she felt it burn clear to her soul. Slowly she knelt beside him. His clothes were rumpled, as if he had been wearing them to bed, and bluish shadows left crescents beneath his eyes. Her trembling finger-tips brushed the abrasive whiskers on his jaw. "Thomas?"

"Damn you, Ginny . . . why did you make me love you?"

The unexpected question, hoarse and vulnerable, wrenched at her fragile emotions. Yet she had no answer. How could she tell him of her own selfishness? That he was everything she had thought Herz would become? That he was everything she had ever needed, before she had known what she needed?

"Do you know how it destroyed me to let you walk away?"

It had destroyed her, too.

"Do you know how sick it made me, imagining you and that . . . that Herz sleeping together every night when it was my bed you belonged in?"

Now was not the time to tell him of the babe she sheltered within her womb. But the tortured grief in his eyes compelled her to say, "Nothing ever happened between Herz and me of the intimate nature."

She thought she saw a slumping of relief. His head bowed so that his chin touched the opposite shoulder. His eyes were glassy. She knew it was not from liquor this time, but sorrow. Over the lump of remorse in her throat, Ginny said, "I never meant to hurt you, Thomas."

"Then why did you? You didn't have to go with him."

"Yes, *Liebling*, I did. If for no reason other than to close that part of my life." She gathered her skirts tight around her legs and lowered herself to the walkway stones, near enough to draw strength from his presence yet far enough away to give him space. "I came to realize that the love I felt for Herz long ago belonged to a sixteen-year-old girl." She touched the pale spot on her finger where her ring used to dwell. The memory of placing it on her husband's finger before the coffin closed brought a sense of peace and finality. "I was young, then. Filled with hopes and dreams. All those hopes and dreams revolved around my husband. I made him into something that he was not. May never have been. But I blinded myself because I did not want to face the possibility that my dreams would not come true."

"So you made it so they did. Ginny the Fixer."

She smiled with sad fondness at her grandmother's description of her. "I never once even looked at another man until you. And I could not accept that you were not my husband, because then I would have to face the ugly truth about myself. That I no longer felt the same way about him. That I was no longer faithful. That I was a terrible wife, an adulteress."

"He left you, Ginny. He never sent for you. He was the one who broke his promises to you."

"But I could not knowingly break mine to him." She looked at Thomas, wondering if he could see in her eyes the love for him she could not hide. Did not want to hide. "If it had been you, would you have wanted me to stay with another man?"

"I wouldn't have let you go in the first place."

"But you did let me go."

"Because it was what you wanted! Because your dedication to the people you love is one of the things I admired most about—" He stopped, looking stricken by his own words. Then he ran his calloused hand through his thick hair. "Ahhh, Ginny . . . I had no idea it would come to this. I wish I'd never started the search for him."

"Why did you, then? I never would have known."

"Because I didn't like the feelings I had when I was around you. Somehow I knew that if I managed to make you a part of my life, I'd never be the same."

"Is that such a bad thing?"

"Yes," he hissed. "I can't go back!"

She heard the anguish, the frustration in his voice. If he could return to the numbness, if he could run behind that wall of emotional detachment, she knew he would in an instant. His admission that he could not gave her a granule of hope that mayhap all was not lost.

"You loved me once, Thomas," she reminded him. "Can you give us a chance to begin again now that nothing stands between us? No secrets, no lies, no past to contend with? Can you ever believe in us again?"

"Do you know what you're asking of me? I cut open a vein for you . . . let you into my blood . . . let you claim a part of me no one ever had before." His voice broke. "I sacrificed everything for you. My farm, my freedom, my feelings . . . I swore no one would have the power to touch any of those things, and you grabbed every single one in your stubborn little hands and wrestled them right out of me."

Moving so close that she could feel the musky heat of his

skin through their clothing, she sought to keep the desperation from her voice. "I know what I am asking. I am asking for the happiness we had so briefly to last a lifetime. It was ours, Tom Heart. In spite of what you may think, it belonged to you and me and the children. And it can again." She stroked his cheek, staring deeply into the green-flecked amber eyes she loved so dearly. "I am free now, in a way that I was never free before."

"How would I know that when you're looking at me you aren't wishing I was Herz and thinking of what might have been if you'd never confused me with him?"

"Listen to your heart, Thomas. The heart never lies."

"Like yours was honest with you?"

"My heart *never* lied. From the moment we met, it called out to you. It simply got your name wrong."

"Give me one good reason why I should trust you again."

One good reason? "Because when Thomas Herz died, Ginny Herz died with him."

"Then what's left for me?"

Sorrow for causing him such misery and uncertainty made her eyes water and breathing difficult. Ginny tenderly cupped his jaw and forced him to look at her. "Ginny Heart—if you will have her."

He closed his eyes, the struggle evident on his face. She held her breath, waiting, hoping, dreaming. Daring to believe. Her beliefs were all she had ever had to hold onto. If they failed her now . . .

Then he opened his eyes. "If I have her, I won't ever let her go."

Her nose and throat filled with tears. She wound her arms around his neck. Enfolding her in his arms, holding her so tightly she could feel their heartbeats become one, she heard him whisper in their native tongue, *"Ich liebe dich, Ginny, mit alle Herzschlag."*

Her arms tightened. She felt the tightly coiled strength of maturity. Pressing a kiss to a spot below his ear, she tasted the salt of life and labor. "And I love you, Tom, with every heartbeat."

"I don't ever want you leaving me again."

"It will never happen. We are heartbound, you and I."

"If we're going to do this, we're going to do it right. That means starting from the beginning, Ginny, with a proper courtship and everything. I don't want you to ever mistake me for anyone else but the man I am. I want you to know without a doubt that it's me you want to spend the rest of your life with, and not a memory."

She longed to tell him that she made that discovery the day she had found him teaching Doreen to dance, though she had not known it then. But she also knew the importance of giving Thomas time to trust in her love. The thought of the baby due in five months' time, though, warned her that time was not their friend. "I am already certain. But what of you? Will you change your mind? Will you regret giving up your freedom to raise a family?"

"I'm more afraid of losing you than of losing that. A few restrictions I can handle. Your leaving I can't."

"Are you asking for my hand, Thomas?"

Pulling back a scant few inches, he said gruffly, "I suppose I better or you'll send the village women after me again."

It was the sweetest proposal she'd ever heard. Forehead pressed to forehead, each cradled the other's face, and Ginny smiled a watery smile of relief and granted wishes and dreams come true. "And not even General Grant and his whole U.S. Army have a chance against them."

As his lips closed over hers, she decided that news of the baby could wait until later. When her blood stopped singing and her nerves quit humming . . .

Epilogue

OCTOBER, 1866

"IN THE NAME of the Father and of the Son and of the Holy Spirit, I baptize thee Sheridan Bertha Heart."

The new minister of Ridgeford, Pastor Gene Mason, trickled water over Sheridan's forehead while the irate squallings of Tom's tiny daughter ripped through the village church.

Doreen bounced her six-week-old baby sister gently in her arms in an attempt to give her comfort while Noble squirmed as only a man unused to infants could squirm, and Evie Mae Mason blotted the tiny blond cap with the ivory cloth her new husband handed her.

Tom looked upon them all while David stood tall and proud on one side of him and Ginny on the other. He squeezed his wife's hand and she smiled brilliantly up at him. Sheridan's birth had been nothing short of a miracle, proof positive that they really did happen. When she had come out with the cord wrapped around her neck, and with no doctor to give him instruction, Tom thought he could understand what Ginny had gone through all those years ago with Doreen's illness.

She'd had Bertha nearby, though. Tom had had no one. And just when he thought he'd lose control, Ginny's soft German voice broke through his panic and coaxed him through the ordeal. All she said was, "I believe in you."

Instinct took over then. Tom gently unwrapped the umbilical cord then cleaned the baby's mouth and breathed life back into her still body.

It had been a miracle, all right. Against all odds, she won the battle for her life. And Tom had known that his daughter could have no other name than that of the valiant Union Major General Phil Sheridan. And her godparents could be none other than their closest friends, Gene and Evie, married just last week, and Noble, who remained true to both him and Ginny.

Behind them, Dolores, Elsbeth, Mary, Vernice, and the rest of the village women sniffled and dabbed at their eyes. The four in the front pew rose and Tom stepped back to make room for them. Predictably, they gathered around the baby and made those silly crooning noises until Sheridan stopped crying.

Of course Tom would never admit it to anyone, but he made those same silly sounds deep in the night when Sheridan awoke for her feeding. And he would sit and watch as Ginny nursed their baby, his chest so swollen with wonder and pride and love that he thought it might explode from the pressure.

As Ginny reached to take the baby from Doreen, Tom wondered how he could have ever thought living a life alone would be better than being surrounded by his family. He had a son, two daughters, and a wife. No, he thought, gazing at Ginny's profile as she exchanged a few words with her friends, he had more than a wife. He had a friend, a confidant, a helpmate and a lover. That so many blessings could be wrapped up in one small imported package still left him in awe, even four months after they'd stood in the very same church and pledged their lives to one another.

"You want me to bring the wagon around, Pa?"

The lump in Tom's throat prevented him from answering David with anything more than a single nod. But once David started out of the church, the tightness in Tom's chest gave way to open laughter at the inch of mismatched socks—one green, one red—showing between his boots and hems. The boy—no, the rapidly growing young man—definitely needed new trousers again.

Taking Sheridan from Ginny, Tom laid her in a woven basket. He ran his finger down one chubby cheek. She vainly ought nourishment. Tom chuckled. "Sorry, sweeting, you'll ave to wait for your *Mutti* to feed you at home."

Soon Tom had the children and Ginny loaded into the wagon nd heading out of the village. Beyond the bridge, ripe fields eady for harvesting stretched between the river and wood-ands. Tufted stems of wheat waved a welcome. Shoulder-high ornstalks created a perfect natural maze that Doreen and David made use of every chance they got. Of course, Blue's apping always gave their location away, Tom thought with amusement.

They traveled past the bluff where Bertha had been laid to est. The white granite marker they'd erected earlier in the ummer jutted from the ground like a beacon against the thick reen grasses. And he thought of her, and her last words to him, Dis is vhere you belong anyvay."

"You have been strangely quiet this morning, Thomas. Is omething troubling you?"

The charming accent brought his attention to his wife once nore. She was even more beautiful to him now than she'd been ne first time he set eyes on her. Because she belonged to him. And he belonged to her. Not a moment passed that he doubted hat. Each day when he came in from the fields she had a tick-to-the-ribs meal waiting on the table, soft skin to smell when memories of the stench of past battles intruded, and warm, loving arms to keep the cold at bay. With Ginny, he ound another freedom, of being a part of something special nd unique.

Bertha had been wrong about one thing. Ginny didn't love oo deeply; she loved as much as those around her needed to be oved. And for Tom, all those years of turning off the ability to eel pain had also prevented him from feeling love. So if he just appened to require more than most, he figured it was only because he had all those years to make up for. "No, I was ctually just thinking that things couldn't be finer."

Smiling, she pressed herself closer to his side. "*Gutt*. For a noment there I feared you might be having regrets."

He tried to keep his eyes off her. But when the scalloped edge of her bodice went slack, and he caught a glimpse of the creamy swell of her full breasts, heat flared to life in his loins.

"I'm feeling something, but it isn't regret. More like hankering to sow some seed."

A comely blush stole into her cheeks, and she glanced behind her to where Doreen and David were settled in the wagon bed, Sheridan's basket between them. "Thomas, you are incorrigible!"

As always, the way she said his name made his pulse leap. For months he'd held back, and the restraint had been raw torture. Now that her confinement had ended, he couldn't wait any longer. "Can I help it if farming is in my blood?" He grinned wickedly, his meaning unmistakable.

In answer, she lowered her lashes and gave him an inviting smile. Laughing for the pure joy of it, Tom snapped the reins. The pair of blacks surged from a walk to a canter back to Heartland, where hopes and dreams and wishes really did come true.

Author's Note

Many of my fondest memories are of the times I spent on my grandma's farm when I was a little girl growing up in Wisconsin.

I can still remember how her kitchen always smelled of poppy-seed cake and she smelled of the fresh bread she baked each morning.

I remember the sense of "grounding" I felt when the family gathered during the holidays, the rooms filled with cousinly chatter. Waiting my turn for my auntie to trim my hair while my other aunties and Mom sat around the kitchen table talking grown-up talk. (I always felt so important sitting there with the "womenfolk.") Of course, my uncles and Dad lazed around in the living room, or they were outside mowing the huge lawn. Then my horde of cousins and I would fight over who got to spin on the tire swing hanging from the tree in the front yard. Or we dug potatoes, which in spite of the fond memory was not fun.

And I remember listening for Santa's sleigh bells on the way to and from her farm.

And the candy jar on the shelf in the living room—how we could never have any sweets until we finished our supper.

And the feel of Grandma's loving arms around me just before we said good-bye.

It's been twenty years since my grandma died, but I still miss her and I never forgot her greatest gift to me—my heritage.

Though *Heartbound* is a completely fictional story, it is special to me because it was inspired by my family—there are too many to name, but they know who they are. I hope you, my treasured readers, have enjoyed this glimpse into our roots. And if the German words were sometimes difficult to decipher, may you overlook that in the name of "story flavoring."